With a jubilant bark, Charlie burst out of the bushes towards me. I let out a sigh of relief as he pranced back and forth, tantalizingly out of reach. Trying to calm down my racing heart, I held out the doggy treat. With a happy yelp, he took the treat from my hand. He only needed two bites to finish it off. Murmuring endearments, I scratched behind his ears as I tried to slip the leash over his head with my other hand. Thinking this was a great new game, Charlie snatched the leash and ran off.

"You've got to be kidding me." I raced after him. "Charlie!"

The leash clenched between his teeth prevented Charlie from barking, so I needed to keep close behind him. But he not only was the size of a small horse, he could run as fast as one, too. Five minutes later, he disappeared. This was ridiculous. Needing to catch my breath, I stopped and fished my cell phone from the messenger bag slung across my chest. I didn't care if Piper was wearing designer stilts. Charlemagne was her dog, and she was going to come in here and track down her monster puppy.

Before I could call her, loud barks broke out to my left. This time I was the one to burst through the bushes. He wasn't getting away again. But Charlie stopped barking as soon as he saw me. I knew now why he had been quiet for the past few minutes. He'd been digging away in the dirt, which he resumed upon my arrival. I looked for his leash and spotted it a few yards away, half buried by the dirt he flung to all sides. I picked up the leash before Charlie could get to it first. As soon as I did, I also spied what appeared to be an animal bone. Most likely a deer.

But when I turned to see what Charlie was digging up now, my heart sank. It was another bone, but not one belonging to a deer. In fact, it was far more than a bone.

It was a human skull . . .

Books by Sharon Farrow

DYING FOR STRAWBERRIES

BLACKBERRY BURIAL

Published by Kensington Publishing Corporation

Blackberry Burial

Sharon Farrow

KENSINGTON PUBLISHING CORP.

http://www.kensingtonbooks.com

KENSINGTON BOOKS are published by

Kensington Publishing Corp.
119 West 40th Street
New York, NY 10018

All Kensington Titles, Imprints, and Distributed Lines are available at special quantity discounts for bulk purchases for sales promotions, premiums, fund-raising, and educational or institutional use.

Special book excerpts or customized printings can also be created to fit specific needs. For details, write or phone the office of the Kensington special sales manager: Kensington Publishing Corp., 119 West 40th Street, New York, NY 10018, attn: Special Sales Department, Phone: 1-800-221-2647.

Kensington and the K logo Reg. U.S. Pat & TM Off.

ISBN-13: 978-1-4967-0488-7
ISBN-10: 1-4967-0488-6
First Kensington Mass Market Edition: November 2017

eISBN-13: 978-1-4967-0489-4
eISBN-10: 1-4967-0489-4
First Kensington Electronic Edition: November 2017

10 9 8 7 6 5 4 3 2 1

Printed in the United States of America

*To the beautiful villages and towns
that hug the eastern coast of Lake Michigan,
especially Saugatuck, Douglas, and South Haven.
Discovering the charm and magical energy
of this shoreline transformed my life.*

Acknowledgments

I'd like to thank my agent, John Talbot, for selling the Berry Basket series so quickly, and for always being supportive. Another big thanks to the wonderful people at Kensington, particularly John Scognamiglio, Karen Auerbach, and Holly Fairbank. A special thanks to my best friend's husband, Randy Mims, who told me everything I needed to know about road rallies. I'm grateful to the Saugatuck-Douglas Historical Society for hosting a meeting at Crane Orchards. The stories told by Crane family members about running an orchard in Michigan's fruit belt were fascinating and invaluable. Finally, a special shout-out to the Oxbow Art School in Saugatuck, which served as my nonlethal inspiration for Oriole Point's Blackberry Art School. I hope Oxbow and its gifted students continue to create beauty for another century.

Chapter 1

I was prepared to do a great deal for my business. Dying my hair raspberry red was not one of them. Now I only had to convince the photographer. For two years, the same photo had accompanied my bio on The Berry Basket website. However, months of badgering by my fashion-forward employee, Dean Cabot, finally wore me down. He so despaired of my old photo that I began to think it might be as hideous as he claimed. So here I was, posing for photos before the store opened, while defending my refusal to look like Batman villainess Poison Ivy.

"I'm a natural brunette," I reminded him for the tenth time. "Accept it. There's no way I'm changing my hair color to match whatever fruit is in season. And we agreed on a nice simple photo to go on the store's website and Facebook page. Nothing glam or bizarre."

"There's nothing glam or bizarre about dying your hair a different color every month," Dean protested. "Look how often Paige Lindstrom changes her hair color."

Paige was a numerologist who worked at Gemini Rising, the town's New Age bookstore. Yes, she currently had pink hair, but before that she'd spent all her life as a Nordic blonde like her ancestors before her. "Paige also has multiple tattoos and body piercings. Should I cover my arms and face with berry tattoos?"

Dean's eyes widened. "Not a bad way to establish The Berry Basket brand. After all, your business is devoted to berries: berry-flavored syrups, wines, coffees, teas, pancake mixes, jams, smoothies, pastries. And not just foods, either. You sell books about berries, jewelry made in the shape of berries, ceramic berry bowls, berry hullers, berry-scented candles—"

"I know what The Berry Basket sells. You don't have to list our entire inventory."

"Marlee, you're 'The' Berry Girl along the lakeshore. And you once produced cooking shows for the Gourmet Living Network. You're one of a kind, so make your marketing platform as unique as you are. Go beyond what's expected." When Dean wasn't working at the shop, he ran a popular blog called *The Dean Report*. The blog's gossipy, irreverent take on life along the Lake Michigan shore had made it a surprising success. I was happy for Dean, even if he now fancied himself an expert on fashion, marketing, and life in general.

"I do agree that dying my hair the color of raspberries would be unexpected."

"You should listen to me," he said. "Customers would visit your social media sites—and this store—just to see what fruit you had dyed your hair to match."

Dean's brother laughed. Slouched at one of the bistro tables near the ice cream counter, Andrew had a ringside seat for my photo shoot. "I'll be first in line if Marlee colors her hair a nice juniper berry green."

Dean aimed his camera at me. "This photo's going to end up as dull as the one it's replacing. You might as well be posing for your senior class photo at Oriole Point High."

"Sounds good to me." I readjusted my blue chef's apron with The Berry Basket logo emblazoned over the front.

"Especially if you can make me look eighteen again. Now hurry up. We have to open in fifteen minutes."

Standing behind my store counter, I held up a white porcelain bowl heaped with fresh blackberries and raspberries. Dean could grumble all he liked. I was the owner of The Berry Basket and his boss. Not that I was immune to his influence; otherwise I wouldn't be posing for dozens of photos holding bags of cranberry granola mix and blueberry beef jerky.

"Let's get a few of you scooping ice cream next."

"No way." I smoothed my hair before he clicked away again. "You've taken pictures of me doing everything but scrubbing the shop toilet. We're done after this."

A sudden rapping on the door signaled the end had come sooner than expected. I sighed with relief. "That's Piper come to regale me with more road rally problems. Let her in."

Andrew jumped up to unlock the door.

"If Piper's here, we may as well call it quits," Dean grumbled.

He was right. When Piper Lyall-Pierce entered a room, she commanded attention—literally. She was a member of the oldest founding family of Oriole Point, along with being the wife of our mayor, Lionel Pierce. Piper was also the richest inhabitant of our lakeshore village. In a town catering to numerous Chicagoans who kept lavish vacation homes here, that was saying something. But even had she been a recent transplant who had married the grocer, Piper would instinctively take center stage. Which she did as soon as Andrew opened the door.

Piper hurried into the shop without a glance at either of the Cabot brothers. That was remarkable since the brothers were tall, auburn haired, and attractive; they were often taken for twins, even though they'd been born eleven months apart. Today they were more eye catching than usual, decked out in matching white tailored shorts, yellow leather boat shoes, and yellow Oxford shirts. Such sartorial splendor seemed a waste; they were required to wear a Berry Basket chef apron over any outfit they had on. Maybe they'd decided to launch the latest fad of the season, something the boys had done since they were in elementary school and convinced their classmates to glue Pokémon cards onto their T-shirts.

"Bad news, Marlee." She marched up to the counter, ignoring the fact that Dean was still trying to photograph me. "We can't use the Grunkemeyer farm for the Blackberry Road Rally."

I groaned. "I wanted to send the poster artwork to the printer this afternoon. Now I'll have to hold off until we pick a new starting location for the rally."

"Tell me something I don't know." Piper flung her Birkin onto the counter. She owned an endless supply of the expensive Hermès bags in every conceivable color. Today her electric blue handbag perfectly matched the linen tank top she wore with her white summer blazer and slacks. When it came to fashion, not even the Cabots could outshine—or outspend—Piper.

"Some tourists from Wisconsin went there yesterday to take photos of his barn," she said. "I told Henry that if his wife painted that enormous portrait of their favorite cow on the barn, it would attract all sorts of attention. Well, one of the tourists tripped over a post auger and cut his leg. There's talk of a lawsuit, even though the man didn't even hemorrhage. But you know how people are nowadays. Worried about tetanus. Ready to sue over the slightest thing."

Having grown up playing in my family's orchards, I knew how sharp the blades of a post auger were. I doubted the cut on the leg was all that slight. "Is the man okay?"

She waved her hand. "Oh, he's fine. Except his lawyer has accused Henry of being criminally negligent. Ridiculous. How is it Henry's fault if some fool can't see a post auger lying in the grass? Now he's afraid a participant in the road rally might get hurt when they visit his farm. So we need a replacement for the Grunkemeyer farm."

I thought for a moment. "How about the Sanderling place? I drove by it last week on the way to New Bethel. It's a little off the beaten track, but that might make things more fun."

Dean cleared his throat. "I don't know how good a choice the Sanderling farm is."

"By the way, I don't like these new road rally rules." Andrew joined us. "Oscar wanted to be part of the rally, but he doesn't qualify."

Oscar Lucas was the owner of Beguiling Blooms, a florist shop in a neighboring lakeshore town. In addition to working part-time for me, Andrew worked at Beguiling Blooms. It was fortuitous that Oscar the florist proved to be as beguiling as his blooms; he and Andrew were now a romantic pair.

"He can be part of it next year when it reverts to being the Raspberry Road Rally," Piper said. "But it's not my fault Mr. Lucas never took classes at BAS. I'm only following the rules."

None of us mentioned that Piper was the one who drew up the rules for this July's road rally—and every one that came before. Soon after she took over the Oriole Point Tourist and Visitor Center, Piper organized the first Raspberry Road Rally. Tourists and residents alike enjoyed taking part in the annual event, especially since the prize money was sizable. This year, however, Piper had dedicated the rally to BAS, otherwise known as the Blackberry Art School.

An art colony since the late nineteenth century, Oriole Point had always attracted artists and bohemians from Chicago; several of them established an art school at the Blackberry Bayou. The summer sessions held in this rustic complex along the banks of the Oriole River were as widely known as those offered at the Oxbow Art School in nearby Saugatuck. This year, BAS celebrated its centenary, and alumni from around the country would arrive soon to take part in the festivities. Ever mindful of a way to boost tourism, Piper decided to honor the centenary by holding a special road rally named after the school. Because she loved to make things exclusive, participation in the rally was limited to students of BAS, past and present. While that included the Cabot brothers and myself, it did not embrace Andrew's beguiling boyfriend.

"I hope Andrew and I aren't disqualified because we work for you, Marlee," Dean said. "Since you're helping Piper run the event, people may assume we know stuff about the rally the other contestants don't. We don't want to be accused of cheating."

Piper plucked one of the berries from the bowl I still held. "Marlee is only helping with promotion. Ruth Barlow and I came up with all the rally clues. I only brought Marlee on board because Ruth had the audacity to break her arm during our final planning stages. But Marlee knows nothing about this rally except where it's scheduled to begin. And thanks to the Grunkemeyers, not even I know that now." She popped the blackberry into her mouth.

"I vote for the Sanderling farm," I said once more, "if we can get permission from Gordon Sanderling."

"I don't see how Gordon could object. It's not even a working farm any longer." She pulled out her cell phone from the Birkin. "I'll give him a call. If he says yes, you and I can drive over there and check things out." Piper shot me one of her rare approving glances. "I made the right decision when I appointed you as my promo person."

When Piper moved off to make her call, Andrew grabbed a few blackberries from my bowl. "If as many people sign up for this thing as rumored, the prize money will be the biggest ever. Dean and I plan to win it."

"Don't start spending that prize money too soon. Tess and I will be stiff competition."

Dean looked at me in surprise. "I didn't know you were signed up."

"How could I not be part of one devoted to BAS? Tess and I attended two summer sessions there as teenagers. Where do you think Tess discovered her love of glassmaking?" Our classes at BAS helped my best friend to become an award-winning graduate at the Rhode Island School of Design, where she met fellow glass artist David Reese. She and David had been a romantic and professional couple ever since. And while my printmaking lessons at BAS had little to do with my present career, it did inspire me to get a marketing degree at NYU.

I went over to the register to count out the day's starting cash and coins. "The other road rally participants and I only know this year's theme, which is 'Art Along the Lakeshore.' After all, ads for the rally have been in the local papers for weeks."

"If the clues are about art, our chances of winning look good," Dean said. "Andrew and I attended BAS for an entire summer. Although I was a much better painter than he was."

Andrew smirked. "Please. You were so afraid of getting paint on your clothes, you only used one color: beige." He turned to me. "His canvases looked like smashed Cheerios."

"Well, you must have been impressed. You copied everything I painted, only in blue."

"Liar!"

"Keep your voices down." I pointed to Piper, who was hunched over her phone by the window. "If the two of you want to increase your chances of winning, why not ride with me and Tess? Up to six people are allowed per car."

The brothers shot matching grins at me. "I can get on board with that," Andrew said.

Dean nodded. "This way, the four of us will have the painting, glasswork, and printmaking clues covered. Assuming those are the types of clues Piper's come up with. Maybe we should find a potter to join us."

"You're overthinking this," I said.

"All settled," Piper announced as she walked over. "Gordon turned me down at first, but I mentioned that Lionel and I are redoing five of our bathrooms this autumn, and we're looking for a company to contract with. That was enough to get him to come around."

"Exactly how many bathrooms do you have?" Andrew asked her.

"Nine. No, ten. I forgot the one in the pool house."

I exchanged amused looks with the Cabot boys. "This has turned out well," I said. "Piper gets to update her bathrooms and the rally has a new starting point. I'll correct the posters and send them off to the printer today."

"I only hope no one taking part in the road rally is superstitious," Dean warned. "The farm is supposed to be haunted."

"What?" This was news to me.

"Everyone knows that." Andrew shrugged. "At least everyone our age does."

I found this a bit insulting. Granted, Piper was closing in on fifty, but I was only thirty. Only six years separated me from the youngest Cabot brother.

"I've never heard anything so absurd." Piper sounded as if she had taken offense as well. "Why would the place be haunted? As far as I know, nothing interesting has ever happened to a Sanderling, on or off the property. And Gordon leads a life as dull as his plumbing business. He uses the barn out there to store surplus pipes and sinks."

Since Gordon ran the largest plumbing supply company in west Michigan, this seemed a logical use of the property. Certainly, none of this lent itself to rumors of a haunting. Of course, I wasn't completely up to date on rumors in our village. Although I was born and raised in Oriole Point, my parents moved to Chicago when I was eighteen, while I headed off to New York University. After graduation, I remained in New York City, thrilled to be working for the Gourmet Living Network. Things became far too thrilling when one of the chefs on a cooking show I produced decided to murder a fellow chef, who also happened to be her husband. The resulting publicity and trial convinced me to return to my hometown two years ago and open up The Berry Basket. I had never regretted it. Not only was my business a success, I was surrounded by friends, my parents were only a two-hour drive away, and I was engaged to Ryan Zellar, maybe the best-looking country boy in the state.

"The only weird thing I remember hearing about the Sanderling farm is that UFOs were spotted there in 1975," I said.

"What next?" Piper gave an exasperated sigh. "Leprechauns dancing in their pasture?"

"Everyone who's ever gone there after dark has been totally creeped out," Andrew added.

"I don't know why anyone would be at the Sanderling farm after dark unless they were a Sanderling." Piper narrowed her eyes at Andrew. "Or trespassing."

"If it isn't haunted, then it's unlucky," Dean persisted. "Even our mom talks about the Sanderling farm being a bad-luck place."

"Why? Because their winery business went bust?" I asked. "If so, that's pretty lame. People go out of business all the time."

"There's a bad vibe out there," Andrew said. "You can feel it. Dean's right. Pick another spot to start the rally. Otherwise you could jinx the whole thing."

Piper snatched her Birkin from the counter. "If you ask me, it's the Grunkemeyers who jinxed my plans by painting that silly cow on the barn. But Gordon has saved the day by letting us use his property. I won't have any ghostly gossip putting a damper on things."

"Maybe we can use the Sanderling farm again for next year's road rally. The theme can be ghosts and ghouls." I made a scary face. "Zombies, too."

"Given how much work we have to do today for the rally, we're moving as slow as zombies." Piper flung open my shop door. "Let's go, Marlee."

"She's right, guys. Before I change the poster artwork, we need to check out the haunted Sanderling farm. But if we're not back by noon, call the police." As I trailed after Piper, I turned to give them a wink. "Or a ghost hunter."

Piper was not happy I insisted we take my car rather than her white Hummer. But she always drove well under the speed limit. I couldn't bear the thought of crawling at thirty miles an hour while every other driver in the county zoomed past us. And as someone who tried to be ecologically friendly, I felt guilty whenever I found myself a passenger in her Hummer. None of us could figure out why Piper had such an affection for the gas-guzzling monster, especially since she and Lionel also owned a new Lexus, a Porsche, and two BMWs. But who had the time to figure out why Piper loved her Hummer? At the moment, I was trying to understand why there was a hulking Great Dane in my backseat.

In fact, I was so surprised when Piper had brought the dog out of her Hummer that I'd simply opened up my rear car door for him without a single comment.

"He's mine," Piper said, taking note of my stunned expression. "His name is Charlemagne."

I kept looking at the dog in the rearview mirror as we now drove up Lyall Street. Like many things in the village, it was named after Piper's family "I never pegged you for a dog lover,"

I said finally. "Especially one the size of a small horse. When did this happen?"

"Lionel's always wanted a dog, but they're so messy and loud. Not that I don't find some dogs quite adorable—especially the small ones—but they require too much attention. And you know how busy I am running the Visitor Center. However, after that nasty murder business last month, Lionel insisted we needed extra protection. Aside from our home security system, of course. We've only had Charlemagne a week. I do admit it was an adjustment at first."

I suspected it was far more of an adjustment for her household staff.

"His previous owners called him 'Charlie,'" she continued, "but Lionel and I thought a dog of such imposing dimensions deserved a grander name."

"He is big." The sound of his panting literally thundered in my ears. And every time I looked at my rearview mirror, a large pair of curious dark eyes stared back at me.

"I must admit I've grown fond him," Piper went on. "Lionel adores him. He even lets Charlemagne sleep in our bedroom, although thankfully not on our bed. Not that all three of us could fit in the bed. Despite his size, he's only a year old."

I glanced over my shoulder. His body took up the entire backseat. "Is he still growing?"

She frowned. "I hope not. Anyway, I have your aunt to thank for him."

A devoted animal lover, Aunt Vicki ran Humane Hearts, a sprawling animal shelter on over twenty acres of farmland in Oriole County. I had fostered a number of animals for her these past two years but managed to avoid adopting any of them. Like Piper, I thought I was too busy to properly take care of a pet. That changed with the arrival of a talkative African grey parrot dubbed Minnie, who was too delightful to resist. Within five minutes of meeting the clever bird, I had adopted her.

"You lucked out. Aunt Vicki doesn't get a lot of purebreds surrendered to the shelter."

"Vicki Jacob has connections, my dear. She had Charlemagne transferred from a Great Dane rescue organization in Indiana. Your aunt delivered him right to our doorstep."

That didn't surprise me. Last year, Aunt Vicki was responsible for rescuing a panther and two lions from some nutty survivalist in the Upper Peninsula. The gorgeous wildcats now resided at a wildlife park in California. I had no idea what had happened to the survivalist.

I snuck another peek at Charlemagne. Having been in my car a few minutes, I guess he decided it was safe to relax. When he threw himself down on the backseat to stretch out, I swear the car shuddered. "I'm not sure we'll need him as our bodyguard today. I don't expect the Sanderling farm to be particularly dangerous. Unless one of us steps on a post auger."

"I'd love to know who told Carol Grunkemeyer she was an artist." Piper shook her head. "You should see that cow on their barn. It's huge. And orange! I swear, it looks like a drunken giant got hold of a paintbrush. One with no artistic talent, by the way."

"I'm sure it's not that bad."

"Why else do you think those tourists wanted to take a picture of it? What an awful thing to have up there for anyone to see driving by. And in a year when BAS is celebrating their centenary. Visitors may think the cow was painted by one of their students. I should ask Lionel if he can find some town ordinance about graffiti. He may be able to force her to paint over it."

"Let it alone, Piper. Besides, the barn is on their property. It's not like Carol painted on the walls of city hall. And I think it's sweet. The Grunkemeyers loved their cow so much, they wanted to immortalize her after she died."

"A shame they didn't have her stuffed." She smoothed down her chin-length blond bob, an unnecessary gesture since her hair was always sprayed and styled to perfection. "At least we'll have nothing like that to worry about at the Sanderling farm. If memory serves, there's a long driveway to the farmhouse and a graveled lot beside it. Should be more than enough to hold all the starting cars for the road rally."

"How many have registered so far?"

"Twenty-nine cars have signed up, but I'm capping participation at thirty-five."

"Why cap it?" I asked. "The more people who register, the bigger the winning pot."

"Too many cars driving helter-skelter along country roads in search of clues can lead to disaster. By the way, I looked over your artwork for the poster. The colors are a bit too saturated. Tone it down before sending it to the printer. Although it's far superior to some of our past road rally posters. Last year, Cindy at the cheese shop volunteered to design a poster and it had to be redone five times." Taking a deep breath, Piper launched into a litany of past road rally mishaps.

I was content to let her take over the conversation. Now that we had left the village limit—and the tourist speed traps our local police had set up—I stepped on the gas, confident I could make good time along Blue Star Highway. The Sanderling farm was about eight miles from downtown Oriole Point, most of it along two-lane country roads. I was briefly tempted to stop by Zellar Orchards and spend a few minutes with Ryan. But it was Fourth of July week and I didn't want to be away from the store any longer than necessary.

Enjoying the summer breeze, I hung my elbow out the window. If Piper hadn't been sitting beside me, I would have plugged in my iPod so I could sing along with Adele, Beyoncé,

Taylor Swift, and Rihanna on my Diva playlist. Instead, I listened
with half an ear to Piper while enjoying the country scenery:
farms surrounded by grassy pastures, cows milling near
wooden fences, undulating rows of apple trees, fields of cornstalks, and blueberry bushes that stretched to the horizon.
Interspersed with the bucolic charm were several barns con-
verted into antique stores or quilt shops, roadside fruit and
vegetable stands, and a one-room schoolhouse now serving
as an art gallery.

I braked at the next crossroad, waving at the teenage girl
who rode past on a shiny black horse. I recognized her as
Courtney O'Neill, the daughter of a nearby blueberry grower.
Gordon Sanderling's property was only half a mile away.

When I turned up the long graveled drive belonging to the
Sanderling farm, Piper was just finishing her tale about the
Raspberry Road Rally of 2009, when two of the cars took a
wrong turn and drove right into Turtlehead Creek.

"No one will end up in the creek this year," I reassured her
as I parked the car near the pebbled path that led to the farmhouse. "That new subdivision blocks access for miles."

Charlemagne let out several deafening barks when Piper
and I got out of the car. With leash in hand, Piper went to
open the back door. While she did, I looked around.

Gordon's acres appeared well maintained. The pasture that
supported dairy cows three generations ago had been neatly
mown, and the farmhouse looked like it had a fresh coat of
gray paint. Numerous tire tracks in the gravel and dirt around
the barn indicated recent activity. A third of the property still
retained the last of the grapevines not destroyed by the
fungus that had spelled doom for the winery. And a thick
wall of trees stood about a hundred yards away on the east
end of the property; dandelions dotted the field between the
house and wooded area. If this was what passed for a haunted
farm these days, kids must be easily frightened.

"Wait, come back!" Piper shouted. "Charlemagne, stop!"

I turned in time to see the Great Dane bound past me. Still barking—this time in joy at being let loose—the overgrown puppy raced across the grass and headed for the trees.

"I'd go after him if I were you," I advised Piper. "And when you get him home, I'd add a dog trainer to your staff."

She stomped over to me. "Look at that dog. He's moving faster than a cheetah. I'll never be able to catch him, especially wearing these." Piper pointed at her five-inch wedged sandals.

"What do you suggest?"

Piper shot me a sheepish look. "You're the only one here wearing running shoes."

I turned to see Charlemagne disappear into the trees. "Why should he come to me? I only met him twenty minutes ago."

She pulled a doggy bone from her blazer pocket. "He'll come to anyone offering a doggy treat. But hurry. I don't want him getting lost on the property."

I took the leash and dog treat from her. "Fine. But while I'm gone, check out the parking area. You might also want to look for hidden post augers." Setting off toward the wooded area, I yelled back, "And next time, wear sensible shoes!"

When I reached the trees, there was no sign of Charlie, except for his excited barking.

"Charlie, come here!" While Piper preferred the aristocratic moniker of Charlemagne, the dog had been called Charlie for a year and would probably respond quicker to that. I headed in the direction of the barks, taking care to step over the roots and uneven ground. A branch caught my shirt and snagged it. Thankfully, I was dressed casual: jeans and a Berry Basket T-shirt.

"Charlie!" I whistled several times. "Come here, boy!"

This elicited another series of barks, along with the angry chattering of a squirrel who stared down at me from the branches of a tree. I wondered just how large this forest was. At first glance I had taken it for a small stand of pine, but it now seemed much denser and included white hemlock, oak, and ash trees, with ferns scattered along the grassy floor. I'd spent enough time hiking in the state forests to recognize the scat of deer, which was evident. I was also having a difficult time stepping over rocks, vines, and an increasingly thick groundcover. I'd already tripped and fallen twice, both times praying I hadn't landed on a clump of poison ivy.

"Charlie, come over here! I've got treats. C'mon, boy." Not only was I frustrated to have lost sight of the huge dog, I began to worry I might get lost. The nearby state forest could well be connected to the Sanderling property. If so, I'd be tracking that dog for miles.

When I no longer heard barking, I stopped. How fast could Great Danes run? Now that I wasn't batting away low-lying branches and stepping on crackling twigs, an unexpected silence greeted me. Only the sound of a rose-breasted grosbeak met my ears. I'd been a fool to come charging into this place alone, especially with my skewed sense of direction. I was grateful it was late morning, although the tall trees allowed in little of the sun. Accustomed to the wide blue vista of Lake Michigan outside my windows, I felt uneasy in this dimly lit forest. Now I knew why the Brothers Grimm set so many of their tales in the woods.

A wild blackberry bush ten feet away rustled. I froze. Was that a deer? Or was Dean right? Was this place haunted? I wished the Cabot boys hadn't mentioned the rumors about the Sanderling farm. I worried about who—or what—might be in here with me.

With a jubilant bark, Charlie burst out of the bushes toward me. I let out a sigh of relief as he pranced back and forth, tantalizingly out of reach. Trying to calm down my racing heart, I held out the doggy treat. With a happy yelp, he took the treat from my hand. He only needed two bites to finish it off.

Murmuring endearments, I scratched behind his ears as I tried to slip the leash over his head with my other hand. Thinking this was a great new game, Charlie snatched the leash and ran off.

"You've got to be kidding me." I raced after him. "Charlie!"

The leash clenched between his teeth prevented Charlie from barking, so I needed to keep close behind him. But he not only was the size of a small horse, he could run as fast as one, too. Five minutes later, he disappeared. This was ridiculous. Needing to catch my breath, I stopped and fished my cell phone from the messenger bag slung across my chest. I didn't care if Piper was wearing designer stilts. Charlemagne was her dog, and she was going to come in here and track down her monster puppy.

Before I could call her, loud barks broke out to my left. This time I was the one to burst through the bushes. He wasn't getting away again. But Charlie stopped barking as soon as he saw me. I knew now why he had been quiet for the past few minutes. He'd been digging away in the dirt, which he resumed upon my arrival. I looked for his leash and spotted it a few yards away, half buried by the dirt he flung to all sides. I picked up the leash before Charlie could get to it first. As soon as I did, I also spied what appeared to be an animal bone. Most likely a deer.

But when I turned to see what Charlie was digging up now, my heart sank. It was another bone, but not one belonging to a deer. In fact, it was far more than a bone.

It was a human skull.

Chapter 2

The Sanderling farm probably hadn't seen this much activity since the summer of 1975 when flying saucers were rumored to be spotted over their pasture. Things grew so hectic after I found the skull, I would have welcomed a UFO. It might have been able to transport me back to my shop in Oriole Point. Instead, I found myself knee deep in police officers . . . again. After the Bowman murder last month, I had had my fill of police and their probing, suspicious questions. Now it looked like I was about to be in for another round of interrogation. Not that I blamed them. If I were the police I'd want to question me, too. I only wish I had answers.

As soon as the industrious pup had unearthed the skull, I called Piper on my cell. Still determined to prevent her white pants and expensive sandals from being damaged, the infernal woman had never even tried to find me. Instead, she waited by the car until the state police arrived and sent them off into the woods in what she hoped was my general direction. By the time they discovered us, Charlie had dug up what looked to be an entire skeleton. I tried to put the leash on him, but every time I got close, he barked and scampered away. In the end, I had no choice but to let him dig as I sat on a nearby fallen log, praying no more bodies surfaced. The only thing to be grateful for were the wild blackberry bushes surrounding me. I ate about five fistfuls of the fruit while trying to avoid the sight of a human skeleton being unearthed.

When the police finally arrived, Charlie had grown tired and lay napping at my feet like an exhausted pony. As drained of energy as the dog, I simply pointed at the exposed skeleton. Charlie and I were led back to the farmhouse driveway, where an Oriole County sheriff van now joined a pair of blue Michigan State Police cruisers. Piper sat in the open doorway of my car, looking both irritated and bored.

"What in the world have you been up to in there?" she snapped at me.

"Oh, the usual. Digging up skeletons."

She grabbed the leash from me. "I thought you had wandered all the way to South Haven. We've now wasted an entire morning because you got lost in there."

"We're surrounded by police because *your* dog ran off and *your* dog wouldn't listen to me and *your* dog dug up a body. So think twice before you try to blame me for any of this."

Before Piper could come up with an offended response, a state trooper led us to a weathered picnic table on the front lawn. She ordered us to sit and remain quiet. There were lots of people bustling about the property now, some heading into the woods, others coming back. An ambulance pulled up, presumably to retrieve the skeleton. I noticed Courtney O'Neill watching all this activity from the road, still astride her horse. There was a small commotion when a Sanderling Plumbing Supply truck arrived and the police refused the company employee access.

One of the county officers was clearly a dog lover. He came back from the backyard shed holding a metal bowl. Emptying the contents of a water bottle into it, he laid it down in front of Charlemagne. The dog lapped it up in less than a minute. I was so thirsty I would have drunk from the water bowl myself if it had been offered.

At least eight police officers now milled about, including the medical examiner. Detective Greg Trejo of the Michigan State Police was among them. He had been part of the Bowman murder investigation, so we weren't strangers, although you wouldn't know that from his brusque demeanor.

"I know that good-looking officer," Piper muttered. "He questioned me last month after the Bowman murder. Suzanne at the police station calls him the 'Latino hottie.' If you ask me, he's a pretty chilly number."

I leaned closer to her. "Who do you think that skeleton is? I hope there isn't an Indian burial ground on the property. The last thing I need is some curse coming down on me for disturbing a sacred burial place. Although this whole grave defilement can be laid at the paws of this big baby here." I reached down and scratched Piper's dog behind his ears. Moaning with delight, he stretched out farther over my feet.

"The Sanderling family have lived here for a hundred years. Don't you think they'd know if there were bodies buried on the property?"

"Maybe all they needed was a Great Dane to dig them up."

She rolled her eyes. "There are no Indians buried on Gordon's farm."

"How do you know? A lot of native tribes settled in Michigan. Especially Potawatomi."

"True. But we're too close to the lake here; soil conditions aren't optimal for the preservation of material." Piper smiled. "Don't look surprised. I majored in archaeology back in college."

"Okay, Indiana Jones. Maybe that skeleton isn't from a Potawatomi burial ground. That means it's much more recent. I'll ask you again: Who do you think was buried in the woods?"

"No idea." Piper cast a jaundiced eye at the police officers on the property. "I hope some Sanderling ancestor wasn't deranged enough to take an ax to a relative. Perhaps the family got snowed in and things got out of hand."

"If you ask me, murder seems an extreme response to lake effect snow."

Her expression turned disapproving. "Let's not even discuss the possibility. Oriole Point has barely recovered from the Bowman murder. We don't need talk of another one so soon, especially during the week of Fourth of July. Besides, a skeleton is no proof of murder. A hunter might simply have dropped dead of a heart attack in there."

"Then who buried him? The deer?"

Before she could reply, Detective Trejo approached us, accompanied by a man from the sheriff's office. Yes, Trejo did qualify as a Latino "hottie" but that was only a surface judgment. His dark good looks and lean muscular frame were offset by a stony expression. He seemed to lack a sense of humor, as well as the ability to make anything resembling small talk. If I were a criminal, he'd scare the crap out of me. Maybe that was the point. At least his companion from the sheriff's office seemed more approachable. He was a slightly husky man in his thirties with curly brown hair beginning to thin and eyebrows that needed plucking. I warmed up to him immediately when he squatted beside Charlie and patted his heaving flank.

"This must be the puppy responsible for getting all of us out here," he said. The dog turned onto his back, inviting a few pats on his belly. After petting him for a moment, he looked up at Piper and me.

"I'm Captain Holt, head of Investigative Services at the sheriff's department. One of you, I believe, is Marlee Jacob."

I raised my hand. "That's me."

"Marlee Jacob," he repeated. "I'm going to guess your mother was a fan of Charles Dickens."

"Good guess." I smiled. "My mom's a professor of English literature at Northwestern. When she went into labor, she was reading *A Christmas Carol*. It also happened to be Christmas Eve. With a last name of 'Jacob,' she couldn't resist naming me after Scrooge's partner, Jacob Marley. I'm thankful I wasn't a boy. I might have been called Ebenezer."

He chuckled, but Detective Trejo didn't even blink. I swear the man was made of granite.

"You have my sympathy," Holt said. "My mother's favorite book is *To Kill a Mockingbird*. She was rereading it for the eighth time when I was born."

My smile grew wider. "She named you Atticus?"

"She did. At least our last name wasn't Finch."

Detective Trejo cleared his throat. "Now that we've gotten introductions out of the way, you may be interested to learn Ms. Jacob was also involved in the Bowman murder last month."

"So was I," Piper said. No matter how unpleasant the connection, Piper Lyall-Pierce refused to be overlooked.

"I seem to recall Ms. Jacob was the one to capture the murderer." Captain Holt nodded in what I hoped was approval. "The next time there's an opening in the sheriff's department, you may want to think about applying."

Trejo's expression grew even chillier. "Ms. Jacob employed a few unorthodox methods to unmask the criminal, including an illegal break-in. I doubt she'd pass the background check."

"I didn't actually break into the house. After all, I had known the—"

"You broke in. And you're lucky the Oriole Point police chief is a generous man who likes your family. I would have had you up on charges."

Detective Trejo grew less attractive by the minute.

Captain Holt seemed amused by the exchange. "I don't

care if Ms. Jacob employed magic to track down the killer. The important thing is that the murderer was caught. But none of us are here today to rehash the Bowman case." He pointed at the woods. "The skeleton buried in there may also be the victim of foul play. Let's concentrate on that right now."

"The person could have died from a heart attack or some sort of seizure," I suggested, hoping Piper was right. Perhaps it was just a hunter who suddenly dropped dead. Lord knows, I did not have time to be caught up in another murder.

"We'll know more when the medical examiner has been able to do her job. And the K-9 unit has just arrived." Holt looked over as officers emerged from a newly arrived sheriff's van. Accompanying them were two German Shepherds, who, fortunately, were leashed. Charlie sat up in obvious excitement at the appearance of the dogs, letting out a thundering bark. The K-9 unit barely glanced his way as they were led toward the woods.

"Do you think there are more bodies buried in there?" I asked him.

"That's what we intend to find out. We also need to know why you and this woman were on the property."

Piper stiffened beside me. Even I would have quailed before referring to her as "this woman." "I am Piper Lyall-Pierce," she announced. "And you should be aware that my ancestors founded Oriole Point."

Trejo turned to Captain Holt. "More important, her husband is Lionel Pierce, a retired executive who was elected mayor of Oriole Point three years ago. His wife currently works at the local visitor bureau."

"I do far more than simply work there." Piper's voice was sharp enough to cut glass. "I run the Tourist and Visitor Center in Oriole Point and there isn't a single thing to do with tourism in our village that I don't oversee."

"She's right," I chimed in. "If some tourist drops their frozen yogurt in the street, Piper is likely to hear about it."

"Exactly," Piper said.

"So you and your husband run things in Oriole Point?" Holt asked. That wasn't as impressive as it sounded. Our lakeshore village only numbered four thousand inhabitants.

Piper sat back. "Many people might say that."

And Piper would definitely be one of them, I thought.

Holt now looked at me. "I'm the owner of The Berry Basket in downtown Oriole Point," I said with no small amount of pride. Piper wasn't the only person who liked to brag. "My shop sells berry-related products, and I've been open for two years. Before that, I lived in New York City, but I was born and raised in Oriole Point. In fact, the Jacobs have been here almost as long as the Lyalls."

"Almost," Piper repeated.

"My family once owned orchards in Oriole County, but they were sold off when I was a child." No reason to tell him that after my grandparents died my father and his sister lost the orchards due to a stunning lack of business acumen. Since then, I had tried to make up for their shocking ignorance by working almost as hard as my namesake and his hard-hearted partner, Scrooge. However, I hoped I was much kinder.

"None of this explains why the two of you are here today," Holt said.

"We're at the farm because of the Blackberry Road Rally," I said. "I'm responsible for promoting the event."

"And I am in charge." Piper sat up even straighter.

"The rally is less than two weeks away," I continued, "and we planned to begin the rally at the Grunkemeyer farm, but that fell through. After Gordon Sanderling gave us permission to use his farm, we came here to make certain the property is suitable. If so, I can correct the info on the poster artwork before sending it to the printer."

"It's an exhausting process," Piper added. "And I still have to visit the rally locations to plant the clues. But first we need to find a suitable starting point for the event."

"This doesn't explain how you ended up in those woods, Ms. Jacob." For the first time, Captain Holt looked like the suspicious law enforcement officers I had come to expect.

I reached down to scratch the Great Dane behind the ears. He fell back against my knees in a doggy swoon. "This puppy got away from his derelict owner."

Piper gave a squeak of protest.

"He took off for the trees like he'd been shot out of a cannon," I went on. "Because Piper's not dressed for tracking, I ran after him. You may have noticed his legs are pretty long. The dog can run, and those woods go on for a lot farther than I thought. When I finally caught up with him, he was happily digging in the dirt. That's when the skeleton showed up."

"Did you disturb the site in any way?" Trejo asked.

I made a face. "Why in the world would I do that? Seeing a skeleton dug up is an unnerving sight. I wanted nothing to do with it. I tried to put a leash on Charlie so we could get out of there, but he wasn't cooperating. That's when I called Piper, and she took it from there."

"Aside from the skeleton, did you see anything unusual at the burial site?" Holt's dark brown eyes gazed at me with the same rapt attention as Charlie's.

"No. But Charlie was flinging so much dirt around, I didn't want to get too close."

"His name is Charlemagne," Piper reminded me.

Holt smiled. "He looks big enough to warrant more than one name."

I smiled back. Holt did indeed make a strong contrast to

the impassive Greg Trejo. As someone named after a literary character, I enjoyed casting people as their fictional equivalents. Looking at the two officers, I had a sudden thought that the trim, unsmiling Trejo seemed the perfect Mr. Spock to Atticus Holt's huskier—and friendlier—Captain Kirk.

"Are we done here?" Piper asked. "We've already been delayed far too long. Whatever was found in the woods has nothing to do with us or the Blackberry Road Rally. Therefore, I'd appreciate it if you would allow us to get on with our plans for today while the police handle whatever is going on in there." She pointed in the direction of the woods.

As always, Piper lived up to my belief that she was the embodiment of a privileged Edith Wharton heroine. Just now, she was being as insufferable as Bertha Dorset in *The House of Mirth*.

Trejo glared at her, but Captain Holt took her attitude in stride. "We need written statements from both of you. Officer Morrison will handle that." He looked over at the young woman who stood a few yards away with a fellow officer.

"I have more questions about this rally," Trejo said. "I thought road rallies were all about driving to certain destinations in the shortest amount of time. What do clues have to do with it?"

"There are all kinds of road rallies," I hurried to answer before Piper could. I didn't need her irritating the police and delaying us even longer. "You're thinking of TSD rallies, or Time, Speed, Distance events, where drivers follow a course and are timed at checkpoints. Our road rally is more of a scavenger hunt. Everyone is given a packet of instructions that contain ten clues leading them to different locales in the county. There's also a task to perform at each location. The first car to solve all ten clues and return to the final destination wins the grand prize."

"Which is?" Trejo asked.

"Cash, of course." Piper looked at him as if he were a complete fool.

"Each person pays a fifty-dollar registration fee," I explained. "With up to six people per car and the rally capped at thirty-five cars, that ends up to a nice chunk of change for the grand prize winner. There are cash prizes for second and third place, too. Not bad for driving around and having fun for a couple of hours. And that is the main purpose of the road rally: having fun."

"Excuse me a moment." Holt went over to two officers who had just returned from the woods. After they handed something to him, all three of them bent their heads to scrutinize it. My heart sank. I'd bet anything it was an evidence bag. I promised myself that I would never let Piper "volunteer" me for anything again.

Holt returned to where Piper, Trejo, and I waited in uneasy silence. He lifted up the clear plastic bag. "I need to know if this belongs to you, Ms. Jacob. If not, do you remember seeing this object when you were at the burial site in the woods?"

I squinted at the bag. Inside lay a charm bracelet encrusted with dirt. I could barely make out the details on the charms, but they were multicolored. "That doesn't belong to me. And I didn't see it when Charlie was digging. Then again, I didn't look at much after I saw the skull." I looked closer at the bracelet. "The charms look like tiny crayons."

Holt nodded.

"So the skeleton belonged to a woman." This knowledge made me even sadder. Such a colorful, whimsical bracelet indicated a young woman had been its owner. Maybe a teenager. What was that poor girl doing in the woods? Or had someone brought her body there?

"We'll know more after the ME report. But it's likely this belonged to the victim."

"Victim?" Piper asked. "Are you saying this was murder?"

"I'm not saying anything," Holt replied, now looking as impassive as Trejo.

"I guess that rules out the skeleton belonging to an ancient burial ground." I put my hand down on the wooden bench and was rewarded with a small splinter.

Holt took a deep breath before answering. "Given the condition of the bracelet and the skeletal remains, I think it unlikely. The burial appears relatively recent."

While I worked to pull the wooden splinter from my palm, a pine green van sped up the long driveway. It braked so suddenly, gravel spit in all directions. The door flung open and Gordon Sanderling emerged.

"Gordon doesn't look happy," I murmured to Piper.

Indeed, the owner of Sanderling Plumbing Supply was beet red and muttering under his breath. A high-strung fellow, Gordon was prone to panic attacks. Last October, he became quite upset when his bid to supply pipes for a new subdivision was turned down at a city hall meeting; EMS had to be called to handle his chest pains. Although at least a hundred pounds overweight, Gordon reminded me of Thomas Barrow, the scheming footman from *Downton Abbey*: dark haired, aloof, and defensive. As far as I knew, he had few friends or romantic attachments, which didn't surprise me. The few times I had encountered Gordon, an air of suspicion and regret seemed to surround him. Maybe the Cabot brothers were right about the Sanderling farm. Maybe it did bring bad luck, at least for its owner.

Growing even redder at the sight of all the police on his property, he headed toward us. "Piper, what is this all about?" he asked, ignoring both Trejo and Holt. "I kindly give you permission to begin your road rally here, and two hours later I get a call from the police telling me a body has been found on my farm. A body!"

"It was a skeleton, not a body," Piper replied, as if the two had no connection.

This only caused him to breathe faster. Any moment, he would hyperventilate. I wondered if they could use a spare evidence bag for him to breathe into.

"A skeleton?" This time, his agitated gaze embraced me as well. "I should have known better than to agree to anything the pair of you are involved with. Especially after that awful Bowman murder."

"I solved the murder," I protested. "Why are you blaming me?"

"I blame both of you for coming on this property and finding bodies. How do you think this will look for my business? I keep my company's plumbing equipment here. And what were you even doing in the woods? Were the two of you planning to break into my house next?"

"Sir, I need you to calm down," Holt ordered. "Ms. Jacob and Mrs. Lyall-Pierce do not appear to be responsible for the dead body buried in the woods. It is you and your family who own the land where the remains were discovered."

"That's not strictly true." Gordon took a deep breath in an obvious effort to control himself. "After my parents died, my brothers and sister sold their shares of the farm and our plumbing supply company to me."

"Then we'll need to speak with anyone in the family who has lived here in the past. Now we'd like you to come with us to where the skeletal remains were found."

When Sanderling opened his mouth to object, Holt added, "That was not a request."

Gordon seemed to see both Holt and Trejo for the first

time, his ire being initially directed toward us. "Of course, Officer. I'll do whatever the police and the sheriff's department require." He shot another resentful glance at Piper and me. "But I refuse to allow the road rally to come anywhere near my farm. You two will have to find another person stupid enough to let you do so. And I want you both off my property as soon as possible."

For once, even Piper didn't have a rejoinder. As for me, I doubted anything I said would make the situation better. I only hoped the Cabot brothers were wrong about the Sanderling farm being a jinx. It hadn't worked out well so far. This year's Blackberry Road Rally had gotten off to an unlucky—and deadly—start.

Chapter 3

Although Ryan greeted me with a kiss, he looked more suspicious than pleased by our sudden appearance at Zellar Orchards. It was one thing for me to drop in on him unannounced, but not with Piper in tow. Ryan had little patience with Piper's "lady of the manor" attitude.

"I didn't expect to see you here, especially with the Fourth only a few days away," he said. "What's up?"

"Just wanted to stop and say hi. We were checking out one of the road rally locations, and Zellars was on the way." I turned to wave at the brown hulk in my car. "And Piper adopted a Great Dane from Aunt Vicki. He's the sweetest thing, even if he barely fits in my car. His name's Charlie."

"It's Charlemagne." Busy texting on her phone, Piper didn't bother to look up from her screen.

Ryan raised his eyebrows at the large canine barking at us from the open backseat window. "Don't let him out. The beagles are running around the fields, and the barn cats are everywhere. Not to mention all the visitors here for U-Pick. Due to the early bumper crop for raspberries, traffic's been heavy all morning. I don't need some monster dog scaring the crap out of everyone."

Piper sniffed. "He is not a monster. Charlemagne is the

exact size he should be for a purebred Great Dane. You're simply too accustomed to those little beagles. And you should know that both breeds are hunting dogs."

"Yeah, and I don't want your dog hunting mine," Ryan said.

"Honestly," she muttered.

Two beagles came tearing out from behind the barn, barking in response to Charlie's loud appearance. All three dogs set up such a racket Ryan grabbed the beagles by their collars and gave them a stern talking-to. When he pointed to the fields, the dogs scampered off, albeit with a last longing look at Charlie.

"I've told Dad that we need to keep the dogs over in the apple orchards for the summer," he said. "They're having too much fun with some of the U-Pickers. The dogs, I mean. Not the people."

He was right about how busy Zellars was today. I had pulled up to the largest barn on the property—one of several—where a driveway led to the extensive berry patches out back. In the summer, this was where a Zellar family member would be stationed to guide cars to the correct U-Pick parking lot. In the short time we stood there, at least five cars drove past us. Like Crane Orchards in nearby Allegan County, Zellars was one of the most successful growers in west Michigan's famed fruit belt. Visitors came from as far away as Indiana and Illinois to pick Zellar cherries, peaches, berries, apples, and pumpkins.

Farther down the road lay the Zellar Farm Pantry, where pies made with orchard fruit were sold, along with apple butter, jams, and jellies. The orchards had been here since 1908, expanding every decade until the Zellars owned over two hundred acres. All five Zellar sons lived on or near the property, as did their parents. As Ryan's fiancée, I was expected to call this home when we married next January. Ryan planned to build a house for us on several adjoining acres, and it was assumed I would be spending far more time in the country than in Oriole Point. The only person who didn't assume this was me.

"Why are you out here directing traffic?" I asked. "Isn't driveway duty for the grandkids and younger cousins?"

"J.J. had to bring more bags out to the U-Pick scales. I'm holding down the fort until he gets back." He glanced over at a car that pulled up the driveway, then stopped. "Hold on."

While he answered the driver's questions about the U-Pick, I turned to Piper. "You're being rude. Ryan's not crazy about you as it is. But texting on the phone without saying 'hi' is something one of the Zellar kids would do. Or Natasha."

"One, I'm not enamored of Ryan, either. I have no idea why you're marrying him." Piper finally switched her phone off. "Two, don't compare me to that ridiculous Russian. She's never had a serious thought in her life. On the other hand, I am trying to take care of business. I texted Barbara Duchovic to see if we could use their farm to launch the road rally."

"Are you crazy? Why did you do that? The bank just fore-closed on their property."

"I hoped they wouldn't have to vacate the premises for at least a month. But she told me they're moving out next week." She frowned. "Bad timing for us."

"Yes. For the Duchovics, too." This road rally was turning into far too big a problem. "Please don't ask anyone else for the use of their farm without clearing it with me first. FYI, families about to lose their home are not on our list."

"We're running out of time, Marlee. Don't blame me if I resort to extreme measures. I hope you have some leverage with Mr. Zellar, even if he doesn't seem to be in an agreeable mood today. Then again, he rarely is."

"That's not true." I refused to let Piper irritate me. The day was problematic enough. "Ryan's one of the most laid-back people I know. Everyone in Oriole County thinks he's a great guy."

"Certainly the women do. Oh, I will admit Ryan is a good-looking man. Almost pretty, with that sandy blond hair and those blue eyes. Why wouldn't the ladies be bowled over by him?" She regarded me with a mixture of pity and disappointment. "Only I never thought you would be one of them. All that female attention is probably why he acts so entitled."

"Entitled?" I couldn't help but laugh. Talk about calling the kettle black. "Ryan is a sweet, unpretentious guy who loves me. And I love him. He'll be my husband in a few months, too. Now for the sake of our friendship, please don't say another word against him."

"Fine. Besides, I have more important things to worry about, like this road rally crisis."

"What's this about a crisis?" Ryan asked as he rejoined us.

I took a deep breath. "We have a little favor to ask."

His expression grew even more guarded. "If you've come to ask us to contribute money to the fireworks fund, forget it. My family's already paying for half of this year's display. Try hounding the O'Neills instead. They haven't paid for anything since the 2006 Hog Roast. The Zellars can't be the town's sole source of money."

Piper cleared her throat. "Lionel and I are paying for the remainder of the fireworks fund this year. We're sponsoring the Halloween parade as well."

"My family is the primary sponsor of the Pumpkinfest," he shot back.

I held up my hand. "Stop. This isn't a philanthropist of the year contest. Ryan, I know you think the road rally is stupid, but the Zellars have allowed the rally to begin here in the past. That's why we thought of you. You see, we've run into a little problem."

Ryan crossed his arms. "How little?"

"Tiny." I squeezed my index finger and thumb together. "We planned to begin the rally at the Grunkemeyer farm, but a tourist walked on their property and cut their leg on a post auger. There may be a lawsuit, and now Henry and Carol are afraid to host the event in case someone else gets injured. Gordon Sanderling agreed to let us begin the rally at his farm, so we went out there this morning to check things out." I hesitated, uncertain how to continue.

"And?"

"Charlie got loose, ran off into the woods, and I went to bring him back." I grimaced. "When I finally caught up with him, I discovered he'd dug up a dead body."

Ryan did a double take. "What?"

"He dug up a dead body."

"It was a skeleton," Piper corrected. "Marlee makes it seem as though Charlemagne unearthed a fully clothed corpse."

"Excuse me, but I'm out there alone in the woods and I come upon a human skull with an entire skeleton attached. Some part of me is still in shock. I'll have nightmares all week."

Piper waved a dismissive hand at me. "Gordon now refuses to give us permission to start the rally there. He acted as though we buried the body in his woods. When, for all we know, he's responsible for the body."

"Oh, he is not."

"Marlee, what do we really know about Gordon Sanderling? If you ask me, he seemed far too angry when he arrived at the farm today. I think he was deflecting attention from us."

"Or he could have been upset I found a dead body on his property."

Ryan didn't look happy. "If this is some sort of sick joke, it's not funny."

I gave him a weary look. "As if I have time to spread macabre stories during the week of the Fourth. I found a skeleton, the police are involved, Gordon is unhappy, and we don't have a place to begin the Blackberry Road Rally. Which brings us to the reason we're here."

"Sorry, Marlee," Ryan said. "But we've hosted the rally three times. Last time, a rally car ran down one of our ducks. Six years ago, several cars took a wrong turn and went into our pumpkin patch. They crushed a quarter of our pumpkin crop. The year before that, one of the drivers had a heart attack as the clue envelopes were being passed out."

I bit my lip. "I'm guessing you're not eager about doing it again."

"The Zellars have washed their hands of the Raspberry Road Rally." Ryan looked hard at Piper. "Along with the Blackberry Road Rally and whatever name you come up with in the future."

Piper turned to me with "I told you so" written all over her face.

I kissed him on the cheek. "We shouldn't have bothered you. Piper and I are responsible for the rally this year. It's our problem."

Ryan hugged me. "Babe, I'm sorry to turn you down," he whispered in my ear. "But my family will kill me if I let the rally anywhere near here."

I hugged him back. "Don't worry. We'll work it out."

"I'd like to know how," Piper said.

"I have an idea," I reassured her. "I'll tell you about it in the car. Why don't you wait for me there while I say good-bye to Ryan?"

Piper shot us a mocking smile. "Young love."

"She doesn't like me," Ryan said with a chuckle as Piper marched back to the car. "Of course, I'm not thrilled with her, either. I think the only friend of yours I genuinely like is Tess."

"I hope that's not true." I loved all my friends, even the ex-asperating ones like Piper and Natasha.

"What I hope isn't true is you being involved with another murder."

"No one is officially saying the body I found was murdered. And it looks like this person died years ago. Aside from a few more questions, the police are probably done with me."

Ryan brushed the hair back from my face. "Last month was bad enough. You were almost killed. Twice. If there's any chance you're in danger again, I want you to leave on a nice long vacation."

"During high season? Never." I squeezed his hand. "But I'm not in any danger, unless you want to count being harassed by Piper."

"Are you okay?" He looked at me with those dreamy blue eyes that always made me catch my breath, like a palpitating heroine in a romance novel. Small wonder the rest of the female population found him so appealing. "Finding the body must have been a nasty shock."

"I'm fine," I reassured him. "But I hope you plan to spend the night at my house. I wasn't kidding about having nightmares."

He kissed me. "I'll be there as soon as we finish spraying the blueberries. It will be late, though, around eight-thirty. And I have to be up early tomorrow. Before six."

"Hey, I'm marrying a farmer. I know all about the hours."

After another long kiss, I went back to my car, then pulled away from Zellars with a last wave. Charlie stuck his head over the seat and licked my cheek with touching enthusiasm.

Piper crossed her legs and arms, assuming a challenging posture. "You said back there you had an idea about where we can begin the rally."

"I do. The owner has to agree, but I'm pretty sure it's a done deal."

"Really? Who is this person?"

I glanced over at her. "You."

Piper's mouth fell open. "Excuse me?"

"It makes perfect sense to start at Lyall House. You and Lionel live on a huge piece of property overlooking the lake. You've got room enough to hold dozens of cars. And the road leading to your home goes nowhere near downtown, so there won't be any traffic problems."

"I can't have all those rally cars at my house," she spluttered.

"Why not? Unlock the gates and assign your staff to supervise things outside. All you have to do is greet everyone on your front steps."

I could see Piper desperately trying to figure out how to get out of this, except it made perfect sense. "I-I refuse to allow strangers to roam through my house."

"No one will go anywhere near your house. The rally participants only leave their cars to get the clue envelopes. C'mon, Piper. You can't ask other families to host the rally without expecting the duty to fall on you one day."

"There must be someone else. Maybe if we went back to the Grunkemeyers . . . "

I gave her a stern look.

Piper sat back with an exaggerated sigh. "Very well. Lionel and I will host the rally this year. After all, we've already done so much for this town. Why not this?"

Relief washed over me. The problem of where to begin the Blackberry Road Rally had been solved, and I could get back to work at The Berry Basket. There was that little matter of the dead body at the Sanderling farm, but how did that concern me? I was just an innocent bystander when Charlie went into a digging frenzy.

As I turned onto Blue Star Highway, I mulled over what had happened today. I wasn't a superstitious person, but discovering a buried skeleton had unnerved me. "Piper, do you think there's any truth to the Sanderling farm being unlucky?

The Cabot brothers could be right. Maybe it is cursed. The last thing I expected to see on the Sanderling farm was a skeleton."

"It certainly was the last thing Gordon expected." Piper scrolled through her phone messages. "And the farm isn't cursed. However, I'm starting to worry this road rally is."

"Why have you never heard rumors about the farm being haunted and unlucky? You know everything that goes on in Oriole Point. How did you miss this?"

"It's all I can do to keep track of the events and people in the village. I don't have time to worry about what goes on in the rest of the county. And that includes the Sanderling farm." Piper finally put her phone away. "Let's stop by my house to figure out how we should direct the rally cars."

"You and Lionel can work on that. I have three big product shipments due any day, and we're setting up a Fourth of July 'Red, White, and Blue' sale. I'm also working with my baker, Theo, on the pastry menu. I found some Colonial American berry desserts I'd like him to whip up for the shop. One of them is a peach raspberry strudel that sounds delicious."

"Well, I have even more to do. You're only responsible for one little store. I have to oversee the Fourth of July events for all of Oriole Point."

"Piper, you're the head of the tourist center, not secretary of state."

"None of you appreciate the weight of responsibility I have shouldered all these years. This entire region depends on tourism—"

"And farming, and fishing, and furniture manufacture—"

This time she interrupted me. "Nonetheless, tourism is the lifeblood of the lakeshore towns and villages. If the tourists don't come, everyone's business suffers. And that includes

The Berry Basket. It is my job to find ways to attract as many vacation visitors as possible."

I grinned. "Lake Michigan does a pretty good job of attracting people all on its own."

"Even the Great Lakes can benefit from my assistance."

"Fine." I refused to argue with a person who thought she was an equal player with Lake Michigan. "But be careful when you visit the rally locations to leave the clues. And when you do, I have a word of advice."

"Which is?" Piper asked impatiently.

I jerked my thumb at the backseat. "Leave the dog at home. This big baby has dug up enough trouble for one summer."

Chapter 4

As I feared, visions of skulls and giant dogs marred my dreams that night. My subconscious had clearly been shaken by memories of that buried skeleton. I woke up three times, breathing hard and shaking. Ryan slept soundly no matter how much I tossed and turned, and it was a comfort to hear him snoring beside me. Although maybe I could have done with a little less snoring. Still, I was grateful for his reassuring presence.

The next morning I dressed quickly, eager to leave for beach yoga. If ever I needed a few relaxing asanas and a session of guided meditation, it was today. Just the walk along the lake on the way to class did wonders for lowering my stress level. I sent up a prayer of thanks that I lived so close to the water.

The Jacobs had owned a charming Queen Anne house on a bluff overlooking Lake Michigan since 1895, and I was the most recent family member to live there. Not only was the view breathtaking, but a long wooden stairway led to our private stretch of beach. I headed down those stairs five days a week to attend yoga class at the popular public beach, only a fifteen-minute walk away. This morning, I was the first student to arrive. After unrolling my yoga mat on the sand, I settled into a lotus sitting position. Rowena, the instructor and owner of the Karuna yoga studio, gave me an approving nod.

The sight of Rowena Bouchet helped nudge me into a Zen state. The twenty-five-year-old always appeared beatific and serene. I'd be happy all the time, too, if I looked like her. Not only did Rowena boast the sleek, trim body of a yoga instructor, she had the most luminous hazel eyes I'd ever seen. And her gleaming blond hair was so long it reached her waist. During yoga, she wore it in a braid, but I'd seen her hair loose a few times; it brought to mind liquid gold. Every time I saw her, I felt like I was setting eyes on Titania, Shakespeare's Queen of the Fairies. A shame she didn't have magical powers and could somehow erase the image of that awful skeleton from my mind. I'd have to rely on my own powers instead, and by the time the other students arrived, I had managed five minutes of much needed meditation.

Normally we averaged a dozen students, but in summer many tourists signed up as well. At least twenty of us now sat cross-legged before our instructor. Although it was early, people were already setting up their beach umbrellas and spreading towels on the sand. Several children ran past us, plastic pails and shovels in hand. Their delighted squeals as they stepped into the water made me smile. Even during the first week of July, Lake Michigan often retained its chill. Depending on the weather, the water temperature might not turn balmy until August.

As Rowena began the session, I turned my gaze from the lake. Before I closed my eyes for Mountain Pose, I noticed two sailboats bobbing on the horizon. Time to focus.

Somewhere in the middle of Triangle Pose, my body relaxed and I was able to view what happened yesterday with detachment. The skeleton in the woods had been buried for years. It was an unhappy coincidence that Charlie had discovered it. A shame he wasn't a smaller dog. Ryan's beagles would have taken hours to dig up that skeleton. I took several deep breaths as we moved into Cobra Pose. The sand beneath my yoga mat felt warm and had a soothing effect, as did the sight of the blue glittering waters of Lake Michigan a few yards away.

As Rowena's soft voice guided us into the stretch of the pose, my thoughts drifted to yet another brush I'd had with murder. Only a few years ago, I'd been a successful producer of *Sugar and Spice*, the most popular cooking show at the Gourmet Living Network in New York City. I had even been the person to discover the husband-and-wife cooking team of Evangeline and John Chaplin at a food expo in Nashville. Within three years of our first meeting, both the show and everyone connected with it seemed headed for TV superstardom. Our meteoric rise came to a crashing halt when Evangeline learned her husband was having a steamy affair with one of the show's interns. A resourceful and vengeful woman, Evangeline used her superb pastry skills to bake a wedding anniversary cake for John . . . with a surprise ingredient of arsenic.

The subsequent murder trial became the cooking world's version of the O.J. case. This spelled the end of *Sugar and Spice*, Evangeline's freedom, and my career in television. After the judge sentenced Evangeline to life in prison, I returned home to Oriole Point, Michigan, and opened The Berry Basket. I hoped to never be involved with crime and killers again. But with the Bowman murder and this grisly discovery in the Sanderling woods, I feared my propensity for being around deadly events had surfaced once more.

"Let's lie back in Savasana for our final minutes," Rowena said, the cries of nearby gulls accompanying her words.

I couldn't help but remember that Savasana was also known as the Corpse Pose, which called to mind my first look at the skeleton. Although I no doubt appeared calm as I lay on my yoga mat, my thoughts were a fevered jumble of dead bodies, skulls, and poisoned cakes. I sighed as I heard the others around me get to their feet. While I might have managed a few moments here and there of peaceful stillness, most of the thirty-minute session had left me agitated and worried. I had a long way to go before I achieved anything resembling detachment.

After exchanging greetings with some of the regulars, I set off for home, yoga mat tucked under one arm. I put my head back and smiled at the clear blue sky overhead. It would be busy in town today, with every hotel, B&B, and private rental snapped up for the long holiday weekend ahead. I chided myself for wasting a minute on the skeleton. It was high season in Oriole Point, I was walking along my favorite lake in the world, and my sales at the end of the day were certain to be impressive.

By the time I reached my small stretch of private beach, I was more relaxed than at any time during yoga class. I shouted hello to my next-door neighbor playing Frisbee with Cleo and Pan, his chocolate Labradors. With a last look at the lake, I headed for the thirty-plus steps of my wooden stairway. Because my beach angled sharply, I had to plow uphill through a sand dune to reach the stairs. It felt as if I were marching through snowdrifts, but it was a great cardio workout. As was my stairway. When I reached the top landing, I bent over to catch my breath.

A burst of laughter greeted me. "You're really huffing and puffing," someone called out. "Maybe you need more than beach yoga to stay in shape."

I turned to see my best friend Tess Nakamura stretched out on one of my white Adirondack chairs. "I have nothing to be ashamed of," I said. "Members of the high school track team have collapsed after running up those dunes."

My other good friend Natasha waved at me from the chair beside her. "I think maybe you need a smaller *lestnitsa*," she suggested. A former Miss Russia, Natasha Rostova Bowman was a beautiful young woman with an instinct for self-preservation and a tenuous grasp of the English language. "I have money now. I will buy for you."

I joined my friends beneath the mulberry tree that shaded my lawn chairs and fire pit. "I'm assuming you offered to buy me a stairway with fewer steps."

"*Da*. But of course."

"*Spasibo*." Expressing thanks was the extent of my Russian. "But that would only make the stairs steeper, causing my hamstring muscles to explode on the way up. Besides, the exercise is good for me."

Natasha pouted in response. "Bah. You must come to my spa for such things."

"You have a spa?"

"*Nyet*, but I will soon. When I find a *zdaniye* big enough. I need much room for all the pretty spa things." Natasha flung her head back, a gesture she employed to allow the rest of us to better appreciate her lush mane of almond brown hair. Once a beauty queen, always a beauty queen, as evidenced by her impeccable make-up, sculpted nails, and designer summer outfit. Because I once had the funds to buy runway wear, I guessed her camel brown shorts and double-breasted belted top belonged to the latest resort collection of Michael Kors.

Natasha could afford it. After marrying a rich older man soon after competing in Miss World, Natasha had lived well for eight years—at least in a material sense. However, her sugar daddy turned out to be a violent brute with too many enemies; one of them murdered him last month. Now Natasha was wealthy, independent, and enjoying her status as a merry widow. I didn't blame her, even if some people in the village were put off by her hyperbolic view of life. But Natasha was bighearted, generous, and entertaining. Too honest and impulsive for her own good, perhaps. And I worried she might run through her new bank account with alarming speed.

I sat in the Adirondack chair facing my friends. "Please don't start buying property without getting expert financial advice. Cole's will has barely been read. You need to think carefully about what you want to do for the rest of your life."

"The rest of my life? Do not be *psikh*. Crazy. I am too young to think like that."

No point reminding her that she was twenty-eight, two years younger than me. I hoped the money lasted until she found her next husband. Natasha seemed like the type who would end up at the altar a good three or four times—an attitude light-years away from both Tess and me. While I planned to marry Ryan next January, there were moments when the idea terrified me. As for Tess, she and David had been a couple since they met as eighteen-year-old college students. Twelve years later, they were as close and loving as ever. And in no hurry to make it legal.

I pointed to my lovely blue house across the narrow road. The bluff and lakeshore view served as part of my front lawn. "I'd ask the two of you inside for coffee and breakfast, but I barely have time to shower. Theo is whipping up new pastries to celebrate the Fourth. Since I found the recipes in a Colonial American cookbook, I have no idea how tasty they'll be. We may need to come up with something new in a hurry."

"No problem," Tess said. "I have a ten o'clock dentist appointment."

"As much as I appreciate the visit, why are the two of you here? Has something happened?" Tess and Natasha only spent time together if I was part of the group.

"We ran into each other at the grocery store an hour ago," Tess replied.

I turned to Natasha next. If she wasn't working at Kitchen Cellar, the shop she and her late husband owned, Natasha usually slept till noon. Since Cole's death, she hadn't worked there at all. "Seems pretty early for you to be grocery shopping, Miss St. Petersburg."

"I must buy food for my *malenkaya kukla*."

"Who?"

"My little doll." Natasha reached for a large white straw purse and pulled it onto her lap. "Her name is Dasha."

Two tiny ears peeked out from the purse. A second later, the rest of the dog's head appeared.

"You have a dog?" First Piper, now Natasha. "Let me guess. My aunt Vicki had something to do with this."

Natasha took the dog out of her purse, showering kisses on its scrunched-up face. "I ask your *tetya* Vicki to find me a dog many months ago, a little sweet one. And she bring me such a beauty two days ago." When she cradled the dog, Dasha closed her eyes in apparent bliss. "We are in love. I dream of a dog just like this. Is she not *prelestnyy*? Adorable?"

"Very *prelestnyy*." I reached out to pet her. "Looks like a Yorkie. Is she a puppy?"

Natasha kissed Dasha again. "She is my puppy, my *rebenok*. My baby. Only seven months old. And I love her."

"At least she'll be easier to carry around than Piper's new dog. She and Lionel adopted a Great Dane."

"Piper has a dog?" Tess asked in obvious disbelief. "Last year, she tried to get Lionel to institute a sunset curfew for dogs. She claimed barking after dark was a form of noise pollution."

"She should expect plenty of noise pollution at Lyall House from now on. Her dog's voice box must be the size of a laptop."

"Wait a second. Was this dog with you and Piper yesterday?" Tess asked.

"How did you know I was with Piper? I meant to call you, but my shipments came in yesterday and things got super hectic. Then we got slammed with customers right before closing. It was after ten before I could lock up. Wait till you hear what happened with Piper and her dog."

This time it was Tess who reached for her purse beside the chair. "As of this morning, all of Oriole Point has heard." She handed me the latest issue of the *Oriole Messenger*. "It says a skeleton was dug up on the Sanderling property. Given the size of a Great Dane, I assume Piper's dog played a role."

Scanning the article, I felt relief at its brevity. After all, there were few details available, aside from skeletal remains being uncovered on the forested section of the Sanderling farm. Unfortunately, the article also claimed Berry Basket shop owner Marlee Jacob was the person to discover the remains; Piper merited a brief mention when the reporter explained she was there checking out a starting location for the Blackberry Road Rally.

"I can't believe it made the paper the very next day," I said.

Tess laughed. "That's how newspapers usually work. Cindy from the cheese shop told me that one of the Sanderling plumbing supply guys was there at the same time the police arrived. It looks like he was the person who contacted the *Messenger*." She raised a wary eyebrow. "This won't go over well at the *Oriole Point Herald*. They've been scooped."

Even though our village was small, it supported two weekly papers. The rivalry between the papers approached operatic proportions, and I feared there would be an inordinate amount of interest directed toward this skeleton business now.

"That is why Tess and I come here after we see newspapers at grocery store." Natasha cuddled her puppy. "We must know you are safe."

"I figured you'd be at morning beach yoga," Tess added, "so we sat and waited for you to return. Are you okay? Finding a skeleton must have been an awful experience."

"I'm fine. Although I could do without the memory of that skull being uncovered." Mindful of my upcoming pastry meeting with Theo, I quickly told them what happened at the Sanderling farm. While Natasha seemed amused, Tess looked troubled.

"Someone must have been murdered and then buried in the woods," she said.

"Most likely many years ago. Which means it's nothing for us to worry about." I got to my feet. "Now I have to hustle my butt into the shower. I have tons I need to get done today."

Tess left the comfort of her Adirondack chair as well. Since she wore black jeans and an Oriole Glass T-shirt, she clearly planned to go to work right after her dentist appointment. "I don't know what's more shocking: you finding a skeleton, or Piper owning a dog."

I grinned. "He's huge, Tess. You know how I try to match up people with their fictional counterparts?"

"All too well. You view me as Elinor Dashwood from *Sense and Sensibility*. And Natasha is Jasmine from Disney's *Aladdin*."

Natasha looked up from cooing over her little dog. "Who is this Jasmine?"

"A beautiful, exotic woman," I told her. No need to mention it was a cartoon character.

"What does this have to do with Piper's Great Dane?" Tess asked.

"He reminds me of the Hound of the Baskervilles. Only lovable."

She didn't look happy. "Be careful, Marlee. You've already stumbled upon two dead bodies this summer. If this keeps up, you may need Sherlock Holmes to get you out of trouble."

The Berry Basket smelled like pastry heaven. As usual, Theo had been baking in my shop kitchen since dawn. The desserts at The Berry Basket were berry themed, with three to four different kinds each day. This morning, he had worked his magic on the Colonial recipe I'd found for peach raspberry strudel. When I entered the kitchen, I headed for the cooling racks. Inhaling the mouth-watering aroma of peach, raspberry, and buttered crust, I grabbed a knife and sliced a small piece. It was still hot, and the baked fruit burned the top of my mouth. But it was delicious. I cut another small piece.

"You should let it cool," Theo warned.

I was too busy savoring my second bite. "You've outdone yourself," I told him. "And the golden raisins make it even fruitier. If this is an example of eighteenth-century pastry, I would have loved sitting down to dessert with Abigail Adams."

He nodded. "You can really taste the ginger."

"The nutmeg, too." I gazed in approval at the sheets of strudel on the steel counter. "Another thirty minutes and this will be cool enough to slice."

"The turnovers are ready to go out front now." Theo nodded at the trays on an adjacent counter. "I filled them with blackberries, raspberries, and the last of the strawberries."

I didn't need to taste those pastries because Theo and I ran a test batch yesterday morning. The mixed-berry and cream cheese turnovers were sinfully delicious, and probably my least healthy offering in the shop. But it was a holiday week. Most people would be pigging out on barbecue, ice cream, and a whole lot of beer. No reason to turn down Theo Foster's rich Fourth of July pastries. It would be unpatriotic.

I scanned the pristine kitchen. Theo Foster was not only a dazzling baker, he was compulsive about cleanliness and neatness. "How about the cupcakes?"

He pointed to the rolling racks where large trays of vanilla-frosted cupcakes were stacked. "There are two dozen left to frost. I'll be done by the time you open."

"It's early. I'll help you." Each of us grabbed a small rack of cupcakes. As per my instructions, the cupcakes were filled with blackberries and raspberries. While these weren't

Colonial recipes, the dark blue and red fillings combined with the white frosting would satisfy my Red, White, and Blue holiday theme. Especially once I stuck a tiny American flag in the center of each cupcake.

We worked in companionable silence for a few minutes until Gillian arrived.

"Greetings, fellow berry lovers." She donned her store apron. "I can smell the strudel from the back parking lot. If they taste as good as they smell, we'll be sold out by noon."

"They're fantastic," I assured her. "When you get the chance, please put the lingonberry jams out on the shelves. My supplier got them to me sooner than expected. I've priced them, so they're ready to go. Same with the tins of strawberry tea."

"Sure thing." Gillian made her way to the adjoining storage room, where the boxes of yesterday's shipments were kept. Before she disappeared inside, she turned to face me. "Maybe it's not such a good time, seeing as we have to open soon, but I wanted to let you know my dad's a little upset." She didn't meet my gaze, which worried me.

Twenty-one-year-old Gillian Kaminski was an earnest, hardworking young woman. A student at Grand Valley State University, she had been my first hire when I opened The Berry Basket two years ago. While she only worked part-time during the school year, she pulled almost as many hours as I did at the shop during the summer. She was dependable, sweet, and far more sensible than either Cabot brother. If she was troubled, something must be wrong.

"Why is he upset? Are things fine at home? Is your mom sick again?"

Gillian bit her lip, looking even more uncomfortable. With her long, curly blond hair, blue eyes, and determined expression, she always reminded me of *Alice in Wonderland.* Just now, she looked as young as Lewis Carroll's Alice, too. "I shouldn't have said anything. It's really none of my business. But Dad called me this morning."

"I don't follow."

"Today's story in the *Messenger* surprised him. His feelings are hurt."

Gillian's father was the editor of the *Oriole Point Herald*, chief competitor of the *Oriole Messenger*. The two weekly papers fought over readership like boxers in a ring. In a small town like ours, finding a skeleton buried on a nearby farm qualified as big news. Because Gillian worked for me, Stephen Kaminski probably thought I would go straight to him with any juicy journalistic tidbits.

"I never spoke to a single reporter from the *Messenger*, and since there are only two of them, I would know. Someone from the state police or sheriff's office must have talked about the discovery. Plus Gordon Sanderling was there yesterday, and at least one of his employees." I bent back to the task of frosting the cupcake in my hand. "After the publicity about the Bowman murder, I'd do anything to avoid talking to the press again."

"I told Dad that, but he's manic about the *Messenger*. They've scooped him."

"The *Messenger* comes out on Tuesday, and the *Herald* three days later. If something newsworthy happens early in the week, they'll scoop your father's paper. But it works the other way, too. If a house burns down on Thursday, the *Herald* is the paper of record."

"I agree, but my dad is still upset. He wants to interview you."

I shook my head. "The only response I intend to give about all this is 'No comment.' And that includes your father."

"What happened on the farm?" Theo now looked as anxious as Gillian. "I don't read the newspaper. How did you find a skeleton?"

This wasn't good. According to his resume, Theo Foster

was thirty-seven years old but looked much younger. He also acted like a boy still in his teens: insecure, uncommunicative, nervous. And in the seven months he had lived in Oriole Point, few had ever seen him in the village. In fact, I would be shocked if he had a single friend. There were times I suspected he had a form of Asperger's. Then again, our village embraced more than its fair share of eccentrics. Theo could simply be a younger version of Old Man Bowman and Leticia the Lake Lady. Whatever happened at the farm, I didn't need to upset my industrious and talented baker. Not during Fourth of July week.

Taking a deep breath, I explained how Piper and I needed to scout out a new location for the Blackberry Road Rally. I threw in a quick description of the road rally and why it was being held in honor of the BAS. I was about to explain what the Blackberry Art School was when Theo surprised me.

"I know about BAS. I was a student there," he said. "Twenty years ago."

"Really? I didn't know you'd ever been to Oriole Point before this winter." I tried to recall the details on his resume. I did remember that his last address was Champaign, Illinois.

He grew even more serious, which was saying something. "I was here the whole summer. My mother thought I should learn more about pottery. I was a potter."

I exchanged glances with Gillian, who seemed as surprised as me. "I had no idea."

"I don't make pottery now. I bake instead." He looked down at the tray of cupcakes he was icing. "How did you find a skeleton?"

"To be honest, I wasn't the one who found it. Piper's dog did."

"Piper has a dog?" Gillian sounded as stunned as Tess had.

Eager to put this whole episode behind me, I described

what happened at the farm yesterday, which was little more than what was printed in the newspaper.

"The police have no idea who this person was?" Gillian asked when I was done.

"The medical examiner could have answers once the forensic tests are done. But it looks like there's little for the police to go on." I paused, wondering if I should mention it. Then again, it would be a tiny scoop for Gillian's dad. "Except for the bracelet found buried with the body."

"Bracelet?" Theo and Gillian asked at the same time.

"A gold charm bracelet, although only the bracelet links are gold. The charms themselves are ceramic and painted to look like tiny crayons."

With a startled cry, Theo pushed himself away from the counter. The violent movement sent the tray of cupcakes crashing to the floor.

"What's the matter?" I asked in alarm.

"I made that bracelet," he replied with a stricken expression.

"What?"

"I made the bracelet at the school that summer. I know who's buried in the woods."

Chapter 5

I didn't want to appear callous, but the last thing I needed was another murder. Even one that was twenty years old. Fourth of July was three days from now. Since the holiday fell on a Friday, it promised to be a long and profitable weekend. Every shop and restaurant would be open later than usual and only festive tourists sleeping off hangovers were likely to get much rest. The long-range weather forecast was also ideal, which meant anyone who owned an Oriole Point vacation home or rented a boat slip at our marina would be in town. And that didn't include the thousands of visitors drawn to our gorgeous beaches. I didn't have a second to waste on anything but business.

After Theo's shocking revelation, however, I had little choice but to inform the authorities. I also needed to get the store ready to open, frost the cupcakes that hadn't been knocked to the floor, and put out the lingonberry jam, strawberry tea tins, and new shipment of ceramic berry bowls. Gillian was not available for those tasks since she was busy speaking with her dad on the phone. I now knew what the headline of the *Oriole Point Herald* was going to be this Friday.

It took over five minutes to calm Theo down. The normally stoic fellow became so overwrought I feared only a sedative would do the trick. If Piper had been here, I would have borrowed one of those Xanaxes she always carried with her. I had no sooner convinced Theo to sit quietly and try to relax when Ryan's sister-in-law Beth showed up to drop off the dozen fruit pies she delivered from Zellar Orchards each morning. I had time to exchange only the briefest greetings with her. My attention and concern were still focused on Theo, who now sat silent and unresponsive on a metal stool near the oven.

I needed to decide which law enforcement agency to call. The Oriole Point police were ill equipped to handle serious crimes, as evidenced by their handling of the Bowman murder. Besides, the remains had been found out in the county, which meant it fell under the jurisdiction of the state police and the sheriff's department. Because I had no desire to enjoy Greg Trejo's Dementor-like presence twice in two days, I retrieved the card Atticus Holt gave me yesterday. Like a heroine from the Old West, I was counting on the sheriff to help me out of this mess. Or, in this case, the head of the sheriff department's investigative branch.

Thankful when he picked up on the second ring, I told him about Theo's claim. Holt assured me he'd be here as soon as possible. I looked forward to handing this whole problem over to him. It was now fifteen minutes past opening and we had six customers lined up outside. As soon as I unlocked the front door, they all headed straight for the ice cream counter.

In the morning, we had a number of people who stopped in for fresh-berry smoothies, available with ingredients such as protein powder, wheat germ, flaxseed, and chocolate chips. Later in the day, ice cream cones and sundaes would be even more popular, but morning Berry Basket regulars craved breakfast smoothies and Theo's pastries. One of us had to man the ice cream counter and power blender, while another took care of the register. Gillian was already scooping black-berry frozen yogurt for a smoothie, a position she was likely to be occupied with for some time. Only I couldn't stay out front to help her, not with Theo catatonic in the kitchen and a sheriff's captain en route.

After ringing up the first of my smoothie-loving customers, I made another phone call. I knew Andrew worked at Beguiling Blooms today, and Dean was in Zeeland interviewing someone for his blog. Tess would be up to her ears in customers at the glass studio, which only left one person to contact on such short notice. I breathed a sigh of relief when my call found Natasha about to have a pedicure at Nirvana Nail Salon just down the block. Before I could finish cashing out the next two customers, Natasha burst into the shop, giving a gracious wave as if she were parading down the stage at Miss World.

"*Dobroye utro!* Good morning! I am here to help sell berries."

Gillian regarded me with an expression of horror. "You're letting Natasha work here?"

"Only until I'm done with things in the back. She'll be fine. After all, she and Cole both worked at their store."

Natasha swept me up in a long hug, followed by kisses on both cheeks.

"You did actually work at Kitchen Cellar, right?" I asked her in a low voice.

She tossed her long hair back. "Mainly I am what Cole called 'window dressing.' But I work sometimes, too. Only I do not have fun."

I touched the computer screen of my register. "And you know how to ring up purchases?"

Natasha shrugged. "Kitchen Cellar is not exact same as Berry Basket computer. But I just hit numbers of what people are buying, *da*? Ding, ding, ding. Is easy."

I felt a stress headache "dinging" its way to me. Three more customers entered the store at the same time I heard knocking on my back door. Captain Holt had arrived.

I took off my Berry Basket apron and handed it to Natasha.

"Here, put this on. I'll try to take care of things as fast as I can. And if you run into trouble, Gillian will help you."

Gillian looked like she wanted to cry.

It was my turn to give Natasha a hug. "*Spasibo*. Thank you for helping me out like this. And I'll treat you to your next mani/pedi."

Natasha slipped the chef apron over her head and tied the belt behind her. It was a shame the apron completely covered her designer summer outfit. "You are my friend, Marlee. My best friend in world. Dasha and I want to help."

A small yip erupted from the white straw purse on the counter, and a Yorkie head popped out to look at me. I'd forgotten about the dog who now lived in her purse.

"I can't have a dog in the shop. Especially since I serve food." My mind raced as to where I could put Dasha. Not in the kitchen, and my storage room was jammed with delivery boxes. I did have a tiny office, even if it currently was awash in artwork I had worked on for the road rally. The knocking on my back door grew louder.

Natasha heard the knocking, too. "Go talk to sheriff man. We will be fine. I keep little Dasha in purse." She laid the purse on the floor at her feet. "My baby stay there. She not move."

With a prayer that the Health Department wasn't about to make a surprise inspection, I hurried to the back room to let Captain Holt in. On my way through the kitchen, I noticed that Theo still sat motionless on the stool. I feared I might have to alert a medical professional.

My worry must have been apparent since Captain Holt's first words were, "Are you all right, Ms. Jacob? You're looking a little pale."

"I've been stressed out since the whole skeleton thing. Now I'm worried about my baker. I'll take you to him." As he followed me, I glanced over my shoulder. "And please call me Marlee. When people use Ms. or Miss in front of my name, I automatically think I'm in trouble." I'd had attorneys and the judge refer to me as Ms. Jacob so many times during the Chaplin trial, I cringed whenever anyone called me that now.

"How long has Mr. Foster worked for you?"

"Since December eighteenth of last year," I answered as we walked into my airy professional kitchen. Before The Berry Basket moved into the building, it housed a business called Cookie Monster for ten years. I was forever grateful the previous owner had outfitted the kitchen with state-of-the-art baking equipment.

Although Captain Holt and I now stood a few feet away, Theo didn't even raise his eyes in our direction. "Theo, I called Captain Holt to come talk to you," I said in a gentle voice, not wanting to alarm him further. "He works for the county sheriff's department. I told him that you might know who the bracelet belonged to."

No response. At times like this, Theo Foster reminded me of the passive and bewildering clerk in Herman Melville's *Bartleby the Scrivenor*. I only hoped things worked out happier for Theo than they did for Bartleby.

"Mr. Foster, I need to ask you a few questions." Holt kept his voice as quiet and nonthreatening as mine. "If you knew the person who was buried in the woods, I understand this may be upsetting. But it appears a crime has been committed and you could have some answers for us." Again no response from Theo. Holt turned to me. "I may have to question him at the sheriff's office."

I shook my head. "Taking him there will make him clam up even more."

"I don't see how that would be possible." Holt allowed himself a rueful grin.

Theo made a jerking movement, as if he had been sleeping and just awoke. "Are you here to arrest me?" he asked in a hoarse whisper.

"No. I only want to ask you a few questions," Holt said. "Unless you've done something I should arrest you for."

Theo flinched. "No, no, no."

I gently touched his shoulder. "Can you tell Captain Holt what you told me? Please."

After a long pause, he answered, "I made the bracelet. I made it for her. For Sienna."

"Who is Sienna?" Holt asked.

"I loved her." Despite the heartfelt sentiment, his voice was devoid of emotion. "That's why I made the crayon bracelet for her. Because her name was Sienna."

"I think I understand," I said to Holt. "Her name was the same as a crayon color, the one that's a brownish orange. It must have been a cute little joke about her name."

Theo shook his head. "The bracelet wasn't a joke. It was a gift. Because I loved Sienna and wanted to make her happy."

"Was she happy with your gift?" Holt asked.

"Yes. She wore it all the time. She must have been wearing it when she died." He now looked at us, his gray eyes wide. "When someone killed her."

Both Holt and I stiffened. "Who killed her?" Holt whipped out a small pad and pencil from his shirt pocket.

"I don't know. There were a lot of them there that summer."

"Why do you say she was killed?" Holt narrowed his eyes at my baker.

Theo's clean-shaven face hardened, and I could see his jaw tighten. While his voice betrayed no emotion, it was clear his feelings about Sienna ran deep. "Everyone said she drowned. But how could she have drowned if Marlee found her body in the woods? I always thought it wasn't true. They lied."

For a moment, Theo looked like the middle-aged man he was, and the wild desolation on his face was wrenching. But as quickly as the despair appeared, it was gone. Theo once more reverted to his impassive, childlike state. "They lied," he repeated.

"Who are these people who lied?" Holt asked. "Do they live in Oriole Point?"

"They did twenty years ago. They were at the school with me."

I remembered how Theo surprised me earlier by revealing he had been a summer student at BAS. "Do you mean the Blackberry Art School?"

"Yes, I was there. So was Sienna. I made pottery. She painted."

"What was Sienna's last name?" Holt had his pencil poised over his notebook.

"A beautiful name. Katsaros." He paused. "Sienna was beautiful, too."

I searched my memory for anyone with that name but came up with nothing. Then again, if something happened to a girl called Sienna Katsaros twenty years ago, I would only have been ten years old. At that age, I spent all my time learning to ride horses and having desperate crushes on boy bands. I looked at Theo, sitting hunched over in what was almost a fetal position. If he was thirty-seven now, that meant he was a seventeen-year-old art student back then. I wondered if he was more open and animated as a teenager. I hoped so. Most students lived at the school compound during the summer session and, like all teenagers, they could be cliquish. Tess and I had thoroughly enjoyed our two summers at BAS, but neither of us were shy or easily intimidated. A socially awkward person like Theo might have had a difficult time there.

Holt wrote something down, then looked up. "Why would anyone kill Sienna Katsaros?"

"She was the best artist at the school," Theo replied. "No one was as good as Sienna. Everyone was jealous. But not me. I loved her."

"Did she love you?" I asked.

"I think so. When I gave her the bracelet, she kissed me." He touched his right cheek. "Right here."

"Do you remember the names of the art students who were jealous of her?" Holt asked.

"I remember the painter. He was a Christian."

"What was his name?" Holt had his pencil poised to write again.

But like morning mist over the lake, Theo appeared to be drifting away from us. The news about Sienna's burial in the woods had upset his fragile equilibrium. "Leah shouldn't have been jealous, though," he said in a bewildered voice. "She could do magic."

This conversation grew stranger by the minute. "Leah did magic tricks?" I asked.

"Not tricks," Theo answered. "It was old magic. Bird magic. She knew how to call birds so they came to her."

Holt and I exchanged confused glances. "What was Leah's last name?" he said.

"I don't remember. It was a long time ago. But I remember the other students called Sienna 'the bane of their existence.' They laughed when they said it, but I could see they were serious. And it wasn't a silly nickname like the others. I looked up *bane* and it was not a nice thing to say about anyone. They were jealous. All of them."

"But not you." Holt didn't phrase this as a question.

"I loved her. I could never be jealous." Theo closed his eyes. "I'm tired, Marlee. I want to go home."

From the moment I sat down with Theo Foster to interview him for the baker position, I'd felt protective of him. He was the same height as me, and I was only five feet seven. He also had a slight, wiry frame, with not the slightest hint of a paunch as he approached forty. And his boyish expression was matched by an equally youthful haircut and an often childlike view of things. Every time I was with him, I couldn't keep my maternal instincts from surfacing. At the moment, my feelings approached mother lioness proportions.

"This may be too much for Theo to take in," I said. "If the bracelet belongs to someone he once cared about, we should give him time to absorb what all this means."

"A young woman was possibly murdered and buried in those woods," Holt said. "And Mr. Foster has given us a name. If the body we found checks out to be someone called Sienna Katsaros, we're going to need a lot more information from him."

"Understood. But not right at this moment." I patted Theo on the shoulder. The poor man was trembling. "Could we speak outside, Captain Holt?"

Holt surprised me with a smile. "Why do I have a feeling you won't take no for an answer?"

I led Captain Holt outside to the rear parking lot reserved for employees and deliveries. The sound of horns from the nearby Oriole River greeted us as a steady stream of boats made their way out onto the lake. Despite the delicious aroma of my pastry kitchen, I felt relieved to be standing in the warm July sun with the sounds of normal village activity all around me.

"I probably should have told you about Theo before you questioned him," I began. "As you can see, he doesn't react as most people would. I suspect he may be autistic, Asperger's syndrome perhaps. Or he could suffer from some other developmental disability. All I know is you can't press him too much. Three months ago, there was a grease fire in the kitchen. He was quick enough to put it out as soon as it began, but it upset him for weeks afterward. Much more than it should have."

"Ms. Jacob—"

"Marlee, please."

He frowned, but his expression remained kind. "Marlee, we have a murder investigation on our hands. So far, your baker has the only pertinent information. And he claims he made the crayon bracelet found with the body."

"Maybe he did. Or maybe there's some other story connected with it. I don't know how Theo views the world. Not that I think he's crazy or dangerous. He seems a gentle soul, and a phenomenal baker. I couldn't ask for a more reliable employee. But in the seven months he's worked for me, I've learned next to nothing about his personal life."

"You must have interviewed him for the job."

"Of course I did. I can give you a copy of his resume. He lived in Champaign, Illinois, before moving here. No wife or children. He worked in an industrial bakery in Champaign for eight years. I called his references there and they all agreed he was responsible and trustworthy."

"Nothing seemed off about him during the interview? Even you have to admit he's odd."

"It's clear you don't live in Oriole Point."

Holt seemed puzzled. "No. I live in New Bethel."

"I know New Bethel. A small town settled by farmers and Christmas tree growers. Oriole Point is a little different. We've been a lakeshore resort for rich Chicagoans since the nineteenth century, and a magnet for artists, Bohemians, and freethinkers. I could introduce you to at least five people who own stores on Lyall Street you might think are certifiable. And wait until you run into Wendall Bowman, also known as Old Man Bowman. He's the uncle of the fellow who was murdered last month. Wendall's our resident Bigfoot hunter. Also I'd advise you to stay clear of Leticia the Lake Lady."

He raised an amused eyebrow. "Why?"

"You don't want to know. What I'm trying to say is that Theo Foster is not even at the extreme end of the Oriole Point oddball spectrum. Yes, he has quirks, and his personal communication skills need work. But he's also a quiet man who's never bothered anyone since moving here."

"Quiet loners can end up causing a lot of harm." Holt took off his cap and wiped an arm across his damp brow.

I had a sudden urge to ruffle his tight brown curls and immediately felt guilty. There was enough on my plate just now; I didn't need to entertain fantasies about Captain Holt, especially with an engagement ring on my finger.

"If Theo does have a social life, I'm not aware of it."

I didn't add that all of us at The Berry Basket had dubbed Theo the "Phantom" since he was rarely seen out and about in the village. If I didn't arrive early at the store several days a week to consult with him, I wouldn't even know he existed . . . except for the fresh-baked pastries stacked on the rolling trays. Theo had the shop key and always came before dawn to do his baking. I'd invited Theo out to dinner with other staff members, but he'd always refused. With time, I hoped Theo might grow more comfortable with the residents of Oriole Point and come out of his self-imposed shell. But I also knew I'd make things worse by forcing the issue.

"Who was your baker before Mr. Foster?"

"Ed Orsini. A wonderful older guy with a genius for Italian desserts, especially cannoli. And I should know—my mom's side of the family is from Naples."

"What happened to him?"

"Last fall, he fell in love with a tourist from Kentucky. After she returned home, Ed couldn't bear to be without her, so he visited her at Thanksgiving and proposed. They married two weeks later. Within days of the marriage, Ed packed up and moved to Louisville." I sighed. "Leaving me high and dry without a baker right before Christmas. I was thrilled when Theo answered my ad. His lack of social skills was unimportant. I would have hired the Grinch if he knew how to make Christmas berry trifle and cranberry cobbler."

"Which I assume Mr. Foster knew how to do?"

"Yes. And far better than Ed." I lifted my hands up. "I was in a bind. I needed a baker immediately and not just for Christmas Week. There's the January ice-carving contest and the winter carnival in February. Both bring in lots of visitors, for which all of us must thank Piper. And I mean that literally."

"I take it you don't bake yourself?"

"Boxed cake. The occasional scone. But I wouldn't foist any of it on paying customers. Although I do have a talent for creating berry-flavored syrups." In fact, *Vogue* had recently featured my homemade blueberry syrup flavored with lavender, and strawberry syrup infused with rosemary and basil. And while it helped that an assistant editor at the magazine had gone to NYU with me, my syrups were also delicious, organic, and unique. This autumn I planned to introduce a raspberry and ginger syrup to both my online and shop customers.

"When I was in your kitchen, I noticed the Zellar pies." His face took on a mischievous expression. "I hope you're not passing the pies off as the work of Theo Foster. I'd hate to have to arrest you for pastry fraud."

"No pretense there. Everyone knows the pies are delivered every morning from Zellar Orchards." As someone from New Bethel, Holt wouldn't know the town gossip I took for granted. "I'm engaged to Ryan Zellar. That means I get a nice price break on the pies."

Holt seemed surprised by this news, but I had no idea why. After all, a diamond solitaire glittered on my left hand. When I glanced down to confirm it, I realized my ring was gone. I suddenly remembered I'd taken it off while cleaning up the smashed cupcakes from the floor. At the moment, the ring was lying on the kitchen washboard, still covered in buttercream frosting. I wondered why he hadn't noticed my ring yesterday at the farm. Then again, he'd been focused on the skeletal remains, not the dubious allure of Marlee Jacob. More important, why did I care whether Atticus Holt was attracted to me? I certainly wasn't attracted to him, even if he did have kind eyes and a curly head of hair I longed to touch.

Holt put his cap back on, officially reverting to sheriff mode. Not a moment too soon. "Did you recognize the name he gave us? Sienna Katsaros."

"No. But that was two decades ago and I was only ten. And my family went to Yellowstone that summer. We were gone an entire month. Does the name sound familiar to you?"

He shook his head. "I didn't even live in Michigan back then. But I'll run a check on Sienna Katsaros. And the department is still waiting for the ME's report. That should tell us a lot more about the person buried in Sanderling's woods."

"Come back inside and I'll give you a copy of Theo's resume. Like I said, I don't think it's wise to question him further at the moment. He's had more than he can handle for one day. I want him to go home and rest."

"Where does he live?" His tone and attitude were now purely professional.

"He rents a small house on the river. I helped find it for him."

"You seem like an especially caring employer." This time I heard a faint note of suspicion. No matter how much I liked his curly hair, I needed to remind myself that Atticus Holt was an officer of the law. And I knew enough to keep my guard up.

"It's hard to find year-round rentals in the village. Most owners only agree to lease their properties from September through May. This lets them charge high rental fees for summer visitors. Because I knew Theo would have a hard time, I worked out a deal for him at Crow Cottage." I shot him a shrewd glance. "This wasn't charity. I was in desperate need of a baker, and Theo was in need of a roof over his head. To quote *The Godfather*, 'It was business, it wasn't personal.'

Speaking of business, I need to return to the shop and focus on mine."

Holt smiled. "I do appreciate a woman who can quote *The Godfather*."

"I told you I was part Italian."

The back door to my store banged open. "Please come inside," Gillian cried. She looked far too frazzled for this early in the day. "Natasha's dog got loose."

I broke into a run. Gillian and Captain Holt were right behind me.

"Where's Natasha?" I asked as we hurried through the kitchen. Theo still sat on the stool, head lowered.

"She realized she'd left her phone at the nail salon and ran off to get it," Gillian said. "You know how Natasha is about her cell phone. Anyway, the dog jumped out of the purse and took after her. But she was already gone and children were in the store and they started to chase the dog all over the shop. I was in the middle of making smoothies and a customer wanted to buy four bottles of berry wine and—"

"I get the picture," I told her as I ran into the shop.

It hadn't taken much time for things to get out of control. At least fifteen customers milled about; some with smoothies, others holding items they wanted to pay for at the abandoned cash register. The air rang with the laughter and excited screams of children. Two adults seemed to be chasing several children about the crowded shop. The contents of a spilled bag of strawberry cake batter lay on the floor, tiny dog footprints evident in the debris. The Yorkie had to be somewhere. Her high-pitched yapping echoed off the walls.

"Has anyone seen the dog?" I asked my startled customers.

A tall fellow in surfer shorts and flip-flops pointed at my front display window. "She jumped in there. But don't blame the dog. The kids were chasing it."

"Don't blame my children," a woman snapped back. She was one of the adults chasing the kids. "That dog has no business in this store. Especially without a leash." She grabbed one of the shouting boys by the collar of his T-shirt. "And where's the owner? I want to lodge a complaint. That dog might have hurt one of my children."

I had no time for manufactured outrage, especially since the children seemed to be having the time of their lives. More important, the dog was the size of my foot and no possible threat to anyone. Although Dasha did need to be on a leash— or zippered up in that purse.

As I hurried past the children racing around the bistro tables, I spotted Dasha. The youthful high spirits in the shop were clearly contagious; the Yorkie ran about the window display like a wind-up toy cranked much too tight. I suspected she had climbed into the window via the tiered shelf of bagged raspberry chocolates. When I reached in and grabbed her, she fought to squirm free. In only a few moments, Dasha had managed to rip the cellophane wrapping off the gift baskets on display, along with leaving an unwelcome surprise on a pile of Berry Basket sweatshirts. This dog needed to be house trained as soon as possible.

Clutching Dasha to my chest, I tried to calm her down. But she had worked herself into a frenzy. Her tiny tongue licked my face faster than the wings of a hummingbird.

With a laugh, Holt handed me a napkin from a nearby bistro table.

While I wiped the doggy saliva from my cheeks, the intrepid Dasha wriggled out of my hands and jumped once more into my display window. Just then, Max Riordan, owner of Riordan Outfitters on the harbor, walked by my store window. He did a double take as I struggled to grab the Yorkie. This time I caught her only because she slowed down long enough to pounce on a bag of blueberry pancake mix.

The door to my shop swung open, and Max peeked in. He wore a wide grin. "Hey, Marlee, I was wondering: How much is that doggy in the window?"

I felt pleased when the bag of pancake mix I threw landed right on his head.

Chapter 6

Five minutes after the parade began, I tripped George Washington. Actually, it was Dean dressed up as our first president, and he had only himself to blame. Against all advice, he planned to walk the entire length of the parade route on stilts. And while his white periwig, breeches, and waistcoat were historically accurate, the addition of eighteen-inch stilts seemed more suited to the circus than the Oriole Point Independence Day parade.

At least I didn't fear injury for Dean's brother. Andrew was decked out as Captain America, replete with helmet, mask, and a snug-fitting blue costume emblazoned with the American flag. I was also glad his boots were firmly planted on the pavement. But since the temperature was eighty-five and sunny, I feared our Marvel superhero might collapse of heatstroke by the time we reached Lyall Street. The costume must have been inflexible, too. He was no help getting his brother back onto those stilts. Instead, Gillian and I dusted George Washington off, straightened his wig, and sent him tottering once more along the parade route.

"And stop trying to strut," I called after him. Dean had tripped after strutting right onto my left ankle, and I resolved to keep the stilted Father of Our Country in front of me for the rest of the parade.

Gillian and I exchanged amused glances before picking up our wicker baskets filled with candy. Except for Theo, the entire staff of The Berry Basket would be participating in the parade. We had even closed the shop for an hour.

As expected, the village was jammed with tourists, the vast majority lining up to watch the parade. If past years were anything to go by, they wouldn't be disappointed. Oriole Point held a bewildering number of parades throughout the year, but Fourth of July held preeminence. At least half the store owners in the village took part, the entire city council, and the high school marching band. We had few restrictions on participation; organizations from the volunteer fire department to the Sandy Shoals Saloon Euchre Club were represented. And the floats ranged from the sublime to the ridiculous.

My personal favorite were the Betsy Ross Babes from Miss Lana's Dance School. Miss Lana herself led a chorus of teenage dance students in a high-kicking number that threatened to topple the red, white, and blue float they rode on. For three years in a row, complaints had been lodged against the provocative costumes of the Betsy Ross Babes. These complaints fell on deaf ears. A guaranteed crowd pleaser, Miss Lana's sexy American flag outfits were again eliciting their usual whistles and cheers, most of it from teenage boys.

I was feeling pretty patriotic myself. Both Gillian and I wore white shorts, red T-shirts, and shiny blue top hats crowned with a pinwheel. Unable to resist a little self-promotion, I had stenciled "The Berry Basket" on the back of the shirts. We also carried baskets filled with wrapped berry-flavored candy to hand out to the crowds lining the streets. Since the lengthy parade route stretched from the public library to River Park, our candy baskets—large though they were—would wind up empty halfway through. To prevent this, Gillian and

I took turns pulling a red wagon that not only held piles of extra candy, but her adorable five-year-old nephew, Skye. I hoped this plan kept us supplied with sweets, but I had my doubts. Every time I looked back at the child, he was unwrapping another piece of candy for himself.

The ring of a bell sounded behind me. I looked over in time to see Max Riordan pedal past in his vintage black tricycle. Unlike Dean and his stilts, Max had ridden the four-foot-tall trike for years, and had yet to be knocked off its high perch.

"Happy Fourth, Marlee!" he cried, looking as gleeful as five-year-old Skye.

I waved back. "Watch out for George Washington."

If those two collided, I hoped someone took a video of it.

Max and I had been friends since kindergarten, and there were few people I felt more comfortable around. Things did get awkward back in our senior year of high school when we briefly dated and Max proposed marriage right before prom night. The proposal was such a shock I refused to go to the prom or to even date him again. Luckily, I moved away to college soon after. By the time I returned, enough time had passed and we resumed our old, easy friendship. I hoped his romantic feelings for me were a thing of the past as well. However, Ryan had never bothered to hide his jealousy of Max. The way I looked at it, the two of them would have to work it out, not me.

Calling out greetings to people I knew, I threw candy to both sides of the street, setting off a scramble as kids raced to see who could snatch the most. We were still at the beginning of the parade route and a tunnel of trees shaded us as we marched downhill to Lyall Street. While tourists made up the bulk of the crowd along the downtown streets, these blocks were residential and I recognized virtually everyone who watched us from the sidelines. Most had brought out lawn chairs and sat on their front curb to enjoy the festivities. A few sipped lemonade and beer, their pet dog lying nearby. Talk about a front-row seat.

Because the road led downhill, I had a bird's-eye view of the beginning of the parade up ahead. As always, the Oriole Point High School marching band kicked off the fun; their drum majorettes high stepping with even more brio than Dean on his stilts. Hot on their heels rode a vintage car carrying Piper and her husband, Lionel. Granted, he was our mayor and had every right to be leading off the parade, his devoted wife by his side, but the two of them had led the parade years before he took office and would no doubt continue to do so long after he stepped down. Every year, they borrowed a different vintage car from the Oriole Antique Car Club. Their parade car this year was a 1929 fire engine red BMW roadster. The choice of vehicle raised a few eyebrows; there were lots of American vintage cars they could have chosen. But Piper's fondness for BMWs won out.

Aside from the Lyall-Pierce German car, most parade floats were patriotic and homespun. Zellar Orchards was represented by a large open tractor filled with bales of hay and a half-dozen Zellars dressed as bucolic versions of Paul Revere and Molly Pitcher. Because Ryan refused to dress up, he chose once again to drive the tractor. A shame. I would have loved to see him outfitted in tight breeches and a tricorn hat.

Right behind me were the cast members of *Grease*, all of them in costume. Oriole Point boasted a first-class theater on Barlow Avenue, begun years ago by native son Daniel Garrett, who went off to New York City to direct plays off-Broadway. He returned each summer to unveil three entertaining productions, with the musical *Grease* starting things off this year. I smiled each time I caught sight of Danny Zuko, Sandy, Rizzo, Kenickie, and Frenchy waving from a pink T-bird convertible. While technically not a patriotic float, the

Pink Ladies and Greasers of the 1950s seemed as American as Thomas Paine. And a lot more entertaining.

"Marlee! Marlee!" Natasha shouted. Beside her was Old Man Bowman. Both of them waved American flags while relaxing in camp chairs on the curb.

I tossed a few candies her way. Old Man Bowman caught them before they hit the ground. Although seventy years old, his reflexes were impressive.

Both had dressed for the occasion. Natasha wore a sleeveless red mini dress and a wide hat decorated with red, white, and blue stars. Her patriotism wasn't feigned. She had been studying for her citizenship test for the better part of a year. As for Old Man Bowman, he had traded his usual khaki cargo shorts for a white pair to go along with his annual American flag T-shirt. He also went the extra patriotic mile by threading red, white, and blue yarn in his white hair, which he always wore in a thin braid down his back. They won the award for Oriole Point's Oddest Couple. None of us were certain if this was a May-December romance, or simply two free spirits linked through Natasha's marriage to Old Man Bowman's nephew. And while both of them had no affection for the late Cole Bowman, I still couldn't figure out exactly what had transpired between them since Cole's death. To be honest, I didn't really want to know.

By the time we reached Lyall Street, Gillian and I had refilled our candy baskets, and little Skye seemed in the throes of sugar overload. With a worried expression, Gillian handed him off to his mother as soon as she caught sight of her along the parade route.

"I'm grateful he still has his baby teeth," Gillian said to me. "Otherwise, my sister would be billing me for future visits to the dentist."

"I'm more worried about his stomach," I said, pulling the

red wagon behind me. "He's probably eaten a pound of candy and there's still the big barbecue in a few hours."

Gillian laughed. "I've seen Skye eat everything from a fistful of beach sand to an entire bag of taco chips. He'll be fine."

As enthusiastic as the crowd was on the way here, everything got louder and more congested once we hit Lyall Street. Like many resort villages along Lake Michigan, the streets leading to the beach and harbor comprised the business district. The Oriole River flowed right through the center of town, making its way past the shops, marina, and our white stone lighthouse before it emptied into the lake. Lyall Street ran right along the river, serving as our small-town version of Fifth Avenue. While our commercial district was only a few blocks long, it boasted a rich variety of unique shops and restaurants, along with a breathtaking view of Lake Michigan. Visitors loved to stroll past the shops and cafés, along River Park and the marina, and right out onto the beach. I was born and raised here and I never tired of it.

At the moment, all I could see were flags and parade viewers three deep along the sidewalk. I hoped Dean had remained upright on his stilts, especially since several parade participants were roller blading. I waved at Aunt Vicki, who was also in the parade, accompanied by some of her rescue animals. She and the volunteers of Humane Hearts were marching to help promote the good work of her shelter. They had set up a tent in River Park for this weekend where people could meet and greet a few of the animals available for adoption.

Although I was having fun, I looked forward to reaching the end of the parade route. I'd been up since three o'clock this morning to help Theo with the baking. Theo only worked Monday through Friday, which meant he put in extra hours on Friday mornings in order to bake enough pastries to see us through the weekend. Because demand was even higher due to the holiday, I came in before dawn to lend him a hand. He was as industrious as usual but barely said ten words to me during the hours we worked together. Even for laconic Theo, this seemed odd behavior. However, the long silences were less important than our goal of producing an absurd number of pastries in a short amount of time. And there wasn't much for us to talk about since I hadn't heard anything further from Captain Holt. I reminded myself that this mystery concerned the police, and maybe Theo. I had a business to run and a parade to enjoy.

Two blocks from the end of the parade route, it became even more enjoyable. The cast of *Grease* jumped out of their convertible and began to dance. A minute later, Gillian and I found ourselves bopping along the street with Danny Zuko and Kenickie. Suddenly I felt like Olivia Newton-John doing the hand jive with John Travolta. The crowd clapped and hooted as we swung our way down Lyall Street, my candy basket left behind to be pillaged by children.

Laughing as the actor spun me about, I felt thrilled to be acting out my teenage fantasy of dancing on Broadway. Surrounded by people having the time of their lives, it felt like nothing could go wrong on this glorious summer day. But as I kicked up my heels, I caught sight of Captain Holt and Detective Trejo watching me from the curb. Since they were both in uniform, I had a sinking feeling the day was about to take a less festive turn.

"Are you sure you don't want a hot dog?" I smeared my own with liberal amounts of mustard and relish.

Trejo looked at me and my hot dog with obvious disapproval. "No thanks. And you should know they're one of the unhealthiest things you can eat."

I waited until I had enjoyed my first big bite before answering. "It's the Fourth of July. Everyone eats hot dogs. Like everyone eats pumpkin pie at Thanksgiving. Or sugar cookies during Christmas."

"I don't," he said curtly.

Somehow that didn't surprise me. Trejo seemed like a man wary of simple pleasures. This didn't seem to be the case for Captain Holt, now enjoying his own hot dog beside me. As soon as I arrived at the end of the parade route, both men had approached me to announce they had news concerning the body in the woods. Since I was starving, I first led them to one of the food trucks lined up along River Park.

Leo's Lakeside Eats was my favorite of the temporary venues open for business during our downtown festivals. Nothing fancy: hot dogs, hamburgers, gyros, and the best chili outside of Detroit. We sat at one of the small makeshift tables set up near the food trucks. Because an art fair was in full swing at the park, people milled about everywhere. The noise level was high.

Clasping his hands, Trejo placed them on the white table. The surface must have been sticky since he immediately pulled his hands away. "Can we talk about the Katsaros case now?"

"Is that what it's called?" I took a long sip of my root beer.

Holt nodded. "The name Theo Foster gave us checked out. Twenty years ago, Sienna Katsaros from Lawton, Oklahoma, was a student at the Blackberry Art School. Three days before the session ended, she disappeared. The school notified the police, who began looking for her. Two articles of her clothing washed ashore on one of the Oriole Point beaches twenty-four hours later. A search-and-rescue team went out on the lake, but no body was recovered. The authorities believed she had drowned, and the probable death was ruled an accident."

"I remember the case," Trejo added. "I was in high school. A lot of attention was paid to the disappearance. It was the only time a BAS student had died during a school session. Of course, anyone who lives here knows there are drowning deaths every summer. People often go swimming in the lake after they've had too much too drink. And out-of-towners don't realize how treacherous a riptide can be. Sienna Katsaros may have been a victim of both."

"Did people assume the girl had been drinking?" I asked.

"Newspaper accounts and police records state she had a reputation for drinking at the school." Holt shrugged. "Then again, she was eighteen and away from home for the summer. She can't have been the first BAS student who partied at night once classes were over."

"Her exact whereabouts that day and night seem sketchy," Trejo said. "The summer session was winding down. A few kids had already gone home. Technically, her age group had to be in their cabins by midnight, but she could have headed off to the beach instead."

"How in the world did she get to the woods at the Sanderling farm? It's miles away. The farm has no connection to the art school."

"It has one," Holt told me. "Gordon Sanderling was a student at BAS that summer."

I nearly choked on my hot dog. Of all the people I would have pegged to be interested in art, Gordon Sanderling would be last on the list.

"Are you certain the remains are those of Sienna Katsaros?" I asked.

"Yes," Trejo stated emphatically. "Because the body wasn't recovered, the Katsaros family insisted on continuing the search. Local law enforcement stayed on the case, and the family also hired private investigators. But after five years, the case had grown cold. Even the family agreed the official cause of death was likely correct. However, the police had dental records of the girl on file. We used them to confirm the identity of the remains that you found."

"Theo was right." Finished with my hot dog, I sat back and wiped my fingers on a napkin. "That means he's telling the truth when he says he made the charm bracelet for her."

"It also made him a prime suspect for a time."

"But why would he admit knowing who the body was if he had killed her? It doesn't make sense." I stopped. "Wait. You said he was a suspect 'for a time.' Does that mean he no longer is?"

"We've looked into the backgrounds of several people these past few days, including Mr. Foster," Holt said. "As he told us, he went back home to Illinois before Sienna went missing. His mother died four years ago, but we spoke to his father, two aunts, and a cousin. All of them swear he was with them that week, which includes the day Sienna went missing. Theo also started a part-time job at the local Baskin-Robbins in Champaign that day."

"Too bad," Trejo said. "He had a great motive."

"What are you talking about?" I whirled on him. "Theo said he loved her."

"Exactly. This awkward, simpleminded boy—"

"He's not simpleminded."

"This odd boy develops a crush on a girl," Trejo continued. "A girl who appears to have been something of a queen bee at BAS that summer. Lauded by the instructors, winning every award. Surrounded by a clique of friends. Someone out of Theo Foster's league."

"He did say everyone was jealous of Sienna," Holt reminded me. "Maybe he was jealous, too. But for romantic reasons."

"If he'd been jealous of her, Theo would have told us. He's the most honest person I know. Sometimes, I wish he wasn't. Never ask his opinion about what you're wearing. Or if he likes your boyfriend." Along with Piper, Theo did not like Ryan.

"It doesn't matter," Holt said. "He has an alibi. The same can't be said for Gordon Sanderling."

I had never had much interaction with Gordon Sanderling.

His business and personal interests didn't coincide with mine. But the thought that he may have killed someone twenty years ago was upsetting. Since I grew up in Oriole Point, the long-time residents were like extended family. I didn't want to believe one of them was a killer.

"Have you questioned him?"

"Yes, with his attorney present. And we'll continue to question him until we ascertain exactly what happened on his property twenty years ago." Trejo's stony features seemed Mount Rushmore–like. "We've also spoken with his brothers and sister now living in Florida. They all seemed as shocked by the discovery of a body on their property as Gordon Sanderling was."

Holt finished off his root beer. "Mr. Sanderling has the only real connection to the victim, given that he and Sienna were at the school together. He's officially a person of interest."

I thought Gordon had a lot to worry about. "Having that huge stand of woods on the property makes it easy to conceal a body."

"Let's not rush to judgment," Holt said. "The Sanderling farm connects to the state forest. If the murderer was a local resident, he would know that. Anyone who wanted to bury a body could access those woods from the Oriole River State Forest."

Sitting back, I rattled the ice in my own root beer. Deep in thought, I was only vaguely aware of all the tourists laughing and moving past our table. "Does the medical examiner have any idea how Sienna died?" I asked finally.

"The body was buried too long ago," Holt said.

"Unless the killer confesses, we may never know how she died," Detective Trejo added.

"Do you think there are other bodies buried out there?" I shivered at the thought.

"The cadaver dogs haven't discovered anything so far," Trejo replied.

Holt pushed his paper plate aside and leaned over the table. "Gordon Sanderling gave you and Mrs. Lyall-Pierce permission to begin the Blackberry Road Rally at his farm. Had you been on his property before?"

"Never. Although it was my idea to start the rally there after our first choice fell through. Because it's not a working farm any longer, I didn't see why he would turn us down."

"Several people in the county claim the farm is haunted." Holt paused. "Cursed even. What do you know about that?"

"The first I heard about those stories was the day I found the body, which seems ironic. Two of my employees warned me the farm was haunted, but they had nothing concrete to back it up with. I'm guessing the weird rumors stem from the UFO incident in 1975."

"Why hadn't you heard any of these rumors until this week?" Trejo asked.

"After I went off to college, I spent ten years away from Oriole Point, except for holidays or family reunions held at our lake house. I wasn't around long enough to hear the latest gossip and rumors. Plus, my parents and I were never friends with any of the Sanderlings."

Trejo raised an eyebrow at me. "Bad blood between the two families?"

"Not at all. We simply had no reason to socialize with them. The only thing we have in common is that the Sanderlings and my family once were in the fruit-growing business. Grapes for them, berries for us. Aunt Vicki and my dad mismanaged the orchard business and lost it to the bank. The Sanderling winery failed because the vineyards were hit with a fungal disease."

"Were you surprised when the other members of the Sanderling family sold their share of the farm to Gordon, and then moved out of state?"

"I have no idea when they left," I told Trejo. "Or why they sold the farm to Gordon. All I do know is when I returned from New York, Gordon was the only Sanderling living there and his focus was on the plumbing business. I hired his company last year for a job at my house, but that's pretty much the extent of my relations with Gordon. At least until this past Monday when he ordered Piper and me to get off his property."

"Mrs. Lyall-Pierce didn't know about these rumors when we questioned her again yesterday." Trejo seemed unhappy by this. "That strikes me as strange. The mayor's wife is reputed to know everything that goes on in Oriole Point. Why not this?"

"I asked her about that. She said she confines her interest to the village, not the surrounding farmland. That makes sense. Piper isn't the bucolic type. Why do you care so much about these silly rumors anyway? Obviously the farm isn't really haunted."

"True," Holt said. "But rumors like that might prevent people from trespassing on the farm or the woods. Something a murderer might find desirable, especially with a body buried on the property."

I sat back as the logic of this dawned on me. "Do you think Gordon began the rumors to keep people away?"

"It's possible someone did," Trejo said. "There's no evidence to prove that person was Gordon Sanderling. But we're far from done with questioning people."

I turned to Captain Holt. "I hope you're careful when you question Theo again. You've seen how sensitive he is."

"We went to his cottage this morning to speak with him," he said. "It didn't go well."

"And I'd describe him as unstable, not sensitive." Trejo looked irritated.

"Was he upset?" This was all too much for Theo Foster to absorb. Even a man who was more balanced would have an awful time learning that the bones of someone he loved had been discovered. And that she had been murdered.

"Quite upset," Trejo said. "Mr. Foster began to shake so much, we feared he was going into shock. But he refused to let us take him to the hospital."

I put my head in my hands. "Poor guy. I'll go over there right now to check on him."

"I was about to suggest that," Holt said. "He seems to trust you. It would also be helpful if you asked him more questions about what happened at the school that summer."

Raising my head, I stared out at the happy crowd. I envied them, concerned only with picnics, art fairs, beach outings, and tonight's fireworks. "I don't know how much stress Theo is able to handle. And on Monday, the centenary festivities for the Blackberry Art School begin. That will remind him even more of Sienna."

"You need to remember to be cautious around anyone connected to BAS." Holt's voice was filled with concern. "If Gordon Sanderling didn't kill Sienna Katsaros, it's possible someone connected to the school did. That means the murderer could be arriving any day."

Chapter 7

I never understood how Crow Cottage got its name. For one thing, it resembled a shack much more than a picturesque cottage. Little time or money had been spent on upkeep in the past thirty years, and it showed. I'd also never seen a crow anywhere near the place, even though enormous crows paraded along every village road. Maybe the crows appeared at twilight or dawn. However, the plumbing worked, the roof didn't leak, and the rent was reasonable. Best of all, Crow Cottage's shabby appearance was offset by a lovely riverine view.

Located on a cul-de-sac accessed by a gravel road, the neighborhood consisted of three houses hugging the shoreline of the Oriole River. As much as I loved gazing out my kitchen window at Lake Michigan, I'm not sure I wouldn't have preferred Theo's view: marshes, gently flowing water, and flocks of swans and Canada geese. There was something serenely majestic about it, and I hoped it had a calming effect on Theo.

If only I felt more serene. Theo wasn't answering his door. His car, a dented blue VW Beetle, sat parked on the dirt space allotted for it by the shed. Was he refusing to come to the door, or was he out taking a walk? Maybe he went fishing. I knew so little about Theo's private life, I couldn't even speculate on what he did in his free time.

I faced the road in front of the cottage. Two single-story houses shared the cul-de-sac, all of them spaced far apart along the river. Several bikes lay scattered over one of the lawns, along with a large plastic playhouse. At least one family with children lived here. Did the noise and activity of children bother Theo? I'd never seen him interact with kids. At least it was quiet, although firecrackers sounded in the distance. For weeks leading up to the Fourth, I heard firecrackers being set off with irritating frequency. Even when I arrived at the shop early this morning—two hours before dawn—the occasional popping of firecrackers met my ears. The teens of Oriole Point must stockpile their money all year just to spend it on holiday explosives.

"Theo," I called out again. "It's Marlee. Are you here?" My frustration grew. All the windows were open. If Theo was inside, he could hear me. I had an uneasy vision of my baker hiding in the closet until I left.

"The police told me they talked to you earlier. I came by to make sure you're all right."

From inside the cottage I heard a voice call out, "Tell the police to stay away."

At least he had finally responded. "The police are gone. It's only me. And Captain Holt and Detective Trejo needed to ask you a few questions." I moved closer to the window, hoping to catch a glimpse of Theo on the other side of the screen. "The police are trying to find out what happened to Sienna. You and Gordon Sanderling are the only ones in Oriole Point who knew her. They have to question both of you."

"No, no, no. I won't talk to them. Tell them to leave me alone!"

This last reply sounded on the edge of hysteria. If only I

had a key to the cottage. Theo shouldn't be holed up alone in there, not while he was in such a state.

"Theo, I'm sorry about Sienna. But finding her body means we could discover what really happened to her. You should want to help the police, not hide from them." I paused. "Only children hide themselves away when they're frightened. And you're not a child. So come out and talk to me."

I was met with another long silence. Just as I was about to admit defeat, the front door opened. Theo stepped out onto his porch, which was little more than a stoop. It came as a surprise to see him dressed in a clean white T-shirt and jeans so freshly ironed they were creased. Except for his job interview, I'd never seen him in anything but his baker's uniform.

"I'll help *you*. I won't help the police." Theo craned his neck, looking right to left, as if expecting to see a squad car suddenly appear.

"Theo, I'm only a shop owner. It's not my job to track down the killer."

"That's not true. You tracked down a murderer last month. Why can't you do it again?"

No use trying to explain that my own life had been in danger. Going after the murderer seemed an act of self-preservation, even if it did nearly get me killed.

"And you found Sienna's body after all this time," he went on. "The police weren't able to do that. It was you."

"That was an accident."

"No. Sienna wanted you to find her. And she wants you to find out who buried her there."

I saw no purpose in arguing with him. "Theo, I came by because I was worried about you. The police said you couldn't stop shaking when they were here."

"I don't want the police to come to my cottage again." Theo wrapped his arms protectively about himself. "I don't like the police. They put people in jail."

"Theo, they have no reason to put you in jail." At least I hoped not. "I know you're upset about Sienna. She was your friend, and you cared about her. Think back to your time at the school that summer. Do you have any idea who wanted to hurt her? How about this Christian boy you talked about?"

"I liked Christian." After scanning the cul-de-sac once again, Theo finally felt comfortable enough to leave his porch and walk nearer to me. "I don't think he would hurt her."

"So his name is Christian. We weren't sure if you were referring to his religion instead."

Theo looked at me as if I were the confused one. "It was his name *and* he was a Christian. He went to church every Sunday. He was the only one in the group who did."

"What else can you tell me about him?"

"He made oil paintings filled with lots of dark colors. I didn't like to look at them too long. The paintings made me sad. And nervous. But he was a good painter. Not as good as Sienna. No one was."

"What was his last name?"

Theo thought for a moment. "I don't remember. They called him 'Blue' sometimes. Because he was sad. Like his paintings."

This wasn't helping much.

"Anything else?"

"He was black."

I fought back a sigh of frustration. First he was blue, now black. "Do you mean he was African American?"

"Yes."

At least I could tell Captain Holt to ask BAS officials about an African American student with the first name of Christian who attended twenty years ago. With luck, he'd get more information out of Christian than he had out of Theo. "Are there any other students you remember from that year aside from Sienna and Christian?"

"Leah."

I thought back to when Theo first mentioned her earlier in the week. "Is she the one who did magic tricks?"

"Not tricks. Real magic. Old magic. She taught me how to call birds. Leah could make them come to her." He lowered his voice to a stage whisper. "One of the bird calls was secret. She used that one to call people."

I didn't know how to respond to that. "Who did she call? Her friends?"

Theo nodded. "I love birds. They're freer than us. Nothing can stop them from flying away. Unless you kill them. Or cage them. But I would never do that."

"I have a bird at home. Her name is Minnie and she talks. She says all sorts of things."

Theo's eyes lit up. "Can I come to your house and see her?"

My mouth fell open. For seven months, Theo had refused every invitation to my house for dinner or a get-together with fellow Berry Basket employees. Who guessed a mere mention of my African grey parrot would override his deep shyness?

"Of course. But Minnie is in her cage sometimes. It's a big cage, though."

"That's wrong. Birds should be free. Free and happy. That's why I feed them. Do you want to see my feeders?" Before I could answer, Theo began to walk to the rear of his house.

Hurrying after him, I felt a sense of relief. All this time, I feared Theo was living a misanthropic hermit's existence in his cottage. But it appeared he had a hobby, something that engaged him during all the hours he wasn't baking at my shop. And when I rounded the cottage, I realized it was a most extensive hobby.

Except for the large metal container that stored heating oil for Theo's cottage, his entire backyard was filled with feeders, from suet holders to Droll Yankees. Some hung from trees;

others were attached to wooden or metal posts. Theo also offered his feathered friends shelter as well. Large purple martin houses towered over the grass, three bluebird houses were nailed to an adjacent wooden fence, and a wren darted into a small birdhouse just six feet away. Our sudden appearance startled dozens of birds at the feeders, and they flew off to nearby willow and birch trees. Given that the property stretched right to the river's edge, I wasn't surprised the only trees were ones that thrived in marshy ground.

Theo took me by the elbow and led me to a green metal chair beneath one of the willows. I was surprised Theo had touched me. If he accidentally brushed against me in the kitchen, he blushed and murmured an apology. Maybe being on his home ground gave him more confidence. There was only one chair in the yard; after I took it, Theo sat on the ground beside me.

He pointed at the bright orange feeders near the water. Baltimore orioles drawn to the orange slices and nectar now returned to their feeding perches. Our appearance had been noted and judged harmless.

"I like the orioles best." Theo never took his eyes from the striking black and orange birds. "That's why I wanted to come to the Blackberry Art School. The school was in a place called Oriole Point. I never saw orioles back home. But I knew if the town was named after them, there must be lots here. And there are. Why is that?"

"This part of Michigan is known as a fruit belt," I explained. "Orioles love fruit, and not just oranges. Melons, grapes, berries, pears, peaches. We grow some of the biggest peaches in the country here. The lakeshore orchards must appear like buffet tables laid out just for them."

"I'm glad." He turned to me. "I read that birds can get drunk by eating berries. How does that happen?"

"When overripe berries fall to the ground, the fruit often

ferments, which makes the berries alcoholic. Birds eating those berries become drunk. If they fly in that condition, they may end up dead. Just like people who drive when they're drunk."

"Just like people," he repeated. "I haven't seen any drunk birds here, but I saw a dead bird once by a berry bush. Maybe it ate too many berries, got drunk, and died. I don't think anyone should get drunk. Including birds." Theo's serious expression lightened. "Oriole Point seems a happy place for birds. And there are so many. Especially orioles."

"The town was founded by Benjamin Lyall in 1830," I said. "The first night he came here, he camped along the river near where Lyall Street and Iroquois intersect. Legend has it that when he looked out his tent the next morning, flocks of orioles were eating the berries of a nearby mulberry tree. He looked on it as a sign and called the town Oriole Point." I laughed. "At least that's what Piper has told every local historian since I was born. Because she's his ancestor, I assume there's a grain of truth to the story."

"I think the story is true." He pointed to a bright yellow bird who landed on a tube feeder. "Look, a common yellowthroat. I don't see many of those at my feeders. Yellowthroats prefer insects."

For a few minutes, I was content to bird-watch with Theo. I, too, had a love of birds. I'd grown up with a trio of cockatiels that I still missed and I'd been a member of the Audubon Society since I was sixteen. Maybe Theo would enjoy bird watching with me and a few local members of the society. Although I was happy to learn he had a hobby, Theo needed to let other people into his rather isolated existence. As wonderful as birds were, he should spend time with more than cedar waxwings and orioles.

"Do you miss home?" I asked finally. "I've been to Champaign once to see my cousin graduate from the University of Illinois. It seemed a very nice place."

Theo tore his attention from the birds for a moment. "It is nice, but there's no lake there. The Middle Fork River isn't anything like Lake Michigan. And the lake makes me happy. I like the river here, too. So many birds live along it. Even swans." He glanced over at the Oriole River, glittering in the sunlight. Two pairs of geese honked as they glided in for a landing on the water's surface. "Michigan has so much water."

How true. We were surrounded by the Great Lakes, the largest concentration of freshwater on the planet. No place in Michigan was farther than six miles from an inland lake or eighty-five miles from one of the Great Lakes. It was no coincidence our state was called a "Water Wonderland."

"Do you miss your family?"

"I miss my dad. My mother is dead. And I don't have brothers or sisters. They didn't have more children after me." He appeared embarrassed by that.

"I'm an only child, too. To be honest, I rather like it. I had no one competing for my parents' attention, so I got all of it. I still do. And you can choose friends who will become as close to you as a brother or sister." I smiled. "I'd like to know more about your family. If you miss your father, you and he must be close. Why did you leave him to move to Oriole Point last December?"

"I had to. They mailed an invitation to me."

"Who did?"

"The Blackberry Art School. It came right after Thanksgiving. That's how I learned about the big celebration this summer. The invitation said all students who had gone to the school were being invited. I had to come."

"Why not just come for the week of festivities? There was no need to move here." I didn't think I would ever be able to figure out how Theo's mind worked.

"I think the invitation really came from Sienna. She's unhappy because I left before she disappeared. And when I found out she was gone, I didn't come back. I should have. I loved her. And she must have cared about me. She was wearing my bracelet when she died." He took a deep, shaky breath. "I should have been looking for her. *And* the person who killed and buried her. I should have been here all along."

"But she died twenty years ago, Theo."

"It doesn't matter. She wanted me to wait in Oriole Point until she gave me a sign. And she did. She led you and that dog to her grave in the woods. When I got the invitation, I knew I had to move back. And I was right, wasn't I? I was in Oriole Point when you found her."

Needing to think, I took the rubber band out of my hair and redid my ponytail. Maybe I should call Theo's father and ask him a few questions. I didn't even know if Theo was on medication, or if he suffered from anxiety or depression. Then again, Theo was thirty-seven and I felt guilty for regarding him as a child, even if his behavior often appeared child-like.

"About this student called Leah, the one who taught you how to call birds. Could she have killed Sienna?"

Theo kept his attention focused on his feeders. "The birds liked her. I don't think birds like people who hurt others or are mean."

"Do you remember Leah's last name?"

He shook his head.

I'd ask Captain Holt to look into school records for a woman called Leah. With luck, both Christian and Leah would show up for the centenary. "Did you know Gordon Sanderling?"

"Everyone at BAS knew Gordon. Like everyone knew Sienna."

"If everyone at the school knew him, he must have been a talented artist."

Theo made a face. "Gordon made silly things. He wasn't

like Sienna. Sienna was the best artist. Everyone knew Gordon because he was handsome."

This time it was my turn to make a face. I couldn't imagine anyone calling Gordon Sanderling handsome.

"Sienna thought Gordon was handsome, too," Theo went on. "She liked him."

I paused. "Did that make you jealous?"

"Oh, no. I loved her and wanted her to be happy. Gordon made her happy. I think he loved her. But not as much as I did." Theo seemed about to say more until the arrival of a northern flicker at the feeders distracted him.

If Theo was correct, Gordon and Sienna had been romantically involved. Things were looking worse for Gordon by the minute. Several blue jays shrieking from the birch trees reminded me of Theo's comments about the girl who called birds.

"Theo, you said Leah taught you bird calls. Was she friends with Sienna and Gordon?"

"Yes. They were in the same Bramble."

That made sense. People were housed according to age at the Blackberry Art School. These groups were called Brambles, each with its own corresponding name.

I had a sudden thought. "Did the students ever visit the Sanderling farm that summer?"

Theo pointed with excitement at a rose-breasted grosbeak. "Look."

"Theo, did you hear me?"

He nodded, his eyes fastened on the colorful bird. "Gordon's family invited two of the Brambles to their farm. It was Gordon's birthday and they had a party."

"Did you go to the birthday party at the farm, too?"

"Yes." Theo finally turned his attention back to me. "His family was nice. And they had a lot of food. More than I've ever seen at a party. They gave us wine, too. Even though some of us weren't grown-ups yet." He leaned a bit closer. "The teachers weren't happy about that."

I thought back to when the Sanderling vineyard went out of business. It was shortly before the summer Sienna went missing. But Sanderling wines continued to be sold out of their cellar for several more years until their supply was gone. Some of those wines must have been served to the BAS crowd.

"Did any of you go into the woods while you were there?"

He cocked his head at me. "Why would we do that? It was a birthday party. We sat at the picnic tables by the barn. No one went anywhere else."

I wasn't certain about that. If the Sanderlings invited a lot of people to the party, it would have been easy for several to slip away. Had the killer been among them and noticed the large stand of woods on the property? "The police need to know about this. It's important."

His expression turned fearful. "I don't want to talk to the police. They'll put me in jail. I won't talk to them, Marlee. Don't make me."

"Theo, I don't understand why—"

"I mean it. If they come here again, I'll run away."

I had never seen Theo so determined. There was no doubt in my mind that he would flee at the first sight of the police. "Okay. But I have to tell Captain Holt that a group of BAS students were at the Sanderling farm the summer Sienna disappeared." I got to my feet.

Theo looked at me in surprise. "You're going?"

"I've been away from the shop too long. But I'm glad you showed me the bird feeders."

He stood up, carefully smoothing down his spotless jeans. "I can get any bird I want to come, as long as they're in the area. I call them. Do you want to see?"

I shrugged. "Sure."

"What bird should I call?"

I glanced over at the unimpressive dwelling known as Crow Cottage. "A crow."

"Crows are easy." Theo shut his eyes and let out a series of piercing catlike growls.

A good two minutes passed while he continued his bird calls, interspersed with occasional pauses. I grew uncomfortable and sorry I had played along with him. But I didn't know how to bring a halt to this whole thing without embarrassing Theo.

Suddenly, I heard a flutter of wings behind me. I peeked over my shoulder. Perched on top of the metal lawn chair was a gleaming black crow. It stared back at me before letting out a piercing caw.

"I thought you were joking," I said in a hushed voice as the enormous bird and I looked at each other.

"I don't like jokes," Theo said. "And I would never joke about birds. They're my friends. Would you like me to call for a nuthatch next? Or maybe a robin?"

Before I could choose another bird species for him to summon, the distant sound of a police siren met our ears. Theo looked at me in horror.

"The police are coming back!"

"No. They're not coming to the cottage." I reached out for Theo as he took several steps backward. "Listen, the siren is getting fainter. It's nowhere near here."

He clapped his hands over his ears. "Tell them to go away. I won't see them. I won't!" Pushing past me, Theo ran out of the backyard. A moment later, I heard his front door slam shut.

I shook my head. This whole visit had ended exactly the way it had begun—with a terrified Theo hiding in the cottage.

Surprisingly, the crow hadn't flown off yet.

"And what do you have to say about all this, Magic Crow?"

Shooting me an inscrutable look, the bird gave another

deafening caw before taking wing. I took that as a signal for me to leave as well. There was no point in trying to talk to Theo again today. He had a fear of the police that I would not be able to calm. And I had a fear as well. I was afraid I'd been drawn into yet another murder case.

Chapter 8

That night I had another troubling dream, but this one didn't include human skulls or monster dogs. Instead, it featured a flock of angry crows fighting over the berries on a wild blackberry bush. At the end of the dream, one of the crows looked in my direction and said something in Greek. Then it bit me on the arm.

An hour after I woke up, the dream still haunted me. And my arm felt strangely sore. Even though I didn't put much stock in dreams, this one seemed significant. And disturbing. I knew if I wanted an interpretation, there was only one person to ask: Natasha. The superstitious Russian slept with a notebook beside the bed to record her dreams, thumbing through her dream dictionaries every morning to figure out what the latest dream meant. And while I hoped the dream heralded good things, violent talking crows seemed the stuff of nightmares.

I called Natasha while sipping coffee as I sat in my Adirondack chair on the bluff overlooking Lake Michigan. The sight of the majestic lake always helped put things into perspective, and I needed reassurance from both nature and Natasha that my dream didn't foreshadow ill fortune. But I felt like dark trouble had already come calling. Murder had a way of upending one's carefully constructed life. And I should know. Beginning with the Chaplin case in New York, I had now been involved with three murders in three years. I only hoped bad things came in threes, and this latest murder would be the end of it.

When Natasha answered, I explained my need for a dream session. Natasha was so thrilled by my request, she temporarily forgot how to speak English. When her Russian at last veered into a language I understood, I described the dream about the crows and the berries. I waited while Natasha retrieved her dream dictionaries. Dasha's high-pitched barking could be heard in the background.

"Let me see," she said after a moment. "Big angry crow who bites you. Berries. And a bird who talks Greek. Do you remember what Greek words this bird uses?"

"No, except for 'Yasou.' And I know that means 'hello.'" I had vacationed in Greece for a month after college graduation, which was long enough to learn how to greet people, thank them, and order food. But that was the extent of my facility with the language. "Why would the crow say something in Greek?"

"The girl buried in woods. Her name is Katsaros, *da*? Is Greek. I have good friend who was Miss Greece. Despina from Thessaloniki. I know what is Greek name. If bird speaks Greek, dream has something to do with dead girl."

Natasha murmured to herself in Russian for a few minutes; the sound of turning pages and Dasha's barks served as accompaniment "What does my dream mean?" I said finally.

"Is confusing. Maybe I not tell you."

"Natasha, you have to tell me. Otherwise I'll think the dream means disaster and bad luck is headed my way." I prepared myself for the worst. "Does it?"

"Depends. Crow is strange bird. How you say? Mystical. To dream of crow is rare. And you have many crows in dream.

This is symbol of people who want to influence you. Be careful. Do not listen to them."

"The crow bit me. Is that a bad thing?"

"To be bit is never good. But crow is smart. Most smart bird there is. If crow bites you, it wants you to pay attention."

"To what?"

"*Ya ne znayu*. I don't know. Berries, I think. You say crows are eating berries in dream?"

"Yes. Wild blackberries."

"Then you must pay attention to such berries."

Since it was blackberry season and the Blackberry Art School was celebrating its centenary, I was already paying an inordinate amount of attention to the fruit. This was silly. I had dreamed of crows because one showed up at Theo's cottage yesterday. Also, my life revolved around berries. Of course I'd dream about them.

"Thanks for the interpretation. But it's almost ten. I have to get to the store."

"One more thing, Marlee. Crows not always good in dream. Sometimes they mean much sadness. And *smert´*."

"*Smert´*?"

"Death."

The last thing I needed to hear was that my dream about crows and berries foretold death. But if I didn't want to hear the truth, I should never have asked Natasha to play soothsayer. Besides, I had never believed in dreams before. This wasn't the time to start.

Luckily, I had a lot to divert me. From the Fourth of July to Labor Day weekend, Oriole Point witnessed a virtual onslaught of tourists. I'd be hunched over my computer records each night trying to figure out what store item needed to be reordered—and how quickly could I have it express shipped. I'd ordered extra quantities of blackberry food products to coincide with the BAS centenary festivities, which began on Monday.

Several BAS alumni had already arrived, visiting the store as soon as we opened on Saturday. Because they were much older than me, I didn't recognize them as fellow students. But they wore purple "100 Years of Art on the Bayou" T-shirts, proving they were here for the centenary. Their high spirits boded well for the upcoming week. So did their enthusiasm for my store-made blend of blackberry and chocolate tea. Three of them purchased a tin of it. I felt confident my shop was ready for the incursion of blackberry-loving visitors.

I'd set up a butcher-block table in the center of the store stacked with blackberry-flavored tea, coffee, jams and jellies, syrups, wine, candy, and granola. A shipment of Asian blackberry vinegar arrived that morning, just in time to include the bottles in my butcher-block display. Blackberry and raspberry pies from Zellars were lined up in our pie case, and Theo had baked heavenly blackberry muffins bursting with ripe fruit. It wasn't even noon, and we'd already sold two dozen. I'd also stocked ceramic berry bowls and mugs decorated with blackberries. Blackberry-themed jewelry, too. Except that every time I looked over at the blackberry charm bracelets, I remembered the crayon bracelet unearthed by Charlie.

Behind the counter three posters greeted customers. Two of them announced the Blackberry Art School centenary and road rally. The other displayed the nutritional and cosmetic benefits of blackberries. For example, eating fresh blackberries can promote tightening of skin tissue—a cost-effective, healthy way to look younger. Because blackberries possess a high tannin count, the fruit also helps to relieve inflammation of the intestines, which makes it a good tea or smoothie for anyone suffering from tummy troubles. And for as long as they were in season, I ate a cup of fresh blackberries each morning, providing me with half my daily vitamin C requirement. A smaller poster by the door related further interesting facts about the fruit, including the other names it is known by: brambleberry, dewberry, and thimbleberry.

No matter how many berry facts I made available on my walls, someone always had a question I hadn't thought to provide information on. I knew instinctively that the woman dressed in white culottes and a bright yellow shirt who approached the cash register had a blackberry question.

"Excuse me, miss," she said in an accent that placed her south of the state of Indiana. "My blackberry plants aren't doing well. I love blackberries, but I can't get any fruit out of them. As soon as I think they're about to ripen, the berries turn brown or shrivel up."

"Sounds like a leaf disease called *anthracnose*. It's caused by a fungus. Take a specimen to your local nursery and they should be able to diagnose the problem." I wondered why she hadn't done so already. As I often reminded my staff, I only sold berry products; I didn't grow them. Although generations of Jacobs had done just that, going all the way back to the eighteenth century in the Netherlands. "If the plant is relatively new, it may have had a virus when you bought it. And make certain your domestic blackberry plant is nowhere near wild blackberries, which carry viruses."

After she left, my thoughts returned to the dream I had the night before. Wild blackberry bushes figured largely in it, as they did at the site of the burial. I closed my eyes, trying to re-create the site in my mind. The images from last night's dream returned, more vivid and disturbing than ever.

"Earth to Marlee."

I opened my eyes to see Dean staring at me with a mixture of concern and exasperation. "Were you talking to me?"

"Ah, yeah. I asked you to quiz me." He held up a coffee table book entitled *The Age of French Impressionism*. "Been boning up on the Impressionists all week. I assigned twentieth-century art to Andrew. If there are any painting clues in the road rally, he and I need to be prepared." Dean rifled the pages of the book. "Go ahead. Ask me about Renoir or Degas."

"Please stop studying for the road rally."

"But Andrew and I intend to win."

"Dean, I took part in the road rally last year. It's just a scavenger hunt. If we drive fast and guess well, we have a good chance of snagging one of the top three prizes. But this is not the SATs. We're supposed to have fun at the Blackberry Road Rally. And speaking of blackberries . . ." I slipped my cell phone out of my apron pocket and searched for Captain Holt's number.

Things had slowed down, and there were only two people in the store aside from Dean and me. I could leave The Berry Basket in Dean's hands for a while. "I'll be gone for an hour or two," I said, waiting for Holt to pick up. "If things get crazy busy, call me."

"Where are you going?"

"I have business to attend to," I replied, then headed into the back room as soon as I heard Holt's voice. No need to let Dean know the business concerned murder, not The Berry Basket. Although Natasha had helped me as best she could, I had my own interpretation of last night's dream. And it required that I return to the scene of the crime.

Chapter 9

On the way to the Sanderling farm, I missed the looming presence of Piper's overgrown puppy in my backseat. If Gordon happened to be at home today, there was certain to be an angry reaction from him when I showed up. With Charlemagne by my side, Gordon might think twice before trying to throw me off his property. But when I turned onto his driveway Gordon's green van was nowhere in sight. However, several law enforcement vehicles were in evidence. There were two uniformed officers in the pasture, and another pair returning from the woods, accompanied by leashed dogs. The search for additional bodies on the property continued.

As soon as I got out of my car, I spotted Atticus Holt sitting on a bench by the picnic table.

"Thanks for meeting me here," I said when he met me halfway. "Since it's Saturday, I was worried you might have the day off."

"It is my day off," he said with an easy smile, "but I've been putting in extra hours on the case. So is Detective Trejo. He and I were at the Blackberry Art School this morning."

"Are you and he partners? I didn't know that was possible. After all, you work for the sheriff's department, and he's a state trooper."

"Both departments are involved in the Katsaros case." He hesitated. "And he's family."

"Family?"

He laughed. "Don't look so shocked. Greg's my brother-in-law; he married my sister ten years ago. They have three kids."

"Wow. I never would have pegged Detective Trejo as a family man." To be honest, I couldn't picture Trejo as anything but an attractive robot. To hear he had a wife and three children seemed as fantastical as my talking crows.

"He's not bad once you get to know him. But he is a little intense. I've tried to get him to ease up a little, especially with people who are witnesses, not suspects. He sometimes treats the guilty and innocent exactly the same."

"Yeah, I've noticed." I looked around. "Is he here?"

"Nope. Just you and me, and two search teams."

"Anything else turn up?"

"Not yet. And we're getting ready to wrap things up tomorrow. Not a moment too soon for Gordon Sanderling. He's been staying away as much as possible while the police are here." Holt gave me a questioning look. "When you called you asked me to take you back to the burial site. Are you certain that's what you want?"

I turned my gaze to the wooded area. Now that I was here, I felt uneasy. A girl was buried in those woods. Perhaps she had also been murdered there. And she was no longer an anonymous pile of bones. She had a name. I knew how young she had been when her life ended, that she was a gifted artist and had a family so shattered by her disappearance they kept up the search for their daughter for five years. And my baker had loved her. When I charged after Charlie a few days ago, I didn't know what was waiting for me in those woods. Now I did. An innocent young girl had been buried there, her killer assuming she would remain hidden forever. But Theo was right: After twenty long years, the victim had been found. And she wanted justice.

"Marlee, you look nervous. You don't have to go back in there."

I took a deep breath. "Yes, I do."

As we set off for the woods, I looked down at my watch. When I chased after Charlie, I hadn't paid attention to how much time had gone by before I'd reached the burial site. I needed to know how long it had taken the killer to bring his victim to the site. Once we reached the woods, I noticed yellow markers placed along the ground, with yellow police tape sporadically wrapped around several trees. The trail to the burial was now unmistakable. Even the branches and vegetation I had tripped over had been flattened, and I could see numerous footprints and paw prints as I followed behind Holt.

"Be careful how you step," Holt called over his shoulder. "The ground's uneven."

"I remember." I glanced up at the towering trees. It was an overcast day, still and muggy. The woods seemed dimmer than before, the trees more close together. As if the forest itself was weary of all the recent intrusion by humans and wanted to shut us out. "Were Sienna's parents relieved to hear that her body had finally been found?"

"Relieved. And devastated. They've never gotten over their child's death. Now the family is being forced to relive the tragedy. Once the forensic tests have been completed, they're flying in to retrieve her remains."

"How terrible and sad," I said. "I don't know how anyone in law enforcement deals with this on a regular basis."

"It's not easy. But if we don't deal with it, the guilty will never be captured and punished."

I hoped the guilty person who murdered Sienna Katsaros would be one of them. And I wanted to help in any way I could. Holt and I spoke little for the rest of the way. It was hot, and we had to pay attention in order to avoid the all too prevalent poison ivy. I'd been lucky I hadn't fallen into a patch when I was here last time.

"This is it," Holt announced as we entered a small clearing.

Checking the time, I noted that it had taken us twenty-five minutes to walk here from the farmhouse driveway. As I suspected, the distance was not so far from the farm that no one would have found this place. But it was distant enough that few people were likely to stumble on it, as I had done.

"The police have been busy," I remarked. The spot where Sienna had been buried was cordoned off, and the ground thoroughly excavated. I noticed paw prints everywhere, obviously left by the cadaver dogs. Other spots had been dug up as well. The police were looking for further clues: another body or a buried weapon perhaps.

Holt watched me as I walked around the clearing. "Why did you want to come here?"

"To make certain of what I saw." I turned to him. "Last night I had a vivid dream about the burial site, and it reminded me of something that might be important."

His expression turned even more serious. "Go on."

I stroked the overgrown bush beside me, then pointed to three other bushes nestled among the borders of the clearing. "These are wild blackberry bushes. I remember eating the berries while I was waiting for the police to arrive. I didn't think anything of it then. Wild blackberries are common around here. But now that I know Sienna went to BAS, it takes on meaning. My dream last night reminded me of it."

"You think there's a direct connection between the burial site and the Blackberry Art School?"

"I do. I think this site was deliberately chosen by the murderer." I scanned the burial site. "And I suspect the murderer is part of BAS."

"We've come to the same conclusion. The only tie Sienna

Katsaros had to this area was the school." He grimaced. "And Gordon Sanderling."

I sat down on the fallen log where I had watched Charlie dig up the body just five short days ago. "It's more than that. Look where the body was buried. A small clearing surrounded by wild blackberries." I bit my lip. "This is hard to explain unless you've been a BAS student."

Holt sat down beside me. "I'm listening."

"The area where the art school was founded has always been covered with blackberry bushes, both wild and cultivated. It's why the bayou and the school were named after the berries. If we had a mascot, it would probably be a giant blackberry bush. Everything at BAS is connected to the berries."

I reached over and plucked one of the blackberries from the bush beside me.

"The cabins at the school are grouped according to age and are referred to as 'Brambles,'" I continued, looking down at the berry. "The Black Butte Bramble houses students aged twelve to fourteen. Those fifteen to seventeen live in the Black Pearl Bramble, while students eighteen to twenty call Black Diamond Bramble their home. Adults twenty-one and up live in the Bayou Bramble cabins, which are more spacious than those assigned to younger students. By the way, those are all names of different blackberry cultivars. Then there—"

"Wait a second," Holt interrupted. "You said students are housed according to age. Theo Foster was seventeen when he was at BAS, and Sienna a year older. According to your description, that would have put them in different housing groups."

"True. But the classes held students of all ages."

"Then there's interaction between the age groups?"

"Yes. And we ate meals at the same time. Still, BAS is as cliquish as high school. The upperclassmen treat younger students with a mixture of affection and disdain. In fact, students aged twelve through seventeen are referred to as

'Drupelets,' while those eighteen to twenty are known as 'Drupes.' Adults are called 'Canes.'"

He swatted away a deer fly. "This sounds like gibberish."

"It makes sense to people who are fruit growers. But even the newest BAS student realizes all the terms are related to blackberries. We're also given berry-themed nicknames by our fellow Drupes and Drupelets."

I saw a hint of amusement in his eyes. "And what was your nickname?"

"Everyone at BAS called me 'Raspberry,' or 'Razzy' for short." I smiled. "I was a bit of a smart ass and liked to give people the raspberry."

He chuckled.

"My best friend, Tess, never makes a decision until she mulls it over about thirty times," I went on. "So her berry nickname was derived from the mulberry; we called her 'Multessa.' The Cabot brothers work for me; they also went to BAS for a summer. Because Dean liked to poke fun at people, he was dubbed 'Poke,' a shortened version of poke-berry. And Andrew apparently hit on every cute guy at BAS. His nickname became 'Wolfie.'" I noted his confused expression. "After the wolfberry."

"If all the BAS students were given berry-related names, I wonder what Theo's was."

"I don't know. I hope he was given one, but it's usually your friends and Bramble cabinmates who name you. It's possible he kept to himself so much that no one thought to give him a nickname." The idea made me sad. "Again, what you need to remember is that virtually everything at the school is linked to blackberries." I paused for emphasis. "Everything."

He shrugged. "We already assumed a person at the school had something to do with Sienna's death. A fellow student or instructor. Maybe a workman who visited the campus."

"Maybe. But I think someone in Sienna's Bramble group

knows what really happened to her. Of course, it depends on how long the group was together. Students can register for weekly and monthly sessions, or stay the whole summer. Near as I can figure from talking to Theo, he was here the entire summer semester: early June to late August. If Sienna and her Bramble mates were, too, that's significant."

"Why?"

"The school is a world unto itself. Kind of like a summer art camp version of Hogwarts—without the magic wands. Those who stay all summer forge strong bonds. And the bonds between Bramble cabinmates can last a lifetime. The two girls Tess and I roomed with our first summer returned the following year. We became as close as sisters. In fact, Emma and Alison are coming in for the centenary and staying with me at my home. Many of us also honored our time at BAS by marking our bodies permanently."

I pulled up one of my jeans' legs and pointed. My right ankle boasted a delicate purple tattoo of four blackberries.

He shook his head. "This sounds less like a school, and more like a cult."

"Leave it to the police to see something sinister in this," I said with a laugh. "It wasn't. BAS attracts kids more creative than those attending most summer schools or camps. And we were given a great deal of freedom. Famous artists taught us, we lived in the woods beside a lovely bayou, and the lake beaches are an easy walk away. Waking up each morning to the smell of pine and paint. Being with your friends all day, creating art, having fun, discussing the meaning of life as only teenagers can do." I sighed with pleasure at the memory. "If cults were that wonderful, I'd join one in a minute."

"So we should pay particular attention to the students in Sienna's Bramble," he said.

"That's the logical place to start. The Bramble cabins each house four students. Those students know you the best." I nodded. "Even Theo referred to Sienna's Bramble yesterday when I visited him. He mentioned two names: Christian and Leah. I'm betting Leah was one of Sienna's cabinmates. And Christian was probably a student in her Bramble group."

"By the way, thank you again for calling me yesterday after you talked to your baker. Greg and I checked the records at the school this morning for the information you gave us. We think the students Theo referred to are Leah Malek and Christian Naylor. Both of them RSVPed to the school that they plan to attend the centenary next week." He leaned forward, his arms clasped over his knees. "We'll question them as soon as they arrive. As we intend to question everyone who attended BAS that summer. Especially those in her age group."

"I'd pay particular attention to Gordon."

"We are. After all, the body was found on his farm."

"More than just on his farm. It was found right here." Frustrated, I gestured to the clearing. "If you're a teenager spending an entire summer at a school obsessed with blackberries, this would be ideal. It's private, it belongs on the property of a BAS student, it's filled with blackberry bushes. A perfect place to hide out with a fellow Bramble member." I narrowed my eyes at the burial site. "Or maybe more than one."

"For what purpose? Sex? Drugs? Partying?"

"All of the above. There are a fair number of chaperones on campus because some of the kids are as young as twelve. However, Sienna's Bramble group would have been eighteen, nineteen, and twenty. I'm sure they were looking for a place to sneak away to. Gordon had to have known about this clearing. Sanderlings have lived here for decades."

"Now we only have to prove it." He shot me a rueful smile.

"Theo said the Sanderling family threw a birthday party for Gordon on the farm that summer. Lots of BAS students were invited. Any of them might have wandered into the woods and found this spot. Or maybe Gordon took some of them here."

"Maybe. But this is no more than conjecture, Marlee. Yes, we found the remains, which we were able to identify. Someone at BAS either killed her, or knows who did. But the murder happened twenty years ago. This is a cold case and we may never solve it."

I got to my feet. The clearing felt more and more like a graveyard, one that we were disturbing with our conversation. "When will the newspapers reveal the name of the murder victim?"

Holt stood up, too. "The forensics results came in yesterday. The big news outlets in the state will include it in their Sunday edition tomorrow."

"And the centenary celebration begins the day after." I put my hand on his shoulder. "Therein lies your only advantage."

"What do you mean?"

"If the murderer plans to attend the centenary, this person should be here by Monday. That will be the first time they hear of the discovery of Sienna's remains. Don't you see? The news will come as a complete shock. Whoever killed Sienna may be thrown off balance by this unexpected turn of events. Perhaps the murderer will make a mistake. One big enough to allow the police to catch him." I recalled Theo's mention of Leah. "Or her."

"There is another scenario." His smile was friendly, but world weary. "The murderer may be so upset by the news that he might feel compelled to kill again."

Chapter 10

On Monday, I could almost hear the gnashing of teeth at the tiny editorial offices of the *Oriole Messenger* and *Oriole Point Herald* as they both got scooped by the bigger news outlets. As Holt had surmised, every news service from Grand Rapids to Detroit carried the story in their Sunday editions. There wasn't a person in the village who wasn't talking about it, especially Gillian. She pestered me all morning about any further details regarding Sienna that she could pass on to her father.

The only ones uninterested in the case were Dean and Andrew. Instead, the brothers had taken to asking me random questions about painting and sculpture. I felt as if I were trapped in an art-themed version of *Jeopardy*. If it hadn't been so busy in the store, I would have sent both of them home. I was thrilled when Andrew's boyfriend called him up with some floral-related emergency. I quickly gave him the rest of the day off. One down, two to go, I thought, as Dean asked me for the name of the woman who posed for Goya in his Naked Maja painting.

"Caitlyn," I replied as I bagged blueberry soap for a customer.

"Be serious." He shook his head at me. "You're not even trying."

"And you're trying my patience. Now stop with the questions and get back to work."

"I only hope Tess is prepping for the road rally. Otherwise we're likely to finish last," he grumbled before heading off to wait on a customer at the pastry case.

When I turned my attention to the next customer in line, I gave a yell at the sight of Emma Kanin, all five feet eleven of her. "You're here!"

"We both are," a voice replied. Much shorter than Emma, Alison Smollett peeked around her friend's shoulder.

I ran out from behind the counter. For the next few minutes, we jumped up and down in a boisterous group hug.

"Where's Tess?" Alison asked after we'd hugged and jumped ourselves breathless.

"At Oriole Glass. Let's go over there right now." I was about to remove my chef apron when I realized the shop was filled with people. The ever-present sound of the blender meant Gillian was making smoothies, and I spied Dean slicing blackberry cobbler for a customer. Three people stood at the counter, ready to have their purchases rung up.

"Sorry, I can't leave. But you know where Tess's studio shop is."

Emma gave me another hug. "Not to worry. We booked our flights to arrive at O'Hare around the same time. After the two-hour drive, a walk around downtown will do us good."

"Both of you are staying with me this week," I reminded them. "I don't want to hear you've changed your mind and booked a B&B or prefer to stay in a BAS cabin."

Alison laughed. "We're staying with you. I've been looking forward to that more than the centenary. It will be like a weeklong pajama party."

"We put together a pajama party grocery list on the drive

from Chicago." Emma looked down at her phone. "Potato chips, chip dip, popcorn, chips, wine, salsa, chips, dark chocolate, chips. Am I leaving something out?"

"Chips?" I suggested.

Swamped with pastry-loving customers, Dean cleared his throat to get my attention.

"You need to get back to work," Emma said. "We'll go bother Tess."

"If it slows down, I'll call your cell. I'd love to have lunch with you guys." After a last group hug, I hurried back to the register.

With a frantic wave of his silver pie cutter, Dean hissed at me. "If another person walks in here, we'll be in violation of the fire code."

"Don't be so dramatic. It's just summer in Oriole Point," I answered while ringing up the next customer. Although, to be honest, it seemed busier than usual. Looking around, I noticed quite a few BAS shirts. The art school alumni were arriving in droves. If this was any indication, the centenary would be great for business. Better than even Piper hoped.

For the next two hours, I looked up expectantly at every person wearing a purple BAS T-shirt. Several I recognized, but many I didn't. And I couldn't help but think that one of these returning students may have murdered Sienna Katsaros.

Emma and Alison held off on lunch until store traffic slowed down for both Tess and me, which meant we didn't sit down to eat until after two o'clock. The afternoon rush over, we were able to find a table at the popular Boatswain, a large moored riverboat on the Oriole River. All of us were starving. In addition to our sandwiches, we ordered crab and artichoke dip appetizers, along with cups of chicken gumbo. Except for

Tess, who requested a proper vegetarian meal of three-bean soup, followed by a sweet potato and quinoa salad.

I sat back, enjoying the first moment off my feet since morning. A double-decker vessel, the Boatswain's outer decks were filled with tables. Because most of the lunch crowd had left, we snagged a ringside table at the railing. The view was appropriately picturesque and waterborne. The sunny eighty-degree day prompted dozens of boaters to take their cabin cruisers, fishing skiffs, pontoons, and whalers out to the lake. And the brisk summer breezes were responsible for the tall elegant sailing vessels streaming past us.

"This is nice." I sipped my iced tea as a schooner, sails billowing, glided only a few yards away. "I love that business is booming in summer, but it means I have to spend lots of gorgeous summer days inside. Sometimes I wish I had a boat like this to sell my merchandise from."

"Like one of those junks in Hong Kong's Victoria Harbor." Emma's glamorous, globe-trotting job involved handling marketing and overseas promotion for Ralph Lauren. If any of us had questions about junks in Victoria Harbor—or the best espresso bar in Budapest—we went to Emma. Or her husband, Stefan, who also traveled around the world for business.

Alison tapped a spoon on her water glass. "Time to get serious. Who has big news they haven't shared yet? We know Marlee's finally getting married this winter. Any wedding dress details? And are you having a berry wedding cake? If so, I hope it's blueberry."

"Things have been so busy at the shop, I haven't had much time to think about it. Besides, we're not having a big wedding. Ryan prefers something small and intimate. Only close friends and family, which includes you and Emma. Remember, he's been married before."

"You haven't," Emma said. "If you want a big fancy wedding, you should have one."

"I don't."

Tess cleared her throat. "For the record, you should know Marlee has a wedding board on Pinterest with over a thousand pins."

I gave my friends a sheepish grin. "Okay, maybe I wouldn't mind a big wedding with the bridesmaids dressed in winter white, and a white chocolate cranberry cake decorated with pine cones, and centerpieces of white branches and hanging crystals—"

"I told you," Tess said.

"What she's not telling you is that I think I'm more excited about having a big party than actually getting married." I sighed. "The whole idea makes me nervous. Maybe there's a reason I'm thirty years old and never walked down the aisle."

"I think you're gun shy about marriage because of the two men who did propose." Like most of my friends, Alison knew the details of my checkered romantic past.

"Max's high school proposal shouldn't count," Tess said. "He was way too young. As for proposal number two, Fergus was not the right guy for her."

"Maybe if he had a different name," Emma added with a wry grin.

There was some truth to that. Fergus Fink was not the name I would have chosen for my beloved. But he'd been a sweet young man, and my first serious relationship after college. I loved him, too. I also loved my job at the Gourmet Living Network. When Fergus proposed during a romantic dinner at my favorite French restaurant, I kept fielding calls over the latest network crisis. He grew angry, I got defensive, and the evening ended with Fergus grabbing the ring hidden in my chocolate mousse and exiting the restaurant. And my life. After that, I vowed to concentrate on my career, along with men as work obsessed as I was. This decision hadn't resulted in much personal or professional happiness, which was why I was back in Oriole Point about to marry Ryan Zellar this winter. If only I felt more confident about my decision.

"Sometimes I think Tess has the right idea," I said. "Why bother to get married at all? Maybe Ryan and I should just live together."

Alison frowned at Tess. "I knew you were a bad influence."

Tess held up her hands. "I have nothing to do with this."

"I'd believe that if there were wedding bells in the future for you and David." Alison was a romantic at heart and something of a traditionalist. Married these past eight years to a doting husband, Alison had two adorable children and was proud to be a stay-at-home mom.

"David and I are happy. I don't see how a wedding would change anything."

"If that's true, why not do it?" Alison was nothing if not persistent.

"We might change our minds if we decide to have children. For now, it's all good. Even my parents have stopped badgering us about getting married. And you know my parents."

Indeed we did. Tess came from a conservative Japanese family. Her parents and grandparents would be thrilled when she finally made her relationship with David legal.

"Alison forgets Tess is a Bohemian." I waved my hand in the air. "Devoted to the pursuit of love, art, and beauty. If this were the Roaring Twenties, she and David would be cavorting in Paris with Picasso and Gertrude Stein."

"Speaking of love, art, and beauty, what's this about the body of a BAS student being found in the woods?" Emma said. "We saw the newspaper headlines about an hour ago. And Tess brought us up to speed when we stopped by her studio."

"I don't think I knew the girl," Alison remarked.

"None of us did," I said. "She disappeared years before we went to BAS."

Emma sat back. "This is sure to put a damper on the school

celebrations. Some of the alumni due to arrive must have been her friends."

"I know one person who went to BAS that summer with her: Gordon Sanderling. He's a local businessman, and his family's lived in Oriole Point for decades." Our server arrived with our gumbo. I waited until she left before continuing. "The body was found on his property."

"It does look suspicious," Tess said.

Our friends stared at us in horror. "The killer is in Oriole Point right now? I thought this murder happened twenty years ago." Emma's hazel eyes grew so wide I feared a contact lens might pop out.

"You need to tell the police," Alison said. "They have to arrest Gordon Sanderling! What if he shows up at the BAS reception tonight?"

"Guys, keep it down," I warned. "We're not the only ones having lunch out here."

Two tables away sat three older women, all of them local residents. One of them was Suzanne Cabot, mom to the Cabot brothers. If Andrew and Dean were the heat missiles of gossip in our small town, Suzanne was the mother ship.

"We don't want to give those quidnuncs anything to talk about," Tess added in a stage whisper.

My friends looked puzzled, but Tess was reminding me that those local ladies were notorious gossips, or quidnuncs. Tess and I met as fifth graders while competing in a statewide spelling bee, one in which we tied for first place. We had been friends ever since, while also retaining our love of obscure and archaic words. It often served as our secret code.

I waved to Suzanne, who waved back. Leaning across the table, I said, "Suzanne's sons work for me. She's also the receptionist at the local police station, where she's probably gleaned a few extra details about the murder."

"Why haven't they arrested this Sanderling person?" Emma asked me.

"Nothing concrete to charge him with, at least not yet. That poor girl was buried on his property twenty years ago. And Theo Foster, my baker, attended the same summer session at BAS as Gordon and Sienna. Lucky for him, he has an alibi. The police are probably looking into Gordon's background, trying to find something incriminating."

"If Sanderling didn't kill Sienna Katsaros, it's possible someone at the school did. One of the students maybe. Or even one of the teachers." Tess appeared ill at the thought.

Alison seemed just as distressed. "I can't believe this. I look back at my two summers at BAS as some of the happiest of my life."

Emma nodded. "I hope a stranger is responsible for this terrible crime, not someone from Blackberry."

"Does this Gordon person seem like a typical murderer?" Alison asked.

Tess and I exchanged glances. "What does a typical murderer look like?" I asked. "As for Gordon, I don't know him all that well. He owns a big plumbing supply company in nearby Holland. And he lives alone on the old family farm."

"Has he ever been married?" Emma looked up from her gumbo.

"Don't know," I answered. "But he probably had a serious relationship at some point. Gordon's in his late thirties, at least six feet two, thick black hair, broad shoulders."

Emma whistled. "He sounds hot."

"Only on paper. He's pretty out of shape. And last summer, I hired his company to replace the copper pipes in my house. I didn't enjoy dealing with him at all. He was abrasive and rude." I perked up at the sight of our entrees. "Lunch has arrived. Let's spend the rest of the time talking about anything other than murder or Gordon Sanderling."

"Fine with me," Alison said. "I have more I want to say about weddings and marriage. I'm not giving up on either you or Tess." She pointed at Emma. "After all, if this party girl finally walked down the aisle, there's hope for anyone."

I welcomed the change of subject. Despite my concerns about marriage, it was a more benign topic than murder. Even if I did suspect it held almost as many hazards.

The lunch lasted longer than anticipated, but I needed the girl talk and the laughs. The Boatswain's legendary giant onion rings were an added bonus. But I had to get back to work, and Tess left early after a phone call from David alerted her a client from Chicago had come looking for her. I handed over my house keys to Emma, with instructions to not let my bird, Minnie, out of her cage until I got home. Standing at the foot of the riverboat's gangplank, I waved to Emma and Alison as they pulled away in their rental car.

"Friends from out of town?"

I spun around and met the curious gaze of Suzanne Cabot. "Yes. We all attended summer sessions at Blackberry Art School. They're here for the centenary."

"Ah yes, the BAS centenary. It's gotten off to a terrible start, hasn't it? Piper must be frantic about that skeleton you found. She's worked so hard to put together events for this week. And now one dead body threatens to ruin everything." She gave a deep sigh.

Suzanne often performed in the winter stage productions at Calico Barn. Unlike the professional actors who appeared each summer at the Oriole Point Theater, the Calico players were all amateurs, albeit enthusiastic ones. Since Suzanne was as animated offstage as she was on, it seemed as if the curtain never came down for her.

"Keep in mind it's a body that's been buried for two decades,"

I said. "It's not like someone was murdered last week. Most of the alumni here this week never knew the girl."

Taking me by the arm, she led me a few steps away. I wasn't certain why. There was no one in the immediate area, and her lunch companions were nowhere in sight.

"I heard one of the people at your table mention Gordon Sanderling. You're probably suspicious about him. If not, you should be. The police have learned Gordon knew Sienna Katsaros. And you found the body on his property. There's talk at the station that an arrest is imminent."

"Could be no more than gossip, Suzanne. The case isn't even in the jurisdiction of the Oriole Point police."

She raised a dramatically shaped eyebrow. Like her sons, Suzanne never left the house without being well groomed. For Suzanne, that included bold choices in make-up and accessories. Today, she boasted Joan Crawford brows and chunky jewelry gleaming like gold bars in the July sun. With her teased reddish brown hair and plus-size figure outfitted in a floral silk jumpsuit, she turned as many heads as her fashionable sons. Although her style choices often made Andrew and Dean cringe.

"The police don't deal in gossip, Marlee."

"I beg to differ. What else have you heard?"

"They're looking into Gordon Sanderling's past. His disturbing past."

Now she had my interest. "How disturbing?"

"He went through an ugly divorce years ago. Someone he met when he went off to Minnesota to attend college. The marriage didn't last much beyond graduation. As far as I know, they never lived in Oriole Point. He went to school in Duluth, and they got married there. The girl was the daughter of a local congresswoman. I think the last name was Poe, like the writer of those scary stories. Gordon must have been unhappy about the divorce because around the same time charges were brought against him."

"What kind of charges?"

"Harassment. Stalking." Her grip on my upper arm tightened. "I heard Officer Davenport talking with the chief this morning. Because they kept their voices low, I could barely make out what they were saying. But a woman accused Gordon of stalking her sixteen years ago. He got divorced around the same time. It must have been his ex-wife who filed charges."

"I'm sure the police will be talking to her."

"That may be difficult." Suzanne paused. "No one knows what happened to his ex-wife."

Although the day was warm, I felt chilled. "What does that mean? Did she go missing?"

"I'm not sure." She looked unhappy. "Everyone's being tight lipped down at the station. It's hard to find out much of anything."

"This sounds bad for Gordon," I said. "Two women he knew in the past twenty years just up and vanished."

"Now one of them has been found." Suzanne leaned even closer. "Between you and me, I wouldn't be surprised if his ex-wife's body is also buried in those woods."

Chapter 11

Fireflies seemed to outnumber people at the Blackberry Art School's welcome reception. Given that over three hundred guests were in attendance, the fireflies were putting on quite a show. And it was dusk: the optimal time for these glimmering creatures to go into their mating display. Everywhere I looked, fireflies twinkled in the bushes, shrubs, and grass. The curved shoreline of the surrounding bayou already made the location scenic and tranquil; the lightning bugs pushed the vista into magical.

"This place is wondrous," Alison said with a touch of awe in her voice.

"It is beautiful." I gazed out at the bayou, its calm surface reflecting the last of the rosy sunset. Also reflected in the water were the strings of white Christmas lights strung over long wooden buffet tables. And a tempting buffet it was: platters heaped with chicken wings, beer steamed shrimp, fish tacos, cole slaw, and three different kinds of salads. I had already sampled everything and was waiting to digest it all before going back for seconds. Especially the blackberry balsamic–glazed chicken wings.

"I'm glad I wore long sleeves tonight. Otherwise the mosquitoes would have eaten me alive." Emma gestured at her white cotton dress. Since she worked for Ralph Lauren, it likely came from his latest spring collection. Although the flared collar and midcalf skirt were the height of summer fashion, I knew it was the dress's white color that helped protect Emma. Having grown up surrounded by water, I knew all the tricks—scientific and homespun—about keeping mosquitoes at bay.

Alison smacked at her forearm. "They're biting me like crazy."

"I told you not to wear black. Mosquitoes are attracted to black and red. Bright floral colors, too." At least I had convinced her not to wear perfume. "And they seem to prefer biting blondes and redheads over brunettes. Sorry."

Alison smacked her leg next. She wore a sleeveless mini dress, exposing enough skin to qualify for an insect smorgasbord. "I guess blondes don't always have more fun."

"Lucky the rest of us are brunettes." Emma winked at Tess and me.

"That dry mountain air in Colorado has made you forget how humid Michigan summers can be," Tess reminded Alison. "We have a lot of water around here, girl." She peeked over our shoulders. "Hold on. Is that Kurt and Denny? I haven't seen them in fourteen years."

She hurried to greet two fellow glass artists from our long-ago summer sessions at BAS. We had all been experiencing similar encounters since arriving at the bayou. Every five minutes, another familiar face from summer school appeared, followed by kisses, shouts, and hugs. I actually burst into tears at my first sight of the woman who taught me to silk-screen.

Next it was Emma's turn to cry out in surprise and delight. "Ali, I think that's the Kleinbender sisters." She pointed at three women standing near the makeshift bar.

After Alison and Emma ran off hand in hand, I turned to see Atticus Holt making his way toward me. He was in uniform once more, signaling he was here on official police business. "We have to stop meeting like this," I said when he reached my side.

He chuckled. "You're looking very bridal tonight."

I glanced down at my white slacks and white silk blouse. "This is a little casual for a wedding."

"But you do have flowers in your hair. White flowers, too."

I reached back to touch the French braid that hung down my back. "One of my houseguests insisted on weaving daisies in my hair. Emma's job revolves around lifestyle tweaking and the perfect finishing touch. As soon as she spotted my garden daisies, I knew I was about to be finished off." I smiled. "Seems a little Boho to me, but it makes Emma happy."

"Me too. You look beautiful tonight, Marlee." As soon as he said this, Holt must have remembered I was engaged. "I assume your fiancé is with you. I'd like to meet him to extend my congratulations on the upcoming marriage."

"You have time. We're not getting married until January."

Holt glanced over at the waters of the bayou, now darkening as night fell. "Until I got here, I thought calling this place Blackberry Bayou was a mistake by some founding father. But it actually is a bayou. I went to college in Louisiana and I know a bayou when I see one."

"The Oriole River takes a long, lazy curve here. Also it's shallow; no more than three feet deep. Great for kayaking. Birding too." I lowered my voice. "Have you learned anything further about Christian and Leah?"

He nodded. "Tina Kapoor, the current BAS president, pulled up that summer's records for us. You were right. Leah Malek was a cabinmate of Sienna's. Christian Naylor belonged to her age group, too. He's thirty-eight years old, born and raised in Chicago. His dad is an architect, a profession the son also took up. Naylor's mother is a well-known nature photographer, and his grandmother was the first African American student to attend BAS."

"Do the Naylors still live in Chicago?"

"His parents and sister moved to Atlanta years ago. But Christian lives in San Diego now, and he's supposed to attend the centenary. Don't know if he's arrived yet. However, I can't go around asking every African American man if his name is Christian Naylor."

He was right; dozens of African American men were in attendance tonight. At first I was surprised one of them wasn't Mayor Pierce, otherwise known as Piper's husband. Since they were Oriole Point's power couple and presided over everything in the village except for kiddie birthday parties, their absence was noted. However, Piper and Lionel had been invited to a sunset cruise on a friend's yacht. A cruise that included another prominent couple: the governor and his wife. Small wonder Piper ditched the BAS welcome reception for such a social coup.

"Has Leah Malek arrived?"

"I spoke with her earlier today. But I don't see her at the moment. I also have the names of the students who roomed with Gordon Sanderling."

"Theo could help you identify Christian," I told Holt. "Only I'm not sure he plans to show up tonight."

I looked out over the crowd. The Cabot brothers currently held court near the fire pit, and I recognized at least thirty local alumni enjoying themselves. Some sat on picnic benches or Adirondack chairs; others strolled along gravel paths that led along the bayou or uphill through the pine trees to the cabins and various art studios.

"I don't see Theo. But there's my fiancé." I pointed to the four people en route to the screened-in gazebo near the dining hall. "The tall, blond guy is Ryan. If he were closer, you'd see how good looking he is. And how lucky I am."

"If you ask me, he's the lucky one."

I felt myself blush, not something I often did.

"I'm surprised he's not with you," Holt continued.

"Soon after we arrived, Ryan and I bumped into three of his cousins from out of state. Neither of us had any idea he had relatives who once went to BAS. Ryan was thrilled to see them, and he hasn't left their side since. Ryan is extremely tribal. And he's not comfortable with anyone outside the Zellar tribe."

"Except for you," Holt said, although it sounded like a question.

I watched Ryan disappear into the gazebo, his arm slung around the shoulders of a cousin introduced to me as Little Pete. "Of course. I'm part of the tribe now."

While I had no qualms about joining the Zellar clan, I hoped Ryan's reluctance to spend time with anyone outside his family would lessen. As an only child, I learned early to make friends and hone my socializing skills. The result was an ever growing network of people whom I regarded as much my family as my Jacob and Rossi relatives. But Ryan was one of five sons, all of them dedicated to the orchards and each other. It was no secret the women who married into the Zellars were expected to accommodate themselves to how the family lived and worked. I had already been told that if I wanted to see my parents on major holidays they would have to come to the Zellar farm and celebrate it there.

When I first heard this, I assumed they were trying to make a joke about how close knit the Zellars were. But the longer we were engaged, the more I realized the family really didn't need anyone outside of those related by blood or marriage. It was like joining the British royal family—or the Corleones. I hinted to Ryan that my complete transformation into a Zellar was unlikely, but he regarded my comments as amusing. This didn't amuse me.

"I heard something earlier today about Gordon Sanderling," I said. "It seems he was charged with stalking a woman about sixteen years ago. Possibly his ex-wife."

His expression turned wary. "Where did you hear this?"

"A friend." I had no intention of ratting out Suzanne. It might get her fired from her job at the police station. "But this person seems confident the rumor is true."

"Rumor is the word for it. And a garbled version, too." Holt lowered his voice as a group of people strolled past. "Marlee, this is an official police investigation. While it's beneficial if you have information that could throw light on the case, spreading unsubstantiated rumors is harmful. Especially to the person being gossiped about."

"It seems pretty serious gossip. I was told Gordon's ex-wife has disappeared."

"This is why gossip can be so damaging to a case. Let me assure you that Gordon's ex-wife is alive and well. She remarried years ago and is about to run for city council in Duluth."

I reminded myself to set Suzanne straight the next time I saw her. But I wasn't willing to totally concede defeat. "You did mention the stalking rumor was garbled. Does that mean part of it is true?"

He stared back at me.

"Okay, okay. I've concluded the question part of the program tonight."

"Good. Now you can answer some questions for me. Exactly how big is this school?"

"A hundred and thirty acres. You can only see a third of it from here. Those uphill trails lead to the workshops and studios. Beyond that are the Bramble cabins where students and faculty sleep. Staying in those cabins was the most fun. Except for the mosquitoes."

"Why weren't you a day student? Ms. Kapoor explained that most local students went home at night."

"Tess and I knew we'd miss out on too much fun if we weren't here all the time, especially after dark. We bugged our parents until they agreed to let us remain on campus all summer, even though they had to pay more tuition. A small price to pay to shut us up."

"You both sound like a handful."

I gave him a wink. "I prefer to think of us as two girls who knew what we wanted and were determined to get it."

"I suspect that's still true. Is it also true the Blackberry Art School is one of the most prestigious art summer schools in North America?"

"Absolutely. The faculty comprises well-known artists and instructors from all over the country: the College for Creative Studies in Detroit, the Rhode Island School of Design, Yale's School of Art, the Academy of Art University in San Francisco."

"No one connected to the Art Institute of Chicago's school?"

I laughed. "Our neighbor to the north snagged that plum. The Art Institute runs the Oxbow Art School in Saugatuck."

"And where are all these blackberries you were telling me about?"

"Follow me." I led him to a long row of bushes that lined the path leading to the bayou pier. "These are blackberry bushes." I touched one of the leafy branches heavy with fruit. Even before I plucked the berries, their sweet fragrance wafted toward me. "Taste one."

Holt ate far more than one blackberry, as did I. The berries were bursting with flavor.

"Tastes like summer to me. Especially summer at BAS."

"Are they wild blackberries?" Holt reached over to pluck a few more.

"No, these have been cultivated by the school." I squinted at the berries in my hand. "This one looks like the Chester Thornless variety. I'm surprised they're doing so well this close to the water. Blackberries like well-drained soil. As for wild blackberries, there are dozens of bushes up by the cabins. And if you like blackberries, I saw blackberry cobbler at the buffet. The school cooks make certain to serve a blackberry dish every day. They're quite creative. I still remember the night we got blackberry chili." I wrinkled my nose. "Not one of their more successful attempts."

"I'll take a pass on the chili, but I wouldn't mind some blackberry cobbler."

He followed me to the buffet, where we were soon enjoying slices of cobbler. Occasionally I lifted a fork as someone called out a greeting to me. It was breezy, which made the humidity more bearable. I smiled as two guitarists began to play near the gazebo. I expected to enjoy myself tonight, but I never thought Holt would be the person I'd be enjoying it with.

"Don't the students ever get tired of the blackberry theme?" He scraped the last bit of cobbler from his plate. "Seems like overkill."

"Nah, we loved it."

"I see now why you run a business called The Berry Basket. You're obsessed."

I craned my neck to look at something over his shoulder. "My phantom baker just showed up." Theo Foster stood half hidden by a pine tree near the path leading to the parking lot. I noticed he wore a purple BAS centenary shirt.

A thin woman with tousled blond hair suddenly swept Theo up in an embrace. Although it was no surprise when Theo didn't return the hug, I was impressed he hadn't pulled away.

"That's Leah Malek," Holt told me. "Theo was telling the truth about knowing her."

"Theo always tells the truth. Or at least the truth as he sees it."

Holt watched them for a moment. "I'm glad Theo showed up. I'd like to ask him a few questions about Christian Naylor."

I put my hand on his arm. "Let me talk to Theo first. He'll

take off the minute he sees you coming toward him. Then he'll hide in his cottage for the rest of the night."

"You're probably right. I don't want to send him into another panic attack in front of all these people. But he has to speak with the police again, whether he likes it or not. I've also been told Gordon Sanderling has been spotted here tonight." He frowned. "Marlee, I don't want you getting any more involved in this. Asking questions could land you in trouble, particularly if you're talking to the murderer."

"Don't worry. Theo is not the murderer."

He shook his head at me. "You're too trusting, Marlee."

"And you're too cautious." I grabbed another slice of pastry. "Have another piece of blackberry cobbler. Fruit and sugar make everything better."

Before he could protest, I was striding toward Theo and the blond woman. Theo appeared visibly relieved at my approach. "This is Leah," he told me when I joined them.

Leah turned an expectant face in my direction. "Hi. I'm Leah Malek. Are you a friend of Theo's? He and I were students at BAS about a thousand years ago."

"It was only twenty years ago," Theo said.

"I stand corrected." She grinned. "It just feels like a thousand."

"Marlee Jacob." I shook her hand. "I own The Berry Basket on Lyall Street. Theo's my baker."

Theo looked over my shoulder at Captain Holt, now making his way to the administration cottage. "I saw you talking to the policeman. I hope you told him to stay away from me."

Leah's smile dimmed. "Tina introduced me to him earlier tonight. He wanted to question me about Sienna. I still can't believe her body was discovered last week. What a horrible thing to happen. And after all this time." She turned a sad gaze in my direction. "Did you know Sienna? Probably not. You don't look familiar."

Before I could say anything, Tina Kapoor stepped onto the wide, polished base of an oak tree cut down years ago. The stump was known as Speaker's Corner, and anyone who stood atop it had to be accorded attention. Although Tina did not need Speaker's Corner to attract notice. A tall woman with a hawkish profile and black hair worn in an elaborate braid, she resembled a Madras version of Louise Nevelson. Her career promised to be nearly as impressive as Nevelson's as well. Not yet fifty, Tina had achieved worldwide fame for her clay sculptures, with recent exhibitions in Berlin, London, and the Whitney in New York.

Tina tapped on her live microphone, and the music and conversation died away. "Ladies and gentlemen, teachers and alumni of Blackberry Art School, I want to welcome all of you back to your artistic home along the bayou."

A wave of applause and cheers greeted this.

"Hundreds of former students have made their way to the beautiful village of Oriole Point once again to celebrate the art and friendships forged here in the heat and glory of past summers. One hundred summers have passed since the first artists came to the bayou determined to make this a learning ground for painters, sculptors, glassworkers, ceramicists, and anyone with an eye for beauty and a hunger to create. And far more than one hundred artists have emerged from our exciting summer sessions."

I glanced over at Theo, who stared solemnly at Tina. He claimed he was a potter once. I wondered how talented he had been, or if he kept any pieces from his summer at the bayou. Or was the memory of that summer too painful to bear?

"As you can see from the schedule posted on the studios and cabins," Tina went on, "we have a number of activities planned for this centenary. I hope all of you spend part of your time in the studios making art. I don't care if you haven't sat at a kiln or picked up a brush in decades. That hunger to create still resides within each of us. Let it reawaken this week." She paused. "Twenty years ago, one of the students at BAS, Sienna Katsaros, disappeared at the end of the summer session. For those who haven't seen today's newspapers, you should be aware the remains of Sienna Katsaros were recently discovered in a wooded area several miles away."

It became so quiet I could hear frogs croaking.

Tina's habitual stoic mask seemed to twist with pain. "It is suspected she met with foul play, which makes Sienna's death even more tragic and incomprehensible. We hope the police finally learn what happened to our Sienna and are able to bring some measure of peace and justice both to her memory and to her family. Now I would like all of you to observe a moment of silence for our youthful friend, our artistic sister, our Sienna."

She bowed her head and we all followed suit. When the long minute passed, I raised my head and looked over at Theo. He was gone.

"Where's Theo?" I asked.

Leah sighed. "I never could understand why that boy did anything."

"He's not a boy now," I reminded her.

"Isn't he? I swear he hasn't aged at all. And I don't think he's changed much in any other way, either. He still doesn't seem comfortable around people."

"I believe he likes you," I said. "And I know he cared for Sienna."

"Ah yes, Sienna. The boy had a huge crush on her. Then again, he wasn't the only one."

This didn't surprise me. The newspapers published a photo of Sienna on the front page this morning. She had been a re-markably pretty teenager: straight dark hair, heart-shaped face, delicate features. And it appeared at least two girls in their Bramble were attractive. Leah boasted a casual, almost brazen, beauty. Although she was far too thin, like a human greyhound.

"He was really upset to learn Sienna's body had been found." I took a deep breath. "In fact, I was the one who accidentally discovered the remains."

Leah looked appalled. "How terrible for you."

"Theo blames himself for not being in Oriole Point when Sienna disappeared. Now he thinks he should have been here all along trying to find her body." I sighed. "Or her killer."

She closed her eyes, as if the idea was distressing.

"It's hard to get information out of Theo," I continued. "And the less I know, the more difficult it is to help him. But he did mention you. And Christian Naylor."

"Yes, Christian was part of our group of friends. There were seven of us: four boys, three girls. But Theo was too young to be a member of our Bramble." She shrugged. "And too odd."

"Why only seven in your group? The school assigns four students to a cabin. I've never known a Bramble cabin to house only three."

"Dawn, Sienna, and I shared our cabin with Amanda Dobson, a watercolor student from Detroit. We all liked her, especially Christian. We were bummed when she had a severe reaction to poison ivy and had to be sent home. It took Christian weeks before he cheered up."

"Is Christian here tonight? If you could point him out to me, I'd be grateful."

"I'm the only one of our group in Oriole Point at the moment. According to my phone texts, the rest of the gang arrives later tonight or tomorrow." Leah's face took on a far-away expression. "Of course, Gordon is here. We had a lovely reunion. I didn't realize how much I've missed him. Now I'm looking forward to seeing the others."

The sudden hooting of a barn owl reminded me of my conversation at Crow Cottage with Theo. "This may sound stupid, but Theo said you taught him how to summon birds. He gave me a demonstration by calling a crow. He described what you did as 'old magic.'"

"Poor guy. Leave it to him to think learning bird calls was magical. It's kind of endearing. But it only proves how out of touch with reality he is."

"You spent a summer with Theo. I hoped you could help me understand him better."

"Marlee!" Ryan emerged from the gazebo and waved. "Little Pete wants to talk to you."

I waved back. "Are you free at all this week? We could meet for coffee or something."

"How about tomorrow for breakfast?" Leah asked. "Eight-thirty maybe?"

"That would be great. Meet me at the Sourdough Café on Lyall Street."

"Done. Anything to help a former Drupe." After giving me a friendly wink, she made her way toward a group of alumni by the bayou pier.

Now to figure out where Theo went. Why did he slip away while Tina Kapoor was honoring the memory of Sienna? Had Tina's speech upset him? I looked back to where Ryan stood waiting. Holding up my hand, I yelled, "I'll be there in a few minutes!"

Not waiting for Ryan's response, I started down the curved path that led to the parking area. It was the only place Theo could have disappeared to without us noticing. I wondered if this was what it was like having a child. I certainly felt over-protective about my baker. And unreasonably worried.

Several people passed me on their way to the BAS campus. I reminded myself there were dozens of cars in the parking lot tucked away among the trees. I would not be alone, even if only three lampposts provided illumination. As I walked among the parked cars, the voices and music from the campus faded. The shadowy lot made it difficult to identify one car from another. But there was enough light to discern two figures standing by a Volkswagen a few yards away. One of the figures was tall and bulky, dwarfing his companion. When I drew near, I was certain the car was Theo's VW. Which probably meant the slight person pressed against the car was Theo.

I heard Theo say in a trembling voice, "I didn't do anything."

The larger figure appeared to grab Theo and give him a shake.

I broke into a run. "Hey! What's going on here?"

Both figures jumped at my appearance. Now that I was close, I recognized the large hulking figure as Gordon Sanderling. His fist was clutched about the collar of Theo's T-shirt.

"Take your hands off him!" Furious, I grabbed Gordon by the arm and yanked him away.

"Are you okay? Did he hurt you?" I asked Theo, who was shaking. At this rate, the poor man would suffer a nervous breakdown.

"He said I was telling lies to the police," Theo said, his breathing jagged and worrisome. "But I told him I didn't. I'm afraid of the police. I would never talk to them. Never."

"It's fine, Theo. You've done nothing wrong. And Gordon won't bother you again."

"I didn't do anything to him," Gordon said.

"Don't lie to me." It was all I could do not to smack Gordon across the face. Yes, I knew this man had possibly killed Sienna Katsaros twenty years ago, but I had inherited an Italian temper from my mother that was difficult to control. "I saw you shaking him. You were threatening him, weren't you? Why?"

"This is none of your business."

I took a step toward him, causing Gordon to take an involuntary step back. "Theo is my friend. I won't allow you to frighten him. He's going through a hard enough time since Sienna's body was discovered. The last thing he needs is anyone making him feel worse."

"You think he feels worse about Sienna than I do?" Gordon gave a hollow laugh. "You're as simpleminded and stupid as he is."

"And you're a rude pig," I shot back. "By the way, don't worry about Theo talking to the police. I'll be the one doing all the talking, starting tonight. Captain Holt will be quite interested to hear how you were threatening Theo."

Gordon swore under his breath. "You don't know what's going on. I was only trying to prevent things from getting out of control."

"You're the one who seems out of control, Sanderling." Crossing my arms, I planted myself in front of Theo. If Gordon made a move toward Theo, he would have to get by me.

"That's where you're wrong. Events are spinning out of control." He pointed over my shoulder at Theo. "And a fool like him could get people killed."

"What does that mean?" I was torn between anger and frustration.

"Maybe he isn't talking to the police, but I suspect he is. The police are questioning everyone about Sienna's murder. Of course they'd question him. And what will they get from your nervous baker? Cryptic, confusing statements that could incriminate other people."

"You perhaps?" I asked.

He shook his head. "Not just me, you idiot. And stay out of

this. Haven't you caused enough grief by digging up Sienna's body?"

"Marlee didn't do anything wrong." Theo amazed me by coming to stand by my side. "Leave her alone."

"Exactly what I should do. Leave the two of you alone to cause all kinds of trouble. And you will if you keep interfering with things you don't understand."

"Then enlighten us," I said. "What don't we understand?"

"That if things spiral out of control, someone else may wind up dead."

Theo took my hand, which surprised me as much as Gordon's statement.

"Is that a threat?" I asked.

"No," Gordon said. "A prediction." Theo and I stared after him as he stalked off, his figure swallowed up by the darkness waiting just outside the narrow reach of the lampposts.

"He frightened me," Theo said.

I didn't want to worry Theo by telling him that I was frightened, too. And I felt as surrounded by darkness as Gordon's retreating figure. Except this darkness would not be over by sunrise. This was a darkness that had lasted twenty years.

Chapter 12

My breakfast meeting with Leah meant I had to skip beach yoga, which was for the best. I hadn't been in a tranquil state of mind since I'd discovered the bones of Sienna Katsaros. Last night's encounter in the parking lot didn't help. Following my conversation with Gordon, I went looking for Captain Holt to tell him what had occurred. Although unhappy to learn I had confronted a suspect, Holt immediately left to track down Gordon with questions of his own. I hoped Gordon said something incriminating during their conversation. If Gordon was in police custody, I'd breathe easier about Theo's safety. And mine.

At least I had a delicious breakfast to look forward to. A favorite with natives and tourists, the Sourdough Café had been run by the Schells for sixty years. The Schells freshened up the country farm décor only about twice a decade, and they changed their menu even less often. But if I had to choose one place to eat breakfast for the rest of my life, the Sourdough Café would be my pick. Working at the Gourmet Living Network had exposed me to some of the greatest chefs on the planet, but I had never tasted eggs, bacon, waffles, or pancakes cooked as divinely as the Schells did at their café. And at a reasonable price, too.

Because of this, I wasn't surprised to see a line of people waiting for a table. Throughout the summer, a wait for a table was the norm. I didn't see Leah among the crowd milling about the front door, so I assumed she wasn't here yet. Best to get our name on the seating list.

Before I could add my name to the pad of paper on the counter, I heard a voice shout, "Marlee, we've already got a table!" Leah beckoned me from the rear of the café.

As I dodged around servers and tables filled with customers, I was glad to see Leah had snagged a booth along the window. The café boasted the longest booths in town, easily fitting eight people. More, if any of them were as thin as Leah. Dressed in tight jeans and a lime green tank top, she seemed even slimmer than she did last night. Her bare arms appeared skeletal. I'd be shocked if her weight topped ninety pounds.

"We've been waiting for you." Leah gestured toward the group sitting at our booth.

Two men and a woman looked up at me. All of them had mugs of tea or coffee in front of them. I wondered how long they'd been sitting here, especially since I had arrived early.

"This is Marlee Jacob," Leah announced. "Marlee, meet my BAS Drupes. The bushy-haired guy is Joel MacGregor, also known as the programming prince of Cleveland."

"Marlee," said the chubby fellow, who boasted a scruffy beard and wavy brown hair hanging to his shoulders.

"The woman next to him is Dawn Vance," she went on. "If you love fiber art, you may have heard of Vance Designs. She's wearing her product. Then again, she never wears anything else."

Dawn smiled at me. "She's jealous because she can't afford my clothes."

"I don't blame her. They're lovely." I found Dawn's tunic top covered with leaf designs in copper, ginger, and garnet quite striking. The ginger hues matched the color of Dawn's hair.

"Thank you," she said. "And I'll finish the introductions. The sleepy man across from me is Zack Burwell. Ignore the bags under his eyes. His plane got in late last night. Although we're having a hard time ignoring his shaved head. I have no idea what that's all about."

"Hi." Zack lifted his coffee mug in greeting. "And shaving my head keeps life simple. One less thing to worry about." Even without hair, Zack was an attractive man, but his guarded gaze made me uneasy.

Dawn scooted over, although the booth held lots of room. "Sit next to me, Marlee."

Once I sat down, all four of them looked at me. "I'm sure Leah told you I'm the owner of a downtown store called The Berry Basket. Theo Foster bakes for me."

"Can't believe Theo is a baker," the rotund guy introduced as Joel said. "Then again, he did spend a whole summer at BAS baking pottery in that kiln."

Zack shook his head. "I thought Theo came from Illinois or Indiana. I'm shocked he's living here now. Is he staying with relatives? Or a group home?"

"There's no reason Theo would be living in a group home," I said. "He's perfectly capable of taking care of himself."

Dawn appeared dubious. "I honestly can't see Theo living on his own."

"He was only seventeen when you were at BAS together. Hard to figure out what people will become when they're older." I felt the need to defend Theo.

"Not always," Joel replied. "Leah teaches fine arts, and Dawn is a walking showcase for her product. We all knew the two of them would be the only ones to remain interested in art. The rest of us wasted our time—and our parents' money—at BAS. Money flushed down the Blackberry Bayou drain. It certainly didn't help me to become a computer programmer."

"There's more to life than paying bills," I said. "BAS gives children and adults a chance to focus on nothing but art and beauty for a few precious weeks. How often will that happen again in their lives? BAS tuition fees seem a small price to pay for such an experience."

"The last thing Joel's parents worried about was the price of tuition. He comes from one of Ohio's richest families." Leah laughed at his scowling expression. "Don't try to deny it."

I looked across the table at her. "Where do you teach fine arts?"

"Pratt University in Brooklyn."

Pratt was a premier art institution in the country. I was impressed.

"I never thought I'd return to BAS. Then an invitation arrived for the school's centenary week. I almost didn't come." Leah's smile faded. "The last memory of my summer here was the Coast Guard finding Sienna's clothing in the lake. It shattered me."

"I was just a kid then," I said. "It only became real when I found the body last week."

The four of them looked at each other; they wore varying expressions of dread, fear, and sadness. There were all sorts of undercurrents at this table making me feel unwelcome—and suspicious. I was happy when Drea, my favorite waitress at Sourdough, appeared.

"Hi, Marlee," she said with a wide grin. "Didn't know it was you this table was waiting for. Should I give everyone a few more minutes or are you ready to order now?"

The others snatched up the menus scattered in front of them

and quickly ordered. By the time it was my turn, I worried I'd have little appetite while among this group. Still, it might seem odd if I only asked for something to drink.

"A chai latte and two eggs, sunny side up. No toast or potatoes." Drea appeared stunned by the brevity of my order. Usually I ate enough food at the café to satisfy a trio of lumberjacks.

Once she left, an awkward silence hung over the table. Joel kept scratching his beard as he stared out the window. He reminded me of a shaggy brown bear: one to be approached with caution. Leah examined her green painted nails as Zack sipped his coffee. It had to be a nervous gesture. I'd seen him empty the mug a moment earlier. When I turned to my left, I met Dawn's steady gaze. She was an average-looking woman with none of Leah's natural beauty. Her chin-length hair framed an angular face, one side of her hair tucked behind her ear, the other side falling in a sleek curve over her other cheek. There was nothing delicate about her features; her nose was long, her mouth wide. I suspected there was little delicacy about her temperament, either. If I was to get any information to help me with Theo, it would most likely come from her.

"Leah told me that all of you had another close friend in your Bramble twenty years ago. A girl called Amanda Dobson. Is she coming to the centenary, too?"

"Not according to the last BAS newsletter." Dawn smiled at my puzzled expression. "Amanda is a professor of botany, at Harvard no less. Her parents are botanists, too. She spent her whole time at BAS either sketching the forest vegetation or hiking through it. We found it ironic when she ended up falling into a patch of poison ivy."

"She had to be sent home," Joel added. "Amanda was mortified at having to explain to her parents how she failed to identify such a common plant. But she's made up for it since."

Zack signaled to Drea for more coffee. "She's some big-deal botanist now. Writes books on the subject, travels around the world gathering plant species."

"Amanda's in the Brazilian rain forest collecting specimens." Leah continued to study her nail polish. "The newsletter announced she'll be part of a PBS special on climate change."

"Even if she were in the U.S., why would she come back here?" Joel's voice rang with bitterness. "There's nothing but unhappiness at the bayou. Then again, she left weeks before Sienna died. Amanda missed out on all the black horror we had to go through. Now we learn Sienna's body has been discovered after all this time. It's like a filthy joke. I think all of us should get the hell out of here today. How much more do we have to suffer over this?"

"Take it easy, Joel," Zack said in a low voice.

Dawn turned to me. "You probably regret meeting us for breakfast."

"Not at all. I wanted to see if any of you could help me understand Theo better. He was quite disturbed to hear Sienna's body was found. I've thought about contacting his father, but it might offend Theo. After all, he's not a child."

"He's always acted like one." Zack gave Drea a brief nod when she refilled his mug.

"Sometimes he does," I said. "But he has thirty-seven years of living behind him."

"Thirty-seven years of living like a child."

I frowned at Zack. "I don't know how you can make such a judgment. You haven't seen him for two decades."

Zack took a deep breath, as if he was counting to ten. "Look, Marlee, I knew Theo better than anyone else here. He and I were ceramics students, which meant we were often in the pottery studio together. I had more than enough occasion to talk with him. Certainly enough to know he wasn't a normal teenager. Although the boy did know how to throw a pot."

"He knew Sienna well enough, and she wasn't a potter. How did they become close?"

Zack snorted, while Joel gave a deep sigh. The two men were getting on my nerves.

"Theo was infatuated with Sienna," Dawn explained. "And they had something in common. He was a surprisingly talented potter. Sienna was a gifted painter. They both received a lot of attention from the instructors."

"Especially Sienna." Finished examining her nails, Leah tossed her long blond hair back in a gesture worthy of Natasha. "None of us could hope to compete with her."

"Sienna cast such a long shadow," Zack said, "it was as if she was the only real artist at BAS that summer. Like we all said whenever her name was mentioned, 'That girl is the—'"

"'—bane of our existence,'" they said in unison.

While they exchanged pained looks, I recalled Theo had used the exact same phrase "the bane of our existence" when he told me how the other students felt about Sienna. Despite their gently mocking tone, the others at the table had been jealous of this girl. Were any of them jealous enough as teenagers to resort to murder?

"You mentioned how talented Theo was. Did the other students resent him, too?"

"Most of the students ignored him," Dawn replied.

"He did trail after Sienna," Leah said. "It was a little creepy. We'd call it stalking now."

The reference to stalking reminded me how Gordon was rumored to have stalked his ex-wife. "If you were all eighteen and nineteen back then, you would have been housed in the same Bramble section. Gordon Sanderling must have been around the same age."

Dawn nodded. "He turned twenty that summer, making him the oldest in our group."

The mood lightened a bit, and Zack actually smiled. "Gordon shared a cabin with Christian, Joel, and me. The chaperones turned a blind eye if he came in after curfew. They were bowled over by him, too."

"He was gorgeous," Dawn said with a wistful expression. "So handsome."

"No, he was beautiful," Leah corrected her. "Half the school was in love with him, including some of the boys. And he had a body only seen on a superhero. Oh, the muscles."

"Don't get her started," Joel warned. "The Gordon hero worship will make me gag."

My mouth fell open. Were we talking about the same Gordon Sanderling? "It's hard to imagine Gordon as a sexy young guy."

"I'll make it easier for you." Dawn rummaged about in her purse and pulled out a photo. "This was taken toward the end of our summer at BAS."

I gazed intently at the seven young people in the photo, all wearing shorts and T-shirts, some stained with paint. I recognized the four sitting at the table with me, even if they were now older. Joel wasn't as chubby back then, and Leah seemed to be a normal weight. A tall black student stood front and center, his arm wrapped around a petite brunette. I looked closer at the girl, who I was able to identify as Sienna from the newspaper photos. She wore a sunny smile, which made her look even younger than her eighteen years. It gave me a wrench to gaze upon the girl whose bones I had stumbled upon. But the real surprise was Gordon Sanderling. In the photo, he stood on the other side of Sienna, a relaxed and happy expression on his face. It was a remarkably handsome face, too. Movie star handsome. I shook my head. If I hadn't been told this was Gordon, I would never have recognized him. And it was only partly due to the weight he had put on. In twenty years, life had done more than aged Gordon. It had ravaged him.

"Gordon has changed." I handed the photo back to Dawn.

Leah threw me a defiant look. "I saw him last night. Yes, he's gained weight, but he's still an impressive man."

"The rest of us haven't laid eyes on him yet," Joel said. "In fact, most of us haven't seen each other since that summer. Although we did keep in touch for the first couple of years."

"We reconnected after the BAS invitations arrived. It took some time trolling social media to find each other," Leah said. "Except for Christian and Zack."

He shrugged. "We speak on the phone once in a while."

Dawn's expression turned rueful. "We've been catching up on each other's lives this morning on campus. It appears we have more in common than our summer at BAS. In the past twenty years, all of us have had marriages that ended in divorce."

Joel lifted his cup with a mocking smile. "Three divorces for me. But who's counting?"

"I heard Gordon was briefly married when he was in college," I said. "Did any of you go to his wedding in Duluth? It would have been less than two years after your summer at BAS."

"We weren't invited." There was an edge to Dawn's voice. "I adore Gordon, but excluding us was rude and hurtful. He knew I'd moved to Minnesota to go to school."

"Strange thing is, most of us were in Minnesota when Gordon had his fancy wedding," Leah remarked. "My family is from St. Cloud, which is only about a hundred and forty miles from Duluth. I was home that year taking care of my mom, who had cancer. And Dawn was living in Minneapolis."

"When we were at BAS," Dawn said, "Gordon told me the Minneapolis College of Art and Design had a great fiber arts program. I looked into it and realized he was right. I transferred from Penn State that same year. And before you ask, I did not transfer to be near Gordon. I made the move purely for academic reasons."

"You were both in Minnesota at that time, too?" I looked over at Zack and Joel.

"I'm a sound engineer," Zack said. "I was on a mid-western tour with a band called Clarion. We were booked to play at Peavey Plaza during the annual Sommerfest in Minneapolis. I read about Gordon's marriage in the paper. The bride's family was a big deal."

Dawn leaned toward me. "He married a congresswoman's daughter."

"What was the name of the girl he married? Ellen? No, it was Elise." Leah snapped her fingers. "Elise Poe. I think her grandfather was a senator, too."

"Too bad the marriage didn't work out," Joel said. "With those family connections, Gordon might have gone into politics himself. It's what he always dreamed of doing."

"Do you know why they divorced?" I asked.

Joel smirked. "The same reason everyone divorces: incompatibility. And I should know."

Our food arrived and conversation stopped while Drea put down the colorful Fiesta plates.

"Why were you in Minnesota then?" I asked Joel after she left.

"I wasn't. I've never set foot in the state. Why should I?"

I decided to concentrate on my eggs and chai. The energy at the table wasn't conducive to friendly conversation. Or enjoying my breakfast.

Dawn poured strawberry sauce over her berries and cream French toast. "How well do you know Gordon? After all, you both live in such a small town."

"His company did some work for me last year. But we've never had a lot to do with each other." I decided not to mention the threatening encounter last night in the parking lot. "And you should know he appears much older than a man in his late thirties. It might be a shock when the rest of you see Gordon, particularly if everyone once had a crush on him."

"Don't insult me." Joel lifted a scornful eyebrow. "Do I look like some impressionable teenage girl? Or hero-worshipping 'bro'?"

"I'll admit to a bit of a man crush," Zack said. "Gordo was smart, funny, athletic."

"I had a full-blown woman crush," Dawn said. "But I never had a chance with him."

"Same with me," Leah chimed in. "Although not for lack of trying. I did everything to get his attention. I even pounced on him on the way to the showers one evening." Her expression softened. "Okay, maybe we shared one delicious moment. Or hour, to be more correct. The next day, I went back to not existing for him. None of us did. Not with Sienna around."

"If Gordon stayed at a Bramble cabin, he was living on campus," I said.

Dawn smoothed the napkin on her lap. "He commuted from his family's home for the first week before deciding to spend the rest of the summer at the bayou. I mentioned to Gordon how some local kids chose to stay on campus. I also told him if he lived on campus, Sienna might pay more atten- tion to him. Sienna was one of the few girls immune to Gordon's charms, at least in the beginning." She sighed. "Maybe it was all an act to make him want her more."

"Hello?" Joel said. "I believe I had something to do with Sienna not running after Gordon. At least for those first few days."

"He's right." Dawn nodded. "I'd forgotten Joel and Sienna were sweet on each other that first week. Although painting *was* the most important thing to Sienna. Even more important than Gordon. The girl spent every waking moment at her easel."

"Not every waking moment," Joel muttered.

"To be honest, I hoped Sienna and Joel would become

more involved with each other. But Gordon won her over. I should have waylaid him on the way to the showers like you did." Dawn pointed a fork at Leah.

"A shame you didn't." She winked. "It was worth it."

"So Gordon was the best-looking student at BAS that summer, and Sienna was the most talented," I said.

"Yep," Joel said between mouthfuls of his Greek omelette. "And Sienna was pretty, too. The prettiest girl there. A lot better looking than Gordon, although you'd never know it from listening to these two."

"As you can see, Dawn and I spent the summer chasing after Gordon," Leah said, "while Joel pined for Sienna."

"Fat lot of good it did any of you." Zack downed the rest of his coffee.

"What were her paintings like?" I asked.

"BAS keeps one or two examples of every student's work," Dawn told me. "Ask Tina Kapoor to show you Sienna's paintings."

"To answer your question," Joel said, "Sienna was a bold, figurative painter, a combination of Eric Fischl and Frida Kahlo. But there was an abstract strain in her waiting to come out. Had she lived, Sienna might have ended up having a career like Fiona Rae."

I gave him a questioning look. "For someone dismissive of an art education, you seem to have kept up your interest in the art world."

"Twenty years ago, I harbored a fantasy of opening my own art gallery. A place where I could exhibit the work of artists as gifted as Sienna. But my summer at BAS put an end to that." Joel's face hardened. "Like it put an end to her."

The other three studied their plates with renewed interest. "I'd think all of you might want to blame Gordon for what happened to her, not BAS," I said. "Her body was buried on his family's property. Maybe he had something to do with her death."

"Excuse me." Dawn's voice suddenly became as sharp as nettles. "Who are you to accuse our friend of murder?"

"Sienna was a friend of yours, too. And her body was found miles away from the school. How did she get from the art school to the Sanderling farm? Did she have a car?"

"None of us had cars," Zack said. "We flew in from out of state or were driven here by our parents."

"As a local boy, Gordon would have had his own car," I persisted.

"What's your point?" Joel's gaze was as unfriendly as his tone.

"Gordon was romantically involved with Sienna, and had access to a vehicle to transport her to his family's farm." I lifted an eyebrow at them. "Where someone buried her body."

"Gordon did not kill Sienna," Dawn said. "He couldn't have harmed her."

"How do you know? You haven't seen him in twenty years. All of you admitted you don't even keep in touch, except for Zack and Christian. People change a lot in two decades."

"Marlee, it's true we don't know what Gordon is like now," Leah said. "But we remember what he was like twenty years ago, which was when Sienna died. And the Gordon who attended BAS with us was no killer." She pushed her plate of pancakes away; I noticed she had barely touched her food. I suspected she kept rail thin by eating no more than a few mouthfuls every meal. "As for Gordon's farm, lots of BAS students knew where it was. His family invited our entire Bramble for a barbecue."

"Yes, I know. Theo told me."

"And not just our Bramble was invited," Dawn said. "Some of the younger ones, too. Over fifty students attended. BAS had to arrange for a local school bus to transport us."

"Never saw so much barbecued chicken in my life." Joel smiled.

"I remember the wine," Zack said. "Even though Gordon's family had shut down the winery business, they had a fine selection in their cellar. Gordo kept us supplied all summer."

Dawn turned to me. "Don't get the wrong idea. The Sanderlings didn't serve wine to the underage students. But Gordon was good at sneaking a bottle or two to his friends."

"By the way, Theo was also there." Joel raised an eyebrow in my direction. "Maybe you should be a little suspicious about your baker."

"Theo has an alibi. He left BAS a week before summer school ended to go home. His relatives in Illinois all swear he was with them when Sienna disappeared."

"His family could be lying to protect him," Zack said.

"And Theo lives in a fantasy world. You told me last night that Theo said I knew magic because I taught him a few bird calls." Leah frowned. "Didn't you think that was strange?"

"Maybe he misunderstood you. I'm sure this will sound ridiculous, but I asked him to summon a crow . . . and a crow suddenly appeared."

Dawn looked at me as if I were insane. "Where in the world did this happen?"

"At the house he rents along the river." I hesitated. "Crow Cottage."

The table erupted into laughter. "I'm betting the place is called Crow Cottage for a reason," Joel said. "Like lots of crows have been seen there."

"Why would he make something like that up?" I asked.

"I bet he heard about my ancestry and fabricated some fanciful tale associated with it."

"Ancestry?" I turned to Leah.

"Don't let my blond hair and fair skin fool you," she said. "I'm one-eighth Choctaw on my mother's side. I wasn't the only student at BAS with Native American blood. Some of us sat around the fire pit at night comparing stories of tribal legends. Theo was always skulking in the shadows. He could have heard us speak about summoning totem animals or something. And I was taught to imitate bird calls by my grandmother. He's right when he says I taught him a few. But only because he asked me to. Theo did love birds."

"Theo also mentioned there was a secret bird call you wouldn't teach him."

Joel grinned at the others. "The secret bird call? At least that one makes sense."

"We liked to party after curfew," Leah explained. "When the coast was clear, we'd give a signal. Because the call of a night heron is distinctive, I taught the others how to imitate it. Sorry, Marlee, there's nothing magical about any of this. Just a bunch of kids wanting to sneak off to the woods to drink and fool around."

I sat back, arms folded across my chest. "Why did all of you come back for the centenary? It must be unpleasant to be here, given your last memories of BAS."

"You're beginning to sound like a policeman. And I don't like it." Joel's cheeks reddened with anger. "I don't like it at all."

Zack shook his head. "Don't let her get to you."

"Joel's right," Dawn said to me. "It's felt like an interrogation since you sat down."

"I told you, I want to help Theo cope with his shock over Sienna's body being discovered. But I'm sure the police will be questioning everyone at this table."

"I was on the hot seat yesterday with some guy called Captain Holt." Leah sighed.

"They've also questioned Gordon," I said.

"Poor Gordon," Dawn murmured. "Hasn't he suffered enough?"

"We came back because all of us have been living with a

ghost for twenty years," Zack said with sudden vehemence. "And we had no idea until yesterday that Sienna's body had been found. I'm not sure we would have returned if we had known. But when Sienna disappeared, our youth and innocence vanished as well. She was our friend. We lived with her all summer. Yes, we were jealous of her talent, but we also liked and admired her. And she was the youngest in our group. We felt protective of her."

Dawn wore a grim expression. "For twenty years, we believed she had drowned. After all, it's only a thirty-minute walk from the bayou to one of the beaches."

"And we were ingenious about sneaking alcohol on campus." Zack now pushed his own plate away. "I drank a lot even then. But Sienna could keep up with me. If she'd lived, I'm sure she would have wound up at A.A. meetings, too. When her clothing washed ashore, all of us assumed she got drunk and went swimming in the lake after we went to sleep."

"The centenary gave us the excuse to return as a group and lay the memory of Sienna to rest," Dawn said. "We were in shock twenty years ago and so young. We never grieved properly. A few days after her clothing was found, the school semester was over and we all went home."

"What about Christian Naylor? Is he coming?" I asked.

"He should be landing in Chicago about now," Zack said. "He took the red-eye. We spoke last night. I wanted to let him know Sienna's body had been found. He was more upset than I thought he'd be. Although all of us are in shock. I had to call my sponsor this morning. The last thing I need is to start drinking over this tragedy again. I've been sober seven years, four months, and three days. I can't risk my sobriety over this. I can't."

Joel leaned across the table. "We'll get through this, buddy. I promise."

Leah laid her head on Zack's shoulder.

Dawn turned to me again. "I don't blame you for being suspicious of Gordon, or even of us. But none of us wished any harm on Sienna. And Gordon would have given his life for her."

"That may be true," I replied. "But someone buried Sienna in those woods. And the same person made it look as if she had drowned by throwing her clothing in the lake."

"Maybe the murderer is long gone," Joel said, before draining his coffee.

"Maybe the murderer never left," I said, thinking of Gordon Sanderling.

"Or maybe he came back to the scene of the crime after twenty years." Dawn's gaze became even more intense. "Maybe he's pretending to be a harmless and simple young man."

"Theo did not kill Sienna." I gave her a challenging look of my own.

Dawn startled me by grabbing my wrist. "No one really knows Theo or what he's capable of, Marlee. I don't think even Theo knows. I'd be careful if I were you. Really careful." She squeezed my wrist so hard, I let out a small cry of pain.

After yanking my hand from her grip, I signaled Drea to bring the check. For the first time, I left my breakfast at the café unfinished. Did Theo's family lie to protect him? And was he even aware of what was truth and what was fantasy? Yet I trusted him more than I did any of these people sitting in the booth with me. Beneath their ready answers and thinly veiled exasperation, they were afraid. Maybe they had been afraid since the day Sienna disappeared. But was it because they didn't know what happened to their friend? Or because they did?

Chapter 13

Although breakfast with Sienna's friends had not been pleasant, the start of the workday promised better things. Moments after I hung the OPEN flag outside my shop door, a middle-aged couple hurried inside and cleaned out the shelf of blueberry and raspberry vinaigrette: eleven bottles of each, to be exact.

"Do you have more in the back?" the woman asked as her male companion lined up the twenty-two bottles they chose on the counter. I tried to read her expression to see if this was a joke, but her eyes remained hidden by enormous amber sunglasses.

"I don't think we have any raspberry left. Blueberry, for sure." I sent Gillian to our storeroom for the last dozen bottles of blueberry vinaigrette.

While Gillian rolled the bottles in bubble wrap, I rang up their purchase. "Are you caterers?" I asked. "Or restaurant owners perhaps?"

The man shook his head. Since the woman only readjusted her sunglasses, it was clear they had no interest in conversation.

"Thank you for visiting my store." I gave them the handled bags filled with bottled vinaigrette. "And I'll be ordering more vinaigrette if you need any in the future."

In response, the woman turned on her heel and swept out of the shop. At least the man gave a curt nod before leaving. Once they were gone, Gillian and I looked at each other.

"What was that all about?" I asked her. "Why would they need so much vinaigrette?"

"Big salad eaters?"

"If they need thirty-four bottles of vinaigrette, they must be bathing in the stuff." I looked down at their credit card receipt. "But at nine dollars a bottle, I'm not complaining."

"When you reorder, remember we need more berry dog treats, too." Gillian said. "Piper bought the last of them yesterday afternoon while you were at lunch. And she brought her Great Dane with her. I swear, he took up half the store. I never knew Great Danes were so huge."

I put the receipt in the register drawer. "I think he's only a little smaller than a Mazda."

The door swung open again as three customers entered. One of them was a sunburnt child who ran to the ice cream counter. Gillian retied her chef apron, ready to scoop ice cream and blend smoothies. "How's the road rally coming along?"

"It's nothing to do with me anymore. I've done my part with the posters. The Blackberry Road Rally is Piper's baby. Let her obsess about it. Along with Andrew and Dean."

"They're determined to win. Last night they planned to watch *Girl with a Pearl Earring* in case there were road rally questions about Dutch painters." A giggling Gillian went off to scoop blackberry fudge ripple ice cream.

My newest flavor of ice cream sounded so good I was tempted to eat some myself. Especially since I'd eaten as little breakfast as Leah Malek had. Because I left the Sourdough Café at nine-thirty, I hoped to catch Theo before he left for the day. But all that greeted me in The Berry Basket kitchen were the sight and delicious aroma of fresh-baked raspberry rhubarb bars (gluten free), blackberry lemon pound cake, and raspberry cheesecake cupcakes.

Ryan's sister-in-law arrived late with the berry pies from Zellars; the cousins from Ohio here for the BAS celebrations had been persuaded to move from the bayou campus to the Zellar farm. Which meant they would probably be spending most of their time at the orchards rather than enjoying the festivities with their fellow alumni. A shame if the visiting relatives missed today's activities: dune buggy rides along Lake Michigan, a beach volleyball tournament, and a luau tonight at the bayou. Thankfully, I had Alison and Emma staying with me. I doubted I'd see much of Ryan until these latest family members went home.

Because I gave Andrew and Dean the day off to attend the dune buggy rides, Gillian and I were kept busy all morning. When things slowed down at one o'clock, I told Gillian to grab lunch for herself. I took advantage of the empty store to eat the hummus and carrots I kept in the refrigerator, along with a scoop of blackberry ripple fudge ice cream. I'd finished spooning the last of the ice cream and was considering a slice of pound cake when the door opened once more.

"Welcome to The Berry Basket," I sang out. But my smile faded when I saw it was Janelle Davenport, my least favorite Oriole Point police officer. Like my earlier vinaigrette-loving customer, she, too, hid behind dark glasses.

I suspected she always wore aviator sunglasses because it made her look tough, as did her muscled and toned upper arms. The tough-cop pose seemed unnecessary for our small village. Until Cole Bowman was killed last month, there hadn't been a murder in Oriole Point for years. Given how the police department had handled the case, that lack of experience showed. Half the police department was part-time, with the other half comprising Chief Gene Hitchcock, Janelle, and an excitable fellow called Bruno. We were lucky Chief Hitchcock was a first-rate law enforcement officer. He balanced out the rest of his unevenly talented squad.

Peeking over the top of her sunglasses, Officer Davenport gazed around my empty store. "I see business is booming."

"This is a berry shop, not an airline terminal. Customers come in waves." I met her cool smile with one of my own. "And business has been good today. If you had a warrant, I'd let you see our receipts. Otherwise you'll have to take my word for it."

"I can't believe you make a living selling these products. Blueberry beef jerky, strawberry coffee, cranberry cocoa, blackberry butter. And these crazy drink mash-ups." She glanced at the bottle of blackberry ginger pomegranate iced tea I'd been drinking with lunch.

"Tastes great. You should try it." I took a long swig. "And I've paid all my bills for two years by selling these berry products. I even make a profit. Amazing, isn't it?"

"I'd call it shocking."

We stared at each other. "Is there an official reason you're here?" I asked finally.

"The Sienna Katsaros case. You were seen having breakfast this morning with four people who attended BAS with her."

"So?"

"So why are you associating with people who are suspects in the girl's disappearance?"

"First, I can meet with anyone I like. Second, the case isn't in the jurisdiction of the Oriole Point police. Third, how do you know I had breakfast with them? Am I being followed?"

"You're not important enough to tail, Marlee. And you know perfectly well no one in town can trip in the street without half the population knowing about it an hour later. Now why were you with these people at the Sourdough Café?"

Although I didn't like being questioned like this, I refused to let Janelle rile me. "I repeat, I can meet with anyone I like. Last time I looked, I hadn't been accused of a crime."

"You did discover the remains of Sienna Katsaros."

"Am I a suspect now?" I couldn't help but laugh. "I was ten when she disappeared. Back then, I was busy watching episodes of *Doug* on Nickelodeon. Murdering people would have cut into my TV time."

An embarrassed flush rose to her cheeks. "I didn't say you were a suspect. But you've now found two dead bodies this summer."

"Both of them accidental. And I did capture the killer the first time."

"Are you planning on a repeat performance? Trying to interfere with a police investigation in hopes of getting a little more media glory if you're successful?"

"Oh, I see. You're worried I'll show up the Oriole Point police again. Don't worry. If anyone gets shown up, it will be the state police. Detective Trejo's handling the case."

"Along with the sheriff department's Atticus Holt," she said. "It appears the two of you have gotten rather cozy. You were seen together last night at the opening ceremony at BAS."

"I guess I am important enough to tail. However, I'm not a suspect in this case and you know it." I leaned over the counter. "And I attended BAS for two summers. I have every right to be on campus conversing with anyone who took a class there. That includes murder suspects."

"Don't be naïve, Marlee. One of them may be a killer. Stay out of this."

"Are you done? Is there more?"

"I'd keep a close eye on your baker. You should remember that a bracelet he made for the victim was found buried with her."

"And you should remember Theo has an alibi for the time of her murder."

"Let's see if it holds up. I've heard your odd little baker was extremely upset when he heard Sienna's body was discovered. Seems suspicious to me."

I was relieved when a customer came into the shop. After waving a greeting, the older man wandered over to a shelf of berry-flavored jams and jellies. "Theo has every right to be upset. He was friends with the dead girl," I said in a quiet voice. "As for his alibi, the sheriff and the state police are satisfied with it. If you're not, get yourself officially assigned to the case. Or else you might upset the officers who are trying to do their job."

"The same applies to you, Marlee. At least I'm a police officer. You're merely a shopkeeper who doesn't want to believe one of her employees might be a murderer."

I looked over at my customer to see if he might be eavesdropping. I didn't need rumors spreading about The Berry Basket and the people who worked here. "He's not a murderer," I said in an even lower voice. "And I don't want this discussed when I have customers."

"You should be more concerned your baker might not be what he seems. The Oriole Point police may not be officially connected to the case, but our help has been sought nonetheless. And we're more skilled than you give us credit for. For example, we've learned Theo Foster was arrested in Illinois fourteen years ago."

"I don't believe it," I said after a stunned moment. "Why would the police arrest him?"

Janelle whipped off her sunglasses. "For committing a crime." Almost as startling as this statement was the sight of Janelle's rarely seen blue-gray eyes.

"What did he do?"

"Broke the law and resisted arrest." She was toying with me . . . and enjoying it.

Although I had every intention of finding out what Theo had been arrested for, I had better sources of information than Officer Davenport. "Whatever he was arrested for, I'm sure it was a misunderstanding."

Janelle rolled her eyes before hiding them once again with her sunglasses. "A misunderstanding, or something unpleasant enough to conceal? I suspect more than a girl's body was buried twenty years ago. Some of the people associated with Sienna seem to have a few buried secrets as well. I'd watch my back the next time you get chummy with the BAS crowd."

Janelle walked out after her dramatic statement, leaving me more confused than ever. Not even my customer's purchase of four jars of lingonberry jam lifted my mood. And while I didn't want to insult or offend my baker, I decided it was time to talk to Theo Foster's father.

I lifted the small tiki god over my head and let out another victory yell. For the past hour, BAS alumni had taken part in limbo contests, each one divided according to age groups. I was proud to be declared the winner in my group. Although I couldn't believe I contorted my five foot seven body beneath the limbo pole without dislodging it. If I'd been larger than a B cup, I would have lost to runner-up Vanessa, whose enhanced breasts finally brought the pole down.

"I never doubted you would win." Ryan stood behind me, his arms wrapped around my waist. "I'll crash at your place tonight if you promise to show me some of your new moves."

"Leave it to you to get turned on by a limbo contest."

"I'm not the only one. Look at them." He laughed at the group of guys watching a pretty blonde in a yellow bikini bend over backward beneath the limbo pole. He was right. Depending on your view of the contestants, doing the limbo was more than a little suggestive.

"Well, I'm thankful my limbo moves have convinced you to give up a night with the Ohio Zellars for me." Indeed, Ryan only attended tonight's BAS luau because Little Pete and his fellow cousins didn't want to miss the fun.

He nuzzled my neck. "I'll take 'limbo love' over my cousins any day."

I almost believed him. Then Little Pete whistled from the long line at the barbecue pit. He held up a beer bottle. "Ryan, they put more ribs on. Come and get it before they're all gone."

"Am I wrong or did you and Little Pete eat a rack of ribs about an hour ago?"

"Those are great ribs, babe. Diego's in charge of the food tonight and he brought his secret sauce. I can't turn down Diego Theroux ribs. Especially when they're free." He gave me a kiss on the top of my head, then sprinted off to Little Pete and the next mountain of pork.

To be honest, I couldn't blame Ryan. Diego Theroux was the chef/owner of San Sebastian, the most celebrated eatery in Oriole Point. The handsome, sexy Diego was also the best man candy along the lakeshore. Tonight his gray tank top and surfer shorts did an excellent job displaying his tanned, muscled body. While the men lining up at the barbecue pit waited for a slab of ribs, I suspected the females clustered around Diego were more interested in the chef himself. I liked Diego and adored his food, but even if I hadn't been engaged to Ryan I would have steered clear of the "Delicious Diego." Men that gorgeous could never be satisfied with one woman. And it would be unreasonable to expect them to.

Tess walked over. "I see Ryan's returned to the rib feeding frenzy. David's gone back for thirds. In about an hour, the man will explode in a flash of pork and sweet and spicy sauce."

David's spiked blond hair made him easy to spot among the throng at the barbecue pit.

Close behind him in line were Ryan and his cousins. "I know this is hard for a vegetarian to witness. Avert your eyes until the last of the ribs have been eaten."

She shuddered. "Thank God it isn't a hog roast, like Piper first suggested to the BAS board. I would have left if there had been an actual pig carcass on display. The only reason David showed up tonight was because he heard Diego was making ribs."

"Can't blame him. David knows there's no chance it will ever appear on your table."

"He's lucky I'm not a vegan . . . yet." She chuckled. "By the way, Alison wants you to know that had she not drunk five piña coladas tonight, she would have won the limbo contest instead of you."

"I won this fair and square." I hugged the tiki god statue. "And tell Alison she's too drunk to realize she even took part in the limbo contest."

"I will when she wakes up. Emma and I left her on one of the Bramble cabin beds. She needs to sleep the luau off."

"She's going to have a lot of company." I watched Andrew try to inch beneath the limbo pole as he held aloft a bottle of craft beer in each hand. He collapsed in a heap of beer and sand, the limbo pole bouncing off his bare chest. His boyfriend, Oscar, helped him to his feet, while Dean jeered from the sidelines. "Between the free ribs and alcohol, the luau's been a smashing success."

"You're right about that. Half the people here seem smashed." Tess shook her head at the next limbo contestant, who tore off his shirt. "It's a good thing the school restricted attendance at the festivities this week to students and alumni over twenty-one."

"I wonder if I should alert Piper about the skinny dipping

in the bayou." I pointed to the water behind me, where excited squeals and splashing could be heard over the music.

"If this luau goes on much longer, the theme may shift from tropical to bacchanal. We should have told Piper that artist types are more free spirited than her yacht club friends."

Tess was right. There was a sexy midsummer night vibe to the festivities. Because of the steamy weather, most guests wore tropical attire, much of it scanty. Outfits included hula skirts, sarongs, shorts, sheer muumuus, and string bikinis. Both Tess and I wore bikinis and short sarong skirts in matching colors: red and white floral for Tess, blue and white for me.

And BAS had taken the tropical theme to heart. Tiki torches flickered every six feet, island music sounded from all corners, the limbo contest was in full swing, and four women danced the hula on the front porch of the administration cottage. We had even been promised a display of fire eating, although I couldn't imagine where Piper had found someone locally to do such a thing. But I had learned to never underestimate Piper. Not only was Piper in charge of the road rally, she had exerted her iron will on the BAS centenary committee. It was Piper's idea to throw a Luau Night, which I blamed on her Christmas trip to Kauai. She had tried to throw a Hawaiian-themed Memorial Day, an idea voted down by the local VFW. The BAS event planners were more easily intimidated, which explained why Dutch and German American hula dancers swayed on the cottage porch, and everyone wore leis of Michigan marigolds.

"Am I wrong or does limbo have nothing to do with Hawaii?" Tess asked as we watched Dean now take his turn under the limbo pole.

"I looked it up. It's the national dance of Trinidad and Tobago. They used to do it at wakes."

"I guess that explains the steel drum."

"Piper needed to fill up the event with as many activities

as possible, so she fudged part of it. Anyway, Trinidad and Hawaii are both tropical. She has us on a technicality."

"Piper pulled it off," Tess said. "People are having a great time. Raucous, even."

I agreed. As packed as yesterday's opening ceremony had been, the luau crowd far surpassed it. All night I looked for the BAS alumni I breakfasted with this morning, but caught only a fleeting glimpse of Dawn and Joel as they walked through the crowd.

"I hoped to see Theo," I said, "but last night must have been too much for him. I don't think he's been around this many people in years. And I called Theo's father earlier today."

"Why? Did he have another panic attack about the police?"

I shook my head. "Officer Davenport paid me a visit this afternoon. She told me Theo had once been arrested. Although it's not as bad as it sounds."

Tess's expression went from puzzled to worried. "Arrested? What did he do?"

"When he was twenty-three, Theo and his cousin took part in a march with an environmental group. They were protesting the dumping of toxic waste near the Emiquon National Wildlife Refuge, which is about a hundred miles from Theo's hometown. According to his dad, the police began to arrest the protestors and Theo got separated from his cousin. When the police tried to arrest him, he put up a struggle. His father had given him firm instructions to not go with anyone but his cousin. Because he resisted arrest, they roughed him up a bit."

Tess winced. "Oh no."

"He was hauled off to jail," I went on. "But he had no ID on him. It took forty-eight hours before his family got him out. Theo didn't leave the house for two years after that."

"Poor guy. He must have been traumatized."

I lowered my voice. "I worked up the nerve to ask if Theo was autistic."

"And?"

"He isn't," I said. "Theo suffered a closed head injury when he was a toddler. It left him with developmental problems. However, except for the years immediately following his arrest, Theo has been actively engaged in the world: going to school, having jobs. He's even had a couple of girlfriends. But he can't handle a lot of stress or unexpected crises."

Tess sighed. "I know how he feels."

I remembered the cold indifference in Janelle's voice when she spoke about Theo's arrest. "I don't like how people are pointing the finger at Theo. During breakfast, his so-called friends from BAS tried to shift suspicion onto him. Then Dead-Eye Davenport traipses into my store with this story of him resisting arrest, and all to make me distrust him. If one more person comes for Theo, I swear I'll shove one of those tiki torches right up their—"

"Will someone please shut the bar down?" Piper literally threw herself into our midst.

"What?" Tess and I asked in unison.

"I've never seen so many drunken people in my life outside of Mardi Gras." Piper flung her arms out as if to embrace everyone within earshot. "Yes, I arranged for an open bar. But I never imagined it would get this out of control. Someone is sure to die of alcohol poisoning if the bar isn't shut down. I complained to Tina Kapoor, but she's on her fourth tequila sunrise."

"Wait. They're serving tequila at the tiki bar?" I asked.

She grabbed my arm. "Don't you dare drink tonight, Marlee. Not after what happened to you at the Strawberry Moon Bash."

Tess giggled as I pried Piper's hand off me. "Don't worry. I haven't had anything stronger than Diet Coke since I got here." No need to tell her there was a little rum in the Coke. There was also no need to remind me about the dangers of downing too much alcohol. I had done just that at last month's bash—although not without reason—with disastrous results. I had no intention of getting even close to drunk for the rest of my life.

"Stop serving liquor," Tess suggested. "Or announce last call."

"These buffoons are so wasted they'd trample me on the way to the bar. Someone has already spilled a bottle of beer over my dress." A dismayed Piper looked down at the stain on her floor-length floral print dress. "I bought this in Kauai and now it's ruined."

"It's beer, Piper," I said. "It will wash out."

Piper's expression turned even more aggrieved. "I never knew art students were so rude. When I tried to make an announcement about the road rally, not a single person paid attention."

I straightened her lei. "Have Lionel quiet them down. He has a wonderful deep voice *and* he's the mayor. They have to listen to him. Tell Lionel to close the bar, too. Although I don't think things are out of control. It's a party. No one's gotten into a drunken fight yet or broken any of the artwork. Everyone seems pretty chill."

"Chill? Oh, yes, everyone is behaving so nicely." Her voice dripped with sarcasm. "Including Kevin Sitko, who made a clay impression of his private parts in the pottery studio an hour ago. He tried to put himself and the clay into the kiln. The drunken moron."

Tess and I laughed. "Too bad we missed it," I said.

"If you want more proof the alumni should never get near alcohol, look at that pair." Piper pointed over my shoulder to where two men stumbled over the grass. Only one was drunk, however. The sober man was a slender African American trying to keep his companion upright.

"Do you need help?" I called out as his friend tripped again.

When both men looked up, the drunken man waved at me. "Marlee, it's all over now. It's over." Then he crumpled to the ground, where he became sick.

"Do you know that disgraceful man?" Piper hissed at me.

My heart sank as I stared at his shaking body on the grass. "His name is Zack Burwell. He went to school here twenty years ago."

I didn't add that only a few hours earlier he had announced, "The last thing I need is to start drinking over this tragedy again. I've been sober seven years, four months, and three days. I can't risk my sobriety over this. I can't."

But by returning to Oriole Point, Zack had risked his sobriety. And I feared the murder of Sienna Katsaros was to blame.

Chapter 14

"Give me that statue." Piper reached for the little tiki god I held. "I want to smack the next drunken fool over the head with it."

"No way." I clutched it closer.

"Then I need to find Lionel so we can leave. I refuse to watch this tropical frat party any longer." She pointed at Zack. "And call EMS if he continues to drink. He'll probably be tonight's first case of alcohol poisoning. But not the last." Piper wasn't totally heartless, however. She pulled a print scarf from a hidden pocket in her flowing dress. "He needs cleaning up. Use this. Lionel bought it for me because the color matched my dress. The poor man didn't realize it was only a cheap batik."

As Piper stalked off, Tess watched Zack with a worried expression. "I should grab a water bottle for him. He needs to drink something that isn't eighty proof."

While she went in search of water, I hurried over to where Zack now sat huddled on the grass. His friend knelt beside him.

I crouched down. The light from the tiki torches flickering over his face showed a pale, defeated man. Like Gordon Sanderling, he suddenly looked a good decade older than he actually was.

"I think you need this." I handed Zack the scarf.

With a trembling hand, he wiped his face, then dabbed at his stained shirt. "I'm sorry," he said in a slurred, weak voice. "I've been drinking."

"Do you want to lie down in one of the Bramble cabins?" I asked.

His friend shook his head. "He needs to be out in the fresh air. And walking around."

This seemed a signal for the two of us to carefully lift Zack off the ground. After a long, uncertain moment, he stood without our help.

"I drank too much." Zack leaned toward me, and I fought the impulse to step back. The alcohol fumes were overpowering. "Why did I do that? I haven't had alcohol in years. But now I'm drunk." He turned to his friend. "Is that true? Am I drunk?"

He frowned. "I'm afraid you are."

Zack swayed on his feet, causing me to grab his elbow to steady him. "Then I must be. Christian never lies to me. Do you lie, Marlee?"

"Only when I have to." I looked over at the man he called Christian. I had suspected who he was the moment I saw him with Zack. "I'm Marlee Jacob. Theo Foster bakes for me at my store in town. I'm also a BAS alumni."

"I'm Christian Naylor. The others told me about you when I arrived today." The way he said it made me think the description hadn't been flattering.

"I hope they told you how concerned I am about Theo. He's been agitated and upset since Sienna's body was found last week."

"Are you surprised? Everyone who knew Sienna is upset." Christian's voice grew sharper with each word he spoke. "We thought this tragedy was over. Now it's all been dug up again.

Literally. The last thing we need is you or the police bothering us with questions again."

"The police spoke with you today?" I asked.

"They talked to all of us this afternoon." Zack looked outraged. "But we told them everything we knew years ago. Why are they asking us again? Did you tell the police to bother us, Marlee?" He took a shaky step toward me. "I bet it was you, Marlee. Asking us those questions at breakfast. You think you're pretty smart. But you're not. You may be pretty, but you're not smart. We are, though." He grabbed Christian's shirt and pulled him closer. "She doesn't know how smart we are. No one knows. No one knows anything, except us. No one."

"Stop." Christian shook him. "Man, why didn't you talk to me before taking that first drink tonight? This makes everything worse. And it was already a god-awful mess."

Zack turned an accusing face to me. "Now you've made Christian upset. What's the matter with you? Isn't it bad enough I'm drinking?" He almost fell, but Christian caught him.

"I had nothing to do with your drinking. I think Sienna's death is to blame for that."

Christian stared at me. The overhead string of white Christmas lights and nearby tiki torches revealed a face I might have described as handsome if not for his pained expression. But he had beautiful eyes. Their light color—probably hazel—proved a striking contrast to his dark skin. And his close-cropped hair allowed no distraction from the impact of his haunting gaze.

"I was told you found her body," he said.

"The dog I was chasing found it. But that's as far as my involvement goes." I paused. "Except for Theo. Because your old school friend works for me, I feel responsible for him."

"You're stupid." Zack laughed, but it wasn't a happy sound. "Theo's not our friend. Who wants to be Theo's friend? Not me. Not him." He jabbed Christian. "Are you Theo's friend, Christian? No, you're not. I guess you're his only friend, Marlee. The girl who sells berries is Theo's friend. Hey, isn't that funny? The girl who sells berries found a buried body. I think that's funny." Again he treated us to his unnerving laugh.

Christian didn't look as if he found this any funnier than I did. "I need to sober him up."

Tess joined us, slightly out of breath. "I couldn't find any bottled water, but I was able to get some iced water for you." She held out a plastic cup to Zack.

"I don't want water." Zack closed his eyes. "I want a drink. Get me a drink."

"Thank you." Christian took the cup from her. "But I think coffee is the better option."

She bit her lip. "Let me see if the staff has coffee urns in the administration cottage."

After Tess left, Christian offered the water to Zack. "Take a sip. To wash out your mouth, if nothing else."

"I told you, I want a drink." Zack smacked the cup, sending it flying to the grass.

Christian swore under his breath. "You've had enough. If I see you anywhere near alcohol again tonight, I'll wrestle you to the ground. And you're in no shape to stop me."

Zack balled up his fists, his stance and expression combative. But just when I thought things were about to get physical, Zack began to weep. Tears poured down his face as Christian pulled his friend into an embrace. The deep sorrow both men felt was as palpable as the humid summer heat. I felt I had no right to witness their shared grief.

"I should go," I said.

Zack raised his head. "Why are you here anyway?" The spittle from his mouth sprayed me. "Christian and I have lots to talk about. Just us. Not you. You don't know anything. Go away!" He shook himself free of Christian's embrace.

"I'm sorry if I upset you, Zack. I hope you're feeling better tomorrow."

"Tomorrow? Why should tomorrow be any better than today?" Zack batted away Christian's attempt to quiet him. "Sienna will still be dead. And I'll still have every reason to get drunk. I will, too. Now go away!"

Before I could do as he asked, Zack shoved me. With a startled cry, I fell backward onto the grass. He'd pushed me so hard, I briefly saw stars when my head made contact with the ground. All I could think was I did not want a repeat of the concussion I'd suffered at the Strawberry Moon Bash last month. Raising myself up on my elbows, I saw Christian grab Zack by his shirt.

"Zack, have you gone crazy?" Christian looked down at me. "Are you okay?"

I fought to catch my breath. "The wind's knocked out of me, but I don't think I'm hurt."

Detective Trejo suddenly appeared. "Stand back. What's going on here?"

While I looked up at him in amazement, I felt strong hands reach under my arms and lift me to my feet. I turned and met the worried gaze of Atticus Holt. "Did he hurt you?" he asked.

"I'm fine."

"Why did you strike this woman?" Trejo's expression was even more severe than usual. If I had been Zack, it would have given me pause. But Zack was too drunk to notice or care.

"Leave me alone!" Zack said as he tried to walk away.

Trejo pulled out a pair of handcuffs. "Stop right there."

Christian grabbed his friend. "Stop, Zack, before you get yourself arrested."

"You can't blame him," I said. "He doesn't know what he's doing."

"That's no excuse for him to lay his hands on you." Holt gently pushed me behind him.

"He fell off the wagon tonight." Christian gripped Zack's

arm so he couldn't leave. "Zack has had a serious drinking problem for years, but we thought he had it under control."

"I am in control." Zack yanked free of Christian.

Trejo spun Zack around and had him in cuffs so quickly it seemed like a magic trick. Zack began to curse and struggle. This was getting worse by the minute.

"Is this necessary?" I asked the police officers. "He didn't hurt me. And you can see he's drunk."

"Drunk and disorderly." Trejo grabbed Zack's upper arm. His grip must have been steel-like because Zack winced. He also stopped struggling. "We can arrest him for that."

Holt turned to Christian. "When we questioned you and your friends this afternoon, everyone assured us there was no problem. Now one of you is drunk and physically attacking a woman."

"I didn't attack anyone!" Zack shouted as Christian stared at the ground in dismay.

"Keep it down," Holt warned.

"I told Marlee to go away," Zack continued. "We didn't want to talk to her about Sienna."

"You spoke about Sienna Katsaros?" Trejo looked over at me.

"I only mentioned how upset Theo's been since I found her body."

"We don't care about Theo," Zack spat. "He's nothing to us. And he was nothing to Sienna. Why is he upset about her? She was our friend, not his. Sienna belonged to us. Not some simpleminded sneak."

"Why do you say Theo Foster is a sneak?" Holt asked.

"Could we get some coffee into him before this continues?" Christian asked in obvious exasperation. "He needs to be sober during any questioning. And have a lawyer present. Zack doesn't know what he's saying."

"Stop talking about me." Although his hands were still

cuffed behind him, Zack tried to pull his arms free. "Leave me alone. Everyone leave me alone."

Out of the corner of my eye, I saw Dawn and Joel run toward us from the direction of the bayou. "What are you doing to Zack?" Dawn cried. "What's happening?"

Dawn took Zack's face in her hands as Joel pulled Christian aside. "What have they done to you?" she asked. "Are you hurt? Why are you in handcuffs?"

"Mr. Burwell knocked Ms. Jacob to the ground," Trejo said.

I now wished I had never gone near any of them. Until I set eyes on Zack tonight, I had been enjoying the luau.

She turned her angry attention to me. "You must have said something to upset him."

"Not really." I regarded Zack with pity. "He had too much to drink and was sick. I tried to help him."

"I'm sure you were bothering him with more questions. It's hard enough for us to be back at BAS, especially with the news about Sienna. We don't need you interrogating us." Dawn glared at the two uniformed officers. "And we don't need you calling the police on us, either."

"I did no such thing."

"We saw a clearly inebriated Mr. Burwell become physically ill," Holt said. "Marlee approached him in what appeared to be an attempt to offer assistance."

"Mr. Burwell grew agitated with Ms. Jacob." Trejo glanced at Holt as if to remind him not to call me Marlee when involved in official police business. "He proceeded to shove her to the ground. That is physical assault. Should she wish to press charges, she has every right."

Joel looked up from his whispered conversation with Christian. "You aren't going to arrest him?" He seemed as upset as Zack. "You can't."

"We can," Holt replied. "If Ms. Jacob wants to file a complaint."

All eyes turned to me. "I'm not going to file a complaint

or press charges. He didn't hurt me. But I do want him to get help." I glanced over at Holt. "Unless you think he would be better off in the drunk tank for the night. You could at least keep an eye on him there."

Dawn shook her head at me. "This poor man is an alcoholic. He's sick. And you want to put him in jail? What kind of heartless monster are you?"

"That's enough," Holt said in a voice severe enough to rival that of Detective Trejo. "Your friend has been drunk and disorderly. We are within our rights to haul him in for that alone. I suggest you leave Ms. Jacob out of it."

Dawn stared at me as the torch light cast flickering shadows along the angular outline of her face. For a startling moment, her visage appeared skull-like. "I see how it is in this town," she said. "You all protect each other. But outsiders like Zack and Sienna are left to fend for themselves."

"Stop!" Zack wailed. "I don't want to hear about Sienna. And take these handcuffs off. I'm going to be sick." A second after this announcement, Zack was once more physically ill. His friends crowded around him, rubbing his shoulders and patting his back.

"Please let him go," I said to Holt. "I don't think he's likely to hurt anyone but himself."

He took a deep breath, then nodded at Trejo.

"If you're really his friends, you'll sober him up." Trejo removed the handcuffs from Zack, who rubbed at his wrists as if he had been restrained hours rather than minutes. "And the police will need to question all of you again tomorrow."

Christian and Joel groaned, while Dawn put an arm around Zack's shoulders. "Fine," she said defiantly. "But only if we have a lawyer present."

"Bring ten lawyers with you, but there are facts about the

case I suspect all of you are keeping from the police." Trejo scanned the group. "And one of you seems to be missing."

"Leah," I murmured to Holt.

Despite how softly I spoke, Dawn heard me. "Your little snitch Marlee is right."

"Excuse me. I simply told them who in your group wasn't here."

Dawn ignored me. "Last time I saw Leah she was speaking with Gordon."

"Gordon is at the bayou tonight?" I asked.

"What's it to you if he is?" Joel said to me with a snarl.

"Leave Gordo alone," Zack said. "Leave all of us alone." He waved drunkenly at the police and me. "Go away!"

Trejo grabbed Zack's arm. "Ms. Jacob, where can we get some coffee into him?"

"Try the administration cottage. The staff might have coffee urns in the office."

"Let's go." Trejo pulled Zack along with him as he marched in the direction of the cottage. Dawn and Christian hurried after them, but Joel hesitated.

"You're making everything worse," he told Holt and me.

"How?" Holt asked. "We're trying to discover what happened to your friend Sienna. If you want to prevent the police from doing that, we have to assume there's a reason behind it. An incriminating one."

Joel sighed. "Did it ever occur to you that we all went through so much hell when she disappeared, we can't stand to go through it again."

Holt was unmoved. "Don't you want to know who killed Sienna?"

"Not really." He gave a bitter laugh. "That sounds incriminating, but I don't frigging care. Maybe it was a stranger who killed her. But maybe it was someone we knew. I mean, how much worse can this whole thing get?"

With a muttered curse, Joel took off at a slight jog after his friends.

Holt turned to me. "I'm afraid this situation can get a whole lot worse."

"I agree. And he knows it, too."

"Is that your new talisman?" He looked down at the little tiki statue I held. Even when shoved to the ground, I had somehow kept my hold on it.

I grinned. "It's the tiki trophy I won for doing the limbo."

"I watched the contest. Most impressive. Although you may have had an advantage. The other contestants looked about as drunk as Mr. Burwell."

"Please don't throw aspersions on my victory. Being drunk is an advantage in going under the limbo pole. Anyway, I'm glad I won. The BAS woodworking students made all the tikis for the event." I held out the six-inch wooden statue. "Aren't these the sweetest carved blackberries you've ever seen? They hand painted it, too. It's a work of art."

Holt traced one of the carved blackberries with his finger. "A work of art covered in berries. Don't imagine it gets any better for you."

"Until the scene with Zack, the night was wonderful." I waved my hand in front of my face. "Except for the mosquitoes."

"It may not have been smart to show a lot of skin this close to a bayou. Not that I'm complaining." His smile deepened, and his expression revealed how approving he was of my blue bikini and snug little sarong skirt.

I had deliberately gone for broke tonight, choosing a sexy little tropical outfit. I also took extra care to arrange flowers strategically in my long wavy hair, which spilled about my shoulders and down my back. Wearing my hair down made me warmer than I needed to be, but the plan was to hold Ryan's attention longer than twenty minutes. For a while it had worked, no doubt due to my wriggling under the limbo pole. Then his cousins and Diego's barbecued ribs intervened. At least my tropical seduction efforts hadn't been a total bust. Atticus Holt regarded me with far more than approval. There was a hearty dose of lust in that gaze, making me feel guilty and grateful. Still, it's never fun when your boyfriend deserts you for pork and hot sauce.

I slapped at a mosquito on my arm. "How long have you and Detective Trejo been here? I didn't know you were at the luau until Zack pushed me. Where were you two hiding?"

"Not hiding. Working. We've spent a lot of time talking with BAS administrators. They've given us the names of the other students who attended the same session with Sienna. With so many different activities scheduled, it's easier to question most of them at an event like this. As far as we know, nothing BAS related is going on tonight except for the luau."

"Then you questioned Zack and his friends earlier today?"

"Ms. Kapoor gave us their contact info. We met with them this afternoon in one of the cabins."

"Was it at all productive?"

"None of them confessed to murdering Sienna, if that's what you mean."

"Do you think one of them did it?"

The look he now shot me was cautionary, not lustful. "You know there's only so much I can tell you. Officially."

"How about unofficially?"

"Unofficially, I want to wish you congratulations on the limbo victory." He chuckled. "Now I'd better join up with Greg. But I want to make certain you weren't hurt. From where I stood, it looked as if Mr. Burwell pushed you pretty hard."

"I'm fine. It takes a lot more to damage me than a simple

shove." I didn't add that just that—and a knock over my head—nearly did me in last month.

"Let me know if you need a ride home later."

"I came with Ryan. He'll see I get home safe."

Holt frowned. "Your fiancé is here? He should be keeping a closer eye on you if he is."

"He lost interest when the next slab of ribs went on the fire." While I said this with a laugh, I felt as irritated as Holt looked. We'd been at the luau for over three hours and Ryan had spent no more than a few minutes with me. I didn't begrudge him the time he spent with his cousins—or even the barbecued pork—but lately I had been feeling like an afterthought in his life. Although if he knew how interested Atticus Holt was in me, Ryan would be hovering over us like a jealous guardian angel.

"The man's a fool for choosing ribs over you," he said in a tone that made my stomach do a little flip.

"I'm going to assume you haven't tasted Diego Theroux's ribs." I thought it safer to return the conversation to the murder case than Ryan and me. "Before you go, have you seen Gordon Sanderling tonight?"

"I got a brief glimpse of him a while back. He made himself scarce when he spotted me. I may have been a little harsh with him last night after you told me what happened in the parking lot. I made it clear he was to stay away from you and Theo."

"Speaking of Theo, is he at the luau?"

"Don't know. But there are several hundred people here. Easy to get lost in this crowd."

"I agree." If I had missed Holt and Trejo here, as well as Gordon Sanderling, I could have overlooked my baker hiding in a corner of the bayou. "Thank you for rescuing me from the inebriated Mr. Burwell. I do appreciate the police gallantry, Atticus."

"Kit," he said. "My friends call me Kit. Only my parents refer to me as Atticus."

On an impulse, I gave him a quick kiss on the cheek. "Thank you, Kit."

I was sure that if the sun were out and not tiki torches, I would have seen him blush. With mixed feelings, I watched Kit Holt stride off toward the administration cottage. After he left, I felt abandoned. Maybe I should join Ryan and his cousins, even if it meant listening to a conversation centered on orchard economics and Zellar family memories. But when I reached the group near the barbecue pit, Ryan and his cousins were nowhere in sight. This was why Ryan hadn't come to my defense when Zack knocked me down. He never knew the incident had occurred.

Pushing through a noisy mob enervated by pork and alcohol, I decided to track down Tess and Emma. Thinking of Emma reminded me that Alison had reportedly drunk so much she had been put to bed in one of the Bramble cabins to sleep it off. I should check on her. This was probably the most this respectable mother of three had partied since her infamous bachelorette party, when she rode piggyback on a male stripper called Muscle Mario.

The farther I climbed up the trail leading to the cabins, the quieter it grew. And the fragrance of the surrounding pine trees soon overwhelmed the smell of barbecue sauce and alcohol. I felt grateful for the change. The dirt and gravel path forked off at various points as I climbed deeper into the surrounding woods. The larger buildings on the right were the art studios. I headed instead for the Bramble log cabins, where students and faculty resided during the summer. Lantern posts stood at regular intervals for illumination, but it was still a shadowy path. First-time students often took a wrong turn, or stumbled on the uneven ground in the dark.

When I reached the first group of Bramble cabins, I stopped.

If Alison had been drunk enough to be put to bed, they wouldn't have been able to get her much farther than this. I walked up to the porch of the nearest cabin and knocked on the door. When there was no answer, I opened the door and looked around. All I saw were four beds, the customary rustic table and chairs, and one of those electric lanterns that sat in the window of each cabin. The lantern didn't afford much light, but it was bright enough to reveal the cabin was empty.

I set off for the cabin directly next door. After my gentle knock received no response, I once more peeked inside. As soon as I did, I bit back a cry. This cabin was not empty, but it wasn't Alison I saw lying on one of the beds. Instead, it was a naked man and woman who were so busy making love they never noticed me.

I quietly shut the door and hurried back to the path. For a moment, I stood there, uncertain and shaken. It wasn't the sight of two people having sex that alarmed me. What bothered me was that I recognized the couple. And while I had not learned Theo's whereabouts tonight, I now knew with absolute certainty where Leah Malek and Gordon Sanderling were.

Chapter 15

"You're mean, Marlee." Since the shop was briefly without customers, Andrew took the opportunity to nag me again. "Why can't I taste some of the wines?"

"Because you need to keep a clear head while we're working. This isn't the BAS luau."

He snorted. "Luau? It felt like St. Paddy's Day in Chicago, only with rum instead of green beer. And did the fire-eaters really get too close to Jenna Meisner and set her on fire? I have a dim memory of something going up in flames."

"That was Jenna, or at least her costume. Her fellow dancers ripped her hula skirt off before she got burnt." I shook my head. "It also brought the luau to a close."

"You have to hand it to Piper. She sure knows how to throw a party."

It had turned into quite a night. I couldn't forget the hula dancer's near immolation, Zack's drunken appearance, or the couple I discovered in one of the Bramble cabins. I hadn't had much time to think about the implication of finding Gordon and Leah having sex. It probably meant nothing more than Leah still carried a torch for Gordon, and a pretty steamy one, too. She told me at breakfast yesterday that she had waylaid Gordon on the way to the showers at the school twenty years ago. They must have been lovers before, even if it was only a brief hookup. I imagined their old attraction to each other, coupled with the grief they shared about Sienna, had drawn them together once more. Whatever was going on between them, I didn't think it was my business. Although I should inform Kit Holt. Or would that make me the snitch I'd already been branded as by Dawn Vance?

"I've never tasted the white currant wine." Andrew eyed one of the bottles on the table.

"And you won't be doing it today until you're done working." After a quick glance at my strawberry-shaped wall clock, I smoothed down my chef apron. "No sips when I'm not looking, either. Otherwise your head will feel even worse."

Andrew had been complaining about his hangover headache since he came to work. He wasn't alone. Alison felt so sick from all the drinking she had done last night she refused to get out of bed this morning. At least we managed to get her back to my house without her becoming ill, like Zack. So far the BAS centenary week had had a less than salubrious effect on everyone. And we still had a few days to go before the celebration was officially over.

As a way of toasting congratulations to the BAS centenary, I'd set up a berry wine tasting. I was now second-guessing my decision. Given how much the BAS alumni had partied last night, offering free wine may not have been the wisest move. Except it was too late to cancel. The two o'clock event had been publicized for weeks and I had stocked an impressive selection of berry wines: blackberry, strawberry, cranberry, blueberry, white currant, and raspberry. I'd hoped to include huckleberry wine, but the last bottles sold out yesterday.

For the third time, I rearranged the wine bottles on the expansive butcher-block table. Once I brought out the platters of cheese and crackers kept in the kitchen, The Berry Basket wine tasting could officially begin.

A squawk rang through the shop, followed by a voice saying, "Give me a kiss."

"Shut up!" Andrew shouted.

His plea was met with a loud "Shut up!" in return.

Cradling his head, Andrew groaned. "Can't you teach that bird to whisper?"

"It would be easier if you taught yourself not to drink so many craft beers in one night." I walked over to the four-foot-tall perch near the window. Unlike Natasha's rampaging Yorkie, Minnie's clipped wings prevented her from exploring the shop. She wouldn't get anywhere near the pastry or ice cream counters. "Don't blame Minnie for only doing what comes natural to her."

"Drinking beer at a luau comes naturally to me, too," Andrew muttered.

"Pay no attention to him," I told my beautiful gray and white parrot as she bobbed her head at my approach.

"Give me a kiss," she repeated.

When I held out my arm, Minnie hopped on. "Mommy loves you," I crooned to her.

"Why did you bring her to work on a day when I have such a splitting headache?" Andrew complained.

"Hi ho, hi ho," Minnie sang.

"Don't listen to the silly man," I reassured her. "As if we knew in advance how the self-indulgent Mr. Cabot is going to be feeling."

"At least I'm trying to prepare for the road rally, which is more than you're doing." Andrew held up a spiral notebook. "I've spent all week trying to figure out what art-related clues we'll have to solve for the rally. And we've got only forty-eight hours left to prep for it."

"You're driving me nuts. There's no way of knowing what kind of clues Piper has come up with. They may be puns, or wacky references we could never figure out in advance, or esoteric questions about the art world." I thought a moment. "For example, where would Dutch painter Piet Mondrian go to find a subject *and* buy fruit? The answer would be Red Tree Market." Andrew looked confused. "Because Red Tree is a painting by Mondrian and there's a farm market called Red Tree on Blue Star Highway."

"Good one, Marlee." He grabbed a pen from the counter and started scribbling. "Let's brainstorm a few more. Actually, you brainstorm the clues and I'll write them down. And get Tess to spitball some clues related to glasswork. By the way, Dean is only studying the Impressionists. He's leaving every other painter to me. The lazy brat. I wouldn't mind if we kicked my brother off the team. Less people to split the prize money with."

I looked at Minnie. "This is why I like being an only child," I told her.

She blinked and replied, "Where are the cashews?"

I removed one of the cashews I kept in my apron pocket for her. "Here you go."

She quickly consumed her favorite snack. "Mommy loves me."

"That she does." I smoothed back the feathers on her head and she shut her eyes in contentment.

The shop door swung open, letting in a couple with two young children in tow. The boy and girl ran over to Minnie and me.

"Does she bite?" The boy put out a tentative hand as if to pet her.

"Sometimes." I raised my arm to keep the bird out of their reach. "Minnie doesn't know you, so don't try to pet her. She may get nervous. But if you let her sit on her perch or on me, she'll be fine." I smiled at them. "And she talks."

Before I could prompt her, Minnie announced, "Peek-a-boo. I see you."

They erupted into giggles, which increased when Minnie added, "How are ya, mate?"

"Mommy, Daddy, can we have a bird?" the girl asked her parents, who had joined us.

"The bird sounds Australian," the mother commented.

"Her previous family was from Australia," I explained. "They lived in the States for a few years, but had to return home. When they ran into problems about bringing an exotic bird through customs, they put her up for adoption. She's mine now. Minnie's never been to Australia, but she does have a few Aussie phrases in her vocabulary." While I had so far counted over three hundred words in her vocabulary, I was certain she knew even more.

"Tie me kangaroo down," Minnie sang.

"Amazing," the children's father said. "What kind of bird is she?"

I looked fondly at the thirteen-inch bird perched on my forearm. "An African grey parrot. They're one of the best talkers. And quite intelligent." With my free hand, I scratched the top of her head. Minnie closed her eyes and murmured, "Scritch."

"Will she be at the store tomorrow?" the boy asked.

I heard Andrew say, "I hope not."

"She's not here all the time." I placed Minnie back onto her perch. Attached to it were two metal bowls, one holding water, the other fresh vegetables. At the base of the perch sat an aluminum pan filled with sand to catch any droppings.

Things had been so hectic, I had hardly been home at all. Feeling guilty for leaving Minnie alone all day, I decided to bring her into work this morning. She also loved talking to people. Certainly she was easier to take care of than Natasha's Yorkie. And if I thought she needed a little nap, I'd move her to the back office, where a large travel cage sat on my desk.

Things had worked out well so far, convincing me to bring her in more often.

The little girl hopped up and down. "Can you get Minnie to talk again? Please."

My bird needed no encouragement. Unless she was eating or sleeping, Minnie kept up a running commentary, interspersed with whistles and perfect imitations of any noise she had heard. Both the children and their parents remained transfixed as Minnie regaled them with phrases, catcalls, and her special rendition of "Ba-ba-ba ba-ba ba-ran." Apparently, her previous owners had a fondness for the old Beach Boys song "Barbara Ann." The delighted children began to sing along, prompting Andrew to down more Tylenol. The Minnie show might have continued for some time had customers not started to arrive for my two o'clock wine tasting.

Needing to oversee the wine table, I moved Minnie and her perch near the closed door leading to the kitchen and storage room. She'd be safely out of the way, and Andrew could keep an eye on her from behind the counter. I placed the perch on a large decorative crate where she could be visible over the heads of anyone in the store, and out of the reach of curious hands.

"Here comes trouble," Minnie called out as a group of women headed for the wooden table in the center of the store, where I had just set down platters of cheese and crackers. Nope, here come paying customers, I thought, and ones who were already examining my berry wine selection with appreciative smiles.

"Could we try this one?" one of them asked.

"Of course. This is a raspberry wine with a dark chocolate finish." I poured wine into the sample glasses lined up. "Because this is a dessert wine, it's usually not paired with cheese and crackers. A raspberry truffle is a more perfect fit." I slid a glass bowl filled with chocolate raspberry truffles toward them. The women crowded round.

The next hour saw my usual summer traffic, along with dozens more drawn in by my sandwich board out front advertising the wine tasting. Andrew was run ragged boxing up berry pastries, whipping up smoothies, and ringing up purchases at the cash register. But I was so busy with the wine lovers, I couldn't help him. Even with the hubbub of a store crammed with people, I could still hear Minnie's nonstop remarks from the back of the store. And whenever she asked, "What's up, punk?" it was greeted with gales of laughter.

Scheduled to last an hour, the wine tasting was so popular I kept it going past that time. But I'd have to call a halt soon. My sample bottles were nearly empty, along with most of the cheese platter. Cindy from the cheese shop had supplied me with the various cheeses I requested, and I displayed a card informing customers that the cheeses came from her store. Even though she had been in business for over a year, Cindy had no idea my fellow shopkeepers and I referred to her store as "the cheese shop," not Cindy's Whey. Over the years, several people had opened—and closed—a cheese store in Oriole Point. A cheese business couldn't seem to make a go of it here, and we fully expected Cindy's to follow suit. It didn't seem worth the effort to learn the name of yet another cheese emporium. But we liked Cindy and had our fingers crossed for her.

For the past few minutes, a distinguished older gentleman had paid particular attention to my three varieties of blackberry wine. He mentioned he was visiting from Oregon, which I knew produced more blackberries than any other state in the nation. If Michigan dominated the blueberry and cherry market, Oregon was the blackberry champ.

While I recommended Brie and Camembert as the best pairings for blackberry wine, I looked up to see Christian Naylor and Zack Burwell at the far end of the table. Busy slicing cheese for my customer, I could only greet them with a nod.

I prayed Zack didn't sample any of the wines. Fortunately, it was crowded, which forced both men to stand behind other customers.

I kept throwing glances their way. Zack looked to be sober, albeit exhausted and pale. And Christian wore a forbidding expression. If they wanted to speak with me, I didn't know how I could manage it. Dean and Gillian hadn't arrived for their shifts yet, and Andrew and I were swamped with customers.

This must have occurred to the two men as well. Zack waved at me finally and said, "Marlee, could we talk to you for a minute?"

"I'm a little busy." I poured a glass of cranberry wine for a customer.

"Excuse me, miss," the gentleman from Oregon asked, "but can any berries be made into wine? I'd love to make homemade wine from my elderberry bushes."

"Wine can be made from almost any berry," I replied. "The basic recipe calls for fruit, yeast, filtered water, sugar, and honey."

He took another sip of his wine. "How long does it take for the mixture to ferment?"

"There are different steps to the process. A month is average for the fermentation process. Most homemade vintners let their wine clarify for a few months before bottling it. But some people don't bother to let it age. They drink it as soon as it ferments."

Everyone crowded about the table listened intently to my explanation, including Zack and Christian. In fact, both men appeared unhappy, which didn't surprise me. The sight and smell of so much wine would be upsetting to a recovering alcoholic and his concerned friend.

"Make certain you enjoy the taste of the berry chosen for your wine," I added. "Some fermented berries can be too sweet, others too bitter. And be careful no insects or bugs get into the mixture. Also, all the equipment and utensils must be kept clean and sanitized throughout the process. But it's easier to make homemade fruit wines than most people think."

Five minutes later, the last of the sample wines had been poured, and only crumbs remained on my cheese and cracker platter.

"I need to end the wine tasting now," I announced, pleased at how many people had chosen to buy the wines they had sampled. "Thank you so much for participating in our event. I hope you've all discovered at least one berry wine that has pleased your palate."

This was met with a brief smattering of applause and cheers. The wine had put everyone in a good mood.

"Zack has something he wants to say to you, Marlee. It won't take long." I jumped at the sound of Christian's voice. He and Zack had muscled their way closer to me and now stood only a few feet away.

"Let me clear off the table first. Both of you can wait in the back of the shop, where it's less crowded. I'll be there when I can."

A couple I recognized from Kalamazoo approached me, and we exchanged friendly greetings. When I glanced over my shoulder, I saw Christian and Zack in the rear of the store. Minnie sat perched a few feet away. Their conversation prompted her to shout, "Shut up!"

After the Kalamazoo couple moved off to inspect the berry pastries, my store traffic increased yet again when two of the performers from the Oriole Point Theater production of *Grease* burst in. Recognizing me from the Fourth of July parade, the actors currently playing Danny Zuko and Kenickie greeted me with shouts and bear hugs. By the time I came up for air, I spotted Christian in line at the ice cream counter, where Andrew appeared to be making an endless number of sundaes.

"This place is busier than Grand Central." I turned to see Zack standing behind me.

"Things aren't always so crazy," I said. "But it is high season along the lakeshore. And when you add the alumni from the Blackberry Art School . . ."

"That's what I need to talk to you about. I can't tell you how sorry I am for what happened last night. To be honest, I don't remember most of it, but Christian told me I got belligerent and angry. He says I pushed you to the ground. He brought me to your store today to apologize." Zack sighed. "We didn't expect you to be holding a wine tasting."

"At breakfast yesterday you told me how you've remained sober for over seven years. If you could do that, a few bottles of berry wine should be easy to resist."

When I placed my hand on his shoulder to give him a reassuring squeeze, I realized he was trembling. Zack suddenly reminded me of Theo; while Zack sought refuge in alcohol, Theo did so by retreating from the world. Both men seemed emotionally fragile and one step away from losing their balance.

"I should never have started drinking last night. It was the worst thing I could have done. You saw what happens when I do. I hope I didn't hurt you. Again, I'm really sorry."

"I'm fine. And thank you for the apology."

"Making amends is one of the Twelve Steps. Waste of time for me, going through the whole dozen. Here I am, back where I started, looking at life through a bottle."

"But you're not back where you started. You just hit a rough patch. Everyone has their weak moments. Don't spend time beating yourself up over it."

"I called my sponsor as soon as I woke up this morning. He wants me to call him again this afternoon. I have a lot of work to do." Zack took a deep breath. "Marlee, I need to talk something over with you. I think it may help me. And Theo."

"What is it?"

"I can't talk about it here," he said in a lower voice.

"As soon as the next shift arrives, we can go into my office. Or maybe you and I can get something to eat. Christian, too."

He looked over at where Christian was pointing to the toppings he wanted Andrew to put on his sundae. "Christian doesn't need to be part of this conversation. Only us."

I was now confused, and a bit wary. "I assume this has something to do with Sienna."

"Everything in my life these past twenty years has had something to do with Sienna. And it needs to stop. I have to stop it; otherwise I'll drink myself into the grave. Although that's exactly what I was doing for years. Drinking myself to death."

This was an incongruous conversation to have in the middle of my store as tourists buying berry jam bustled all around us and Minnie sang "Ba-ba-ba ba-ba ba-ran" every thirty seconds. I felt in over my head and uncertain of how to proceed.

"There's an art exhibition set up today at BAS. I planned to go there after work. We could talk at the school."

He visibly paled. "Not there. The place will be crawling with alumni."

"So is most of Oriole Point this week." I nodded at a trio of women who now entered my store, all of them sporting the school's purple T-shirts. "Hard to avoid them."

When Zack saw the BAS alumni, he averted his face. "How about if I meet you this evening at your house? Christian's rented a Jeep. I'll see if I can get the keys from him for an hour or two."

I had no intention of meeting Zack at my house, especially alone. While I felt sorry for him, I didn't trust him. And because he seemed determined to avoid running into any BAS alumni, finding a place in town where that wouldn't happen was tricky.

Then I recalled the road rally clue I brainstormed with Andrew earlier today.

"How about the Red Tree Market on Blue Star Highway? It's a farm market halfway between here and South Haven. Because they also run an ice cream parlor, they're open until ten on summer nights."

He didn't seem convinced. "Do a lot of tourists go there?"

"Yes, but they're usually the ones renting houses for the week or the summer. Not likely any BAS alumni would be there."

Zack considered this for a moment. "Okay. Let's meet around nine. I should be able to lose the others by then. And you won't be able to miss me. I'll be driving Christian's yellow Jeep." He looked up. "He's coming. Don't say anything about this to him. And please don't bring anyone from BAS. Or your police friends."

"Fine." Of course, that still left a lot of people I could ask to accompany me tonight.

After Christian returned with his ice cream, the three of us said our good-byes. Christian seemed relieved, obviously believing that the purpose of their visit today—Zack's apology to me—had been accomplished. But as I watched them leave the shop, I knew there was unfinished business looming ahead.

I could call Kit Holt and have him lurking in the vicinity of Red Tree Market. Except that might escalate things if Zack caught sight of him. Better to ask Ryan to come with me; my orchard cowboy was more than capable of subduing Zack if he became aggressive. Then again, what if Zack had been the one to murder Sienna? Maybe he wanted me out of the way because I was asking too many questions. But if I mysteriously died, or disappeared, as Sienna had twenty years ago, even more suspicion would fall on him and his fellow Bramble members.

No, he had valuable information he wanted to pass on to me. And he knew I would give this information to the police.

My thoughts were interrupted by Minnie asking, "Where are the cashews?"

I made my way to her perch at the back of the store. I was as happy as Andrew to see that Dean and Gillian had arrived for their shifts. And Minnie was happy when I lifted her down from her perch and gave her another cashew.

"Don't tell her," Minnie said. "Don't tell her."

"I haven't heard this phrase before," I said to the bird, who gazed at me with her head cocked to one side. "Did you hear someone say this today?"

"Don't tell her," Minnie repeated. She gave a piercing whistle before adding, "You're a fool. You're a fool. Don't tell her."

I waited to see if she had any other new phrases, but Minnie began singing, "La-la-la-la-la." Besides, I had a good idea where she had heard these new sayings. After all, I had seen Christian and Zack talking near Minnie's perch while I was occupied with my customers. Zack had probably been warned not to talk to me. No wonder he was anxious to keep our meeting private.

The cell phone in my apron pocket vibrated. Expecting the call to be from Emma or Alison, I was surprised to see Theo's name on my screen. He never called me.

"Theo?" I asked. "Are you okay? Is something wrong?"

"Marlee, the police are here! Make them go away."

"Is it the state police or the sheriff's department?" If Holt had gone to see Theo without taking me along, I would be severely disappointed in him. "What did they say to you?"

"Nothing. I didn't see them. They're hiding. But I know they're here." Theo's breathing became ragged, and I feared he was crying. "Help me, Marlee. I can't see them, but I think they're hiding in my shed. Or maybe they're hiding in my car.

I'm afraid to go outside. They'll take me to jail. And I can't go. I can't!"

"Calm down. I'll be there as soon as I can. Everything will be fine. I promise."

Except, if Theo was now hallucinating about the police, things weren't fine at all.

Chapter 16

Minnie serenaded me all the way to Crow Cottage. Because I didn't want to leave her at the store, I hurriedly put my bird in her traveling cage, where she sang "Ba-ba-ba ba-ba ba-ran" nonstop from the backseat. As I sped to Theo's house, she repeated this chorus like an old vinyl LP stuck in a groove. I needed to expose her to other catchy tunes. And soon.

When I parked in front of Theo's cottage, Minnie stopped singing long enough to ask, "Wassup?"

"I have no idea," I replied as I got out of the car.

A quick scan of the cul-de-sac showed no state trooper cruisers or sheriff vans in sight, but at least Theo's blue VW was still here. I'd been afraid he might make a run for it before I arrived. The only signs of activity were a guy mowing his lawn and a woman in the distance jogging along the river. My concern deepened. Why did Theo think the police were here? Did he suffer from bouts of paranoia, maybe even schizophrenia? I prayed Theo's frantic phone call was the result of some simple misunderstanding. Perhaps he'd heard the sound of a siren in the distance again, or spotted a police car. Anything other than my gentle baker had lost complete touch with reality.

With a heavy heart, I made my way to the cottage. Before

I reached his front porch, I stopped. A police cap and shiny badge lay on the rubber doormat. I blinked to make certain I was seeing correctly. A second look told me the police badge and hat were not authentic.

When I knelt to examine the objects better, the door swung open. "I told you," Theo said in a stage whisper. He stuck his head out and looked from side to side. "The police are here."

"No, they're not." I stood up. "They never were. The badge and hat are fake. The kind of thing kids use to play dress up. These don't belong to a police officer."

"Are you sure?" He stared down at the objects with an expression of dread.

"I'm sure. You can come outside, Theo. There's no one on the street except for me and a neighbor cutting his grass." I beckoned to him. "Really, it's safe to come out."

He didn't look convinced. "Maybe they're hiding. Maybe the police want me to think these are only toys and are waiting for me to leave my house. They want to arrest me."

"No one wants to arrest you. And the police aren't in the habit of dropping off toys."

He took a tentative step onto the porch, staring at the items as if they were poisonous vipers ready to strike. "But why did someone leave them here? I don't understand."

I was as unhappy about this turn of events as Theo, but for different reasons. "As a joke maybe," I suggested. "Not a very nice one, either."

"A joke." His face changed to one of stubborn disapproval. "I don't like jokes. Jokes are mean." Theo snatched up the hat and badge. With a speed that surprised me, he jumped off his porch and sprinted to the back of his house.

"Where are you going?" I ran after him.

I should have warned Theo not to touch the hat and badge. Any fingerprints on them would now be compromised. They were compromised even further when Theo flung the objects into the Oriole River.

When I reached his side, he pointed at the shimmering water. "Next time someone brings a police hat or a badge, I'll throw it in the river as soon as I see it."

So much for evidence. "When did you find the hat and badge on your porch?"

"Right before I called you."

"Did you hear a car drive up? Or anyone moving around outside your house?"

"I didn't hear anything. After lunch I lie there and watch the birds." Theo pointed at a faded green hammock suspended on a metal frame. "Sometimes I fall asleep. I did today."

"After you woke up and went back to the house, you found the hat and badge on your front mat?"

"Yes. It frightened me. I thought the police came to take me away." His voice lowered to a whisper once more. "They did once. Did you know that?"

"I spoke to your father, Theo. He told me how you were arrested at a protest march."

"I marched with my cousin to help the animals. And the birds. It was a good thing to do. My family said so. Then the police came and got angry because I didn't want to go with them. But Dad told me never to go with anyone." He shuddered. "They put me in jail. For a long time."

No doubt his two days locked up in jail had seemed like an eternity to him. It would seem pretty endless to me. "That was a terrible mistake, and it should never have happened. But no one is going to take you away now. Besides, the police didn't leave those things on your porch."

"Who did?"

"Someone who knows how afraid you are of the police." I bit my lip at the memory of Theo telling Gordon about his fear of the police during their encounter in the parking lot.

As if he read my mind, Theo said, "I told Gordon I was afraid of them."

"Yes, I remember. He might have told the others. Sienna's Bramble friends." I began to pace back and forth. This latest turn of events was troubling, and I worried things had grown dangerous for Theo. The police would have to be told, but I'd just reassured Theo they weren't coming. Yet how was I supposed to keep him safe if I didn't call the police? Whoever left the hat and badge meant to frighten Theo. I recalled Gordon's words to Theo and me two nights ago. "Maybe he isn't talking to the police," Gordon had said, "but I suspect he is. The police are questioning everyone about Sienna's murder. Of course they'd question him. And what will they get from your nervous baker? Cryptic, confusing statements that could incriminate other people."

I turned to Theo, who watched me as if I were an interesting bird species visiting his feeders. "Whoever left those things believes you know something about Sienna's murder."

He appeared confused. "But I don't know anything. That's why I've been asking Sienna's Bramble friends about her."

My fear for him increased. "When did you do that?"

"At the BAS parties. The first night I talked to Leah. And I asked Gordon about Sienna when I went to the parking lot. But he got mad. When I was at the Hawaiian party, I talked to Christian and the others."

If the killer wasn't nervous before this, he or she probably was now. "Theo, I never saw you at the luau last night. Where were you?"

"By the bayou. I watched you win the contest. You were very good. But I left after that. The mosquitoes bit me too much." He held out his arms, which were covered in mosquito bites.

"What did you ask all of them?"

"I wanted to know if they saw Sienna the night she went

missing." His expression turned disapproving. "I told them I wasn't happy they didn't protect her like I had."

"How did you protect Sienna?"

"Every day after class I followed her to make certain she didn't get into trouble. And to see that no one hurt her." He lifted his chin. "Sienna was my friend. She liked me and she liked the bracelet I made her. I shouldn't have gone home. When I left, there was no one who could watch out for her."

"But why did she need protecting?" I asked.

"Because she was younger than her friends. She was little. The others were much taller and bigger." He shook his head. "They treated her like she was a grown-up. But she wasn't."

Theo knew something significant, but how to extract the information from him? "How did they treat her like a grown-up?"

"They had parties after everyone went to bed." He moved closer to me. "Leah would use her special bird call and they would all come out. They would go into the woods together."

"The woods around BAS?"

He nodded.

"What did they do?"

"Drink. Dance. And they kissed each other." He flushed red. "They did other things."

Because Sienna's Bramble had initially been composed of four females and four males, I wasn't surprised the eight of them had paired off. I was curious about the specifics, however. "I know Sienna and Gordon were a romantic couple. And Christian was fond of a girl called Amanda, but she left the school early."

Theo nodded. "The girl who loved plants. She went into the woods to draw."

"What about Zack? He's the bald one."

"He had hair twenty years ago. Lots of hair. Almost the same color hair as Andrew and Dean. What happened to his hair? Did he get sick and lose it all?"

"He shaved it off." I rushed to go on, not wanting to dwell on Zack's hair, or lack of it. "Did Zack care for one of the girls more than the others?"

"Leah," Theo answered without hesitation. "She liked him, too. Only she liked Gordon more. But Gordon loved Sienna, so Leah spent a lot of time with Zack."

I thought about the group dynamics. "Does this mean Joel and Dawn were a couple?"

"Maybe," Theo said. "They hugged once in a while. But Dawn watched Gordon and Sienna when they didn't know she was there. I think Dawn loved Gordon more than Leah did."

"What about Joel?"

Theo scrunched up his face, as if he smelled something he didn't like. "Joel got angry all the time. And he yelled. Especially at Gordon."

"Why?"

"He liked Sienna, too. I watched them the first week we were there. They were happy together. That was before Gordon moved to the school."

As I feared, there was jealousy in the group over both Sienna's talent and Gordon's affection for her. Shades of the Evangeline Chaplin trial. Was envy behind every murderous deed? "Were you surprised Gordon took Sienna away from Joel?"

"No. Gordon was handsome. Like a prince in a fairy tale. Of course, Sienna would go with a prince and not with someone like Joel. Or me. But I wanted her to be safe. I followed them when I could. To make certain Sienna would be all right."

"And was she?"

"No one hurt her when I watched. Gordon was usually with Sienna. Maybe he was watching over her, too. But he should have stopped her from drinking. Sienna drank more than the others did. Even more than Zack, the man with no hair. I didn't remember his name until I saw him again. He drank every night when he was a student here. Sometimes he got sick. So did Sienna." Theo looked puzzled. "Why did they keep drinking if it made them feel bad?"

"I don't think they could help themselves," I said with a sigh. "Do you remember what they were drinking? Beer, wine? Something harder, like whisky or vodka?"

"I wasn't close enough to see what was in the bottles Gordon brought."

That brought my pacing to a halt. Gordon had indeed raided his family's wine cellars that summer, and why not? He had access to an entire vineyard's bounty. "Did they go off to the woods to party every night?"

"I don't know if it was every night. They went to the woods late. Sometimes I was tired and fell asleep in my cabin."

"Did Gordon have a car back then?"

"Not a car. What they called a little van. Black. With the family name on it."

It was no surprise Gordon had access to a vehicle twenty years ago. In this case, the family business's minivan.

"Sometimes I couldn't follow them because they all drove off in Gordon's van." Theo looked even unhappier. "I worried about Sienna when they did that. I couldn't protect her."

"That means they didn't always party at the school. They could have snuck off to the beach." My suspicions deepened. "Or to the woods on Gordon's farm."

"Do you think they took Sienna to where you found her body?" Theo asked.

"Someone brought her there. And she probably wouldn't have gone with anyone except her Bramble friends."

"Did one of them kill her?" His voice grew sharp. "One of her own friends?"

"I don't know." I began to pace again. "It's also possible she wasn't killed at all."

"But Sienna is dead," he cried out in alarm. "You found the body. She's dead."

"True. But you described how she drank heavily almost every night. So much so that she often got sick. What if she literally poisoned herself with alcohol during one of these parties?"

Tears welled up in his eyes. "Like those birds who get drunk from the berries and die."

"Yes. If any living thing drinks too much alcohol, it dies."

"Then her Bramble friends didn't kill her?"

"I didn't say that. I said it was possible she died accidentally." Lost in thought, I stared at the goldfinches fighting for a place at the sunflower seed feeders. "If it was an accident, her friends may have panicked and tried to cover up her death."

"They lied?"

"Oh, I bet they're all lying about Sienna's death. The only question is: Are they covering up a tragic accident, or a murder?" I took a deep breath. "You have to tell the police about what you saw at these secret parties where Sienna got drunk."

His eyes widened in fear. "I can't talk to the police. I won't."

"I'll talk to them first. I'll call the detective from the sheriff's department, Captain Holt. He's nice. You can trust him. And I'll be with you."

"I don't want to, Marlee."

"You do want to find out what happened to Sienna, don't you? Think how important it will be for her family to finally know the truth. After all, would Sienna have let me find her body in the woods if she didn't want everyone to know how she died?"

He shut his eyes. After a lengthy pause, he said, "You're right. I'll do it for Sienna."

"Good. Now I want you to do something for me. Go into

the cottage and pack some clothes. Until the BAS centenary is over, I don't want you staying by yourself. Whoever left the police cap and badge was doing more than playing a joke. They wanted to scare you. And I don't want you here alone when this person decides to frighten you again."

"But I don't want to go home to Illinois. I want to stay here and help Sienna."

"You're not going to Illinois. You're moving in with me for a few days. I have a house on the lake with plenty of bedrooms. You'll be safe there."

When I began walking toward the front yard, I felt relieved to hear Theo close behind.

"I can't do that, Marlee. It wouldn't be right. We're not married."

I chuckled. "This is a friendly invitation, not a romantic one."

"But I can't leave my birds. Who will feed them?"

"We'll stop by every day to fill the feeders." By this time we had reached his front porch. "Now please hurry and pack. I told my friends I'd meet them at the BAS art show tonight."

"I don't want to go to the art show. I don't want to see Gordon again."

"And I don't want you to, either," I told him. "That's why I need to get you settled in before I leave. No one will know where you've gone. If Captain Holt is at BAS today, I'll talk to him about what you told me. All you have to do tonight is relax at my house and watch TV." I smiled. "Or even bake. May as well get a head start on tomorrow's pastries."

"Marlee, you are a nice person," Theo said. "But you're not family. I can't stay with you. My father wouldn't like it. He knows I live at Crow Cottage and I should stay—"

"Tie me kangaroo down," a familiar voice rang out.

Theo looked around in alarm. I'd forgotten about Minnie.

The sound of a phone ringing was followed by "Helloooo. Where's the dog?"

"Who's saying that?" Theo asked with obvious trepidation.

"Minnie." I nodded toward the open windows of my car. "I brought her to the store today. She's in her cage at the moment, but I'm sure she wants to get home so I can let her out."

Upon hearing my voice, Minnie asked, "Where's Mommy?" This was followed by three whistles, the meow of a cat, and the sound of someone smacking their lips.

Theo's worried expression changed to one of bliss. "Minnie's your talking bird?"

"Yep, the singing one, too. And you can talk to her all night at my house. Although I'm sure she'll dominate the conversation."

He looked like a child who had just been gifted with a new puppy. "I want to meet her. Let me get some clothes and we can leave." Theo ran into the house before I could say a word.

The same couldn't be said for Minnie, who launched into another chorus of Ba-ba-ba ba-ba ba-ran.

Chapter 17

Like the day after Mardi Gras, vestiges of the previous night's luau remained. Discarded leis lay tossed over bushes, the charred remains of a hula skirt blew about the grass, and the limbo pole sat propped against the wall of the dining hall. The air also smelled faintly of barbecued pork. Aside from that, the rustic campus of the Blackberry Art School looked as it usually did. People painted at easels, sketched the shimmering bayou, or wandered among the striking sculpture pieces placed among the flower beds and blackberry bushes.

"Everything looks peaceful," I remarked to Emma and Tess. "Hardly seems possible there were two cases of alcohol poisoning last night, and a hula dancer who caught on fire."

"Let's hope the road rally goes off without a hitch," Tess said as we made our way up the winding path to the alumni art exhibit. "Otherwise Piper will take to her bed for weeks."

"Speaking of taking to her bed, how long before Alison recovers from last night's partying?" I asked. "When I got home today, she was huddled under the sheets with the shades drawn. All she wanted was weak tea and a damp cloth to put over her eyes."

Tess giggled. "How Victorian. She'll need a fainting couch next."

"She's embarrassed, although I'm sure her stomach and her head feel awful. Ali hasn't done anything like that since her bachelorette party." Emma brushed aside the branches of the bushes lining our path. "Too bad all of you missed today's activities here. We had kayak races after breakfast, a big picnic lunch on Oriole Beach, followed by a talk on campus by Luther Callan. He was incredible."

Luther Callan was the most famous artist to emerge from BAS. For four decades, he had been a giant in the art world, with his paintings found on the walls of the Museum of Modern Art and the Tate Modern. "I even spent some time with my watercolors after his talk," she continued. "And I haven't picked up a brush in years. But being around someone like Luther is inspiring."

Because of the centenary, BAS alumni were encouraged to use all the facilities on the campus, which included a first-rate printmaking studio. Ever since my attendance at the opening reception on Monday night, I had been itching to once again get my hands on the school's linoleum blocks, etching press, sharpening stones, and brayers.

I sighed. "I'd love to spend a few hours silk screening. But there's too much going on right now for that. And if Captain Holt isn't here tonight, I'll have to meet with him tomorrow. At least that gives me more time to prepare Theo to speak with the sheriff's department again."

"Are you sure it was a good idea to leave your baker at the house?" Emma had been there when Theo and I had arrived an hour ago. "He seems like a nervous type. And eventually Alison will get out of bed and wander into the kitchen. They might feel uncomfortable around each other."

"Theo feels uncomfortable around everyone." Tess shrugged. "Except for Marlee."

"They'll be fine. I stopped by the shop to pick up baking supplies on the way home. Theo will be kept busy baking." Although I wasn't certain how much baking would get done. I had left Theo sitting cross-legged on the floor, gazing up at Minnie in utter fascination as she sang, spoke, and danced along her perch. I knew from experience that "The Minnie Show" could be quite engrossing. And lengthy.

"By the way, your friend Piper has excellent taste," Emma said. "I saw her this afternoon. She was wearing a piece from my boss's resort collection. Here I thought I'd be the only one at BAS decked out in the latest Ralph Lauren." She looked down at her navy linen summer skirt and matching silk halter top.

Because I knew Emma would be sporting designer duds again, I'd taken the opportunity to change into a strapless jumpsuit of yellow seersucker when I went home to drop off Minnie and Theo. I'd also twisted my long hair into a loose chignon and donned enormous gold hoop earrings for a little drama. I didn't want Emma to think I'd grown so negligent about my appearance that I wore nothing but jeans and my Berry Basket apron . . . even if that was largely true.

At last, we reached the largest building on campus, which stood on a wooded knoll overlooking the bayou. Constructed to resemble a historic white barn in Oriole County, the structure was the size of an expansive ski lodge. The alumni's art exhibit had been set up inside, with towering metal sculptures ringing the exterior wooden walls. According to the centenary invitation, one art piece from every student would be on display; I wondered what long-ago print of mine they had chosen to exhibit.

When we entered, we were met with a crowd of people, all lit by the warming rays of the late afternoon sun. Birdsong could be heard through the open doorways and windows, while the air was perfumed with the aromas of pine and paint, a combination that always signaled Blackberry Art School to me.

I gazed upward. The barn studio was two stories high with a railing along the open second floor and a skylight illuminating the interior like a medieval cathedral. Every inch of space was taken up with paintings, watercolors, sketches, sculptures, mixed-media installations, pottery, glasswork, photographs, and much more. I felt tears sting my eyes. To think the natural beauty and unique spirit of Oriole Point had inspired all this.

"They have the artwork grouped according to summer sessions," Emma said.

I craned my neck to see better over the crowd. "I think our year is on the other side."

When we reached the tall southern wall, the three of us smiled at the sight of what we had created as boisterous teenagers.

"Better than I remember." Tess stared at her fluted amber glass vase. "Although the lip is clumsy. I think I used the wrong carbon rod. Of course, I was only fifteen."

Not surprisingly, her work as a teenager was more sophisticated than ours. However, Emma's watercolor of the sunset over the bayou and my silk-screened blueberries were nothing to apologize for. I also found it amusing my artwork had been inspired by berries. We chuckled over Alison's black ceramic bowl decorated with turquoise dots. The only clay our friend had learned to successfully throw that summer was a bowl; all of them covered in turquoise dots. Turquoise was still her favorite color.

While Tess and Emma checked out pieces created by the rest of our Bramble, I decided to see what BAS had exhibited of Andrew and Dean. As expected, each brother's work was represented by an oil canvas: Andrew's an abstract swirl of different shades of blue, Dean's an exact copy in beige and cream. I suspected the Cabot boys never had any serious interest in painting, but only wanted to hang out with the artsy bayou kids for a summer.

I glanced down at my watch. Ryan was supposed to meet me here at seven. And I expected Little Pete and the Ohio cousins to be with him. They were a friendly bunch, and I didn't mind, especially since BAS was hosting a fish fry tonight. I had called Ryan to ask him to accompany me to my meeting with Zack. Although he agreed to come with me, I sensed his disapproval. Because Ryan was also a big perch fan, I hoped he would be in a better mood once the fish fry was under way.

After exchanging words with several local alumni, I scanned the barn in search of Sienna's Bramble friends. The next best thing would be finding the artwork of Sienna Katsaros and her fellow students from that session. I had a particular interest in seeing what Theo had produced all those years ago.

It took a while before I realized their year was exhibited upstairs. When I reached the top floor, I stopped cold. At the far wall hung a large oil painting at least seven feet wide. Unlike the oils of Andrew and Dean, this had technique and passion behind every brushstroke. As I walked closer to the painting, a sunbeam from the skylight hit it in such a way that a corner of the canvas became invisible behind the illumination. It had an unsettling effect given that the subject of the painting was a young woman painting at an easel. Because the slim, brunette girl resembled the photos of Sienna, I knew it was a self-portrait. But the sunbeam kept obscuring her face, as if the ghost of Sienna wanted to hide from my curious gaze by wrapping herself in sunlight.

"I told you she was talented." Joel MacGregor came to stand beside me, his attention fixed on the painting.

"I see now why she won all the prizes that year."

"The most gifted of anyone here. Maybe the nicest, too. I

don't think that happens often. Most talented people are full of themselves. Arrogant, entitled, egotistical."

"I don't think you have to be talented to be full of yourself. Or arrogant."

Joel threw me a jaundiced look. "You do love to challenge people. I'm glad you weren't a student here when I was. We wouldn't have gotten along. You irritate me."

"The feeling's mutual."

He snickered. "Yeah, you definitely would not have fit in with our Bramble group. You probably weren't even a talented artist."

"And you're a real charmer." I narrowed my eyes at him. "I'm curious. What was your berry nickname back then? Everyone gets one. What was yours? Given your engaging personality, I'm trying to think of a berry with an unpleasant flavor."

"Ha-ha." Crossing his arms, Joel returned his attention to Sienna's painting.

"No, really. I'm curious. My nickname was 'Razzy' because I did this a lot." I made a loud raspberry sound.

"Why does that not surprise me?" He screwed up his face for a moment, as if deciding whether to tell me. "I choked on a fish bone the first week I was at the school. So my nickname was taken from chokeberry."

"You were called 'Choke'?"

He smirked. "They pronounced it 'Jhoke,' to make it closer to Joel. Stupid tradition. I don't know why any of us went along with it."

"How about Christian? What was his berry name?"

Joel nodded at a landscape filled with rain-swept trees and a dark sky glowering overhead. "That's Christian's. What do you feel when you look at it?"

The landscape vibrated with an uneasy energy. I could see why Christian's paintings had disturbed Theo. I did think

Christian was talented, and I admired the bold thickness of the brushstrokes, the fierce mounds of paint that stood a half inch from the surface, and the sense of doom imparted by the approaching storm.

"Sad." I recalled how Theo had said Christian was blue when I first visited him at Crow Cottage. "He was nicknamed after the blueberry, wasn't he?"

"Yes. Back then, we didn't know Christian suffered from clinical depression." Joel seemed disgusted. "There were a lot of things we didn't know that summer."

"Even as teens, you must have known Zack drank too much."

"We all drank too much. But Zack was the worst. 'Wino' was his idiotic berry name."

"After wineberry," I murmured.

"He wasn't half bad as a potter, at least when he was sober or not suffering from a hangover. That's his work over there." Joel led me to a pedestal around the corner where three pieces of pottery were displayed. One was a large raku platter, another a green pitcher, and the third a blue oblong bowl.

"The raku is Zack's. Like I said, he was an okay potter. But Zack wasn't as good as your strange little baker. You might be interested to know the blue bowl was made by Theo."

I moved closer to examine the most polished piece of pottery in this section. The sapphire blue bowl had a sweeping, even daring, flow to it. And the feathery half-moon shapes decorating the bowl's surface gave it a surprising elegance. I first assumed the shapes were an abstract design, but a closer look revealed the curves of white were actually birds gliding over the blue surface of the bowl as if soaring in a ceramic sky. Like Sienna's painting, Theo's bowl hummed with beauty, grace, and intention. It was the work of a true artist, and I felt saddened that neither of them had been able to use their talent beyond summer school.

"What a shame Theo stopped making pottery," I said.

He snorted. "Sienna never stopped praising him. The girl was much too sweet."

"Why was she kind to him? The rest of you take every opportunity to make insulting comments about Theo. Yet Sienna appears to have genuinely liked him."

Joel ran a restless hand through his tangled shoulder-length hair. "Her younger brother was autistic. And Sienna adored her brother. Theo reminded her of him."

The more I learned about Sienna Katsaros, the sadder her untimely death seemed. She had been a gifted, loving, kind young girl. How tragic such a promising life had been brutally cut short. "Do you know what berry inspired Theo's nickname? Assuming he had one."

"'Cloudberry.' Sienna gave him the nickname because his head always seemed to be in the clouds. We called him the 'Cloud Boy.' A polite way of saying he was simpleminded."

"Please stop saying that. It isn't true. Why are you determined to belittle him?"

"I'm being honest. If you don't like what I have to say, then leave me alone."

"You're the one who approached me tonight."

"Big mistake," he said with a mocking smile. "Which I shall rectify by walking away."

With a sense of relief, I watched Joel disappear into the crowd. Although part of me wished he had remained a bit longer. I hadn't learned all I wanted to from him. And I still hadn't caught sight of Kit Holt or Detective Trejo tonight. I doubted they had finished their investigative work at BAS. As I had told Theo, either one of Sienna's Bramble had murdered her, or they were somehow complicit in her death, which could have been accidental. That latest theory seemed more likely. The only motive for killing Sienna would have been jealousy over her relationship with Gordon. But why kill her just as she and the rest of the BAS students were about to go their separate ways?

Since I was standing in the area devoted to the session Sienna had attended BAS, I searched for the pieces belonging to Dawn and Leah. After reading a dozen identifying tags, I found Dawn's white and burgundy wall hanging, its woven surface decorated with a large mandala and a thin border of tiny stars. But no matter how long I stared at it, it didn't give me any insight into Dawn's character.

While searching for Leah's artwork, I stumbled upon a mixed-media piece by Joel. It seemed a confusing jumble of Barbie dolls, gardening tools, newspaper print, and dried grasses. Yet there was a surprising wit to the decorated wooden box. Along with a touch of whimsy. I couldn't imagine how the sour Joel of today ever created such a piece.

"Now where is Leah's?" I murmured.

A moment later, my eyes fell on a wall tag with her name on it. Beside it hung a pretty watercolor of Adirondack chairs along the banks of a river. No people appeared in the painting, but several gorgeous Canada geese took center stage. When I bent to examine her signature in the corner of the piece, I noticed a small goose painted beside "L. Malek." Thinking back to my discussion with Joel about the berry nicknames, I wondered if Leah had been nicknamed after the gooseberry. Perhaps she had a fondness for the birds, which were seen everywhere along the river and bayou in Oriole Point. After all, she did teach Theo bird calls. She was probably a bird lover like Theo and me.

If Joel was here, maybe the others were, too. As I scanned the crowd, I spotted Gordon Sanderling watching me from the other side of the exhibition space. Even though I was surrounded by dozens of chattering people, I grew tense when he walked toward me. If only Kit Holt would once again show up. He'd become my personal law enforcement genie.

"You can't help yourself," Gordon said when he reached me. I found him physically intimidating. Not surprising given that he was much taller than I was, and many pounds heavier. It was like a gargantuan boulder had rolled to a stop in my path.

"What do you mean?"

"There's an entire barn filled with artwork from decades of BAS seasons. Yet here you are, paying close attention to the pieces made by Sienna and the rest of us."

"I was curious." I took a deep breath. "I wanted to see if what the seven of you produced twenty years ago held any clues as to the people you've all become."

"Liar. You're hoping to find clues as to how Sienna died. Did you? I'm betting you didn't." He shook his head. "That's because all you'll see are pieces of art created by teenagers during one long-ago summer. Nothing more. But you'll keep digging up the past, hoping to find something incriminating. You're worse than the police."

The mention of the police reminded me of the badge and cap left at Theo's. "Did you pay a visit to Theo's cottage today to leave him a little gift?" I didn't shrink from his hostile gaze. "Or should I refer to it as a threat?"

"I don't know what you're talking about. Although I'm beginning to think you're as out of touch with reality as Theo is."

"Maybe you should call him 'Cloud Boy,' like all of you did twenty years ago." I noticed Gordon seemed surprised I knew this. I jerked a thumb at Leah's watercolor behind me. "And I'm guessing Leah's berry nickname was taken from the gooseberry."

Gordon looked as if he wanted to leave my presence as much as Joel did, but he was made of sterner stuff. "How astute. But then you went to BAS. You know about the berry nicknames. Yeah, Leah was called 'Goosey' because she loved to paint the geese on campus."

"Since you were the oldest in your Bramble group, your nickname was probably derived from the elderberry."

"Sorry, Sherlock. Dawn got the elderberry nickname." He seemed pleased I'd gotten it wrong. "I may have been older than her, but Dawn was the most mature of all of us. And I doubt even your wild guessing would be able to come up with the berry that inspired my nickname."

I stared back at him. He had jowls, a double chin, and a hooded gaze. Yet now that I'd seen the photo of Gordon as he'd been two decades ago, I could glimpse echoes of the remarkable good looks he once possessed. "You were nicknamed after the beautyberry. They probably called you 'Beauty.'"

I knew I was right by the shocked expression on Gordon's face. "As for Sienna's berry nickname, that's easy," I went on. "I've been told she was so talented that everyone at BAS called her 'the bane of their existence.' Her nickname came from the baneberry, didn't it?"

Gordon's face twisted with so much pain and hatred that I caught my breath. I fought the sudden urge to flee. "Stop talking about Sienna. You have no right."

"I mentioned you, Leah, and Theo, not just Sienna. As for Christian, Dawn, Zack—"

"You've already worked your charm on Zack. He's hitting the bottle again."

"Zack's drinking because he still hasn't gotten over what happened to Sienna."

"And what happened to her? Tell me."

"I don't know. Maybe she was murdered."

"And who murdered her? Do you think it was me? Zack perhaps? Maybe Leah or Dawn? Then there's Christian and Joel." His expression turned even more bitter. "Let's not forget Theo. Yes, his family swears he was with them the day she disappeared, but where's the proof?"

"Theo did not kill Sienna. He had no reason to want her dead."

"Really? And what's the motive behind Sienna's murder? Maybe that's what you should be searching for, not imaginary clues left in the artwork of teenagers."

I was about to reply when Gordon turned his attention to something over my shoulder.

"What's wrong? What are you staring at?" I followed his gaze to a mixed-media installation near the piece made by Joel. "Is that yours?"

Gordon nodded, his face ashen.

The tag beside the large installation piece called it "The Faux Generation," identifying Gordon Sanderling as the artist. I didn't understand why he appeared troubled. Maybe he was embarrassed by what he'd produced as a twenty-year-old. While it didn't seem to have any real thought behind it, it wasn't that bad. A small kitchen faucet protruded from the top of a large wooden board decorated with felt trees, a ball of twine, deer antlers, rusted gears, old coins, empty wine bottles, and a stuffed pheasant. As if the work wasn't odd enough, the stuffed bird was impaled with a large shiny knife.

"Why are you upset? Was this a piece you didn't like?"

"My artwork never included a knife," he said hoarsely. "Someone put it there."

I frowned. "The BAS administrators should know someone is vandalizing the art."

But Gordon didn't seem to have heard me. Instead, he slowly backed up, his eyes never leaving the knife plunged into the bird.

"Gordon, are you all right?"

After a last stricken look, he rushed down the exhibit gallery stairs and disappeared. I turned to Gordon's artwork again. Did the same person who left the badge and police cap at Theo's door also place the knife in the stuffed bird? If so, the knife was as much a warning as the badge and cap had been.

And if Sienna had been murdered, the knife meant her killer was here.

Chapter 18

While Gordon had been frightened by the dagger in the stuffed pheasant, I was more disturbed at the sight of a shotgun lying on the truck's backseat.

I turned to Ryan. "Since when do you carry a gun in your pickup?"

"Since you called earlier today asking me to come with you to this meeting." He briefly took his eyes off the road to throw me a stern look. "A meeting with a stranger who may have had something to do with that girl's death twenty years ago. You're lucky I didn't bring a shotgun for you to carry. Not that you'd know how to use one."

"Of course I don't. I'm not Annie Oakley. And I'm against hunting."

He chuckled. "You do know me and my brothers go deer hunting every year."

"Don't expect me to eat any venison when you get back."

"You will eventually. My family's been cooking up venison for generations. We'll wear you down. One day you might even want to come hunting with us. Beth joined us one weekend with her bow and arrow. She brought down a doe."

"For the record, I am never shooting a doe. Or any other animal."

"Well, I'd certainly prefer you hunt for game than hunt for killers." His smile vanished. "This is a stupid thing we're doing. Meeting up with this Zack guy. Although now that I've learned he shoved you last night, I might shove *him* around."

"Please don't. He didn't know what he was doing. I told you, Zack's an alcoholic. And he fell off the wagon."

"No excuse for him to lay his hands on you. If I'd been there, I would have punched him. I don't know why you didn't come looking for me right after it happened."

I saw no reason to explain that he had been gorging on pork ribs and Zellar family gossip at the time. At least for the moment, he had left his cousins back at the BAS fish fry, although I doubted he was happy about that. This evening was not turning out as planned. My conversations with Joel and Gordon hadn't just left me troubled; there was something about the berry nicknames that nagged at me. I was repeating them to myself when my phone alerted me to a text.

"Let me guess," Ryan said. "One of the Cabot boys is asking about the road rally."

"Not this time. It's the officer from the sheriff's department I told you about." I scrolled through Holt's text message. "I called him about Gordon's art piece being vandalized. He's at the fish fry right now. Kit and Detective Trejo spoke with Gordon after we left."

"Kit?"

"Captain Holt's first name. Actually it's Atticus, but his friends call him 'Kit.'"

Ryan lifted an eyebrow at me. "Exactly how close are you with this guy?"

"Kit Holt is one of the lead officers on the Katsaros case. Along with Trejo."

"I don't notice you calling Trejo by his first name."

"Believe me, Greg Trego isn't the type you'd care to be on a first-name basis with. Anyway, I've spent a fair amount of time with both of them this past week. Whenever I learn something new, I call them."

"I'm guessing you call 'Kit' first."

I threw my phone back into my purse. "I'm helping Kit Holt and the other law enforcement officers with the case. And you know my tolerance for the jealous boyfriend act is low. So please stop before you say something you'll regret." Indeed, I spent a lurid and well-publicized year in court after being dragged into the Chaplin murder trial back in New York. A murder triggered by a jealous spouse. It left me skittish about any signs of jealous behavior.

Ryan surprised me with an affectionate smile. "Sorry, babe. But I can't help myself. I know other guys are looking at you all the time. Why wouldn't they? You're beautiful." He caressed my bare shoulder. "Even if you do have your mom's Italian temper."

"This is why you should be glad I *don't* know how to shoot."

We both laughed. I reached for his hand and gave it a squeeze.

As the first raindrops fell, I turned from Ryan to look out the truck's window. The rapidly darkening sky was not only because of the approaching sunset. The rain that had been predicted seemed to be right on time. I hoped the storm held off until after my meeting with Zack. I also hoped Ryan didn't make a habit of carrying shotguns in his truck whenever he felt threatened. Although I shouldn't have been surprised Ryan brought a gun.

Oriole County was predominantly rural, filled with farms and orchards. And the state forest swarmed with hunters every autumn, as did some of the private hunting grounds in the area. Every family owned at least one shotgun, usually more. I'd gone to school with lots of boys who hunted and fished. And a fair number of girls as well. But once my parents and I moved to our house on the lake, most of my time was spent in a village populated by artists and free spirits. Then I went to live in New York City, where I'd grown accustomed to men who boasted degrees from Ivy League schools, along with an expert knowledge of the stock market and which bars made the best artisan cocktails. My urban romances had not ended well, however, and I wasn't longing for a return to tailored business suits and big-city cynicism.

In fact, what had attracted me to Ryan was his sheer intoxicating maleness. Michigan didn't have cowboys, but the Zellar brothers were the closest thing to it. All five of them were tall, handsome, muscular, and tanned. And although they were alpha males, none of them possessed a domineering or mean streak. Yes, Ryan's tendency to be jealous was worrying. And he continued to assume I was in total agreement with the plans he was making for our future, despite my protestations. But he and I were in our thirties. Both of us wanted a long-term relationship, especially since he went through a bad divorce six years earlier. Now seemed the perfect time to take the next step. We loved each other, and there was definitely sexual chemistry between us. I'd be a fool not to marry him. At the moment, I was wondering if I'd been a fool to ask him to accompany me to my meeting with Zack.

"When we get to the farm market, let me do all the talking," I said to Ryan. "Zack doesn't know I'm bringing anyone and you might make him nervous."

"We're the ones who should be nervous. I'll pull the truck up to him in the parking lot and you can talk to him from where you're sitting. This way, I've got the gun at arm's reach."

"Ryan, we don't need a shoot-out at the farm market. Besides, he isn't going to kill us in front of everyone. And the sun hasn't even set yet. It's still light out." But due to the approaching storm system, that was no longer true. We lived so far west in the state that sunset along Lake Michigan

arrived later here than it did in the rest of the Eastern Time
Zone. However, the thickening clouds had now put us into
twilight.

"If this rain keeps up, it will get dark fast." Ryan hit the automatic button to close the truck windows. A moment later,
he switched on the windshield wipers.

"Dark or not, there are sure to be people at Red Tree. We're
perfectly safe talking with him in the market. And the farther
we get from your shotgun, the safer I'll feel." I looked at it
again. "I'm assuming it's loaded."

"A gun's not much good if it isn't." Ryan braked to a stop at
a four-way flashing light. "I'm serious, Marlee. Stay out of this
business after tonight. The state police and the sheriff are on the
case. They don't need some shop owner getting in their way."

"I'm not getting in their way," I said as Ryan began driving
once more. "And Zack came to me. I think he wants to give
me information to pass on to the police."

"I don't care what he wants. Meeting with a drunken stranger
about a possible murder is crazy." He shook his head. "I
would have thought you'd had enough close calls after the
Bowman murder."

"There have been no close calls for anyone this time," I reassured him as Red Tree Farm Market came into view. "Besides, I'll be too busy for the rest of the week to get involved
after this. The road rally's on Friday."

"Good. I can't wait for the BAS centenary to be over. Although it's been great seeing Little Pete and the others. And
the food at the luau was great. But I don't want to spend my
time worrying about your safety."

"I'll be fine," I said as we pulled into the parking lot. The
market itself was a large roofed space open on two sides. Inside
were open crates of fresh fruit and vegetables. Pails of cut sunflowers lined the outer walls of the market, and a refrigeration
unit that contained pies and locally sourced grass-fed beef

ran along an inner wall. Attached to the market was a small building that held an ice cream parlor, with lots of picnic tables outside.

The rain now turned into a steady downpour. Luckily, it was no more than twenty steps to the shelter of the farm market and the adjacent ice cream parlor. Armed with the umbrella Ryan kept in his truck, I ran for cover. Ryan trotted after me, ignoring the rain that caused his dark T-shirt to cling to his upper body. If I wasn't so bent on looking for Zack Burwell, I would have taken a few moments to enjoy the tempting sight.

Once inside the market, I checked out the people wandering among the crates of fruit and vegetables. I also eyed the picnic tables. Despite the rain, many of them were filled with families enjoying sundaes and ice cream cones under the striped table umbrellas. I didn't see Zack anywhere. I recalled how he said he'd be driving Christian Naylor's rental car: a yellow Jeep. At least I wouldn't be able to miss him when he did show up.

"Is he here?" Ryan asked.

I shook my head. "We're a little early. He'll probably show up soon."

"Do you want a milkshake? We left before I had a chance to get to the dessert table."

"Sounds good to me." I had a fondness for the Red Tree's strawberry milkshakes, even if The Berry Basket used all natural ingredients and Red Tree didn't. Occasionally, those unhealthy additives were exactly what my taste buds craved.

After Ryan and I got our shakes, he and I waited beneath the white awning that ran along the front of the building. I was thankful there was no wind because the rain suddenly came down in buckets. If we'd been driving, we would have had to pull over until the downpour lessened. But the awning protected us from the rain and it was quite cozy standing there with Ryan as we made small talk and sipped our milkshakes.

I took a quick glance at my watch. It was well after nine o'clock. Zack was a no-show.

The lights around the market flashed three times.

"That's it." Ryan finished the last of his shake. "Looks like they're closing a little early because of the rain."

"Sorry to make you waste all this time for nothing."

He smoothed back my hair. "Anything to keep my girl safe."

A wave of tenderness swept over me, and I pulled him toward me for a kiss. This led to several more, each one growing more ardent.

"Definitely time to go home," he said in a husky voice. "I know you've got three houseguests. How about a fourth?"

I hugged him. "Any time."

The downpour had slowed to a steady shower. Huddled beneath Ryan's umbrella, we ran back to the pickup. Like two high school kids, we made out for a few minutes in his truck. I never could resist the combination of a warm summer night, a strawberry milkshake, and a cute boy. Only in this case, it was a cute man. My man.

When Ryan finally started up the truck, I sat back, relaxed and happy. As the rain streamed down the windows, I closed my eyes, ready to enjoy the drive back to my house. I had no idea what made Zack change his mind. Nor did I know who had stuck that knife in Gordon's art piece. But I'd done all I could. Ryan was right. It was time to stay clear of the whole Sienna case, along with the people who once called themselves her friends.

As we drove down the two-lane highway, Ryan switched on his radio and Miranda Lambert's hit song "Heart Like Mine" came on. Both of us began to hum along, but the relaxed mood was broken by the wail of sirens. I sat up as the sirens grew closer.

"Police." Ryan looked in his rearview mirror, swerving onto the shoulder as two police cars sped past.

"Hope it's not an accident. The rain came down pretty strong for a while. I'm sure it made driving hazardous." I was relieved the rain had slowed to a light shower.

At the next turn at Blue Star and West Pine, two parked state police cars and several troopers came into view. So did a car smashed against the wide tree that stood guard there.

A wave of fear washed over me. "Pull over, Ryan."

"Are you crazy? It's a car accident. This has nothing to do with us."

"I think the vehicle might be a yellow Jeep."

Ryan pulled onto the shoulder of the road and rolled to a stop. I jumped out as an ambulance drove up. One of the troopers waved at me. "Get back in your vehicle, miss."

"Officer, I may know the driver. We were supposed to meet someone at the Red Tree Farm Market, but he never showed up. And I expected him to be driving a yellow Jeep."

We both turned as if to verify the crumpled vehicle was indeed a yellow Jeep. I caught a partial glimpse of the driver, unmoving and covered in blood. I felt faint as the EMS attendants began to extricate the man from the car.

"Is that the guy you were going to meet?" Ryan asked me.

"I don't know." All I could see now were the backs of the rescue team. I wasn't certain I wanted to see any more than that.

"What else can you tell me?" I heard another trooper say.

I looked over to see an officer speaking with a distraught older man with a clipped white beard. "I can't say much more than I've told you. The Jeep was in front of me."

"Was the driver of the Jeep speeding?" the officer asked.

"No." The bearded fellow shook his head. "The rain was coming down like a hurricane. Could barely see past my wipers. Only a fool would be going fast in that kind of weather.

Then a fool did just that. Someone sped past and nearly ran me off the road."

"Did you see the accident?"

"As best I could with the rain pouring down. This person tried to pass the Jeep next. But it mistook the distance between the two vehicles and sideswiped it instead. Sent the driver of the Jeep right into a tree." The man shuddered. "The other person kept on driving. Didn't even slow down. If the crash victim is dead, that speeding driver should be charged with murder."

"What can you tell me about this speeding car, sir? License plate? Model?"

"Like I said, I could barely see out my window because of the rain. And it was dark due to the storm clouds. I only saw a vehicle speed past me. It all happened so quick."

Ryan cleared his throat. "Officer, we believe my fiancée may know the man who was driving the crashed vehicle. His name is Zack Burwell."

Unable to watch the EMS people pull the driver's body out, I focused instead on the state trooper. For the first time, I wished Detective Trejo had shown up for this emergency.

The trooper turned his attention to us. "Does Mr. Burwell live in the area?"

"He's visiting from out of state." I dreaded my next question. "Is he dead?"

The officer threw me a suspicious look but must have seen the concern and fear on my face. "He was breathing when we got here. But his injuries look critical."

Ryan patted me on the back while I shut my eyes and uttered a quick prayer. I heard the sound of men walking toward me. I didn't know if I wanted to see what condition Zack was in.

"Miss, we need you to tell us if this is Mr. Burwell."

Steeling myself, I opened my eyes. The crash victim was strapped to the stretcher, a white sheet covering most of his body. My knees buckled and Ryan grabbed me by the elbow.

"Do you know this man?" the trooper asked as they wheeled the gurney past us. "Is the crash victim Zack Burwell?"

"It's not Zack." I felt stunned. "But I do know him. His name is Christian Naylor."

Chapter 19

I was grateful Oriole Point Hospital had recently been renovated. Especially since the updates included a spacious ER waiting room. The space was needed tonight. State troopers and members of the sheriff's department marched back and forth from the waiting area past the automatic doors leading to the ER exam rooms. There were six law enforcement officers in attendance, including Kit Holt and Detective Trejo. Sienna's old friends from BAS were here as well, with the worrying exception of Zack. Gordon, Leah, Joel, and Dawn had drawn four armchairs into a circle and sat huddled together near a bank of vending machines.

BAS president Tina Kapoor held court in the opposite corner of the waiting area, surrounded by four members of the school planning committee. I was indirectly responsible for her being here. Given the seriousness of Christian's condition, his next of kin needed to be informed as soon as possible. Only I didn't have the phone numbers for any of Sienna's former BAS friends. I had no choice but to call Piper and ask her to pass on the upsetting news to Tina.

Once Piper got over her initial shock, she launched into an impassioned tirade about how all her efforts for the BAS centenary were being ruined. Aware that Christian might not make it through the night, I hung up on her. This was not the time for Piper's ego to take center stage. A reporter from the *Oriole Point Messenger* was also in the waiting room, moving from one beige couch to the other, asking questions. Gillian's father was about to be scooped again.

Since arriving at the hospital, I'd done nothing but answer questions put to me by everyone from the art school administrators to Detective Trejo. In turn, I had alerted Tess and told her to pass the news on to Emma and Alison. I'd wait until I got home before relating any of this to Theo. I'd already been to the chapel, and considered going back again. Meanwhile I paced, restless and worried, as we waited for the outcome of Christian's surgery.

I wasn't pacing alone. Both Detective Trejo and Kit Holt flanked me as we walked from the circular information desk to the floor-length windows that looked out on a meditation garden. Both men were true to form: Trejo stoic and brusque, Holt reassuring and friendly. But this time Holt seemed puzzled to see me here. And as unhappy with my reason why as Ryan had been.

"Agreeing to meet Zack Burwell, or any friends of Sienna's, was foolhardy. You should have called me as soon as he made this request." It was the fifth time Holt said this to me.

"You should have called both of us," Trejo corrected. The state police at the accident site had instructed Ryan and me to follow them to the hospital. Soon after arriving, Holt and Trejo had shown up. While it was nice to see familiar faces—in particular Kit Holt's—they also felt entitled to lecture me. And I was not in the mood for lectures. I still hadn't gotten over my shock that it was Christian who was in the yellow Jeep tonight, not Zack. He must have been coming to meet me at Red Tree Market. But why him and not Zack, as we had arranged?

I looked over at the wide doors that led to the ER exam rooms. "When we will know if he's going to make it?"

"It could be hours," Trejo replied. "Now tell us again why you were at the Red Tree Market tonight."

With a sigh, I launched into my explanation of how Zack had visited my shop earlier.

"Was Mr. Naylor with him?" Holt asked.

"Like I said before, they were together. I thought they came so Zack could apologize for his behavior at the luau. Which he did. But when Christian went to buy ice cream, Zack asked me to meet him tonight. And he didn't want Christian to know about our meeting. Somehow Christian found out."

"Why do you say that?" Holt asked.

"It's the only thing that explains what Christian was doing tonight only a half mile from the farm market. He and the other alumni who knew Sienna are staying on the BAS campus. Except for Gordon. Why would Christian be on Blue Star Highway heading in the direction of the place I agreed to meet Zack at? It doesn't make sense. And where is Zack? The others are here." I waved at the group on the other side of the room.

Dawn, Gordon, Leah, and Joel were now holding hands. Their heads were bent and I wasn't certain if they were whispering among themselves or praying. I hoped it was the latter. Christian needed our prayers. Joel raised his head and caught me staring at them. When he shot me a vicious look, I understood why suspicious people spoke of giving someone the "evil eye."

"They blame me for this." The thought made my spirits sink even further.

When Trejo and Holt looked at the group, Joel averted his gaze. "You weren't the one driving the car that sideswiped Mr. Naylor," said Holt, "and they know it."

"They also know their buddy Zack is nowhere to be found," Trejo added.

"What if something awful happened to Zack, too?" The

idea made me even sicker. "This is one unlucky group. First, Sienna disappears and is found years later buried in the woods. Then a mysterious driver runs Christian off the road. Now Zack is missing."

Holt shook his head. "Not missing. At least not yet. According to Leah Malek, he left the BAS fish fry at approximately half past eight. He told her he had a headache and wanted to take a long walk. She assumed he was suffering from a hangover due to last night's drinking and didn't think there was anything strange about him leaving."

"I think he left to come meet me," I said.

"And what was Mr. Naylor doing on Blue Star Highway?" Trejo wore a skeptical expression.

"Maybe he was coming to see me, too."

"If everyone was on their way to see you, why did no one ever show up?"

I met Trejo's frustrated gaze with one of my own. "Christian probably would have shown up if someone hadn't tried to kill him."

"Then you believe the driver who sideswiped Mr. Naylor did so deliberately, and with malicious intent."

"Yes, I do."

"Why?" Holt asked.

"It's connected to Sienna's murder." I looked over again at Sienna's old friends. "I think all of them know exactly what happened to their friend twenty years ago. And they're covering for each other. Either Zack or Christian was about to come clean tonight. Now Christian is fighting for his life, and Zack is missing. Seems like the group is being killed off one by one. And don't give me your icy state trooper stare, Detective Trejo. You know I'm right."

Holt and Trejo glanced at each other. Surprisingly, it was Trejo who broke into a smile. "I may agree with you, Ms. Jacob. But until we have proof, I prefer to keep my poker face. Now excuse me while I speak with Mr. Sanderling and his BAS buddies once more."

I turned to Holt after he walked away. "If that's his poker face, it must be like playing cards with Dracula."

"He's frustrated. We both are. The last thing we want is for another dead body connected with BAS to turn up. That's why I wasn't happy to hear you had agreed to meet Mr. Burwell alone tonight."

Not again, I thought. "But I didn't go alone. I asked Ryan to go along. And he's more than enough protection." At the moment, he didn't seem like the best security. Accustomed to rising at dawn, Ryan was now snoring in a comfy chair by the window. I was glad Trejo and Holt were here. I'd been dealing with the fallout from Sienna's death by myself and it was draining. Especially with the bad vibes directed at me from Gordon and his friends.

The vibes in the waiting room shifted over into frantic with Piper's noisy arrival. "This is unacceptable," she announced. "I can't imagine what apocalyptic event will take place next."

Holt and I both took deep breaths as Piper headed straight for us. Two steps behind walked her husband, Lionel. It was like watching Queen Elizabeth enter a room, trailed by Prince Philip. I had a suspicion that when Lionel's turn as mayor ended, Piper would run for office next.

"They are an odd couple," Holt murmured as the couple drew near.

"Because Piper is a blond WASP and Lionel is African American?" I asked.

"No. Because Mayor Pierce seems urbane, gentle, and civilized. And his wife is—" He seemed at a loss for words.

"A crazy, demanding narcissist?" I finished for him.

"That sounds about right."

Piper descended on us in all her embattled and self-serving

glory. "Please tell me that you have no further bad news about Mr. Naylor." She aimed a warning look at Holt.

"We know little more than we did when Mr. Naylor was brought to the hospital. He has suffered multiple injuries: four broken ribs, spinal bruising, a broken collarbone and shoulder, a punctured lung, and internal bleeding. But the doctors are primarily concerned about his head injury. He could be in surgery for another two or three hours."

If he survives that long, I thought to myself. For a moment I felt sympathy for Piper. I had been looking forward to the BAS centenary. It was a chance to reconnect with old friends, revisit teenage memories, and enjoy a boost in business. How did everything fall apart so quickly?

"Have his family been notified?" Lionel asked.

"We're tracking down his parents and sister in Atlanta," Holt answered. "His friends from BAS told us that he's divorced with no children. No information on his ex-wife."

"If anyone knows personal details about Christian, it will be Zack," I told Holt. "They were the only ones from their BAS summer who kept in touch."

"We'll certainly ask Mr. Burwell for this information, as soon as he shows up," Holt said. "Meanwhile we're trying to contact his business associates in San Diego. Unfortunately, Mr. Naylor's cell phone was destroyed in the crash, so we can't use the information stored there."

Lionel furrowed his brow. He was an imposing man with a distinctive profile and large dark eyes. At the moment, he seemed almost Lincolnesque. "If Mr. Burwell is missing, perhaps something untoward has happened to him."

Piper sniffed. "Or he is behind the accident today. Marlee told me how Mr. Naylor's car was sideswiped. Out of all the people who drank too much at the luau, Zack Burwell was the worst. And I'd bet he was drinking tonight. He probably went after Naylor in his car while drunk behind the wheel."

"Why would he do that?" I asked Piper.

"I have no idea. I do know I don't enjoy being hauled out of bed at midnight because something awful has again happened to a BAS student. Bad enough Marlee found a skeleton last week. Then one of my hula dancers went up in flames because of an untrained fire-eater. Now another person connected with the school is lying at death's door. At this rate, there won't be anyone left to compete in the road rally."

"We may have to cancel it. If Christian dies, I don't see how we can do anything else."

Piper looked at me as if I had suggested we hold our annual Oktoberfest banquet at Burger King. "You can't be serious. I've spent months coming up with clues for the event. And thirty-five cars will be competing Friday night. The rally has been promoted as far away as St. Louis. We cannot cancel it. Absolutely not. If I did, who do you imagine will come to Oriole Point to take part in next year's rally? No one."

"But if Mr. Naylor—" Lionel started to say.

"We are not canceling," Piper interrupted in a steely voice. "Even if I fall off the bluff and die before Friday, the Blackberry Road Rally will go on." Her blue eyes bored into mine. "Do you understand, Marlee? No matter what, one of us will see the rally proceeds as planned."

"If you say so." I gave her a warning look. "Although maybe neither of us should stand too close to the bluff before then."

Holt grinned but stopped as soon as he glanced over Lionel's shoulder. A man with a shaved head walked by the information desk. Although his hands were stuffed in his jeans pockets, he appeared to be shaking.

"Mr. Burwell," Holt said in a loud voice.

Zack turned in our direction. The bright lights in the waiting room revealed how ill he looked. There was a yellowish cast to his face, and dark circles beneath his eyes. For a moment he froze at the sight of Holt's uniform. Then he saw me and seemed to recoil even more.

Dawn cried out, "Zack, thank God you're here. We've been worried sick."

She jumped out of her chair and ran over to him. As she threw her arms around his shoulders, Gordon, Leah, and Joel hurried after her. By the time Holt and I reached Zack, he was surrounded by his BAS friends, all of them murmuring words of comfort. Taking up the rear was Trejo, who observed them with a taciturn expression.

"Mr. Burwell," Holt repeated. "We need to ask you a few questions."

"Can't you leave the poor man alone," Dawn said as she held Zack in a tight embrace. "He and Christian were close friends. How do you imagine he feels?"

Zack looked at his friends with dismay. "Is Christian dead?"

"No, no." Leah took Zack's hand. "He's in surgery. Christian's still alive. He's alive, Zack."

When Zack began to sob, Gordon cursed under his breath. He and Joel joined the two women as they made a protective circle around the distraught man. Zack appeared on the verge of completely breaking down. Could he really have tried to murder his friend? It didn't seem possible.

Trejo pushed through the knot of people around Zack. "We need to know your whereabouts tonight, Mr. Burwell. If you won't speak to us here, we'll have to take you in for questioning."

That set the four of them to protesting so loudly the receptionist at the information desk rushed over to quiet them. Watching them clustered together, I felt as if I were looking at a close-knit family. They were protective of each other and looked on everyone else as outsiders. But I wondered if what bonded them was their summer at BAS, or the secrets they shared.

"Why are you doing this right now?" Gordon asked Trejo after the irritated receptionist had walked away. "Our good friend is in critical condition. All we can think about is whether or not he's going to survive. This isn't the time for questions."

Dawn threw him an approving look. "He's right. It's indecent to bother us now."

"I don't know what I'll do if Christian doesn't make it," Joel said in a hoarse voice.

Leah blinked back tears. "Don't say such a thing. He's not going to die."

With a loud moan, Zack held his head as if it weighed a hundred pounds. It seemed like an even heavier weight lay on his shoulders. Despite their emotional state, I felt uneasy by the events of tonight. Like it or not, I had been dragged into this by Zack. I'd never have been at the farm market tonight if not for his request to meet with me.

"Zack, did you tell Christian about our meeting tonight?" I said.

Everyone turned their attention to me now. "What are you talking about?" Dawn asked.

Leah looked confused. "Why would Zack meet with you? You're nothing to us." She made it sound as if I were no more than a troublesome insect they would all love to swat.

Joel glowered at me. "The last thing any of us wants is to spend more time with you."

"Joel's right," Gordon added. "You've been worse than any police officer. You and all your questions."

I had the feeling Holt and Trejo would be lecturing me again after this was over. "I do have one more question. Who do you think stuck the knife in your artwork at the exhibit?"

Leah gasped, while Joel turned to Gordon. "What is she talking about?" he asked.

Before he could answer, I explained what had occurred at

the exhibit earlier today. With her hand covering her mouth, Leah ran off to the restroom. The others looked grim.

"You won't be happy until something terrible happens to all of us." Dawn shook her head at me.

"Again, you're blaming the messenger. I had nothing to do with Sienna's death. Nor did I have anything to do with Gordon's vandalized artwork or Zack getting drunk at the luau. As for tonight, Zack is the one who came to me and asked for a meeting."

"And why would he do that?" Joel asked.

"Ask him." I waved at Zack.

Holt stepped closer. "Mr. Burwell, why did you want to meet with Ms. Jacob tonight?"

Zack stared at me for a tense moment. I was close enough to smell alcohol on him. He had been drinking again.

"I don't know what she's talking about," he said. "I never asked to meet with Marlee. She's lying."

Chapter 20

My jaw dropped. "Are you actually going to stand there and deny you asked me to meet you tonight?"

Zack couldn't look me in the eyes. "Why would I want to meet with you?"

"Exactly what I asked you earlier today. You said you needed to discuss something with me." I gestured to the Bramble friends clustered about him. "And you didn't want any of them to know about it."

"You're deluded." He looked over at Dawn, who squeezed his shoulder in sympathy. "I did go to her store today with Christian, but only to apologize for knocking her down at the luau. That's all I said to her. But she's as weird as Theo. Finding Sienna's body must have pushed her over the deep end."

When Gordon, Dawn, and Joel nodded in agreement, it was all I could do not to give every one of them a swift kick. "You're a liar, Zack," I said. "And a coward."

"And a most disgusting drunk," Piper added, only to be shushed by her husband.

"All of you are liars," I went on. "You're lying about Sienna, and now you're lying about what happened to Christian tonight."

As the Bramble group erupted into outraged cries and curses, Kit Holt pulled me to the side. "Marlee, please leave this to Trejo and me."

"He's lying, Kit," I said. "I swear he is."

"I believe you."

Gordon broke from the group and approached us. "See here, Captain Holt. You too, Detective Trejo. My friends and I are sick of being treated like criminals. Neither of you can prove we've done a thing wrong, and you know it. Meanwhile you let this unstable woman make wild accusations. If this keeps up, I may bring charges of harassment against her."

"Are you certain you want to bring up harassment charges, Mr. Sanderling?" Holt asked in a voice that held a hint of a threat.

"If so, any history of harassment in your background may also come to light," Trejo said.

Gordon stiffened. Dawn now switched her support from Zack to Gordon. Taking his arm, she said, "Let them threaten and bluster, Gordon. It's not our concern. All that matters right now is Christian's welfare. Marlee and her police friends can go to hell."

Before my police friends or I had a chance to respond, Lionel declared in his booming voice, "I believe we are about to have an update on Mr. Naylor's condition."

A tall doctor in surgical scrubs made his way over to us, accompanied by one of the state troopers. By the time he reached our tense group, everyone else associated with BAS in the waiting room had joined us. Only Ryan remained on the couch, snoring peacefully.

"I understand none of you are family members," the surgeon began. "However, the police have informed us that many of you are friends of Mr. Naylor and would—"

"Doctor, please," interrupted Leah, who had just returned from her tearful visit to the restroom. "Is Christian still alive?"

"Yes, Mr. Naylor survived the surgery."

I felt a wave of relief. Tina Kapoor hugged her fellow BAS administrators.

"What is his condition?" Dawn clutched even tighter to Gordon's arm.

"Critical. He's in recovery, and will be transferred to the ICU."

"What does that mean?" Joel asked.

"Mr. Naylor suffered trauma to the brain. To give the brain time to heal, he has been placed in a medically induced coma."

Joel winced, while Leah burst into tears once more.

"How long will Mr. Naylor remain in a comatose state?" Holt asked.

"It depends on how quickly the swelling on his brain recedes. To take him out of the coma too soon could result in the brain shutting off function to the injured areas. Depending on his response to the medication that monitors his blood pressure, Mr. Naylor could be kept in a coma for days, even weeks. Some patients remain in a medically induced coma for months."

A groan went up from all of us. Trejo and Holt exchanged somber glances. Christian would be unable to answer their questions anytime soon. Poor Christian. If Charlie and I hadn't found the remains of Sienna Katsaros, Christian would not be fighting for his life right now. Even though I had nothing to do with Sienna's death, I felt guilty for the unwanted role I had played.

"Doctor, can we see Christian?" Zack asked in a shaky voice.

"I recommend waiting until the morning. As I said, he's still in recovery."

"We may as well wait here," Gordon suggested. "I won't be able to sleep anyway."

Detective Trejo cleared his throat. "Since no one is ready for sleep, this will be a good time to answer a few more questions."

If looks could kill, Trejo would have died instantly from the glances thrown his way.

I turned to Holt. "Do you need to ask me more questions?"

He led me away so we wouldn't be overheard. "You've already told us everything at least ten times. They've told us everything as well, only I think they're omitting the truth. If we keep at them, it's possible one of Sienna's friends will say something they shouldn't." He smiled. "And thanks for calling me earlier tonight about the knife in Sanderling's art piece."

"Did you check it for fingerprints?"

"It's at the lab. We've begun to question anyone who had access to the art exhibit. And I'm afraid we'll have to speak with Theo again, too."

"Theo is staying with me until the centenary is over." I had informed Kit about the fake police badge and cap left on Theo's doorstep, along with Theo's description of the drunken midnight parties of Sienna and her friends. But I hadn't mentioned he was now my houseguest. "Although I might have Theo stay with me for an extended period. Just to be sure he's safe."

"You need to stop worrying about him, Marlee. Theo's a grown man. You also need to stop worrying about this case. We'll handle it."

I lowered my voice. "What about Gordon? I told you I'd heard a rumor about him stalking some woman years ago. And you and Trejo just implied the same thing."

He looked heavenward. "I know I'm speaking English, but she's not listening."

"I am listening. What I'm hearing is there's something suspicious about Gordon's background. I know that he married a girl he met while attending Duluth College. And that her mother was in politics. The divorce must not have been pleasant if she filed charges of harassment against him."

Holt shot me a disapproving look. "You're fishing."

"I am." I lifted a questioning eyebrow. "Did I catch anything?"

"Let's say you have a nibble. Gordon was married only a year. During that time, there were rumors of harassment and stalking. But it wasn't Gordon who was guilty of the harassment. It was another person."

"I don't understand."

"A woman appears to have been obsessed with Gordon back then. This individual stalked both him and his bride for months. Probably trying to frighten the wife enough so she'd leave him. Which she did. We spoke to Gordon's ex-wife this past week. She's remarried but still lives in Minnesota. Kept her maiden name to help her budding political career. Her mother is now a state senator, and Ms. Poe told us she plans to run for city council in the fall."

This seemed like a clear break in the case. If a woman stalked Gordon back then and it had anything to do with BAS, there were only two possible candidates. "What was the name of the woman who harassed Gordon's wife?"

"No one knows. The harassment consisted of anonymous threatening notes and messages. Both Gordon's and his wife's cars were vandalized numerous times. Along with their apartment."

"This woman sounds crazy."

"Well, I haven't met a lot of emotionally stable stalkers."

We exchanged rueful smiles. "If the stalking is connected to BAS," I said, "that narrows the list to Dawn and Leah. Probably Dawn. After all, her company, Vance Designs, is based in Minneapolis. She's been living there for the past twenty years. Dawn would have been in close proximity to Gordon and his wife. Did the couple ever move to Minneapolis?"

"No. And they were still living in Duluth when they divorced."

"Doesn't matter. It can't be that far from Duluth to Minneapolis." I bit my lip in frustration. "Although Leah told me at breakfast that her family is from St. Cloud, Minnesota. She was taking care of her mom at the time Gordon got married. It must be either Dawn or Leah. They both had a crush on Gordon. And I told you how I discovered Leah having sex with Gordon in one of the Bramble cabins."

Holt shrugged. "It's possible one of them became so fixated on Gordon she did harass the newlywed couple. But the harassment could have nothing to do with Sienna's murder. From all accounts, Gordon Sanderling was quite a good-looking guy. Voted most popular and most handsome by his high school senior class. It wouldn't be surprising if a girl at Duluth College became obsessed with him while he was there. Anyway, we have no idea who stalked Gordon and his bride eighteen years ago. We have a much better chance of figuring out who ran Christian off the road tonight. That may lead us to whoever buried Sienna's body in the woods."

I looked over at Sienna's friends. They stood in a tight group, facing Detective Trejo with stubborn and resentful expressions. "Zack knows. It's why he wanted to meet me."

"You exposed him tonight in front of the others." He shook his head at me. "If one of them is a killer, he's in danger."

"I'm sorry. But he took me by surprise when he lied to my face." I sighed. "Maybe you can arrest Zack. I smelled alcohol on him, which means he was probably drinking and driving. If he's in police custody, the killer won't be able to get to him. Once he's away from his Bramble, he might admit something." I gave him a beseeching look. "It's worth a try."

"I can't arrest someone because he walked into a hospital smelling of alcohol."

I watched as Dawn led an unsteady Zack to a chair. He'd been sober as a judge this afternoon at my wine tasting. What had happened between now and then to cause him to drink again? I thought back to what his berry nickname had been at BAS: Wino. How terrible it must be to wrestle with addiction from such a young age. And then to become friends with a young man whose family had just closed down their winery. I wondered how much free wine Gordon had been able to supply to his Bramble friends that summer. Probably an inexhaustible amount. Again the list of berry nicknames repeated in my brain.

I turned my attention back to Holt. "I feel partly responsible for this. After all, I did find the body. I only wish I could figure out exactly how Sienna died. I want to help, Kit."

"You'll help us more by stepping aside." He pointed at Ryan sleeping on the couch. "Your boyfriend has the right idea. Wake him up and have him drive you home."

After Holt walked away, I did wake Ryan. Only I didn't ask him to take me home. Instead, I asked him to drive me to The Berry Basket.

"Is this our last stop of the night?" Ryan asked with a yawn. "If not, we have to find a twenty-four-hour Dunkin' Donuts because I need some strong black coffee."

"This won't take long. I want to grab a folder from my office." I sat beside him in the pickup, searching for the store keys in my purse. The rear parking lot was empty, save for the three cars that belonged to the tenants who lived above the stores.

"What's so urgent about getting it now? You'll be back here in a few hours for work."

"I'm taking the morning off. But there may be something

in my office to answer some questions that are bugging me. I'd like to check it out before I forget."

Ryan yawned once again as I got out of the pickup and hurried to unlock the back door of the shop. When I made my way into the kitchen, the delicious aroma of cobbler and muffins greeted me. I noticed a plastic-wrapped tray filled with the remaining blackberry lime muffins Theo baked earlier in the day. I made a mental note to grab a few for Ryan before leaving.

After I switched on the light in my small office, I didn't waste any time. The bottom file cabinet drawer held information about all the orchards, vineyards, and farms in Oriole County. I often contracted with these local businesses for products. Thanks to Piper, several folders were devoted to those farms or orchards no longer in operation. Eight months ago, Piper cleaned out the visitor bureau's collection of brochures, newsletters, and local ads relating to defunct businesses and long-ago events. I'd snapped them up before she tossed them in the trash. A lot of the old tourist and commercial brochures had interesting images I wanted to keep on file. I thought I might incorporate some of them in future Berry Basket ads and posters.

Brochures about Sanderling Vineyards were in there, as were ads and newsletters devoted to my family's former orchards. Beside the desk sat a pile of blue Berry Basket tote bags sold in my store. I grabbed one and stuffed the file folders in there. I got to my feet, eager to return to the truck and my sleepy fiancé.

The sound of the door banging open told me he was fully awake. "Marlee?"

"I'm in my office, Ryan."

A few moments later, Ryan appeared at the office door.

He looked disheveled and upset. Had he finally realized how late I was keeping him up?

"We can go home now," I said quickly. "I found what I needed."

"Great. Now all we have to do is find my shotgun."

"What do you mean?"

"Remember how you didn't like me having a shotgun in the backseat of the pickup?" Ryan took several deep breaths as if trying to keep calm. "Well, don't worry. It's gone. Someone stole it."

Chapter 21

A disturbing night turned more stressful after the theft of Ryan's shotgun. Although we didn't know who took the gun from his truck, it had been in his backseat when we'd arrived at the hospital. Since we'd been in the ER waiting room for more than three hours, someone had to have snatched it during that time.

The police needed to be informed. Ryan insisted on taking me home before he filed the report, a decision prompted by remarks from me about how foolish it was to bring a loaded gun to the farm market. Although Ryan clearly regretted doing it, he wasn't in the mood for any cranky reminders. My only excuse is that I was exhausted and drained by the previous few hours. I'm sure both of us couldn't wait until he dropped me off at my house.

Despite this recent unsettling event, I fell asleep as soon as my head hit the pillow. I couldn't even wait up for Ryan. I did stay awake long enough to make certain Theo was fast asleep in the third-floor bedroom. Because the other bedrooms were on the second floor, Theo had the third floor to himself. He was lucky. His room boasted a turret window, one of my favorite spots in the house. And there was a soothing energy to the light-filled space, with its pale mint green walls and bleached wood floors. Seagull figurines also decorated the white chest of drawers and dresser. I hoped Theo appreciated the avian accents in the room. I also hoped he'd still be here when I woke up, especially since he had finished his Berry Basket baking last night while I was gone. When I'd gotten home, I'd found the kitchen counter covered with the tarts, cupcakes, and muffins Theo had whipped up for the store.

In the morning, the first thing I heard was Theo's voice from downstairs, followed by Minnie demanding, "Give me a kiss." With a relieved smile, I headed for the shower. If he was talking with Minnie, the conversation could last for hours. I had slept too soundly to notice when Ryan had gotten into bed, but I knew he'd spent the night. And not just because his side of the bed was a tangle of sheets. His dirty underwear lay tossed in a corner of the bathroom.

After showering and getting dressed, I hurried downstairs. The smell of fresh brewed coffee made me quite happy. As did the sight of Ryan, Emma, and Alison sitting on stools around the kitchen island. Theo stood near Minnie's perch by the window, his attention focused on whatever she was currently chattering about. They all looked so welcoming in my sunny yellow kitchen, I wished I could forget about buried bodies and the secrets buried with them.

"She's up," Alison announced. "It's about time."

I laughed. "This from someone who spent yesterday in bed sleeping it off."

"I made up for it by cooking breakfast. Sausage, waffles, poached eggs, fresh squeezed orange juice. I even threw together a fruit bowl: cantaloupe, blackberries, lime, mint, and ginger."

"Don't be too impressed. She Googled the fruit bowl recipe from Martha Stewart an hour ago." Emma got up to put bread in the toaster. Being Emma, she also stopped to rearrange the sunflowers in a tall vase on the counter. "And your baker is responsible for the muffins."

"Paleo blackberry," Alison said. "Thank you for making them, Theo."

"You're welcome," Theo said in a solemn voice. "But no one can have more than two. The rest are for the store."

"I called Andrew. He should be here in five minutes to pick up your pastries," I told Theo. "His boyfriend let him borrow the van from Beguiling Blooms." Although Gillian and Andrew were scheduled to open The Berry Basket, Theo's pastries needed to be taken to the shop. And my car wasn't the best vehicle for delivering long trays of muffins and tarts. It might be time to trade in the Malibu for an SUV.

Theo was so engrossed with Minnie I don't think he heard me. Every morning I took Minnie from her cage in the living room and let her preen and prattle from a tall wooden perch by the kitchen window. Ryan must have brought her to the kitchen while I was upstairs. I wasn't surprised to see Theo beside her. Since Theo's plate of half-eaten breakfast sat on the adjacent counter, I assumed this was where he felt most comfortable having his own meal.

"Did you sleep well?" I asked Theo as I filled a plate with sausages and a waffle.

He nodded. "You have a wonderful house. And I like Minnie. She's very friendly."

"Talkative, too."

"Is Christian okay?" Theo asked.

"I told Theo what happened last night," Ryan said. "Since he knew the guy years ago, it seemed only right he should be told."

"Of course." I smiled at Theo to reassure him. "Before I took a shower, I called the hospital. Christian is still in a coma, but his condition has stabilized."

"Then he won't die?"

"I don't know, Theo. No one does. But things look better than they did last night. I think Christian has a good chance of surviving."

"I hope he lives. Christian is a nice person." Theo sighed. "But he was always sad. Maybe he knew this would happen to him one day."

After scratching Minnie on the head, I went to join the others at the island. I sat next to Ryan, who stopped eating long enough to give me a kiss.

"What happened at the police station last night?" I asked.

"I filled out a report. And got charged with a misdemeanor."

I expected this. Although I knew little about firearms, I didn't think it was legal to drive around with a gun in the backseat.

"You must have a gun license," Emma said.

"Doesn't matter." Ryan drained his coffee mug. "A firearm has to be kept in a case and placed in the trunk. And I shouldn't have had it loaded. I knew better, but I wanted extra protection when we went to meet this Zack fellow."

"Will you have to go to court?" My guilt meter began to rise. Ryan wouldn't have been riding around with his shotgun if not for me.

"Nah. I just had to pay a penalty. One hundred dollars."

"Let me reimburse you," I said.

"Don't be silly. I'm the gun owner, not you. I know the law. And I don't care about the hundred dollars. But I do care about losing my gun. I've had it for nine years."

I spooned fresh berries onto my waffle. "It was stolen when we were in the waiting room."

Alison wiped her fingers on a napkin. "Who do you think stole it?"

"Not a random stranger. I bet it was someone at the hospital with us last night."

"You're thinking the thief is one of those irritating friends of the dead girl?" Ryan asked.

"Yes. Except for Gordon, they're all staying in cabins at the bayou. And we left the campus tonight in your truck. Whoever stole your gun probably sideswiped Christian, too."

"Peek-a-boo, I see you," Minnie sang out.

"If you believe one of Sienna's friends stole it," Emma said, "you should tell the police."

I heard Theo make a strangled sound. "Theo, why don't you take Minnie into the sunroom? She likes to watch the bird feeders in the backyard. And she'll sit on your shoulder while you carry the perch out there."

With a grateful look, Theo hurried to do as I suggested. "You're a doll," Minnie remarked as she left the room perched atop my baker.

"Let's keep any mention of the police to a minimum around Theo," I said.

"Marlee, this situation is scary. You need the police more than ever," Emma said. "There could be an insane murderer running around. Someone who now has Ryan's gun."

"I think she needs to stop being paranoid," Ryan said. "Christian got run off the road by a reckless driver going too fast in a bad storm. And the shotgun was lying in plain view in my backseat—with the windows left half open. A dishonest creep took advantage of my carelessness. There's nothing insane or murderous about any of this."

Rather than reply, I sipped my orange juice. Yet another thing Ryan and I didn't see eye to eye on. I was certain we were dealing with insanity or murder. Or both.

As much as I loved Ryan and my friends, I was glad when they finally left the house. Ryan was already an hour late getting to the orchards, while Emma and Amanda planned to attend today's body-painting contest at BAS. With the dirty plates stacked in the dishwasher and Theo happily keeping Minnie company in the sunroom, I had time to go through the folders I'd taken from my office. After spreading the contents on the cleared-off kitchen island, I rifled through them until I found the brochures for Sanderling Vineyards, one printed for each year they had been open. I noticed the brochures became glossier and more professional looking as the years progressed. The early brochures held only basic information about the business: location, hours, types of wines available. But seven years in, the business had expanded to include wine-tasting dinners, tours of the vineyard, and weekend courses called Winemaking 101.

I read over the course description, which promised to teach registrants how to become their own vintners. My fingers gripped the brochure tighter when I saw students could learn the secrets of homemade wine using local grapes. Or berries.

During my wine tasting yesterday, Christian and Zack had looked upset when I mentioned how easy it was to make wine at home from various fruits. I thought it was their distress at Zack being exposed to the sample bottles of wine. But what if they'd had a bad experience with homemade wine—in particular, wine they might have created themselves during their summer at BAS. Gordon's family had shut down the winery only a year earlier. Their vintner ingredients and tools would still have been on-site.

I ran into the other room to grab a notepad from my home office. Sitting down once more at the kitchen island, I wrote down the berries that had inspired the nicknames given to Sienna and her Bramble friends: Gordon—beautyberry; Dawn—elderberry; Joel—chokeberry; Zack—wineberry; Leah—gooseberry; Christian—blueberry; Sienna—baneberry.

I froze. Although Minnie's whistles from the sunroom reminded me I wasn't alone, I suddenly felt afraid. Staring at the notepad, I knew with absolute certainty how Sienna Katsaros had died.

Wine made from any of these berries would be safe to drink except for one: baneberries. She had died from drinking poisoned wine. With a shaky hand, I wrote *POISON* in big letters next to Sienna's name and berry.

My suspicions were correct. Her fellow BAS friends knew the circumstances of her death and had tried to cover it up. About to reach for my cell phone, I heard a noise in the kitchen. Still looking at my list, I said, "Theo, you'll never guess what I just discovered. I only wish I'd put it together sooner, especially since I know so much about berries."

When he didn't answer, I lifted my head. But the person who met my startled gaze wasn't Theo. It was Zack Burwell. And Ryan's shotgun was clutched in his hand.

Chapter 22

Seeing Zack in my kitchen was so unexpected I became temporarily speechless. Since he stood in the open doorway that led to the living room, he must have entered via the front door. A front door left open again by Ryan. Like most Oriole County residents, Ryan saw no reason to lock doors or windows. A shame he hadn't spent ten years living in New York City, as I had; it would have taught him to be less trusting of his fellow man.

"This is a surprise," I said finally.

He lifted an eyebrow. "You look more shocked than surprised."

"You have shown up unannounced. And carrying a gun. I also didn't hear you knock."

Zack approached the kitchen island. "The front door was open and the screen door unlocked. Seemed like a friendly gesture to whoever stopped by."

"It would be." I paused. "To my friends. What are you doing here?"

"I wanted to return this." Zack raised the shotgun, and I got ready to run out of the room. I was relieved when he placed the weapon on the island. Lying atop the scattered brochures and ads, it suddenly appeared even more deadly. I swallowed hard when I remembered Ryan had told me the gun was loaded.

"So you were the one who stole it out of Ryan's truck last night."

"It was a stupid thing to do. I got spooked after I learned Christian had been run off the road. I thought I needed a way to protect myself." He looked sheepish. "I'm sorry about calling you a liar last night. Only I didn't want the others to think I was going to rat them out. Anyway, I saw your boyfriend's truck in the parking lot. When I walked past, I spotted the gun."

"How did you know it belonged to Ryan?" Although *Zellar Orchards* was painted on the side of Ryan's pickup, I had never mentioned to Sienna's friends that I was engaged to a Zellar.

"I watched you and him leave the BAS fish fry in his truck. I was sitting in Christian's Jeep in the parking lot there. It was my plan to follow you to the farm market where we were supposed to meet." He pursed his lips in disapproval. "Until I saw you had no intention of coming alone, even though I asked you not to bring anyone."

"You told me not to bring the police or any BAS alumni. Ryan is neither."

Zack pointed to one of the stools on his side of the island. "I need to sit down." He fell onto the stool as if he weighed as much as Gordon Sanderling. The morning sunshine showed every premature wrinkle on his face. I also doubted he'd slept. Zack wore the same clothes he had on last night; his jeans and burgundy T-shirt had been wrinkled and stained even then.

"You don't look well," I said.

"I'm not well. When I was thirty-one, I was diagnosed with cirrhosis of the liver."

I quickly did the math. "You told me you stopped drinking seven years ago. Did the diagnosis prompt it?"

"Yes. And I was doing better until I came back here. I didn't think it would be as bad as it was, returning to BAS. Maybe it wouldn't have been if Sienna's body hadn't been found. I couldn't hold it together after that. And once I begin drinking, it's hard to stop. You saw what happened at the luau."

"I smelled alcohol on you at the hospital last night."

He nodded. "I had a bottle with me while I was waiting in the BAS parking lot. Needed a few sips to give me courage. But when I saw you were bringing someone to our meeting, it freaked me out." His gaze turned accusing. "I started to take more than a few sips. Christian found me sitting in his Jeep. He was upset to see me drinking again and wanted to know why. I had drunk just enough to confess I'd agreed to meet you. And how I was going to tell you what really happened twenty years ago." Zack sighed. "That morning, the two of us had discussed telling an outsider the truth, but Christian thought it was too dangerous."

"What did Christian say when he learned you were going to do exactly that?"

"He offered to come with me. Said I was right. We had lived with lies far too long. Christian is a good man. A decent man. Naturally, he's the one fighting for his life and I'm still going strong." He took a shaky breath. "It's my fault he was in the accident. I was half drunk when he found me; then I refused to go with him to meet you. I got out of his Jeep and ran away like the coward I am. Christian must have decided to meet you himself. And he probably told the others before he did. If he planned to come clean, he would have been up front about it."

I looked down at the shotgun lying between us. Moving as carefully as if I were dismantling a bomb, I picked it up. "Do you mind if I put this somewhere else?"

He waved his hand. "You can bury it in the sand, for all I care. I don't want it now."

Because I feared the gun was still loaded, I took it around

the corner into my walk-in pantry. Wishing the pantry had a door, I laid it on an empty bottom shelf. A quick peek through the back parlor revealed that Theo still kept Minnie company in the sunroom. Good. I didn't want him involved in whatever Zack had come here to do. But since he had surrendered the gun, I assumed he planned nothing violent.

When I returned to the kitchen, I asked, "Why did you want the gun in the first place?"

"Dawn texted me to say Christian had been in an accident. I knew then he'd gone to meet you." Zack shut his eyes. "And I knew in my gut he had been run off the road as a warning. I was afraid I'd be next. When I walked past your boyfriend's pickup and saw the gun, it seemed like a sign. I grabbed it and put it in the trunk of a car I borrowed from Tina Kapoor's assistant."

At that inopportune moment, Minnie let out a deafening series of whistles, followed by a long series of "lalalalalalalala."

Zack sat up as if he had been electrified. "What the hell's that?"

"Minnie, my talking bird," I said. "She's in the sunroom." I saw no reason to tell him Theo was in the house, too.

He pushed the stool back and stood up. "Maybe we should go out there to talk."

"Maybe I should call the police first."

"Are you afraid of me? That's ridiculous." Zack gestured with one hand, brushing against the brochures scattered on the kitchen island.

I suddenly remembered what was on the notepad. "You can't blame me for being a little afraid." To divert his attention, I stacked the brochures into a neat pile.

"It's me and Christian who should be afraid," he replied.

"Speaking of Christian, I'm surprised you're not at the hospital."

"There are other ways to protect my friend than sitting at his hospital bedside."

"Why do you and he need protecting?" I moved my hand toward the notepad. I didn't want him to see the word *POISON* beside Sienna's name.

"What's this?" Zack snatched the notepad from me.

My mind raced as I thought of how I could protect myself and Theo if I had to. Before I could come up with a defense scenario, Zack shocked me by bursting into laughter.

With a last guffaw, Zack looked up from my list. "You have been busy, haven't you? Digging around for dirt, like you dug around and found Sienna's bones."

"Which I suspect one of you buried there. Or maybe all of you did."

"What else do you suspect?" Zack appeared calm.

"The other day, Joel admitted at breakfast how your Bramble friends used a special bird call to alert each other. A signal to let everyone know it was safe to run off and party. And you had these midnight parties pretty often. Of course, Gordon provided the wine. Wine that you and Sienna seemed to have overindulged in. She often became sick from her heavy drinking. But then, Sienna was a petite girl; alcohol would work faster on her than on you. I also know not all of these late-night parties were held in the woods at the BAS campus. Sometimes, Gordon drove the gang to the Sanderling farm in his family's van."

Zack shook his head. "Theo's been talking to you. We were afraid he would. The little sneak. Always watching from the shadows, following us around. We caught him a couple of times, but it never stopped him from doing it again."

"He was looking out for Sienna. And he was right to be worried. Sienna died two days after Theo went home. Poisoned by the baneberry wine she drank. But Theo couldn't have saved her the night she died because all of you went off to Gordon's farm, didn't you? Theo wouldn't have been able to follow."

He sighed. "No. Theo didn't have access to a car. Gordon's

farm was off limits to him. Even if he had followed us, there was nothing he could have done to save her. We tried. Believe me, we tried. All we could do was watch her die. How were we supposed to know baneberries were poisonous? Gordon said his family made wine out of all sorts of fruit, berries included." His voice was filled with bitterness. "Too bad you weren't there that summer with us. Sienna would still be alive. After all, you're the berry expert, aren't you?"

"I certainly would have stopped you from making baneberry wine. Who came up with the idea of making your own wine? I'm betting the plan was to drink it at the end of summer at your own private graduation party. Obviously held in the woods on Gordon's property."

"It was Gordon's idea," he said. "But he only wanted to make blackberry wine. The rest of us agreed later it would be more fun to make wines based on our berry nicknames."

I pointed at the notepad he still held. "All the berries on that list grow in the region. Even if the harvest time was autumn, Gordon's family would have had access to frozen berries. As for baneberry, it blooms in May and June. The timing would have been perfect."

If someone had intended to kill the girl, this method was perfect, too.

He threw the notepad onto the counter. "Sienna drank her wine quickly that night. Even faster than me. I've never been so frightened in my life. Frightened and horrified. One minute she was laughing, having a good time. The next minute she was in convulsions. It wasn't an easy death. Not easy at all." Zack put his face in his hands.

After a long pause, I said, "Why didn't you call the police? Or tell Gordon's family?"

Zack lifted his head. "We were teenagers, except for Gordon. And we thought we'd be blamed for Sienna's death. Plus, we'd been drinking almost as much as Sienna had that night. None of us were thinking straight. Sienna was dead. We couldn't bring her back. But no one knew where we were. Gordon's family was fast asleep in the farmhouse. They never had any idea we sometimes went on their property to party. And no one at the school suspected we were off campus. If we buried her body in the woods, who would ever know?"

"No one." I paused a long time before adding, "Except for the six of you."

He ran his hands over his shaved head. If he'd had hair, I suspected he would have been pulling it out. "If you only knew how many times I wished I had thrown myself in the lake that night, instead of Sienna's clothes."

"Whose idea was it to cover up her death? Was the decision unanimous?"

"Gordon wanted to call the police, but we wouldn't let him. We acted like scared, stupid kids. Hell, we *were* scared, stupid kids. Dawn finally took charge. Gordon was wild with grief. He loved Sienna. Really loved her. And she loved him. He'd convinced her to transfer to Duluth College so they could be together. Their romance had become more than a summer fling."

I wasn't surprised Dawn had taken charge. As Gordon told me yesterday, she was nicknamed after the elderberry because she was the most mature one in their group. "You seem to believe Sienna's death was an accident."

He regarded me with horror. "Of course. My God, you don't think one of us killed her?"

"Then why did you assume someone ran Christian off the road last night? Why did you need to take Ryan's gun for protection?"

"I told you, I freaked out. I wasn't thinking like a rational person."

"That's bull. You asked to see me because you wanted to confess the truth about Sienna's death. When Christian was almost killed on the way to meet me, you automatically assumed someone was willing to do anything to stop him. And you're worried you'll be next."

"Maybe." He shook his head. "I don't know. Twenty years ago, the six of us agreed to take the secret of Sienna's death to our grave. If the truth ever came out, it would tear our lives apart. We'd covered up our friend's death, lied to the police, lied to Sienna's family. We needed to keep silent. If one of us confessed, the others would be implicated. And our lives have been ruined enough by that night. There was no purpose in completely destroying ourselves."

"Then why are you willing to tell the truth now?"

He gave a hopeless shrug. "I can't live with the guilt any longer. My sponsor believes my drinking problem grew worse because of what happened that summer. Of course, he doesn't know the sickening truth. But he knows enough to realize something terrible occurred. And it's not only my life that's a wreck. Christian suffers from crippling depression. Gordon's an obese shadow of his former self. Joel is filled with rage. Leah has an eating disorder."

I thought back to Dawn's confident demeanor and professional success. "Dawn seems to have thrived."

"Why? Because she has an eye for textiles?" He snorted, as if my statement was hard to believe. "Dawn is a woman of extremes. Dangerous extremes. She chased after Gordon all summer. It never sunk in that he preferred Sienna to her."

"But Leah pursued Gordon, too."

"Not the same thing at all. Leah was turned on by Gordon. The same way she was turned on by me that summer. Dawn became obsessed."

"Obsessed enough to stalk Gordon and his bride for the better part of a year?"

He shut his eyes, as if exhausted. "Yeah, Dawn harassed Gordon and his new wife. After she moved to Minnesota to be near Gordon, she believed they'd find a way to be together. Dawn had been royally pissed off when she learned Sienna planned to transfer to Gordon's college. After Sienna died, she thought she finally had a chance with him."

"Zack, it looks to me like Dawn had a strong motive to want Sienna dead."

"But none of us knew Sienna had decided to move to Minnesota until a couple of days before that last party. And we began making the wine weeks earlier, back in June. Right after Amanda Dobson left. I swear, Sienna's death was a tragic accident."

I recalled the Chaplin murder trial I had to sit through for the better part of a year, particularly the chilling testimony from the betrayed Evangeline Chaplin. She'd been serene and confident as she'd testified how she had no choice but to poison her husband with arsenic when she learned he was having an affair. And her composure never wavered, even when various experts described how brutally painful a death caused by arsenic was for its victim.

"You don't understand how killers think, Zack. I had a front-row seat to a murder trial and you'd be surprised at what people can convince themselves of. Especially if they're already unbalanced. Dawn hounded Gordon and his bride until they divorced. Doesn't that prove how sick she was? And probably still is."

Zack glanced up as the sound of Minnie laughing like a hyena met our ears. She'd picked up her latest imitation after watching an Animal Channel documentary with me.

"If all of you knew Dawn was harassing Gordon and his wife," I continued, "why wasn't she charged with anything?"

"You still don't get it. We share a secret that could destroy us. That's a lot of power to have over each other. Gordon knew right away it was Dawn who was behind the calls, the notes, the vandalism. She even admitted it when he confronted her.

Gordon was so desperate he contacted the rest of us to see if we could talk some sense into her."

"I assume that didn't work."

"If Dawn couldn't have Gordon, no one else would, either. Gordon did threaten to report her to the police. But she swore to tell the authorities what really happened the night Sienna died. Gordon backed off and kept quiet. He let her destroy his marriage." His expression grew even bleaker. "You may have noticed he never remarried. He doesn't dare."

I had no idea how this group had the arrogance to call Theo the odd one. Sienna's friends seemed as strange as Leticia the Lake Lady. "Someone in your group was willing to kill Christian in order to stop him from talking to me. I think it's Dawn. She's shown how unbalanced she is."

"She's not the only one," Zack said. "Joel has a violent temper. We even nicknamed him after the chokeberry because he tried to choke Gordon when we were BAS students."

This startled me so much I knocked over my empty juice glass. "What? Joel told me he was named after the choke-berry because he choked on a fish bone."

Zack rolled his eyes. "He lied. Joel got the name after he attacked Gordon during one of our drinking parties. It took four of us to stop him from literally choking Gordon to death. We weren't surprised, though. Joel adored Sienna. He worshipped the ground she walked on. But she chose Gordon."

Shades of the Chaplin murder. "Then Joel could have killed her out of jealousy."

"Looking back, I wonder if Joel's anger was more about injured pride than jealousy. Joel comes from a wealthy family. The stereotypical rich boy who's had everything he wanted from the day he was born. Until Gordon took Sienna away from him." Zack gave me a weary look. "Joel never forgave Gordon. I don't think he forgave Sienna, either. And he hated Gordon after that. Oh, he tried to hide it. He acted as if losing Sienna was no big deal. However, Joel has a big ego, and a temper to match. Not a good combo. It's too bad. When he's in the right mood, Joel's a lot of fun to be around."

I found that hard to believe, but my standards for friendship were obviously higher than Zack's. "It looks like either Joel or Dawn might be willing to kill to prevent the truth about Sienna from coming to light."

"It's Joel and Dawn who have always kept the rest of us in line. Late last night, they sat Leah and me down and warned us not to say anything." His voice lowered, as if they were in the room listening. "Both of them were against us attending the BAS centenary. But Christian and I needed to come back for closure. Leah, too. When they learned we were coming, Joel and Dawn decided to return as well. They were afraid the rest of us would say something incriminating when we got here and the memories flooded back." His laugh sounded more like a sob. "And they were right. Especially with Sienna's burial site being discovered after all these years. It can't be a coincidence. Sienna wanted you to find her. Sienna wants the truth to come out."

I didn't tell him Theo also shared that belief. As for me, I believed both Joel and Dawn had a reason to kill Sienna. She was Dawn's chief rival for Gordon's affections. And revenge against Gordon may have been Joel's motive for murder. After all, how better to wound your enemy than by destroying something he loves?

"Marlee, I can't live with this threat hanging over me any longer. I came here to give you the gun back and to ask you to call your police friends. This has gone on long enough. Christian may die because none of us had the guts or decency to be honest. It stops today." He clasped his hands before him, as if praying. "And I might need a little police protection until they figure out who ran Christian off the road."

"When they do, I'm sure it will be the same person who poisoned Sienna."

"I told you, the baneberry wine was a terrible accident," he said. "None of us knew those berries were poisonous."

"That's not true."

Zack regarded me with a hint of alarm. "What are you talking about?"

"You keep forgetting about the eighth member of your group: Amanda Dobson. She was a botany major in college. All of you mentioned at breakfast how she wouldn't be attending the centenary because she's off on a research trip. You *had* a berry expert with you that summer, at least in the beginning. Did Amanda know about your wine-making plans before she left?"

He seemed unsettled. "Gordon suggested making blackberry wine the week before she left. But Amanda never knew about our plan to make berry wines based on our nicknames. We didn't decide on that until after she'd been sent home with a bad case of poison ivy."

I tapped the counter nervously. "Way too convenient. The one person who could have warned everyone about the toxicity of baneberries finds herself shipped home. And because of poison ivy, no less. I'm no botany major, but even I recognize poison ivy when I see it. How did someone as schooled in plants as Amanda Dobson fall into a bed of poison ivy?"

"They were horsing around."

"Who?"

Zack looked up at the ceiling, as if trying to jog his memory. "Sienna, Joel, Gordon, Amanda, and Christian. They went hiking in the woods on the BAS campus after dinner. I was sitting around the fire pit with Dawn and Leah when they got back. Amanda was upset, but the others were laughing. They thought it was funny Amanda got pushed into a patch of poison ivy. She was always warning people to watch out for it."

"Wait a minute. You said she was pushed."

"Yeah, they were chasing each other around. I think Joel had a frog he was scaring the girls with. Anyway, she said she was pushed. I don't remember by who."

"It was Joel." Theo stood in the doorway. And he gripped Ryan's shotgun with both hands. "Joel pushed her."

Zack shot to his feet, causing his stool to topple over. "What is he doing here?"

Trying to remain calm, I walked over to Theo. "Give me the gun, Theo. It belongs to Ryan. He'll be happy you found it for him."

Theo glanced down at the weapon. "It was in that little room in the hallway. I don't like guns. But I heard Zack. I thought I might need the gun in case he tried to hurt you."

"Thank you. But no one is going to hurt anyone today," I said as Theo handed the shotgun to me. This time, I placed it in a nearby broom closet, which, mercifully, had a door.

"Why is he here?" Zack asked again.

"Because he's my friend and I invited him." Which was more than I could say for Zack. I turned to Theo, who stood watching Zack as if he was were an enemy combatant. "You said it was Joel who pushed Amanda Dobson into the poison ivy. How do you know that?"

"I saw Sienna walk into the woods with the others," he replied, "so I followed to keep her safe. Joel used to bother her sometimes. I wanted to make sure he didn't bother her again. He didn't that time because Gordon was there. But Joel bothered Amanda."

"How?" I asked.

"She didn't like frogs. Joel found a frog and chased Amanda with it. It was not a nice thing to do. Christian and Sienna tried to stop him, but he yelled at them. He really scared Amanda with the frog. She fell twice. But the third time she fell, it was because Joel pushed her. That's how she ended up in the poison bushes." Theo sounded disapproving. "She got sick and had to go home. Christian was sad when she left. So was Sienna."

"He's right about that," Zack added. "We all liked Amanda. And it was only a few days after she left when we began to make the wine. Only this time, we decided to use our nickname berries, instead of the blackberries Gordon had wanted."

"You keep saying the rest of you wanted to make wine based on your nicknames," I said. "But do you remember who first came up with the idea?"

I watched Zack's expression slowly turn to one of revulsion. "Joel," he said in a hoarse voice. "It was Joel's idea. He was sick of the blackberry theme and thought we should be more creative. To be honest, he didn't have to try hard to convince the rest of us. Making wines based on our berry nicknames did seem a more creative way to end the summer." Zack shook his head. "Yet another reason we all feel so guilty."

"When the police do contact Amanda Dobson, I bet she'll tell them how Joel asked her about the different berries in the area. Especially which berries were poisonous. And once she told him what he needed to know, he found a way to get her off campus. Quick."

Theo's pale face grew even whiter. "Did Joel kill Sienna?"

"It looks like it. I think Joel was so angry at Sienna and Gordon that he waited to kill her all summer. For two months, he knew a poisoned wine was being made just for her." A cold chill swept over me at the horror of what he had done. "Joel probably took sadistic pleasure out of it."

Zack leaned against the island. "I feel sick."

Because Theo didn't look too good either, I steered him to a stool at the counter and made him sit. "Joel may have decided on such a method of murder because it took weeks to literally come to fruition. Had he been able to win Sienna back, he would have found a way to destroy her wine before she could drink it. Instead, she grew closer to Gordon, even announcing she was transferring to his college that fall. It signed her death warrant."

With a cry, Zack looked up. "Then it was Joel who ran Christian off the road?"

"You did say it was he and Dawn who made certain all of you stuck to your decision to never tell the truth about Sienna's death. You and Christian were the first ones to test him on how far he was willing to go to keep this secret buried."

"The bastard. He killed Sienna *and* tried to kill Christian. I'll murder him myself!"

"I think there's been enough murder." I welcomed the sound of Minnie singing "Ba-ba-ba ba-ba ba-ran" from the back of the house. At this moment, I needed a hint of normalcy.

"Don't you see?" Zack said. "If Joel was insane enough to murder Sienna, he won't stop at killing any of us to keep himself safe. Hell, Joel will punish us for simply trying to tell the truth."

"But Joel is the one who needs to be punished." Theo sounded as angry as Zack. "He should go to jail. Forever."

"Agreed," I replied. "Now we have to figure out a way to make that happen."

"I know how." Theo lifted his chin before saying something I thought I would never hear from his lips. "I'm going to call the police."

Chapter 23

This time, I was the one who dreaded the call to the police. Theo and I faced hours of further questioning. And Sienna's friends would be interrogated even more thoroughly. Now that I knew for certain one of them was a murderer, the prospect was daunting. When we all came face-to-face at the sheriff's office, I felt as if I were looking at a firing squad. Until I realized Dawn, Gordon, Leah, and Joel were more frightened than I was. The secret they buried twenty years ago had finally been exposed to the light, just as Sienna's bones had. Small wonder they appeared shell shocked. And defeated.

Zack repeated his story about how Sienna's body was buried in the woods after she died from drinking the wine. Halfway through Zack's confession, Gordon began gasping for air; within minutes, he was in the throes of a severe panic attack. Leah became physically ill when Zack described how they'd removed Sienna's shorts and top in order to throw them into the lake. A livid Dawn accused Theo and me of stirring everything up. Of course, lawyers were called, which dragged out events until well into evening.

Throughout the endless day, Joel said little. But his hateful stare betrayed his seething rage. Only Theo was calm. It was as if now that the dark secret about Sienna's death had been unearthed, his anxiety and fear had vanished. He spoke without hesitation about how he had seen Joel push Amanda into a poison ivy patch. This finally elicited a response from Joel, who remarked, "Are you going to arrest me for chasing a girl with a frog? Good luck with that."

As the hours dragged on, I longed to be back in my shop, concerned only about how much raspberry jam I had in the back room, and whether I needed to place an order for more cranberry tea. Yet when the proceedings ended, I felt alarmed when no arrests were made.

"How can you let them leave?" I complained to Kit Holt, who had been part of the questioning. "They admitted that Sienna died in the woods after drinking baneberry wine. And that they threw her clothing into the lake to make it look as if she drowned. They admitted it!"

While Gordon denied Zack's story at first, he soon broke down and confessed. As did Leah. Their confessions rattled Dawn so much, she felt compelled to give her version of events, one in which she tried to minimize Gordon's involvement. Only Joel refused to admit any complicity in Sienna's death. He did grow nervous when he was accused of having known baneberries were poisonous. Perhaps because the accusation caused the other members of the Bramble to react to the news with shock. Roused out of his anxious stupor, Gordon lunged at Joel, his face twisted with rage. It took two deputies to pull him away.

Zack was right. None of them thought Sienna's death was anything but accidental. Except for Joel. He blanched when Holt informed him they were trying to track down Amanda Dobson during her research trip along the Amazon. If she confirmed he had knowledge of the toxicity of baneberries that summer, charges of murder would be brought against him. I watched all of them troop out of the station. Only Joel remained behind, huddled with the lawyer who had been hastily called. Although he pretended to be deep in conversation with his attorney, he probably stayed behind in order to make certain the others had left. I suspected Joel was afraid of what would happen when Sienna's Bramble had him alone. When Joel did leave, he sent Theo and me a last hateful look.

Theo had noticed. "Joel wants to hurt us," he said, "like he hurt Sienna."

He was right. The man was a cold-blooded killer. And a madman. "Why can't you arrest all of them for lying about Sienna's death?" I asked Holt.

"That's up to the county prosecutor's office. It's even possible they won't be charged. Most of them were teenagers at the time. They panicked and did something terrible and stupid. But they aren't responsible for her death." He frowned. "The same can't be said for Joel."

Theo and I exchanged frustrated looks. "Joel should go to jail," he said. "He killed Sienna. She would want him punished. So would her family."

"We'll do our best, Theo," Holt reassured him. "But we need corroborating testimony, which Amanda Dobson may be able to supply. Meanwhile, I want both of you to be careful. Zack Burwell claims Joel has a violent temper. He's feeling trapped right now, and a trapped animal is the most dangerous."

"Don't worry. Theo's staying with me at the house, along with Ryan, Emma, and Alison. And I'll make certain both of us keep busy at the store tomorrow. Theo can get another head start on the weekend baking." I gave him a wink. "I'll even bring Minnie to keep us company."

This got a smile from Theo.

"Plus I'll be taking part in the Blackberry Road Rally tomorrow night," I continued. "There's a mob of us competing in that, which is good. Safety in numbers." A thought occurred to me. "Why don't you join my team, Theo? You know Andrew and Dean. It will be fun."

Kit nodded in approval. "Good idea."

Theo took a moment to consider this. I was ready for him to turn my offer down. But he surprised me for the second time that day by replying, "Okay. I've never been in a road rally."

I breathed an audible sigh of relief. Until the sheriff's department arrested Joel, I would be peering over my shoulder. But with the road rally, I had an hour or two of carefree fun to look forward to. Although I feared Andrew and Dean would commit murder themselves if we didn't win.

Despite the drama leading up to it, the Blackberry Road Rally was about to start. The Sienna Katsaros case had not led to its cancellation, and Piper had not been pushed off a bluff, as she had sarcastically suggested. Although Piper's expression as she surveyed the dozens of cars lined along her sweeping drive indicated she wished all of them were lying at the bottom of the bluff that bordered the property. Piper maintained strict control over her gated estate, and too many strangers now intruded on her private domain.

Not that any of the rally participants would be able to get within twenty feet of her spectacular Italianate mansion; six servants stood guard on the perimeter. To make certain no one came close to Piper's front door, her housekeeper, Carmen, stood on the porch with a surprisingly obedient Charlemagne at her side. Whenever he barked, I noticed Carmen had only to say a few words before he quieted down. Who knew the patrician housekeeper was also a dog whisperer? It was Piper who was misbehaving, shooing away anyone who even attempted to speak with her. At least her husband was more gracious, taking the time to greet each rally driver and wish them well.

It was no surprise he had won his mayoral reelection in a landslide.

A horn beeped and I looked over at my car. One of the Cabot boys struggled to get my attention again. They had downed too many caffeinated drinks at Coffee by Crystal in preparation for the rally. And they were energetic enough without the added espresso.

I waved at Dean, who hung out the car's back window. "Piper hasn't passed out the clue envelopes yet!" I yelled. "Now stop beeping my horn!"

Shaking my head, I turned to Kit Holt. "You'd think the grand prize money was a million dollars. Heaven help us if we come in second or third. And if we don't even place, I'll have to go into the witness protection program."

He chuckled, and I noticed the cute laugh lines around his brown eyes. I had to stop paying attention to things like that. Or that Kit looked even more attractive when not in uniform. Since he was off duty this evening, he wore khaki pants and a snug gray summer pullover that revealed more muscles than I would have guessed. I wished I was outfitted in something a bit more attractive than jeans and a purple BAS T-shirt. But everyone riding in my car had decided to dress identically to show we were team players. I also reminded myself I was engaged. . . and not to Kit Holt.

"I'm glad you'll be driving with your friends tonight." He glanced at my car, where Tess waited in the front passenger seat, with the Cabot brothers and Theo crammed in the back. "And I have news: We tracked Ms. Dobson down in Brazil two hours ago. She finally arrived at a town with Wi-Fi."

"What did she say?" I crossed my fingers that whatever she said incriminated Joel.

"She remembered how Gordon Sanderling thought it would be fun if they made their own blackberry wine. More important, the day before Amanda got pushed into the poison ivy, Joel had a long conversation with her about the region's berries: which ones made good wines, which ones didn't."

"Did she tell him about baneberries?"

"Yes." His expression grew somber. "She told Joel that Sienna should not eat the berries she had been nicknamed after. Amanda warned him baneberries were poisonous. He also wanted to know how quickly a person might die after eating baneberries, which she thought morbid. Amanda said she was purposely explicit about the effects. She knew the group was excited about making berry wine, and she wanted to make certain they knew which berries should not be used."

"Exactly what Joel wanted to hear. All he had to do was figure out how to get Amanda off campus. Being surrounded by all those woods made it easy." I felt repulsed at how coldly he had planned the murder of Sienna. "It's a good thing the rash from the poison ivy caused her to be sent home. Joel might have come up with a more lethal way of getting rid of her."

Static crackled through the air. Piper stood on the top step of her flagstone porch, a speakerphone in her hand. Charlemagne let out several excited barks, only to be quickly silenced by Carmen. To celebrate the occasion, Piper had outfitted herself from head to toe in Blackberry Art School purple: purple silk blouse, purple capris, purple braided sandals, even a purple and white scarf, which flowed behind her in the evening breeze. It also looked like she was wearing every amethyst she owned. Piper's impeccable sense of style and good taste had failed her tonight. I blamed all the stress leading up to the road rally.

"Attention, attention," she announced. "It is almost seven-thirty. Drivers, please pick up your team's envelope from the check-in table. Once you do, return to your vehicles and begin the hunt for the road rally clues. Keep in mind these envelopes do not contain your first clue; instead, they hold a clue as to where to pick up that envelope. This prevents cars from simply following each other for the entire rally."

"Interesting," Holt remarked. "I was wondering how road rallies got around that problem."

Piper cleared her throat. "I do hope at least one person on each team has remembered to bring a camera phone, as was specified on your registration sheets. Photos will be necessary to prove you have successfully visited all ten clue destinations. For those who choose to drop out during the race, instructions can be found in your envelope. Everyone else will follow clues to the ten chosen destinations. When you reach a destination, there is a task to accomplish. After you have performed all ten tasks, you are *not* to return here."

Holt leaned toward me. "You know she wanted to add *ever*."

I elbowed him in the ribs.

"The road rally concludes on the campus of the Blackberry Art School, where a picnic dinner will be provided," Piper continued. "The first three cars to arrive at BAS after performing the required tasks will be declared the winners. However, those not finished by ten p.m. should return to BAS. We don't want cars careening about the countryside in the wee hours of the morning. Now drive carefully, put on your detective caps, and enjoy the Blackberry Road Rally."

Before I could join the drivers streaming to pick up their envelopes, Holt took me by the arm. "Marlee, I have more to tell you. We assigned an officer to watch over Mr. Burwell, but Joel might try to lash out at you or Theo. It's wise to keep a lot of people around you."

I gestured to the dozens of cars. "I think I have that covered."

"This is serious. After the sheriff's office spoke with Amanda Dobson, deputies were sent to BAS to take Joel into custody. He was gone, along with his rental car and luggage. Because Sienna's friends were instructed not to leave the area until further notice, we now have a warrant out for him.

I hope he's heading for an airport; that way he doesn't pose a threat to you or Theo. But we don't know where he is. Or what he has planned. I want you to be careful when you're driving out there. A normal fugitive would be on his way out of the state, or trying to hide. But I don't think Joel MacGregor has ever been normal. Or sane."

"Marlee, why haven't you picked up our envelope?" Dean shouted from the car.

Andrew opened the back door to add, "We can't let the others get a head start. Not after all our studying."

I smiled at Holt. "I'll worry about the crazy Mr. MacGregor when I'm finished with the road rally. Right now I have to deal with the crazy Cabot brothers."

As soon as I returned to my car with the envelope, Andrew snatched it from me. "Start the engine. We're wasting time." He ripped the envelope open.

"Shouldn't we read what's inside first?" I asked.

"We can read it while we're driving." Dean peered over his brother's shoulder.

Up to this moment, Theo had sat silent in the backseat. Now he leaned forward and said, "They call it a road rally race, Marlee. You should start racing."

Tess grinned. "He's got you there." She buckled her seat belt. "Let's go."

With a shrug, I started my car, gunning the motor. We squealed out of our parking space.

"That's what I'm talking about," Dean said.

Looking over my shoulder, I asked, "Where do we pick up the first destination clue?"

When I turned front again, I cringed. I'd driven too fast down the driveway and barely missed hitting Piper's wrought iron gate post. I refused to let the fervor of the Cabot brothers push me into driving recklessly. The memory of Christian's crumpled Jeep was too fresh.

"Pull over for a second," Dean said once we reached the road. "We shouldn't keep driving if we don't know what direction to go in."

After I came to a stop on the shoulder, I said, "Need I remind everyone that I wanted to read this clue while we were still at Piper's house?"

He ignored me. "Okay, listen to this. 'Your first clue will be found at a favorite spot for patriotic Audubon members.' What's going on? I thought all the clues were art related."

"This isn't fair," Andrew said. "We read those art books for nothing."

"John James Audubon was an artist," Theo said.

The brothers looked at him with expressions of mild shock. They had been less than thrilled when I'd invited Theo to be part of our team. As far as they were concerned, Theo would be no help at all; even worse, they would be forced to split any prize money with him.

"Theo's right," Tess told them. "Audubon was a painter."

"A famous painter, too," I added. "*Birds of America*. Duh."

"Hey, I studied French Impressionists," Dean said. "Audubon doesn't sound French."

Tess stared at him in disbelief. "Seriously? He was born in the French colony of Haiti."

"Forget about the gaps in Dean's knowledge of art history." I took the clue from him. "Let's try to figure out where patriotic bird watchers would go around here."

"I don't know anything about birds," Andrew grumbled.

"Eagle Pier," Theo said quietly. "Bald eagles nest there."

I laughed. "Theo's right again. American bald eagles do nest by the pier. And it's only a five-minute drive." I leaned over the seat to shake Theo's hand. "Congratulations. You've solved our first clue."

A shy smile crept onto Theo's face.

Andrew threw an arm around Theo's shoulder. "I knew it was a good idea to add you to our team."

Theo's smile widened. So did mine as I started up the car once again. We may not win the Blackberry Road Rally, but it looked like Theo would have a new friend or two by the time it was over. That was worth a lot more than the prize money.

In order to not dampen everyone's spirits, I didn't mention that the grand prize looked to be slipping away. A red road rally car holding a group of older BAS alumni had been one step ahead of us all evening. We were playing catch-up. But our team had nothing to be ashamed of. By the end of the first hour, the five of us had turned into clue-solving machines: methodical, focused, supportive. The Cabot brothers shocked Tess and me by actually remembering some art-related fact they had studied.

I was also pleased to learn Theo's expertise extended to more than birds. He solved the clue to our fourth destination: "When you run out of pottery material, think about heading here." Although it made sense that a former ceramic student would correctly guess the Claymore Family Diner, located only a half mile from Theo's Crow Cottage.

All in all, the rally had been a welcome distraction from Sienna's murder, and I was having fun. Even though the sun was setting, we still had a good twenty minutes of light left as the skies turned dark rose. Fireflies glimmering in the farm fields provided a different sort of illumination. The rally was almost done. Just in time, too. My stomach grumbled. I couldn't wait to set eyes on that picnic awaiting us at the Blackberry Bayou. We had just finished photographing Tess as she held up a turkey feather at our ninth clue destination. Now we sat in the parked car, waiting to hear where we should drive next.

Waving a piece of paper, Andrew intoned, "The final clue."

"Oh, get on with it," his brother said with exasperation. "If the red car gets any more ahead of us, it will be embarrassing."

It seemed I wasn't the only one who realized we no longer had a chance to win. I was cheered by the fact that no one was giving up, not even the Cabot brothers. And second prize was better than no prize at all.

"What does the clue say?" Theo asked.

Andrew cleared his throat. "'If Chihuly's business runs into trouble, he should go here for financial consultation.'"

Tess and I looked at each other. Dale Chihuly was a famous glass artist from Seattle. The clue had something to do with glass.

"Glassware galleries are too obvious." Tess bit her lip. "And auto collision repair shops wouldn't make sense."

"Glass and financial consultation," Dean repeated.

The five of us sat silently as night fell on the cornfields. The only sounds were crickets and the cries of whip-poor-wills.

"Leave it to Piper to write a clue involving finances," Andrew finally said. "She probably had her banker come up with it."

"Excuse me. I'm having a lightbulb moment." Everyone turned their attention to me. "The clue could be referring to the Glass-Steagall Act."

"Huh?" Andrew said.

"Glass-Steagall was an act passed by Congress in the nineteen thirties as a response to the bank failures after the Depression."

Dean held up his hands. "How do you know things like that?"

"I read. I went to college." I shrugged. "And I dated two Wall Street bankers when I lived in New York."

Dean chuckled.

"There's an abandoned motor home park on Glenn Avenue," I continued. "It's called the Steagall RV Resort."

Tess high-fived me. "Yes."

I turned on the ignition. "Second or third place, here we come."

Five minutes later, I spotted the red car turning off Glenn Avenue. If the red car had just left Glenn, I was right about the Steagall RV Resort being the last clue destination. My only concern was the team in third place. More than once I'd caught a glimpse of an SUV trailing far behind us on one of the country roads. Luckily, I couldn't think of any way they could pull ahead. Unless there ended up being a literal race to the finish.

When we arrived at the abandoned motor park, I had barely rolled to a stop before everyone piled out. A single empty RV remained, dirty and ramshackle. It looked as if it had been neglected for a hundred years, instead of only five.

"Now what?" I asked Andrew, who held the clue envelope.

"It says one of us has to be photographed in front of the resort sign."

Like synchronized swimmers, we ran to the weathered sign still standing by the side of the road. "You figured out the clue, Marlee," Theo said. "It should be you in the picture."

I quickly posed in front of the sign. "Go ahead."

But as Andrew photographed me, I noticed the headlights of a vehicle as it turned onto Glenn Avenue. "Uh-oh," I warned. "I think that's the team that's been behind us all night."

"We can't let them catch up," Tess cried.

"Whoever it is, they really want to win," Dean said. "They must be going eighty."

The photo taken, we ran for my car. By this time, the SUV we had spotted had just turned up the motor park driveway.

Andrew pounded the headrest of my seat. "No way are we

going to lose to this clown. We've been ahead of them all night. They're not beating us."

However, they still had to photograph one of their teammates in front of the sign. That gave us a good minute. Maybe two. And I knew these country roads well. If these alumni were from out of town, they didn't have a chance of beating me back to BAS. Snapping my seat belt on, I stepped on the gas. As I shot past the approaching team, there was an instant when my headlights illuminated the front seat of the vehicle.

I gasped. "Oh no. This isn't good."

"What's the matter?" Tess asked.

I turned onto Glenn Avenue so quickly, my car fishtailed. In the rearview mirror, I saw the SUV turn around.

"No one on that team got out to take a photo," Dean said. "Someone should tell them they can't win unless they take the photo."

"He's not interested in taking a photo of the sign." I was torn between watching the road and checking the rearview mirror. "He's interested in me. And Theo."

"What are you talking about?" Andrew sounded frustrated, and a little afraid.

Theo tapped me on the shoulder. "It's Joel, isn't it?"

"Yes. I saw him when I drove past. One of you needs to call the state police or the sheriff's department. Now!"

"What should I say?" Dean leaned over the seat.

"Tell them the man who murdered Sienna Katsaros is chasing us."

Ignoring the alarmed cries from all around me, I stepped on the gas, watching the needle go past seventy. If Joel hit optimal speed on the open road, his big shiny SUV could well overtake my little Malibu.

"I need to change the game," I said. "I have to surprise him."

"I don't understand. What are you going to do?"

But I had no time to answer Tess. Instead, I took a deep

breath before swerving off the road and onto the dirt driveway leading to a farmhouse. A chorus of yells went up as I burst through a locked gate. The SUV followed right behind me.

"Game on, buddy," I told the driver pursuing us in my rearview mirror. "Game on."

Chapter 24

Tess covered her eyes. "Please don't hit a cow."

"I don't think there are any cows out here." I veered left. "Whoops. That was close."

"Was it a cow?" Tess wailed.

"No. A farmer." I glanced at my rearview mirror in time to see a man shake his fist at me. I sighed in relief when Joel narrowly avoided hitting him as well.

"The nut job is right behind us," Andrew warned. "And he ran over a chicken."

Tess's shriek was deafening. This was too much for a vegetarian to take.

"No, wait." Andrew paused. "The chicken just lost some feathers. It's still alive."

"I don't care about chickens or cows," Dean said. "A crazy man wants to run *us* down."

"He'll have to catch us first." I scanned the property I'd crashed onto: one barn, two sheds, tractor equipment, and a penned area of goats. I needed to steer clear of the goats. Tess would never forgive me if I ran down a goat. I wouldn't forgive myself, either. But beyond those goats lay green fields stretching into the distance. I was happy to see the crop was alfalfa hay. Driving around pumpkins and through cornstalks would have been too tricky. But my car could easily plow through alfalfa.

"Here we go." I drove onto the field, hearing my tires crush the grasses beneath me. I'd compensate the farmer for whatever part of his crop I ruined. If I survived.

"Do you have some kind of plan, Marlee?" Andrew asked. "Because he's gaining on us."

Gripping my steering wheel, I began to drive in a zigzag fashion, swerving right, then left, then right again. My passengers fell side to side with each sharp movement. I spied a tractor parked up ahead. "Hold on, guys."

"To what?" Dean cried.

After swerving once more to the left, I made a sudden turn to the right. I was going so fast, my car skidded sideways for several yards. Just before Joel could barrel into us, I stepped on the gas and Joel shot past, missing us by inches. I made a dangerously close turn around the tractor, heading back the way we came.

"I have an emergency dispatcher on the phone," Dean yelled from the backseat. "They want to know where we are."

"On an alfalfa farm."

"They need more information than that." Tess cringed as we nearly ran over the chicken again.

"We have to get back on the road so I can see a sign." I groaned to see the farmer waving a rake at me as I made turn after turn on his property to avoid Joel's SUV.

I heard Dean tell the dispatcher that we'd just left the Steagall RV Resort and were now trampling a lot of alfalfa on a nearby farm. "Here, I'll take a photo of where we are," he said. "Damn it! I dropped the phone out the window."

"Don't you dare touch mine," Andrew warned. "It has the road rally photos on it."

To avoid killing the irate farmer, I turned left, crushing more alfalfa on my way off the property and onto a dirt road.

As soon as I did, I saw a car in my lane up ahead. I was coming up on it much too quickly. And Joel was close behind. I got in the other lane to pass the unsuspecting driver, only to be met with the headlights of a car coming right toward me. Tess let out a strangled scream as I swerved onto the shoulder, scraping the side of my car against a tree. A low-hanging branch knocked off my side-view mirror.

Both cars blared their horns when I sped past them. I winced as my speedometer inched past ninety. I spotted a crossroad up ahead. "Quick. There's a sign. Tell me what it says."

Tess crouched forward, and I was sure everyone in the backseat followed suit.

"Did anyone see what road we're on?" I asked after we drove past.

"Are you kidding?" Andrew asked. "We're going faster than the speed of light."

I cursed aloud at the sight of cars in each lane up ahead.

"Hang on." I turned off the road once more, this time plowing through tall grass, up and down a small gully, and onto another farm field. My car hit something on the ground, and I saw my left hubcap go spinning off into space.

I frowned at the sight of cornfields. Cornstalks would slow me down. But I had little choice. I drove into the corn, which sent corncobs flying through the open car windows. I had to get us out of the cornfield. Joel's vehicle was bigger and had more power. He had the advantage, which was confirmed when Theo shouted, "He's right behind us!"

I blindly turned right, hoping the field ended soon. When it did and we burst out of the cornstalks, I almost wept with joy; my joy was short-lived as Joel appeared once again. I saw a large barn up ahead and stepped on the gas. I was so intent on heading for the barn, I didn't see the pond. A second later, we found ourselves splashing through water. Thankfully, it was shallow, and I got us to the other side without the engine stalling.

"Where are we going?" Tess asked in a shaky voice.

"If I can get past that barn, there should be a road on the other side," I replied. "Along with a street sign somewhere. We need to tell the police exactly where we are."

Cows appeared out of the evening shadows and we screamed. A chorus of frightened moos chimed in. Pressing on my car horn, I terrified these gentle creatures so much, they literally ran off in all directions.

"I've never seen cows run," I remarked.

"I wish I could do the same," Dean moaned.

But I was too intent on avoiding the harvester up ahead to reassure him. I sped by unscathed, only to brush against an unhitched wagon. The impact spun us around once more, and a hoe from the wagon flew into the air, cracking my rear window. I joined my passengers in screaming once again, but the sight of Joel headed right for us propelled me into action.

"Is anyone hurt?" I barely avoided hitting Joel's vehicle as I made my escape.

"We're too frightened to care!" Andrew shouted.

My hands gripped the steering wheel like iron. I was going to get my friends to safety, even if I had to drive through every farm and cornfield in Oriole County. And at the end of it, I hoped to run right over Joel with my battered Chevy.

"What is that?!" Dean yelled from the backseat.

An enormous cow stared down at us from the side of the barn, a lovestruck expression on her face. It was silly, gaudy, and the most beautiful thing I had ever seen. I now knew exactly where we were.

"That's Carol Grunkemeyer's painting of her favorite cow," I announced.

"It looks ridiculous," Andrew said as we approached the barn.

"Well, it looks like salvation to me, sweetie." Unfortunately, I had to not only be alert to what Joel was doing behind me, I needed to avoid the usual detritus found on the Grunkemeyer farm. I'd already swerved around a bucket, two lawn chairs, and a pile of feed bags. We were almost at the barn when I caught sight of yet another object lying in the grass. I smiled. The Grunkemeyers' negligence was about to work in my favor.

I aimed my car directly for the post auger, waiting until the last second before swerving to avoid it. Joel was going too fast, however. He'd hit it for sure. Especially since he was sure to be distracted by the unexpected sight of that giant orange and white cow.

"Tess, look out your window and tell me what happens."

Knocking off a corncob that had landed on her lap, Tess stuck her head out the window. "He ran over something. It looks like a tool. A tool with sharp teeth."

"That is a post auger, my friend." I made a sharp turn, which sent everyone leaning to the side. "Grab my cell and call Kit. He's on my contact list."

"Who's Kit?" She scrambled to get the phone out of my purse.

"Captain Holt." I stepped on the gas and drove straight toward the open barn. Having been here before, I knew I could drive my car through the barn without hitting anything. And it was safer than trying to avoid the objects cluttering their field. "Tell him we're at the Grunkemeyer farm, but we're on our way to the BAS campus."

"We are?" Tess asked.

"We are."

While Tess told Kit that we were en route to BAS with Joel

hot on our trail, I drove through the barn. I felt thankful no animals, people, or farm equipment lay in my path. But Henry and Carol stood near one of the walls, staring in shock at the sight of a car driving past them. I had time for no more than a beep of my horn and a wave before I drove out the other side. As soon as I did, I spotted Blue Star Highway up ahead.

"Where's Joel?" Theo asked. "He didn't follow us."

I hoped hitting the post auger had gashed open one of his tires. But I didn't have time to search for him. The faster I got on the highway, the sooner I'd reach the BAS campus. I turned my car toward the front drive to the farm, narrowly avoiding two startled ducks. Before I could get too far, a pair of head-lights came at me from the side. Joel had gone around the barn, driven close to the driveway entrance, and waited for us.

"I hate that man," I muttered.

Since he blocked my path to the driveway, I had little choice but to head for the wooden fence. The Grunkemeyers were not going to like this. I knew they were proud of their new split-rail fence, which I now split totally apart as I crashed through it and onto Blue Star Highway.

My passengers yelled again as one of the flying pieces of wood hit my front window on the passenger side. If I made it through this alive, my car repair bill would be enormous. Not to mention all the money I owed the Grunkemeyers—and that alfalfa farmer. When I sped past the drive Joel had blocked, I saw him turn onto the highway.

"You lost another hubcap," Andrew said.

"Two," Theo added.

"I don't care if we lose the last hubcap, along with the bumpers." I looked over my shoulder. The cracked rear window made it difficult to see what was going on behind us, as did the encroaching night. "Is he still going as fast as he was before? The post auger should have blown out his tire."

"He's chasing us," Dean said, "but not as fast. I think one of his tires was damaged."

"Good. Because we can't speed like this down Blue Star Highway. There will be too many cars. I'm sure to hit someone."

Tess held up my cell. "Guys, I'm still on the phone with Kit Holt. He's sending police to BAS."

"Now we just have to get to the bayou," I said. "I'm going to lead Joel straight to BAS. There's only one way in or out. If he keeps following us, he'll be trapped. With luck, the police will get there before we do."

"He's getting closer, Marlee," Theo warned. He sounded the calmest of anyone in the car.

"What are we going to do if we can't stay on the highway?" Andrew asked.

"Take a shortcut." Without warning, I made a wide turn at the next intersection, my high speed forcing me to drive through the gravel parking lot of a roadside fruit market.

Tess covered her face as I knocked over a stack of crates. Peaches flew into the air. Joel's headlights appeared in my rearview mirror. The damage from the post auger had slowed him down but hadn't stopped him. If I maintained my speed, I thought I could outrace him. I just had to avoid hitting anything else. My car was now shaking from whatever damage I had sustained from my bucolic version of the Indy 500.

I pressed down on the accelerator, causing Tess to moan.

"We're going way too fast, Marlee," she murmured.

"So is he." I slowed in order to make the next turn without flipping over my car but sped up again for another long stretch. I spotted blueberry bushes to my right. It was the O'Neill farm, and I knew there was an open access road that divided the middle of the property. A few moments later, I turned down it, happy to see there was a delay before Joel's headlights appeared behind me.

When we emerged on the other side of the property, I

headed in the direction of Oriole River Road. I could make good time now unless something got in my way. I had no sooner thought this when a deer decided to cross up ahead. Again I pressed on my car horn. I missed the frightened doe by no more than an inch.

"My hair has gone white," Andrew said. "I know it."

When I saw an open pasture ahead, I turned onto it.

"Not another farm," Dean complained. "Can't we just stay on the road?"

"I'm taking another shortcut." It would be my last. As soon as I got on the other side of this property I'd be on West Pine; from there it was only a few miles to Blackberry Bayou.

"What are those strange lights in the sky?" Theo asked.

"I don't care about anything in the sky right now." I was too aware of Joel gaining ground.

"Hey, wait a second," Dean said in alarm. "Are we on the Sanderling farm?"

"We are." I winced when I hit an unseen hole in the dirt, which increased my car's worrying shimmy.

Andrew and Dean gasped. "Oh no, I bet those lights are UFOs!" Andrew shouted. "Remember all those stories of UFOs being spotted here in 1975. Maybe they've returned!"

"Would you please calm down," Tess said with exasperation. "It's a plane. Definitely not UFOs."

"If only they were UFOs." I sped along the edge of what was left of the Sanderling grapevines. "We might get abducted and Joel would never catch up with us."

"That isn't funny," Dean said. "This place is haunted and we—"

"Are now safely off the property." I turned onto the road on the other side of the farm. "It's only a few miles to BAS. And if I keep up this speed, we'll be there in about three seconds."

After that, I stopped looking at my speedometer. I didn't

want to know how fast I was going along Oriole River Road,
a road comprising two narrow lanes. It also climbed upward,
a result of the lake's sand dunes, which gave the area its varied
elevations. As I started along the uphill road, I glanced in
my rearview mirror. Through my cracked rear window, I spied
Joel's SUV. It appeared to be weaving. All I had to do was
keep a clear head and get this car to the bayou.

I let out a cry. A happy one this time. "Look behind us.
Those are police flashers in the distance."

A cheer went up from everyone. "We can slow down now,"
Tess said. "Joel can't escape, not with the police right behind
him."

"Joel knows he's caught. But he's determined to get rid of
me and Theo first." Proving my statement, Joel's vehicle now
drew much closer to us.

I increased my speed. The road to the campus had never
seemed longer, or more winding. When I came upon a car up
ahead, I honked my horn before passing in a flurry of dirt and
gravel. Joel was right behind.

I was going so fast that when I hit the speed bump at the
entrance to the BAS parking lot my car briefly achieved alti-
tude. I didn't have time to join my passengers in screaming.
Not with people strolling around the parking lot, and a killer
hot on my trail. I drove through the lot, one hand pressed
continuously on my horn. As I raced past, I saw people rush-
ing to all sides, shouting and covering their ears.

Suddenly, I was on the BAS campus, which was filled with
people sitting at picnic tables. While trying to avoid a trio of
musicians now running for their lives, I knocked over a small
buffet table laden with pies.

"What are you doing?" Dean cried. "There's nowhere to go!"

"Yes, there is." Taking a deep breath, I pressed my foot to
the floor. And drove straight into the bayou.

Water gushed through my open windows, but I kept the car

going until it finally ran aground on the shallow bottom. I heard shouts from behind me and another splash of water.

Because the bayou was only a few feet deep, there was no danger of drowning. The only danger was Joel. All of us sat motionless and silent as water seeped in through the open car windows. I was too drained to even look behind me to see what had become of Joel. All I knew was that we weren't alone. Hundreds of people were on campus, and it seemed like all of them were splashing through the water toward us.

The first person to stick her head through my window was Piper. "What in the name of God do you think you're doing?" she cried. "Have you completely lost your mind?"

"No," I said after a moment. "But the man chasing us has."

Before she could continue to berate me, Theo said, "I want to get out of the car."

"Amen," Andrew muttered.

Then the cavalry did indeed appear. Or my version of it. Kit Holt pushed aside Piper, and I smiled at the sight of his face. It was such a cute face, too. And right now, there was no one I would rather have seen, not even Ryan. "Are you hurt?" he asked.

"Can we please get out of the car?" Theo repeated. He was beginning to sound agitated. I didn't blame him.

"Where's Joel?" I asked as Kit helped me exit through my window. It was easier than trying to open the car doors in all this water. I waited anxiously until all of my passengers were safely taken out of the car and standing in the bayou with me. Everyone looked fine. Stunned and exhausted. But otherwise fine. A stricken Andrew still clutched the road rally envelope in one hand and his cell phone in the other. Tess and Dean held each other and wept. Theo tried to squeeze the water from his soaked T-shirt.

I heard splashing and looked up as Detective Trejo and Tina Kapoor approached.

"Mr. MacGregor hit a boulder on the edge of the bayou and flipped his vehicle," Trejo said. "Knocked him out, but he's coming around. His air bag went off, so he'll live." Trejo gently took my arm; Kit had hold of the other. "Given what he did to Sienna Katsaros—and that he tried to kill all of you tonight—he'll spend a lot of that life in prison."

"You poor things look exhausted," Tina said, clucking over us. "Let me find towels to dry you off."

"Absolutely." Piper was not to be overlooked at her own Blackberry Road Rally. "We'll get some food and drink into all of you while the police clear this mess up." She waved at the flashing lights on land, the overturned SUV, and the hundreds of BAS alumni crowded along the bayou's edge and wading into the water.

"Are you sure you're not hurt, Marlee?" Holt looked at me with touching concern.

I shook my head. "And no one else got hurt tonight, either. Although given how I drove, it's a miracle we're still alive."

Dean looked up from his tearful embrace with Tess. "Don't listen to her. Marlee is the greatest driver in the world. The greatest."

Tess sobbed. "And she outraced a murderer."

Theo splashed over to me. "Marlee went very fast. We even drove through a barn *and* a fence. And we didn't kill any of the animals. Not even the chicken."

"My fans." I gave Holt a shaky smile. "But if you'd asked them about my driving ten minutes ago, you would have gotten a different response."

Trejo chuckled. "I guess we need more speed traps out in the country."

"Well, we can't stand in the bayou all night." Piper looked down with chagrin at her wet capris. "Here, come with me." She reached out a hand to Andrew, who wordlessly gave her his phone and clue envelope. I suspected Andrew was still in shock.

All of us began to slosh our way out of the bayou. When we passed the overturned SUV, I barely spared a glance as the police dragged out a semiconscious Joel. People crowded round as soon as we reached shore. The first to greet us were Emma and Alison, who seemed even more in shock than Andrew. I wondered if Ryan had come to the picnic with his cousins. If so, how long would it take before he learned it was his fiancée who had come crashing through the BAS picnic before landing in the bayou.

Holt led me to the first picnic table we came to, and I collapsed onto the bench. Theo sat beside me and took my hand. I looked over at him in surprise.

"Thank you for catching Sienna's killer, Marlee," he said in a low voice. "It was an important thing to do. For Sienna. And her family." He screwed up his face and I thought he was about to cry. "And me."

I took him in my arms, and we both wept. Theo mourned the loss of the girl he had cared for so long ago; I cried over the tragic waste of such a young, promising life. And for the unending grief it had caused her family and loved ones. As the Chaplins had taught me, murder was the darkest, most unforgivable, of crimes.

We broke apart when Kit knelt before us and held out napkins. Theo took one and blew his nose, while I wiped my eyes with the other. "Thanks. You're always around when I need you," I told him.

"I wish that were true. You were on your own tonight during the road rally. I should have been there."

"You couldn't have come with us," Theo said. "There was no more room in Marlee's car."

I gazed out at my poor little Chevy awash in the middle of the bayou. "You know, I was thinking about replacing my car for something bigger. I guess that decision's been made for me."

"See, the evening hasn't been a total waste," Kit said with a laugh.

I heard a loud whoop of joy.

Andrew ran up to our picnic table, looking happier than I had ever seen him. "We did it, Marlee! Thanks to you driving so fast, we did it. We got here first!"

He handed me a fancy certificate. And a check. I whooped with joy as well. It appeared the evening had turned out better than expected, for we hadn't just caught a killer.

We won the Blackberry Road Rally.

Chapter 25

The following week no one talked about anything but the Blackberry Road Rally. Specifically, my wild drive through the countryside with a killer in pursuit. Every news outlet in Michigan reported how Joel MacGregor had been arrested for the murder of BAS student Sienna Katsaros. He was also charged with trying to kill a carful of road rally participants. Not the sort of publicity Piper envisioned for the event. Thanks to everyone packing an iPhone, the road rally chase soon went viral after alumni at the picnic posted video of me barreling onto the campus at eighty miles an hour, then plunging into the bayou. I watched the YouTube videos with horrified fascination. How I avoided running over dozens of people that night I will never know.

Being Internet celebrities thrilled the Cabot brothers as much as the grand prize money did. Tess and I were appalled. Theo didn't understand why anyone who hadn't been at the rally would even care. I did make Gillian happy by granting her father an exclusive interview for his paper. This upset the editor of our town's rival newspaper. I hoped she wouldn't carry a grudge.

Our brief fame burned even brighter when a national morning show interviewed my entire road rally team. Except for Dean, who took too long to get ready for the satellite feed and missed filming altogether. As for Piper, she decided even lurid publicity was better than no publicity. It helped that the morning show wanted to interview her, too.

After we were done filming, Piper turned to me with obvious frustration. "I'll never be able to follow this. People who register for next year's road rally will expect all sorts of excitement. And I doubt we'll have another mad killer joining the festivities."

I gave her a jaundiced look. "We can only hope."

Since I'd been dragged into two murder cases this summer, I wasn't all that confident there wouldn't be fresh mayhem next year. And I had to admit it was hard to top headlines like: BLACKBERRY ROAD RALLY TEAM RACE FOR THE WIN—AND THEIR LIVES!

At least Joel was finally behind bars, although his wealthy family hired an expensive legal team to take up his defense. I prayed justice was indeed blind, especially to the MacGregor money. There was an additional attempted murder charge filed against him; this time for trying to run Christian Naylor off the road. Police had tracked down a witness driving in the opposite direction that rainy night who saw Joel's SUV force Christian's Jeep into a tree.

Amanda Dobson arrived two days after the road rally. She surprised me by being a vivacious, pretty woman, with a fondness for profanity. Not what I had expected from a renowned botanist. Her testimony about how Joel asked detailed questions about the toxicity of baneberries solidified the case against him. Along with her account of how he pushed her into a bed of poison ivy. I found her far more likable and warm than the rest of Sienna's Bramble. Then again, she hadn't spent the past twenty years covering up her friend's death.

The fate of those Bramble friends was uncertain for a time,

especially Christian. But after ten days, the doctors deemed it safe to bring him out of his coma. Christian remembered nothing of what had occurred the night of the accident. Although I heard he took comfort in the fact that his sister and parents were by his bedside when he regained consciousness.

The Katsaros family arrived in Oriole Point shortly after the road rally. Their main purpose was to retrieve Sienna's remains, but they insisted on meeting with Leah, Zack, Gordon, and Dawn. I have no idea what transpired during their private talk. However, as Holt had predicted, the county prosecutor declined to press charges against them for covering up what they believed was an accidental death. Their youth at the time of Sienna's death was a factor. He'd also taken into consideration the wishes of the Katsaros family, who asked that no charges be brought.

It was a compassionate gesture on their part. Joel needed to go to prison for his crime, but the others had been frightened teenagers. And the guilt they carried these past twenty years had been its own form of punishment.

"Is the Bramble gang free to get on with their lives?" I asked Kit Holt and Greg Trejo when they came by my shop to update me on the case. In the two weeks since the road rally, I'd seen both men every day. They were starting to feel like close friends. Even Detective Trejo.

"Naylor remains in the hospital here," Trejo said. "When he's strong enough, he'll be transferred to Atlanta, where his parents live. This way they can be close by during his recovery."

"Zack Burwell left for North Carolina last night. Let's hope his A.A. sponsor there can keep him sober," Kit said as he enjoyed the boysenberry sundae I had made for him. Of course, Detective Trejo refused my offer of Berry Basket ice cream. "And Dawn Vance reportedly caught her flight back to Minneapolis this morning."

I ate a spoonful of my own raspberry sundae before replying.

It was almost noon and ice cream seemed the perfect lunch. "That woman needs help just as much as Zack does. She used to be a crazy stalker. I wish the court had ordered her to undergo psychological counseling."

"Not our problem." Trejo eyed the customers in my store. His suspicious expression suggested he was waiting for one of them to shoplift. Did this man ever relax?

Kit looked up from his sundae. "It also appears Gordon Sanderling has had his fill of Oriole Point. He put his farmhouse up for sale. I'm betting he does the same with his company."

I thought about all the cursed and haunted rumors concerning the farm and wondered how easy it would be for him to sell it.

"And you might be interested to hear that Leah Malek and Sanderling are officially a couple," Kit continued. "We've learned he and Ms. Malek plan to take an extended vacation together in the Caribbean."

"That is news. But not surprising. She's had a thing for him since they were teenagers." I finished off my ice cream. "And I don't blame them for taking a vacation after all that's happened. I'm doing the same. And right in the middle of summer tourist season, too."

Indeed, when I announced my plans a few days ago, it was met with general shock and disbelief by my friends and fellow shopkeepers. No one who owned a business in Oriole Point took a vacation during high season. And I was more work obsessed than most.

"I need a break," I added. "So does Theo. That's why we're vacationing together."

"Seems strange to me," Trejo muttered.

"Can't believe you're going on a road trip." Kit chuckled. "Don't you want to stay off the road for a while?"

I did understand why a road trip seemed like the last thing I'd want to do. But after being chased by a killer, I needed

pampering and home-cooked meals. That meant driving to
Chicago, where my parents lived. Just as they had done when
I left New York after the Chaplin murder trial, Mom and Dad
were happy to get my bedroom ready in their Wicker Park
town house. Since I was bringing Theo, they had also readied
the guest room.

Actually, he was bringing me in his VW Beetle. My sturdy
little Malibu had been pushed to its limits at the rally, but the
car had performed as valiantly as any BMW owned by Piper.
In fact, it had helped save our lives. Ryan removed the steering wheel for me before it was towed away. It now hung on a
wall in my sunroom. And a new vehicle would be waiting
for me at the dealership when I returned. A cobalt blue SUV,
with *BERRY BASKET* painted on the sides.

I glanced up at the clock, expecting Theo to arrive any
moment. Given the dimensions of his car, I had packed light.
I hoped he kept his car in good working order. After visiting
my parents, Theo and I planned to head for Champaign,
Illinois, where Theo could spend time with his own family.
He couldn't wait for his father to meet me. I looked forward
to it myself. It was time I got to know Theo better. And via
people who loved and cared about him. Not the disaffected
members of Sienna's long-ago Bramble.

I didn't even feel nervous about leaving Dean, Andrew,
and Gillian to run the shop while I was gone. Okay, maybe I
felt a little nervous, but I knew Gillian would see to it the
Cabot brothers behaved. Because Theo was making the trip
with me, the store's pastry offerings would be greatly reduced.
However, Ryan promised to have extra Zellar pies delivered
to my store each morning. Best of all, Gillian offered to stay
at my house and babysit Minnie. I had a feeling both of them
would enjoy the experience.

Kit finished his sundae. "Best ice cream I've ever eaten."

"Of course it is." I took his dish from him. "Made at a local dairy with organic ingredients." I shot a reproving glance at Trejo. "Healthy, too."

He smirked. "As healthy as ice cream is allowed to get."

Before I could argue the point, Gillian and Dean arrived for their shifts, followed immediately by Theo. He wore another freshly pressed pair of spotless jeans and a green T-shirt with a picture of a pelican on the front. "We need to leave," he announced. "My dad told me to never drive into Chicago close to rush hour."

"Chicago's in a different time zone," Trejo reminded him. "You gain an hour."

Theo ignored him. He still felt wary around the police. "Marlee, we can't drive at rush hour. Dad said I wouldn't like it."

"I never liked it much myself." I laughed, removing my Berry Basket apron.

"Wait. I have a going-away gift for you. Reading material for your road trip." Kit Holt handed me a small package wrapped in white paper covered in raspberries.

I gave him a hug. When I tried to pull away, he pulled me close for another embrace. After we broke apart, Trejo, Gillian, and Dean looked at us with odd expressions.

"Marlee, we have to go," Theo said in a frustrated voice.

Grateful for his reminder, I made my farewells to Dean and Gillian, accompanied by a flurry of last-minute instructions. Anxious to leave, Theo ran out to his car and turned on the engine. When I got in beside him, he took off before the passenger door slammed shut. It felt like I was about to embark on another road rally race. As we drove up Lyall Street, I second-guessed my decision to take this trip. Tourists crammed the downtown area. Should I really be leaving my store for a whole eight days at such a time? Maybe I was being a wuss. Yes, last month's Bowman murder and the Blackberry Road Rally had been traumatic. But I could have taken a day off and relaxed at home with Minnie. Did I really need to run to my parents in Chicago?

Theo turned onto Blue Star Highway. "Thank you for asking me on this vacation," he said. "It was a nice thing to do. You're a kind person. Sienna would have liked you."

"I'm sure I would have liked her, too."

"Now I understand what you told me when we watched birds at my cottage."

Puzzled, I looked over at him. His attention remained on the road. "What did I tell you?"

"That if we don't have brothers or sisters, we can ask people we like to be a brother and sister to us." Theo shot me a tentative glance. "Will you be my sister, Marlee?"

This time, I was the one to look at the road. I didn't want him to see the tears that sprang to my eyes. "I'd like to be your sister very much. That means you're my brother."

"Of course. We're family now. So it's good we're on the way to meet your parents. And my father. I'm happy we're doing this."

"So am I." My misgivings about leaving the store now seemed silly. This trip was the right thing to do. Maybe the best thing I'd done all year.

As if he knew a barrier had been crossed, Theo's customary shyness vanished. It takes two hours to drive from Oriole Point to Chicago, and Theo talked during most it. Yes, it was mostly about birds and his favorite TV shows, but I found the conversation more interesting than many of my talks with Ryan. Which only increased my bridal jitters.

So did the gift from Kit Holt, which I unwrapped as Theo drove us over the Skyway Bridge. I looked down at the book Holt had bought for me and laughed.

"What did the sheriff man give you?" Theo asked.

"*Wind in the Willows*, a children's classic featuring an enthusiastic motorist by the name of Mr. Toad." Fluttering the pages, I stopped at the title page where Kit had written in the book. I read aloud the inscription: "'To Marlee, my favorite reckless driver. Congratulations on your race to victory. But I hope you slow down for blueberry season. Your devoted deputy, Kit.'"

"He likes you," Theo said with unexpected gravity. "He likes you a lot."

"I like him, too. We're friends." I closed the book. The word *devoted* gave me pause. Primarily because it pleased me so much. I reminded myself again that Ryan and I were in love and about to spend the rest of our lives together. I needed to keep Kit Holt firmly in the friend category. Otherwise there was certain to be trouble ahead.

Sitting back, I watched as we drew nearer to Chicago's magnificent skyline. What lay ahead at this moment was an actual vacation, which I rarely made time for. I'd worry about Kit and Ryan when I returned to Oriole Point for the start of our blueberry festivities.

I peeked down at the book in my hands and smiled. Despite Kit's hope, I had a feeling things weren't about to slow down for blueberry season. Not one bit.

Blackberry Cantaloupe Salad

When Marlee's houseguest Alison made breakfast for everyone, one of the dishes she put together was this refreshing blackberry cantaloupe salad. What she didn't mention was that this recipe works equally well with strawberries or blueberries.

2 cups fresh blackberries
½ cantaloupe, cut into 1-inch pieces
1 tablespoon sugar
1 teaspoon grated peeled fresh ginger
½ teaspoon grated lime zest
2 tablespoons fresh mint leaves, thinly sliced

1. Combine all ingredients in a large bowl except the mint.
2. Cover and let stand 30 minutes. Or refrigerate for up to 2 days.
3. Stir in mint right before serving. Serves 4.

Blackberry Balsamic Drumsticks

At the BAS opening-night dinner, blackberry-glazed chicken wings were a crowd favorite. Here's how Marlee cooks up her own version at home with drumsticks.

6 chicken drumsticks, skin on
1 cup fresh blackberries, rinsed
¼ cup balsamic vinegar
1 cup water
1½ tablespoons chopped fresh rosemary
¼ cup sugar
2 tablespoons whole-grain mustard
2 tablespoons butter
Salt and pepper

1. Combine blackberries, butter, water, sugar, rosemary, and vinegar in small saucepan. Cook over medium-high heat. Stir until sauce is slightly reduced, approximately 10 minutes.
2. Remove pan from heat and stir in mustard, salt, and pepper. Let marinade cool.
3. Place drumsticks in Ziploc bag. Add cooled marinade and seal. Toss to coat.
4. The next day, preheat oven to 375 degrees. Remove drumsticks from marinade. Place on cookie sheet wrapped in foil. Discard marinade. Bake 25 minutes, turning once. Makes 2 to 3 servings.

Paleo Blackberry Muffins

Because many of Marlee's customers follow either a gluten-free or Paleo diet, she makes certain Theo whips up several GF and Paleo baked goods each week.

2 cups fresh blackberries
2 cups almond flour
4 eggs
2 tablespoons organic raw honey
½ teaspoon baking soda
1 teaspoon apple cider vinegar

1. Preheat oven to 350 degrees.
2. Combine dry ingredients in a medium bowl.
3. Place eggs, honey, and vinegar in a separate bowl and mix.
4. Combine contents of both bowls and stir. Add blackberries.
5. Spoon batter into greased or paper-lined muffin pan.
6. Bake 15 minutes, or until slightly browned. Let cool before transferring muffins to wire rack. Makes 10–12 muffins.

Blackberry Lemon Pound Cake

When Janelle shows up at The Berry Basket with disturbing news, Marlee is about to reach for a slice of Theo's blackberry lemon pound cake. Rest assured that once Janelle completed her unpleasant visit, Marlee did indeed find a little comfort in eating a slice of this delicious cake.

½ cup butter, melted
1 cup sugar
2 large eggs
Grated zest and juice of 1 lemon
1½ cups all-purpose flour
¼ teaspoon salt
½ cup milk
1 teaspoon baking powder
1 cup fresh or frozen (do not thaw) blackberries

Glaze
¼ cup lemon juice
¼ cup icing sugar

1. Preheat oven to 350 degrees. Combine butter and sugar in a large bowl and stir. Add eggs, lemon zest, and juice and mix until well blended.
2. Stir together flour, baking powder, and salt in a small bowl. Add half to butter/sugar mixture and stir until blended. Add milk, then remaining dry ingredients. Stir until combined. Don't over mix. Gently fold in blackberries.
3. Pour batter into greased 8 × 4 inch loaf pan. Bake 50–60 minutes, until golden and springy to the touch. Cool in pan on wire rack. Mix lemon juice and icing sugar; drizzle over cake while warm.